KATHRYN HAIG

Secret Sins

HarperCollins*Publishers*

HarperCollins*Publishers*,
77-85 Fulham Palace Road,
Hammersmith, London W6 8JB

This edition published by HarperCollins*Publishers* 1993
1   3   5   7   9   8   6   4   2

A catalogue record for this book is
available from the British Library

ISBN 0 00 224332 6

Printed in Great Britain by
HarperCollinsManufacturing Glasgow

CONTENTS

ACKNOWLEDGEMENTS

My thanks to David Whately-Smith who patiently translated and corrected German phrases for me.

Lines from 'The Desert Song' by Romberg, Harbech and Hammerstein and 'Someone to Watch Over Me' by George and Ira Gershwin, reproduced by kind permission of Warner Chappel Music Ltd/International Music Publications Ltd.

Lines from 'She Don't Wanna' by Jack Yellen and Milton Ager, © 1927 Advanced Music Corporation, USA, reproduced by kind permission of Lawrence Wright Music Company Ltd, London WC2H 0EA.

Every effort has been made to contact the copyright owners of material included in this work. In the instances where this has not proved possible, the author and publishers offer their apologies to and would be pleased to hear from those concerned.

For Hugh and Rachel

Jedoch das Allerschlimmste
Das haben sie nicht gewusst,
Das Schlimmste and das Dümmste
Das trug ich geheim in der Brust.

But the worst of all my failings
They have not even guessed,
For my worst, my greatest sin is
Kept secret in my breast.

                                        Heine

PROLOGUE

When did my children grow old? I scarcely noticed. I must have looked the other way for the space of a heart-beat and when I turned back, their hair was grey – my little ones had turned into parents and then into grand-parents.

What did I expect – that they should ask my permission to grow?

There are children's voices in my garden still, but different voices, different children. English names, English voices. Loud, confident, sometimes quarrelsome, sometimes squealing like indignant piglets, sometimes giggling in a secretive huddle. Now and again, they go too far – a little one is knocked down, perhaps, or something is broken – and then I get angry with them. Not for long. They're only children, after all, thank God.

One of them might climb on my knee and wind bony, brown arms around my neck, whispering, wheedling, all soft, damp kisses and grazed knees. They tell me their secrets, their joys and sorrows, knowing that I've plenty of time to listen (where am I going to rush off to, at my age?).

So many children. They used to smell of warm milk, bread and butter, apples and boiled eggs, of Pears soap and of Seven Seas cod liver oil. Now they smell of Big Macs and French fries (not all the time, thank goodness!), Matey bubble bath and fluoride toothpaste. Delicious!

Oma, they call me – Grandma – but I never carried a child within my body. I couldn't. Not afterwards. A blessing, perhaps. Now, instead of three or four grandchildren, I have a couple of dozen.

David and I fought for the right of their grandparents to be noisy or naughty, to be loved and secure, to be – just children.

Karl and Ulli. Klara and Rosina. Recha and Johann. If I close my eyes, I can see their faces looking back at me, aged beyond their years, eyes that have seen too much, trusting so little in their distorted lives, but trusting us because their parents have told them to. In my dreams, they walk hand in hand in a crocodile behind me, clutching their little parcels, on their way to the good people who would take them in.

Jew and Christian. Catholic and Protestant. Pole, Russian or German. They were all children. They were all *my* children.

The letter has an Israeli stamp. I turn it over and over in my hands, feeling the limp airmail paper, smoothing its crinkles flat beneath a broad thumb, sniffing it suspiciously, like a cat with a rat that may or may not be dead. I lay it on the table and flatten it, trying to decipher the words through their pale blue covering. They tell me no more than the envelope has done – an old person's handwriting, spiky, familiar yet curiously foreign – like my own. I turn it over. The pre-printed lines for the return address have not been filled in.

The children are wrangling again. It's like listening to a flock of starlings settling to roost for the night. They swoop, soar, tumble, squabble, peck, soar again. Someone has cheated someone over a game of French cricket. Their voices reach me, urgent, righteous, demanding that I come and sort it all out. For once, their voices fail to move me. For once, they must solve their own problems.

The envelope isn't full. It's skinny, one sheet, no more. I hold the letter up to the sun, squinting, but all I can see is a halo of splintering, bright light.

Well, open it, for goodness sake – why don't you?

Because I'm afraid. Because it has been too long. Because I stopped hoping so many years ago. Because I'm too old to stand another disappointment. When you're young, you can bear it because there's always another day, another year. When you're old, you can count the days left, and there's no time for false hopes and dreams.

There have been too many hopes raised and smashed. I can't take any more. But God is good and I never stopped praying. Now . . .

Better, maybe, not to open it at all.

ANNE

The Homemaker

I've always thought that if our parents had behaved differently, we should all have turned out very differently too. There was a time when I thought that was a most profound idea. Now I see that it's terribly hackneyed. It's a philosophy of convenience. That doesn't make it any less true, however.

The children of lovers are orphans. That's another cliché – but how true, how true. The reason one is taught to despise clichés is because they lack originality, not veracity.

Mother used to say that Pa saw her at a party when they were both four years old and that he never wanted anyone else from that day onward. She used to say it with the sort of inward-looking smile I thought enigmatic when I was a romantic girl, but found frightfully aggravating when I grew up. It was a distant, self-satisfied smile that used to say – I thought – 'Try as you might, children, you will never know love as I have known it.'

'I wore dark green velvet,' she used to tell us, the words never varying, as though she recited a well-loved fairy story, 'with a coffee-coloured lace collar and tiny pearl buttons down the front. My hair was in ringlets – it was naturally curly. I do so wish that one of my daughters had inherited my curls. Your dear father stared at me and asked his nanny, "Is she real, Nanny, or is she a princess?"' And here Mother would give a little, modest laugh, like a summer shower rattling against the window. 'He asked me to marry him when we were five, but of course, we had to wait for a few years!'

A fairy story, but when you hear it over and over again, it palls. Believe me. There is nothing more boring than someone else's grand passion. A magic circle, and it's so very cold outside.

We were such lucky children: a beautiful house, plenty to eat, pretty clothes, toys, books, ponies. What more could we want? Lucky children.

Olive is just old enough to remember when Pa had two hands. She says he used to lift her up to the ceiling and she felt as high as heaven. She would look up into the bright lights, then down into his laughing face and pull his black moustache.

'Ow, ow! If you want a moustache so badly, miss, you'll just have to grow one of your own! You can't have mine.'

I expect he used to do the same for me – I just don't remember – but Clare and David were never lifted up to the sky. By the time they were born, our father was in France and when he came back he only had one real hand. The other didn't belong to him.

When I was a little older, old enough to know what happened between a man and a woman who loved each other enough to have babies, I used to wonder about Pa's hand. What did he do with it when he came to Mother's room at night? Did he stroke Mother's clotted-cream skin with it? Did he hide it behind his back and caress her with a warm hand alone? Did he leave it behind, safe in its shagreen case with the maroon velvet lining?

What was it like? How could she bear it?

One day, hiding in the bothy, I whispered this awful thought to Olive. Before the war, when the stables had been full of horses, the grooms' boys had slept in the bothy, like a sort of dormitory. Now, when all but our ponies had gone and only one man was needed to look after the Daimler, it was empty and became our secret meeting place.

Olive stretched out on the mouse-nibbled mattress. 'Oh, that,' she said with a superior smile. She crossed her legs at the ankle and even in her drooping white socks and scuffed sandals, their slender shapeliness was obvious. She folded her hands under her head, last summer's cotton frock straining at the seams. Even I could tell that she was beautiful, with her thick, tawny hair and eyes to match. Just now, sitting in a dusty sunbeam, she lounged like a well-fed lioness in the fork of a tree, content for the moment, but one knew that later she would rouse. She was beautiful and somehow – I could sense it, smell it, taste it – disturbing.

My discovery made sense of the stares and sniggers of village boys, on the rare occasions when we were allowed to walk down to the shop for sherbet. (Nanny thought it made us bilious, but sometimes Pa would slip us a penny or two, so that we could indulge. That first explosion in the mouth as the sherbet whooshed up the liquorice straw always snatched the breath from me, but, oh, it was such bliss.)

It was Olive they were staring at, not me. Already, I knew that. Not for me the nudges and winks, the open-mouthed, adenoidal worship.

There was one in particular. I remember him well, a big, bold boy, better fed than the rest, with a thatch of tow-coloured hair. His father had been a farrier who, after the war, had converted his forge to a garage, with hand-pumped petrol and walls plastered with tin signs trumpeting the benefits of Mazawattee Tea and Spratt's Dog Cakes. The boy mended punctures and his mother

19

served teas to charabanc parties. We could always tell when a charabanc had been through on a trip to the Devil's Punchbowl – the lanes were strewn with broken glass from the beer bottles tossed out of the vehicle.

This lad was braver than the others. Sometimes he would skim a pebble towards us, harmlessly, across the dusty street. Once he was coming out of the shop as we were going in and he held open the door with a lordly flourish. Olive shamed me by completely ignoring him. She didn't even say thank you, but I did and the boy turned nearly as red as I.

When she spotted the boys, Olive would draw herself up and toss her head, like a princess in ankle socks. She'd turn and talk vivaciously to me, in a voice quite unlike her own, high and clear and carrying.

'Come along, Anne,' she'd say, 'there's absolutely nothing to linger for here.'

I'd scuff my feet in the dust and follow, my face alight with embarrassment, my shoulders hunched in an attempt to look as different from Olive as possible.

It was very hard not to stare. Only a few weeks earlier, she'd been as flat as I still was. Yet there they were, suddenly, two soft, round swellings, the promise that one day soon she would look just like Mother.

I looked down and away – anywhere but at her chest. Olive laughed and stretched her arms higher. The swellings weren't soft and round any more, but hard, pointed, unfriendly.

'You're too young to understand,' she said.

'I'm not, I'm not. I know all about it.'

'You are. You proved it – worrying about Pa's hand. It's simply not important. Mother doesn't even notice it's missing when they're doing . . . you know . . . that.'

'How do you know?'

'Because it's a great passion, silly. You don't notice little things like that when you're in the grip of a great passion.'

'You mean, like Titania and Bottom? She didn't even notice he had an ass's head.'

'Exactly. What's a missing hand, compared to an ass's head?'

I stretched out on the mattress too, on my tummy, thinking about it all. It was all so difficult, mysterious and vaguely smutty; connected, in a curious way, with the sidelong glance of the tow-headed boy and with being made by Nanny to sleep with our hands outside the bed covers – if she found us with our hands under the blankets, no matter how cold the night, she'd pull them out, while we sleepily protested, and slap us on the wrists. I never understood why, nor why she was particularly cross if she found David like that. It was all to do with closed bedroom doors and whispers and raised eyebrows when I asked the wrong questions.

I felt as if the sun, although screened by net curtains of cobweb, was burning a hole between my shoulder blades. Curly horsehair, having worked its way through the mattress ticking, prickled my chest and thighs. There was a smell of mould and mice and piss. The pressure of Olive's body was warm, all the way down my right side.

I closed my eyes and tried to imagine that she was a man and we were in the grip of that mysterious grand passion. Nothing, nothing. I screwed my face up with the effort.

'It's no good,' I burst out, with a puff of pent up breath.

'What?'

'I just can't imagine ever actually wanting to do it. It's such a ridiculous thing to do.'

'Oh, I don't know . . .'

I sat up suddenly. 'Olive! You haven't . . . ?'

'No, of course not, stupid. When would I ever get the chance, anyway? There's forever someone treading on my heels, saying don't do this, don't do that. But I think about it . . .' Her eyes were closed and I had to strain to hear what she was saying.

'Anne?'

'Mmm.'

'Do you ever get feelings?'

''Course I do. All sorts.'

'No, I mean . . . special feelings. Lower down than in your tummy, sort of warm and hollow and wanting something, but you don't know what you want.'

'Sounds frightful. Take care you don't let on to Nanny or she'll get out the Gregory's Mixture.'

'No, this is nice. Too nice to talk about, really, even to you. I want and I want – but I don't know what it is. Don't you ever feel like that?'

'No, I don't.' I swung my feet to the floor, feeling suddenly angry, excluded from Olive's growing-up world. 'And I don't believe you do, either. I think you're just being stupid. You're making it all up.'

'No, I'm not. You're so clever – how do you know what I feel? You're only a little girl, after all. Why don't you go and play with the littlies . . .' She gave me a shove between the shoulder blades. 'Go on. Run along and play, little girl. I don't want you here.'

Was it that summer David caught measles or was it the one after? No, no, it was definitely that year. I remember because at last our parents had agreed to let me go to a proper school. I'd begged and begged.

'Lots and lots of girls go to school. Why can't I?'

'But there's no need, Anne darling,' Mother would answer. 'Mademoiselle can teach you all you need to know. You like her, don't you?'

22

'Yes, yes, of course . . .'

'Well, then.'

'. . . I'm much cleverer than Mademoiselle. Well, she's better at French, but so she jolly well ought to be. But I know heaps more history and Shakespeare than she does. Honestly.'

'Be good, sweet maid, and let who will be clever.' Mother quoted pompously.

'Why do people always say that to me?' I almost screamed, but held myself back. That wasn't the way to get what I wanted. That wasn't the way Olive would have gone about it. All screaming would achieve would be a trip upstairs for a dose of one of Nanny's noxious mixtures. Oh, but I felt like shrieking out loud.

'. . . but that's not the point. I want to wear a uniform and play proper games and carry my books in a satchel and do prep and ride a bicycle and have chums of my very own . . .'

'Goodness! You've been reading far too many school stories, it seems. I'll have to speak to Mademoiselle quite seriously about your reading list.'

But I knew she wouldn't. She wasn't interested enough.

'And David will be going to prep school soon – just because he's a boy – so why can't I?'

'Olive doesn't want to go. Neither does Clare.'

'Yes, she does, but that doesn't count, because she doesn't really want to go to school, only not be parted from David. But I *really* do . . .'

I was beginning to whine but, although I knew it was the worst possible way to persuade my parents, I couldn't help it. It was the way I felt.

'Arthur, will you talk to this child? I really can't cope with all this nonsense.'

Mother swivelled in her chair to appeal to Pa. Her neck, back and thigh formed a long, sinuous line under

23

a cobweb of a gown. Pa put down his newspaper and left the window seat to join us. Even in my misery, I noticed that he didn't just stand beside Mother, like a father should. He circled her neck with both his hands and, with his real thumb, he softly rubbed the bump at the top of her spine. Mother arched her back and pressed against him.

'What's all this about, Anne?' he asked, his voice much harder than the one he usually used to me. 'I can't have you upsetting your mother, you know.'

'I'm not upsetting her – she's upsetting me. I want to go to school. I want to go so badly.'

'But why?'

'I want to be . . . I want to be ordinary.'

Pa burst out laughing.

'It's not funny. It's not funny,' I stormed. 'If you won't let me go, I'll run away . . .'

'I've heard of children running away from school,' he chuckled, 'but this is the first time I've ever heard of someone running away *to* school. What do you think, darling?' He bent his head and placed his lips softly on Mother's hair. 'Shall we let her go?'

'Please. Please, say yes. Olive will soon be married, I'll go to school and so will David and then there'll only be Clare and she's so quiet. You can pretend you've only got each other. It'll be lovely for you. Please let me go.'

Mother and Pa gave each other one of those stunned looks that, once I became a mother, I found myself too often exchanging with my husband.

All that long summer, loafing around Bramleigh Court, I ached, physically ached for September to come. It was too early for cubbing and the ponies were grass-fat and sluggish. Once our morning riding lesson was over, the day stretched ahead, long, hot and empty. Picnics were childish. Tree houses weren't fun any more. I didn't believe there were wild animals in the shrubbery. I was too young for Olive, too old for Clare and David. The twins were digging a tiger trap among the roots of the rhododendrons, hacking at the hard earth with their little seaside spades, their faces, as identical as could be in boy and girl twins, scarlet and sweaty. It was seven and a half inches deep by the end of August. Olive used to take out the punt and lie all day, out on the island under the willows, reading and dreaming. Last year, she would have asked me to go with her.

Mother and Pa used to come down from Saturday to Monday and then the house was livelier, because they brought their friends with them. Sprawled on the deep-cushioned window seat halfway up the stairs, I would watch them on the terrace below. What were they doing? What were they saying? What did they mean?

Years later, on a cruise, I saw the shadow theatres of Indonesia. The flickering, black images had their own stories to tell, of their names and histories, their code of behaviour, their customs, in movements that were unchanged by time. To the natives, the story pattern was in their blood, interwoven with the thread of their lives. To an outsider, to me, it was a baffling mystery.

Watching my parents and their friends was a bit like that.

Peering down from an awkward angle, I would watch them below me moving to some undiscovered choreography – the glance, the shrug, the hand trailing across a bare shoulder. There were catchy tunes from a portable Decca. Someone would dance a few steps in a look-at-me-everybody sort of way. 'After You Get What You Want, You Don't Want It' was always a favourite, or 'When I Wanna, You No Wanna'. There were shrieks and lunges and clumsy chases. A woman might be caught and dumped, squealing, on a garden-bed. But did her struggles mean anything at all? Did she really want to be rescued? What was really happening?

Under the laughter was a tension and an excitement that even I, far above them, could sense.

Was this what being a grownup was all about?

Sometime during the afternoon, my father would catch my mother's eye. It didn't seem to matter what they were doing or who they were talking to. The look passed across the space as if no one else was there. It was a physical thing, as though one had put out a hand to touch the other. First Mother would drift away, followed, a few minutes later, by Pa. No one but me, it seemed, even noticed they'd gone.

Between tea and cocktails, people would become bored. The men would start arguing – I couldn't hear what they were saying, but could tell by their flushed faces and jerky gestures. The women would yawn and file their nails ostentatiously.

I got bored then, too, and would turn back to the page I'd marked in *For the School Colours*. I understood the life between these pages. It was so simple. The rules were clear, unlike the complex, unsatisfying games going on below me.

The island really was an island, a tiny one, in the middle of the lake, connected to the shore by a willow-pattern bridge, hung with wistaria. Olive liked to punt there, although she could have walked. She would lie in the punt, pulled into a secret cave made by the fronds of weeping willow. It was shady in there, cool and green. The light flickered off the water and sparkled through the shifting leaves.

It wasn't fair. Why should I be the one left out? David and Clare had each other. Mother and Pa didn't need anyone else. Olive was quite satisfied with her own company. That left me.

It was too hot to move, too hot to breathe. The garden was limp with exhaustion. The sun seemed to have sucked all the oxygen out of the air and left only dust that made me sneeze. I was plagued by hay fever, that summer and every summer, with a constantly runny nose and rheumy eyes – a plain child, I suppose, flushed and uncomfortable.

I stumped across the bridge to the island. Why should Olive have it all to herself? It wasn't fair. It wasn't *her* island.

I suppose I must have made quite a lot of noise, but they didn't hear me.

The punt was bobbing gently on the still water. I looked down into it. Olive's skin was dappled with light, green and gold, enchanted. Her flesh looked cool and marbled, her tilted little breasts firm, somehow too perfect to be real. But she was real. The sunlight caught and gilded the down on her arms and legs and the coarser curls, only a few, between her legs.

She was smiling. I knew that smile. When Olive's lips were sweetly curved and her amber eyes mere slits of pleasure, I knew she was about to strike out, like a cat who lies in the sun with paws tucked neatly under. Don't imagine that the cat is snoozing as you run beneath her nose, little mouse.

The tow-headed boy put out his hand. Even from where I was, I could see that it was trembling. He looked so miserable. His coarse flannel shirt was stained with dark half-moons under the arms and a damp stripe ran down the back. His legs were encased in heavy woollen trousers and he wore thick-soled boots. His face was flushed a dull, ugly red.

His hand hovered just above Olive's right breast.

'Don't you dare,' said Olive, her voice sharp and

27

heartless as the Snow Queen I remembered from nursery story time. 'You don't really think I'd let you touch me with hands like yours?'

He looked so big, so strong, so dangerous. Olive stared straight into his face, held his gaze, challenged him and won. Suddenly, he was a shame-faced boy again.

'You've got hands like a navvy,' she went on, relentlessly. 'Your nails are all broken. Who do you think you are?'

'I know what you are,' the boy said, almost incoherent with disgust and his country accent. 'I know what you are and you needn't think I won't let on, because I will. I'll tell everyone what you are.'

'No, you won't. You wouldn't dare. They'd only laugh at you, poor boy.'

He scrambled out of the punt, rocking it almost over. He didn't see me, standing in the bushes, as he blundered past, lumpish with misery. I could hear his heavy boots pounding across the bridge as he broke into a run, back to the village.

> She took me to her elfin grot,
> And there she gazed and sigh'd full sore,
> And there I shut her wild, wild eyes
> With kisses four.

The knight must have run like that, fleeing from his *belle dame sans merci*, leaving her triumphant by the lake. But that was romance. There was nothing at all romantic about this. This was just disgusting. I watched him go and knew how cold his awakening must have been.

I ran too, as far and as fast as I could, until the breath was whistling in my throat and there was a bitter taste of bile on my tongue and I couldn't tell if it was tears or sweat that trickled down my cheeks and into the corners of my mouth.

I didn't know what I was running from. All I knew was that I had to get away from the strange sensations the sight had aroused.

When I went upstairs that night, I found, lying on my bed, my book that I had dropped on the island as I ran away. But we never, ever spoke about it.

Olive didn't go back to the island for the little left of the summer holiday. She was good company for me.

In the cupboard in my room at our house in Mount Street hung my uniform. All summer long, I thought of it hanging there: the purple blazer and tam o'shanter that would mark me as a pupil of Glendower School. It wasn't quite as exciting as going off to a seaside board-ing school, but still . . .

I pestered the life out of Nanny. Yes, she'd sewn my name tapes onto everything. Yes, she knew how to get to Cromwell Road. Not that she needed to, because Cleeve was going to drive us there each morning and take us home each afternoon. And because going for a walk was such a ritual of London childhood, he'd let us down in the park opposite the Hyde Park Hotel, we'd walk uphill as far as Knightsbridge Barracks, and he'd drive us the rest of the way.

I'd been to my new school once, for a visit. I'd met the headmistresses, Misses Lloyd and Cornwall. I'd sniffed the intoxicating mixture of chalk, gas and cabbage. The clatter of shoes on the elaborately-tiled hall floor, the screech of chair legs, the pounding of the piano in assembly had all excited me beyond description.

I'd even made a friend. We'd queued on the basement stairs at eleven o'clock for the one tiny lavatory, while a nice maid called Ada stood at the door saying, 'Hurry along, dear, there are lots more girls waiting'. I'd been standing behind a thin, fair girl called Daphne and we'd made a promise to share a double desk when school started again in the autumn. It was going to be wonderful.

Then David and Clare caught measles.

Of course, it was a tragedy for David. But again, of course, we children couldn't be expected to realise that. David and Clare did everything together, so it was no surprise when they came out in spots on the same day.

They were very ill. No one had time to think about Olive and me for a day or two. Nanny was too busy giving them cold sponge baths to reduce their temperatures. Hour after hour she sat during those first two days, sponging their little red bodies, getting up only to change the water or attend to her most urgent needs.

'Are they going to die?' I whispered to Olive.

'Of course not – not with Nanny sitting there – they wouldn't dare!'

We took ourselves off to bed, quiet as mice, and no one checked if we'd washed or brushed our hair or said our prayers.

When someone finally did remember us, we were both sent back to Mount Street, with May the nursery maid to look after us, out of reach of infection, but in quarantine for three weeks.

I opened my cupboard and there were the purple blazer and the dashing little tam o'shanter. I lay down on my bed and wept. I must have been there for an hour before May found me.

'What's all this, then?' she asked. She perched on the edge of the bed and, with awkward kindness, put her hand on my shoulder. 'It's all right. The twins'll be better soon. We all got it in my family when I was little – nearly drove my mum round the bend having six spotty children at one go – and we all got better. No need to cry.'

'I know they will,' I snuffled. 'I'm not crying about that.'

'What then? Must be somethink pretty awful to make all that row about.'

'I can't go to school.'

'Is that all? You just got to hang on a bit longer, that's all. Not long now.'

'I won't. I'll never get there. I know I won't. Mother and Pa'll change their minds. Or David and Clare will die and we'll all go into mourning and go to live in the horrid country always.'

'Really! What a thing to say! And I thought you were such a big girl, Miss Anne. You're behaving like a spoiled baby.'

'Something will stop me going. I just know it. You'll see. I hate them for catching stupid measles. I hate them.'

'Well,' she said, taking her hand off my shoulder, 'that's not very nice, is it?'

'I don't feel nice. I feel awful inside.'

''Ere, you're not going down with it too, I hope.' She put her rough little hand on my forehead. 'Your head's all hot.'

So in the end, all four of us had measles, one after the other. By the time the quarantine restrictions were lifted, it was nearly Christmas. Mother drifted into the nursery one teatime and looked round at her pale and listless family.

'Oh dear,' she sighed, 'what a dismal sight. Now listen, darlings, your father and I have had a marvellous idea. We're going to spend the winter in France – all of us together – won't that just be fun? No more nasty sleet and smoky fires. No peasoupers. Just lots of lovely sun and scrumptious food. And when we come back, we'll all be healthy again. It'll be such a delicious treat. Now – what do you think of that?'

'And will David be better when we come back?' Clare asked.

'Of course he will. You all will.'

'But he will be able to hear again, won't he? Promise?' Clare persisted. She had Mother hooked on her extraordinarily steady, bright blue gaze.

Mother looked a little startled. She glanced across at David. He was lying on his tummy on the hearth rug, fiddling with his Meccano, but without the energy to make anything worthwhile. The firelight glinted on the nickel-plated spars.

'David?' she said softly and he sat up at once and looked at her.

Mother smiled, relieved. 'You'll all be as fit as fleas, I promise. All you need is some sunshine.'

But she hadn't seen what I'd seen. Clare had nudged her twin with her foot to catch his attention.

I never did go to school.

It was all such an adventure that it almost – almost – made up for not being at school. Mademoiselle had been 'let go' with a good reference. 'No point in taking her,' Nanny had said triumphantly, watching over the banisters as her rival for our affections struggled downstairs with her luggage. 'Taking coals to Newcastle, that would be.'

We set off from Victoria one dank December morning on the ten o'clock boat train. We were well spread out: our parents had reserved a table and armchairs in the drawing room atmosphere of the Pullman car; we children with Nanny and May were in a first class carriage; Mother's maid, MacDowall, had a seat of her own in second class and Mother's jewel case chained to her wrist.

'That's a silly idea,' Clare pointed out. 'Everyone knows that French jewel thieves stop at nothing. They'll just cut her hand off – simple.'

Nanny made us stay out on the platform with May while she boarded the train, with the air of a mountaineer. She took from her bag two huge, freshly laundered, white sheets and fastened them with safety pins to the seats. Only then would she let us into the compartment.

'You can't be too careful, I always hold,' she said darkly, 'what with smuts and you don't know what all else. The sort of people who travel in first class these days aren't always all they might seem.' She began removing our coats and hats, gloves and leggings, and stowing them, neatly folded, in the luggage rack. 'Not like before the war – ladies were ladies and gentlemen were gentlemen in those days.'

The journey, the whole idea of living in a foreign country, was an absolute nightmare for her. As well as the provisions she'd brought for the journey, she'd packed a hamper which travelled in the luggage van, full of the essentials of English nursery life. I'd watched her pack it. There was tea, of course (Lipton's), Huntley & Palmer biscuits (Osbornes), enough Bengers for an army of invalids, Pear's soap, Bovril, Bird's custard, Horlicks, Scotts Emulsion and I don't know what else.

'Though how I'm to be expected to make a drinkable cup of tea with no decent water and heaven only knows what sort of milk, I don't know.'

'We're not going to Darkest Africa, Nanny.'

'You can laugh, young lady, but let me tell you that you'll be laughing on the other side of your face when you get a poorly tummy from all that oily food.'

Before catching the *train bleu* to the Riviera, we stayed for a few days in Paris. Mother had some important shopping to do – simply none of her winter clothes were suitable for a milder climate. So Pa took two suites, one

33

above the other, in the Hotel Meurice, overlooking the gardens of the Tuileries.

'It's not like a proper park, is it, dears?' complained Nanny. 'All gritty paths and rude statues. Not anything like Hyde Park or Kensington Gardens. Think of the Dell and Peter Pan.'

'But Achilles is just as rude – you never complain about him and there are goat carts here and puppets – it's wonderful,' Clare said with enthusiasm.

'It's more than one person's work to keep the twins clean,' Nanny went on as though Clare hadn't spoken. 'They come in all dusty and with their shoes covered in doggies' little mistakes. I can't be doing with it.'

Mother went to Molyneux and Lanvin. She went to Vionnet in the avenue Montaigne. I can still remember her wearing that wonderful Vionnet, a shimmering waterfall of silk jersey that moved as she moved, with a plunging back and crusted beading on the shoulders that must have cost the eyesight of a dozen seamstresses. She bought a jumper suit of caramel cashmere from Paquin, so cleverly understated that it must have cost a fortune, and from Callot Soeurs a motoring coat of squirrel-trimmed scarlet leather with a matching scarlet helmet that I privately thought made her look like Mr Toad on the rampage.

While Nanny gossiped with other nannies in the Parc Monceau or sat in the Tuileries, watching David and Clare riding in the goat carts, Mother dragged Olive and me around Galeries Lafayette.

'It'll be such fun,' she said, 'now that you're old enough to go shopping. My two big girls. Won't we just enjoy ourselves?'

And we did. It was the first time Mother had even acknowledged that her daughters were growing up. We both felt much too old to have a Nanny, although we consoled ourselves by saying that she was needed for the twins. Before too long, Olive would be coming out. And after that, I only had to hang on for a couple of years. It couldn't come soon enough.

What a step up from Gorringe's. I stood at the bottom of the central staircase and looked up into the glass dome of Galeries Lafayette – burnt orange and peacock blue and livid green. Each circular sales floor had metal balconies of stylised Art Nouveau flowers impossible to recognise, poppies maybe, or lilies – old-fashioned perhaps, but still gorgeous. I felt like a queen as I began the climb to the appropriate floor.

My pleasure in the new, grownup clothes was quite ruined by the sight of myself in the cheval glass, standing next to Olive.

We've always been compared – always. It isn't fair.

Olive was *made* for the slender, low-waisted fashions. Nanny called her 'Tin Ribs', but I *longed* to deserve that nickname. The belt of my frock had settled not quite low enough, somewhere between my midriff and hips, on the little pads of flesh that cushioned my pelvis. As a result, the bodice, which should have hung straight, developed wrinkles in the most unflattering places.

Olive wore a smart, supple, tan tweed that brought out the hint of copper in her new, short hair. My frock was bilious green. Olive had said I ought to wear green – she said it went with my mousey-brown hair and tea-coloured eyes. I had believed her. After all, Olive had such a marvellous touch – a tweak, a ribbon, a flower and she could transform the plainest frock. So I'd insisted on green and had turned to the glass eager to see the new me. I looked as though I'd been dredged up from somewhere very deep, draped in seaweed. It hadn't looked like that on the mannequin.

I turned away from the sight.

'Oh dear,' said Mother, 'what a surly expression. I'm

35

sure I never looked like that whenever my mother bought me a new frock. Aren't you pleased?'

'Yes,' I snapped.

'Then why the scowls? Really, Anne, you do have a most fearsome glower. It's so unfortunate. Quite alters your little face. If you don't manage to cure yourself of it soon, no one will dream of marrying such a sour-puss.'

'No one will dream of marrying me anyway, while Olive's around,' I mumbled.

Fortunately, Mother was discussing a minute alter-ation to the hem of Olive's frock with the vendeuse. But Olive heard me. She stuck her tongue out. She bloated her cheeks and forced out her tummy, seeming more grotesquely like me than I did myself. I got my own back. I trod on her toe as we were going out the door.

When we got back to the hotel, Mother went off to rest before dinner. Nanny and the twins weren't back, which was unusual, because they normally had nursery tea. Olive and I settled to a hostile truce. She occupied the table, playing patience, and I retreated to the railed, open window with my new Angela Brazil. It was freez-ing out there and damp, my breath curled up in smoky spirals, but I wasn't in the mood even to breathe the same air as Olive. If Mother hadn't been resting, I'd have gone downstairs and taken sanctuary in her suite, but Mother's little rests were sacred.

How it had hurt, Olive's parody of my size. I knew I wasn't fat – well, certainly nowhere near the Bessie Bunter class – but there was no shape to me. I was strong and compact and, somehow, solid. Just a typical English schoolgirl, I suppose. Yet Olive had managed, in one quicksilver, heartless gesture, to make me feel abnormal.

'You're a growing girl,' Nanny would say when I

36

moaned. 'You'll shed your puppy fat when you're good and ready.'

Yes, but *when*?

The tears of self-pity that brimmed over seemed hot enough to scald my cold cheeks. Very quickly, they cooled down and left stiff, icy tracks on my skin.

I would just stop eating, that's all. I'd starve and starve until I was sylphlike. I'd wear the slinkiest black imaginable and have Mother's old-fashioned diamond brooch made into a smart pair of clips and be sultry and mysterious behind an eye-veil. People would say, 'Who's the woman with the wonderful figure?'. And it would be *me* – Anne Northaw.

Below in the gardens, most of the children were going home in the early winter dusk. It was cold enough for my breath to form little frozen droplets of condensation on the scarf I'd bundled around my neck, but I wouldn't shut the window. The Guignol theatre had closed its doors. The donkeys and goats trooped away. The traffic on the rue de Rivoli had a different sound, an amusing, evening sound. I could see Nanny hurrying through the trees towards the hotel. David and Clare each held one of her hands. She was walking very fast towards the gate flanked by those more-than-life size statues of a bull and a lion rending and being rent by hunting dogs. When I leaned out of the window and waved, they didn't wave back.

Nanny whirled into the room, whipped off the twins' coats, hats and gloves and sent them to wash their hands, then set the kettle to boil on her little primus stove before unpinning her own hat. The cups and saucers clattered together as she laid them on the table, as though her hands were shaking beyond control.

Clare was back almost immediately.

'Have you scrubbed your nails?' asked Nanny, but absently.

37

'David's been sick,' Clare announced, with some relish, 'all over the carpet.'

David had stepped into the road in front of a taxi. He hadn't been hurt, beyond a grazed knee, but there'd been a frightful to-do, with Nanny shouting at the driver and Clare screaming blue murder and assaulting the poor man with her little fists. We didn't know this until later, of course. First there was all the hubbub of cleaning up the mess. Then a doctor was called, but he said that David had only had a little shock and that he'd be better after a good night's sleep.

Pa leaned over David's bed. He was wearing his silk dressing gown over his evening clothes, without his dress coat. The stiff shirt front buckled as he bent over the bed. His patent shoes twinkled in the subdued light. I couldn't remember when I'd ever seen Pa in one of our rooms, no matter how much one or other of us may have vomited. Just to see him there impressed on me the seriousness of the occasion. Not until then did I realise what might have been and the security of my world trembled. There were four of us, but there might tonight have been only three.

'Feeling better, old man?' Pa asked.

David just nodded. He was so pale that his eyes seemed to have sunk into deep holes – like an Eskimo's fishing holes in the ice.

'That's a brave little chap.' Pa gently brushed a strand of hair back from David's forehead. 'Not a very clever thing to do, was it? Poor old Nanny. She's had no end of a fright.'

'I'm sorry,' David whispered.

'Never mind. All over now. Just you have a good sleep and you'll be right as rain in the morning, you'll see.'

Later that night, I had to get up to go to the lavatory. As I passed through the twins' room, I noticed a mound at the end of David's bed. It was Clare, wrapped up in her eiderdown.

'Whatever do you think you're doing? Go to bed,' I whispered. 'It's the middle of the night.'

'I'm keeping an eye on David,' she said.

'Don't be silly. He's asleep.'

'Pa told me to. He said, "Keep an eye on David, old girl. I'm relying on you, remember."'

'He didn't mean all the time, stupid. He knows you've got to go to sleep sometime. Come on – bed!'

In the tiny glow of the night light, I could see just the top of Clare's fair head above the huddle of quilt. She was steadfast, her face turned towards David, her little body hunched and determined.

'He didn't hear it, you know, Anne.'

'Who didn't hear what?'

'David. He didn't hear the taxi. He was looking the other way and he didn't hear it.'

I fell in love with Provence. I didn't expect to. I really meant to hate it – why should I be there when I could have been at Glendower School? – but my pursed lips and ferocious frown didn't last much beyond the first week at le Mas de St Armou. It had once been a fortified farm, almost a hamlet in itself really, honey-beige stone and baked earth, crouching on the summit of a dark green hill, with views over a *maquis* of cork oak and thyme-scented bushes to a navy blue line of sea.

The central room was long, dark and low. Mme Honorat, the housekeeper, threw open the shutters on a row of windows one by one and pushed back the white muslin curtains, letting in that astonishing light. The furnishings were dark and well-polished, but the chair rungs were worn by rubbing feet and the central table scarred with knife marks. At the far end was a pair of glazed doors, leading onto a flagged loggia. It seemed to me to be everything a room ought to be.

'*Ça vous plaît?*' Mme Honorat asked.

It pleased me, at least, very much indeed.

Nanny, however, was rather less pleased by her new surroundings. Upstairs Clare, David and Nanny had been allocated the largest room, the one above the central living room. It was bright and white, with lime-washed walls, rag rugs on polished chestnut boards, tiny window embrasures and high double doors leading onto a balcony over the roof of the loggia.

Nanny looked around her new domain and we could all tell by the pursing of her lips that she was not at all pleased, not one little bit. 'There's no mantelpiece,' she said, 'wherever shall I put the nursery clock?'

She had never, she said, since she was a nursery maid, lived in a house where every drop of water had to be carried upstairs and it was a little late in the day to be starting now. Unhygienic, that's what she called it, but that's foreigners for you. There were no nice, big cupboards to hang the clothes and no bookshelves.

'And don't be surprised,' she continued, 'if we lose one of the little pets over that awful balcony. Those railings don't look any too safe to me.'

We were town children set free. Even at Bramleigh Court, although it was in the country, we had to follow a set programme of naps and walks and mealtimes. At le Mas de St Armou it was at last acknowledged that Olive and I were too grown up for nursery discipline. We were given French lessons for two hours every morning by the old curé from the village below. After that we were free to wander, hatless and with bare, scratched legs.

I give the impression that we lived like gypsies. Of course, that's not absolutely true. Mother and Pa thought they were living a very bohemian life, but they still needed to employ a surprisingly large number of people to make that life comfortable. As well as the staff we brought from England – Nanny, May and Mac-Dowall – I remember Mme Honorat, Mme Esquillon the cook and Lisette who seemed to do everything else that needed doing; there was old Aurore, with face and hands seamed like the bark of a cork oak, who took away our washing and brought it back smelling of the rosemary bushes she had draped it on to dry; the terra-cotta pots of scarlet geraniums and crinkle-leaved cistus were watered by Claude, with the gentle, simple, gap-toothed smile, who pushed his bicycle up the long hill every other day and freewheeled back down it again, a smoke signal of red dust following him.

I learned to love the shape of the landscape, the bare vines on quilted fields, the fierce silhouettes of hilltop villages, perched like hungry birds above the vineyards. I learned to love the colours, too, all so much more daring than at home – red rocks and purple sea, orange roof tiles and navy sky. If a child had slapped those colours on a painting, one might have said, 'No, no, darling, that's not right. Look, do it this way . . .'. But the child would not have been wrong, just as van Gogh had not been wrong.

It was difficult to believe that Christmas had almost arrived. This part of Provence is protected from the mistral by higher hills to the north. We found it cold enough at night for a snapping fire of vine trimmings and pruned fruit tree logs, yet roses still bloomed over the supports of the loggia.

Aurore, in her nasal Provençal accent that sounded always as though someone was tweaking her nose, taught us about the tradition of the *crèche*. In pride of place, in the centre of the long walnut table, we set our crib with its Holy Family. Hurrying to join them came the tiny clay figures, the *santons*, with their naive, eager

41

faces and their hands full of gifts for the Child – *l'homme à l'oie* and *la femme à la poule*, *la femme au fagot* and *la femme à la coucorde*, *la bohémienne* and *Grasset et Grassette*, arm in arm under their umbrella.

I have them still – '*ces petites fleurs que l'on ceuille en hiver*', the poet Mistral called them. I take them out of their cotton wool wrapping and turn them in my hands, remembering. Here is *lou Boumian* with his knife, but it's all right, he's only going to use it to cut the bread he's just stolen from the baker. Here is *Moussou lou Maire* with his tricolour sash of office and his little waxed moustache. And here is David's favourite, *lou Ravi*, the simpleton, his empty hands raised to heaven because he has nothing to give but his love.

'That's Claude,' he would say and certainly there seemed to be an unexpected affinity between the old man and the little boy. David would follow him around, carrying a little basket into which Claude would put the deadheads he had snipped off the flowers. Clare would stand in the shadows watching them, scuffing her feet in the dust. Then suddenly she'd be unable to bear any more. She'd dart out, her voice shrill with jealousy, and drag David off on some invented expedition.

'Bit old for dolls, aren't you, old chap?' Pa queried, watching David as he rearranged the crib yet again.

'They're not dolls,' David answered, turning a stubborn, protective shoulder on the scene, 'they're people.'

'Dolls are dolls,' said Pa, 'and I'm not having any son of mine growing up into a pansy. Go on, out into the fresh air and kick a ball or something. Off with you.'

He gave David a sharp smack on the bottom – a playful one, of course – and sent him out into the garden.

As I handle the little people, I can hear Aurore's cracked voice again, in her almost unintelligible dialect, pronouncing the Christmas blessing: '*E prièr se sian pas mai qu'au mens sieguen pas mens!*' If the coming year be not better, pray that it be no worse.

On Christmas morning, we all went down, squashed into the hired Delahaye tourer that Pa drove at breakneck speed around the hairpin bends, to the little Anglican church in St Raphael, for a service that seemed to compress the essence of the day into its joyful simplicity. On the way back, we passed a little lake, no more than an *étang*, where a flock of flamingos fed, every shade of rose on blue.

For the twins' sake, and for the sake of Mme Esquillon, we had the traditional Provençal Christmas meal, *le Gros Souper*, for luncheon on Christmas Day instead of before midnight mass on Christmas Eve. I don't think our cook was very impressed by this arrangement, even though it was meant to spare her to spend time with her family. She thought it was flouting tradition. I could hear her banging and clattering in the kitchen – the English were doing it all wrong – but Mother just smiled her serene smile as she popped her head around the door.

'Everything all right, Mme Esquillon? Fine, fine. It all looks too wonderful for words.'

There was celery salad, a garlic and herb soup, said to be able to save your life, but after a while kill you, a dish of salt cod with spinach and garlic, lots of little dishes of vegetables – endive, chard, spinach. And of course, *les treize desserts*, thirteen desserts symbolising the presence of Christ and the twelve apostles at the family table: four sorts of dried fruit and nuts, *les quatre mendiants* in their brown garb; fresh fruit to symbolise the products of the earth – pears, melon, oranges; the dried apricots called *pistoles* because they look like golden coins; the sweets – quince conserve, nougat both black and white, glacé fruit from Apt; finally, the dates,

43

at the centre of the table, representing Christ Himself, because on the flight to Egypt only the date palm opened its boughs to shelter Him.

We dragged the long table into the sun in a sheltered corner of the garden. All the children, even the twins, had been allowed wine with the meal. We were heavy and silent, quite tipsy with light and food and wine. David and Clare, twisted in their chairs, sat back to back like little book ends. The sun beat down on the back of my neck and the scent of the rosemary crushed every time I moved my leg was pungent. I looked sleepily round my family, narrowing my eyes against the brightness, and thought how beautiful they all were. I loved them very much that day.

I don't remember that we were ever really a family at Christmas again.

Winter slipped happily into spring and the mimosa bloomed. My parents seemed to have no wish to go back to England. The original plan had been to spend just the winter in France, until we all had roses in our cheeks again. But with the spring, like returning swallows, visitors from England found us and it seemed to become harder and harder to go home.

Now people were coming out to spend time with us for all sorts of reasons:

'Frightful winter – I feel quite washed out – need some sun and sand.'

'Freddie has been quite beastly to me. Do you mind if I hide down here for a while, just to teach him a lesson?'

'Have you all been hibernating? Aren't you coming home? Oh well, if the mountain won't come to Mohammed, eh . . . so here I am!'

And now the garden was filled with the same, lounging people I recalled from Bramleigh Court and the

44

mysterious, grownup dance was just as baffling as I remembered.

No one got up before noon. The garden was mine in the early morning. After that, in all the secluded corners lay bodies, sleek as seals, bare as babies. The sight of all that adult flesh revealed made me cringe with embarrassment. The smell of coconut oil overpowered the scent of thyme and rosemary. The gramophone ground out its tinkling tunes all day and silenced the crickets at night.

There were trips to the beach, when we all piled into several cars and roared down to the coast, past fields where the vines were putting out leaves and lavender spikes were beginning to colour. We'd tumble rugs and parasols and picnic baskets all over some peaceful cove.

The women would tie their hair up in brilliant turbans to protect their pin curls. It made them look like a flight of exotic butterflies pausing for a rest. Then they'd roll down the straps of their bathing costumes and lie down with a sigh. Pleasure can be awfully exhausting when it's pursued so single-mindedly.

The men would rush into the sea with a yell and a spurt of hot sand and a thrashing of water. Always competitive, always on edge. Then they'd see who was fittest, who could swim farthest, fastest . . . anything, to make the women lift their heads from the sand, put on the round sunglasses which reduced their faces to arched brows and mouths like gashes. Anything, to make them take notice . . .

When they came out, there'd be music and sometimes dancing on the hard sand by the water's edge. I'd huddle under my towel, in the broiling sun, on the edge of the laughter, knowing that if I stood up, if I tried to run and dance, my new breasts, that somehow hadn't turned out at all like Olive's, would jiggle and bounce beneath the shrunken striped wool of my costume.

45

'I've got the most appalling spot.' Olive squinted into the dull, freckled looking glass. Her pointed face was twisted with the effort of seeing herself clearly.

'Only one? You're lucky!'

'But it's right on the point of my chin. Oh, how ghastly. I can't possibly be seen like this.'

'Who's looking?'

'I don't know what's the matter with you these days, Anne.' Olive talked at me through her reflection. 'All you do is mope and grouse.'

I shrugged and rolled over onto my tummy, with a book propped up on the pillow in front of me.

'Do you think Mother might lend me something to put on it?'

'Makeup, d'you mean? Pretty unlikely. You're much too young to paint your face.'

'I'm not!'

'You are so!'

'Anyway, this is abroad – it's different. So there!'

'You couldn't hide that thing under makeup, however hard you tried, it's just like a volcano,' I snorted. 'Why don't you go and ask Nanny for a nice mustard poultice for it. Get her to slap it on good and thick and hot.'

'Oh, I hate you! What's the good of having a sister like you. You're such a bore.'

'And what's the good of having a sister like you – all airs and graces . . .' I shouted at her back just before she slammed the door. '. . . and spots!' I yelled, but the door had already closed.

She managed to get round Mother – I knew she would, she always could. When Olive appeared for dinner that night, I was already down. I watched her come down the steps into the garden, timing it perfectly, the last to arrive. I watched the reaction she aroused in the others.

46

To those smart, jaded men and women, sated with doing nothing but pleasing themselves all day, Olive was a novelty, a diversion, a rarity. She was that only distantly remembered thing – someone who still enjoyed being alive.

She looked so fresh, in a frock – a girl's frock, not a woman's frock – of pale yellow cotton, with a wide collar and with short sleeves and a short, flirty skirt that showed off her slender, golden limbs. Her fair lashes had been darkened, discreetly, for the first time and it was astonishing how vividly amber her slanting, cat's eyes had become. She ought to be able to see in the dark with eyes like that, I thought. You had to look very closely to see that the spot on her chin had been darkened with an eyebrow pencil to become a beauty spot, an asset instead of a disfigurement.

It was a disturbing combination: the budding woman dressed in a frock that could have been worn by a child younger than Clare and not looked out of place. Disturbing and – as I see it now – sensuous, dangerous. Olive was like a butterfly that summer, one that has already discarded its chrysalis and sits waiting, crumpled, for the life force to flood through it, to pump its wings full of colour and beauty.

Golden skin, golden eyes, golden dress. She stood like a shaft of sunlight on the darkening steps.

I saw how the men looked at her, hungrily, greedily, as though she had been laid out on a plate especially for them. The women – and this I couldn't understand – looked at her hungrily, too, as though they would like to eat her, to open their painted, vermilion mouths and pop her in – no more than a tasty titbit, an *amuse-gueule*.

I didn't understand then. I'm sorry to say that I do understand now, only too well.

'Well, well, who looks like a million dollars tonight?' Ferdy Cray drawled. 'Come and sit by me, sweetheart.'

'No, I don't want to, not with you. I'm going to sit beside . . .' Olive paused dramatically '. . . the handsomest man here.'

She spun round, her head on one side, considering, playing them as skilfully as a practised coquette. Where did she learn that look? When did she learn how to get what she wanted? Had she any idea what she was doing to them all?

The women were watching, waiting. Did they welcome her to the sisterhood of predators, or did she threaten them with the freshness and youth they had long ago bartered in a worthless bargain?

And each man was certain, when her eyes met his, that he would be the chosen one. I could see them, squaring their shoulders, pulling in their waists. She stopped, made a little movement towards Pa – and I saw him give a small, nervous, relieved smile, as though saying, 'Yes, but she's still only my little girl after all,' – then she plumped down beside Guy Tarver.

Ferdy gave a little titter.

There was a mass sigh of pent-up breath, of anti-climax, of disappointment.

Olive wriggled on the seat she now shared with Guy.

'Move up,' she commanded.

And the apprentice woman was suddenly a child again, tanned and coltish, with drooping ankle socks and her hair clipped back in a tortoiseshell barrette. She was just my sister again. But she had given warning and the warning had been noted.

Guy looked startled. Yet he must have been certain that he would be the chosen one. Didn't he know that he was the most attractive – no, that's the wrong word, not attractive, because he didn't set out to attract, not like the other men – didn't he know that he was the most beautiful man there?

No, probably not. That was part of his charm. He

was dressed like everyone else, casually, in white knitted polo shirt and white flannels, with a school tie – some rather minor public school tie, I shouldn't wonder – knotted around his waist. But his grace invested those simple clothes with a special significance. They could as easily have been the spotless robes of some saintly crusader or the tunic of Greek athlete.

Oh yes, he was beautiful. They said Stephen Tennant was the most beautiful man in England. I always thought Guy Tarver gave him a good run for his money.

He was tall and very slender, slight even, but his supple elegance made the other men look bulky and clumsy. Until that night, I hadn't really noticed him. He had been just one of 'them'. Now I looked more closely at the man Olive had chosen.

His soft, dark hair had been allowed to grow longer than was usual in those days, in a manner that said 'artistic', and flopped across his forehead in a most engaging way. His arm was draped across the back of the chair, really quite close to me and I noticed that his hands were narrow and long fingered. I always think a man's hands are so important. I could never bear a man with pudgy hands to touch me. His profile is famous, of course, stunning in its purity, a gift from the gods, Oliver Messel called it once. Anyone who has ever picked up one of his books from a shelf would recognise Guy Tarver's profile. Even when he was an old man, with features crumbling under the attack of wild living and bad temper, he would insist that his profile as a young man must remain on the back cover of every book. It wasn't vanity, not really, although people were quick to accuse him of that. It was all he had left by then, I suppose. Poor Guy.

He had a way of looking at you, I remember, that made you feel as though every silly word you uttered

49

was very important to him. It wasn't just to do with his fine, dark eyes, though they were dazzling enough to sweep any maiden off her feet. It was the way he looked directly at you as you spoke, the way he inclined his head, as though to catch every word. There was a stillness that surrounded him. For just a little while, he would give you his whole attention and leave you grateful for every second.

He looked at Olive that way. No wonder the silly girl's head was turned.

Bunty Harwood leaned over to Olive in a confidential way. The smoke from the cigarette held in her lips made her eyes screw up in self-defence. She spoke through the corner of her mouth, lipping each word, and the ash from her cigarette spilled, to nestle in the cleft of her bosom, like grubby dandruff.

'I rather think you've picked up more than you bargained for there, darling,' she warned and then went into whoops of laughter, kicking her heels up like a child.

'Oh, but we young people must stick together, don't you think?' answered Olive with a smile of astounding sincerity. Good heavens, did she know what she was saying, could she really be as innocent as she looked? 'Otherwise we'd be outnumbered by you all!'

Bunty and every other woman there bridled, but halfheartedly, as though they weren't quite sure what they had heard, but were pretty certain it was offensive anyway. My father coughed into his illegal pastis.

'Didn't I just hear Mme Esquillon call us in for dinner,' he said hurriedly.

I went to bed directly after dinner, while everyone else was still drinking coffee. I couldn't stand the sight of Olive preening and primping. Anyway, there wasn't anything for me to stay up for. No one wanted me. No one made room for me on the edge of their chairs.

50

I went up early most nights, to read or draw, but on every other night, Olive had come up at the same time. The room seemed very silent without her. I missed her chatter as I cleaned my teeth and brushed my still-long hair. But now Olive was a woman, she had been acknowledged publicly as one. And I was left behind in the limbo of lost childhood.

Actually, it wasn't all that late when she followed me upstairs. The tinny thump of the gramophone leaked through our open window. I could just make out a few of the words sung in Mistinguett's plangent voice.

Je ne vends pas mes fleurs, Messieurs, moi je les donne
En tout bien tout honneur. Oui, je le dis sans peur
Avis aux amateurs: quelles sont les personnes qui désirent
*   ici*
Le bouquet que voici?

I was old enough now to understand how suggestive the words were. I buried my face in my pillow to shut out the sound, but it was too hot, and I was soon out again.

Someone had started up a game of Mah Jong in opposition to the music.

'Oh darling,' I heard a shriek, 'how naughty! You've pinged when you should have ponged!'

'They've started dancing,' Olive said, through a mess of chalk as she scrubbed her teeth. 'I didn't want to stay.'

'What's the matter?' I sneered. 'Did your precious Guy tread on your toes?'

'He's not my Guy – not yet – and he's a very good dancer, if you must know.'

'Oh, of course, he would be, your eggs always have double yolks!'

51

Olive giggled. 'You sound just like Nanny. I wonder if that's what you'll be when you grow up.'

'And I suppose you're going to be photographed for *Tatler* and get married in St George's, Hanover Square to a very rich man and have two boys and two girls.'

She spat vigorously, picked up her hairbrush, dragged it casually through her hair a couple of times, then dropped it.

'I rather thought that sort of thing would be more in your line. To conform, to do what's expected – that's what you've always wanted, isn't it, Anne?'

'Doesn't everyone? Don't you?'

'I don't know,' she said slowly, stopping with her frock half peeled off. Her elbows stuck out at impossible angles. Her skin was taut and white over prominent ribs. 'I don't know. I just feel I want to do something special with my life – not just get married and dance and play bridge every day. I want to do something . . . something beautiful. I want . . . to do and be and have . . . everything.'

'Everyone wants something – I do, too.'

'Ah, but the things you want are such easy things. You think it's a lot, but your hopes are so small. You don't ask for much, so you're bound to get them, don't you see? But the things I want are far harder . . .'

'Oh, what utter twaddle!' I flung my pillow at her, but she caught it neatly and threw it back at me with a much better aim.

I was pretending to be asleep when I heard Olive stir as though she raised herself onto one elbow.

'Anne?'

'Mmm?'

'Are you awake?'

'No.'

'Guy said the oddest thing at the end of dinner. Mother asked me to pour the coffee and, when I had filled his cup, he put his elbows on the table and just stared – you know the way he does – it's eerie. Then he said – what was it? – he said I purged the air of pestilence. Everyone shut up, just like that. You could have heard a pin drop. It was so embarrassing!'

'He said what?'

'It's a quotation, or something.'

'Well, it's wasted on you, then. You've never read anything more challenging than Chick's Own in your life. And not that, if you could help it!'

'Beast! Oh, Anne, don't you know it? You never have your nose out of a book. You must know it. Please.'

'It's Twelfth Night, if you must know – Duke Orsino talking about Olivia – but I can't remember it all. Something about being pursued by desires.'

'Oh!'

'What a soppy thing to say – I didn't think he was that stupid.'

There was a long silence. I closed my eyes and willed them to stay closed.

'Anne?'

'Shut up!'

'Olivia's a much nicer name than Olive, don't you think? It's got more class, more of an air to it.'

'No.'

'I'd much rather be called Olivia.'

'Same difference.'

'Not to me, it isn't.'

She went to sleep at last and left me in peace. I kept the light on for a while, listening to the sounds below. I lay on my back, staring at the ceiling, wondering if we would ever go home again.

To give me something to do, to make me fall asleep, I began to trace with my eyes the length of each ceiling beam, counting the knotholes as I went – it was even more boring than counting sheep.

That's when I noticed the little black scorpion squeezing itself out of a crack in the ceiling. Once it had emerged, it sat still for a while, hooked and malevolent, black on white. I stared hard and willed – willed – it to walk a little further and drop onto Olive as she slept.

Oh, of course I didn't mean her to be hurt. Of course not. But it would have scared her into fits. If I were really lucky, she'd have wet herself with fright. Serve her right.

But given my luck, the scorpion would probably have gone for an even longer stroll and fallen on me. So I lay perfectly still and willed it back into its crack again. I lay there for hours, petrified that if I moved, I'd attract its attention, and the bloody little thing just sat and looked back at me.

Olive was always stubborn, even as a child. If she set her heart on something, then nothing Nanny could do would quiet her yells until she got it. And even if she didn't like it, after all – even if the toy or book she'd screamed for had been broken in the fight – once she got her hands on it, nothing would make her give it up. She might toss it aside later in disgust, but none of us would be allowed to pick it up again.

'Olive, darling,' Mother said sweetly one morning after breakfast, 'we hardly see each other these days, you're so busy. Why don't we have a quiet morning together? Wouldn't that be nice?'

'But I was going swimming with Guy.'

'You went swimming with him yesterday.'

'We were going to go early, before it gets too hot and then Guy wants to take a run to St Tropez to see a friend who lives there.'

'To see a friend? Well, he'd hardly want to drag a little girl along, now would he?'

'He doesn't have to drag me and I'm not a little girl, Mother.'

Oh, Olive guessed what Mother was doing, all right. Her little mouth was tight with mutiny. I knew that look very well, but I don't think Mother had seen it for a long time.

Mother just ignored the last protest. 'Everyone else is going out, but I've a tiny headache. It would be lovely to have a quiet time together and have a little chat. We could sit out in the garden, in the shade, away from the littlies.'

'Anne will be here. She always is. Why can't she keep you company?'

'Because I've asked *you*, Olive,' Mother returned, with just a trace of asperity creeping into her oh-so-reasonable tone. 'Is a morning of her time too much to expect from my eldest daughter? If so, do let me know and I shall make an appointment through your secretary to see you.'

There was no one quite like Mother for making you feel in the wrong.

'But . . .'

Naturally, there were no buts. Mother and Olive were both specialists in the art of getting what they wanted. But Mother had had more practice.

Pa and the others went off to the beach. Guy went to see his friend. The house was extraordinarily still. It so rarely was. The windows were open, but the shutters were closed, with scarcely a breath to stir the muslin curtains. Already the air was heavy, pungent with thyme, bitter with rue. From the house came the slow swish-swish of Lisette's broom and Clare's voice, honey-sweet, wheedling David into joining her in some prank. They sounded very far away.

I didn't mean to listen. I really didn't. I was just wandering around the garden, looking for a cool spot. There was a book laid open and flat on the grass. I hate to see books like that. It breaks the spine and loosens the pages. So I went to pick it up and put it away. It was a fat volume of Shakespeare's plays, open at Twelfth Night. I knew exactly what Olive had been looking up – if it hadn't been in Act One, Scene One, she'd have got lost and never would have found it without my help!

> O, when mine eyes did see Olivia first,
> Methought she purg'd the air of pestilence;
> That instant was I turn'd into a hart;
> And my desires, like fell and cruel hounds,
> E'er since pursue me –

How like her! She'd been sitting here, reading the lines over and over again, lapping up Guy's compliment, like a cat with a saucer of cream. Olivia, indeed! Wouldn't it just make you sick?

I blew the dust and grass off the pages, before I straightened out the book. Mother and Olive were in the arbour.

'Now, you know that isn't what I meant,' I heard Mother say patiently. 'I simply said that it might be a good idea if you saw a little less of Guy, that's all.'

'Why?' demanded Olive and I could just imagine the stubborn set of her mouth, the way she would look down at her feet and scuff the grass. 'I like him. He's the only one of all those old fogies who doesn't treat me like a child.'

'That's just it. You *are* still a child and it isn't entirely . . . oh, dear . . . entirely suitable for a girl of your age to spend so much time with a young man.'

'How Victorian! I can't believe what I'm hearing,' Olive scoffed. 'That sort of attitude may have made sense when you were young, but that was before Adam and Eve got thrown out of Eden and this is 1924, Mother darling!'

'Don't be cheeky,' Mother rapped. 'I don't want to have to forbid you to see him, but you really must be more sensible. Can't you see? You're practically flinging yourself at his head – spending every day with him, swimming, motoring, dancing. Have you no pride?'

It was true. I had seen them. I had watched Olive wade out of the sea one day. The sun had dried her skin almost immediately and left a skim of white salt on honey-brown arms and legs. Her hair was bleached by the summer sun and she flicked it out of her eyes, laughing. She looked so healthy and wholesome compared to the weary butterfly women on the beach. Guy was waiting for her at the edge of the water. The surf lapped around his bare, brown ankles. For a moment, just for a moment, they were still. They just stood and looked at each other. There was such intensity in their stillness and the silence between them was full of whispers. I could hear their echo, but they made no sense to me. Guy didn't touch her. He didn't have to. The air between them crackled. There was nearly enough static to make my hair stand on end. Then Olive bent down and flicked a handful of water over him and the spell was broken. They ran up the beach laughing.

I was left with a very funny feeling inside. I didn't understand that at all, either.

'He likes my company.'

'Darling, darling, of course he does. What man wouldn't enjoy the company of a pretty girl? Any pretty girl. It's fun and very flattering, I know, but it doesn't mean anything to him, not really. After all, you've only just met. You hardly know him.'

'Enough to be sure.'

'To be sure of what?' Mother said sharply. 'To fancy that you're in love? Don't be so ridiculous. What can you possibly know about love at your age?'

'You always told us that you and Pa fell in love when you were only four. I'm fifteen already. So why can't I?'

Poor Mother. One had to feel sorry for her, caught up in the web of her own storytelling. If she could have known, would she have embroidered her perfect love story in quite such detail? I could hear her filling in the silence by pummelling the cushions of her garden chair with a heavy hand.

'That was different,' she said at last.

'Why? Why was it different?'

'Well . . . well, because our families had known each other for simply ages . . . our parents were old friends . . . everyone agreed that it was suitable.'

'Oh, I might have known.' Olive's voice was quavering, gruff and aggressive because she hurt so much inside. She was on the verge of tears, but she was damned if she was going to give Mother the satisfaction of scooping her daughter up and kissing the sore place better. 'I might have known. It's all about family, isn't it? Isn't it? Then why ask Guy here in the first place, if you think he's not good enough to mix with us?'

'Just because one spends a few days in someone's company, it doesn't mean that one is prepared to have him in the family, Olive. Not that it will ever come to that. It's just a little holiday fun for him, with a silly, pretty girl – no more than that. You're making too much of it.'

'*I'm* making too much of it . . . ?'

'He's frightfully good-looking, of course, and witty and clever . . .'

'Guy. He has a name. Guy. Why don't you ever say his name?' Olive muttered.

'. . . and they say his books are quite the coming thing. But who is he? Who are his people? What do we really know about him? Can't you see how you cheapen yourself?'

'You should have thought of that before –'

'Before what? Olive, he hasn't . . . he hasn't touched you, has he . . . Olive?'

'No,' Olive shouted, 'no, he hasn't. But I wish he had . . .'

The end of an idyll. It had to come, I suppose. My parents had become bored, in time, with their Provençal hideaway. One can only play at being gypsies for so long. Frittering one's life away can be frightfully boring.

The excuse was that David needed to go to school. He needed some sort of preparation for life. And so he did, poor chap. So did I, but what effect had my desires ever had on my parents and their selfish pursuit of pleasure?

We arrived back in the rain at Mount Street, well into September and, because our preparations had been accompanied by the usual fluster and chaos, late for the start of the new school year. There was a flurry of visits to Daniel Neal for a uniform, sewing on of name tapes and packing of trunks – Nanny looked happier than I'd seen her look all year – and then David was packed off to prep school on a crumbling Sussex clifftop, chosen because the sea air would be so good for his health. 'The southerly aspect and sea airs have proved ideal for growing boys. Brighton enjoys thirty-two per cent more winter sunshine than Kew. The water supply is pure and healthful, being drawn from deep chalk wells . . .' the illustrated prospectus told parents. David was the only one of the family who still looked peaky after a summer of sunshine.

I can see him still, standing in the hall on a grey, late

September morning, in his stiff, royal blue blazer with sleeves that covered his hands and grey shorts that overlapped long, grey stockings with royal blue cuffs. His hair had been slicked back by Nanny in her long-running battle with the cow's lick that always went its own way. His grey and blue hooped cap was in his hands and he was slowly turning it round and round. Through the open door, I could see Cleeve roping David's trunk onto the back of the Daimler. Leaves from the lime tree were spinning down, as though touched by Midas's unwelcome gift, gilding the flat cap of Cleeve's uniform, sticking to his damp shoulders. The air smelled of smoke, of death and decay.

'Do you mind if I give you a hug, David?' I asked. 'After all, it may be the last one. When you come back at Christmas, you'll be much too grown up to want a hug from a mere sister!'

He just nodded.

I gave him just a quick one. Within my arms, his fine-boned body was quite unresponsive. Then Mother came downstairs, adjusting the short veil on her hat.

'Come along, darling, time to be off.'

She held out her gloved hand. Like a tortoise emerging from its shell, David's hand appeared from the sleeve of his blazer. I ran upstairs to the nursery to catch a last glimpse of the motor. Clare was in the window seat, her face pressed hard against the glass and steam from her breath like a halo around her golden head. Through the car window, I could see David. His mouth was open, and his little hands were hooked round the half-open window, like the paws of a small, captive animal. Clare gave a whimper, only one, cut short by Nanny saying briskly:

'Now, now, no more of that nonsense, Clare dear. I had more than enough of your tantrums last night. What can't be cured must be endured. You can come and help me put all these stockings into pairs. That'll soon take your mind off things.'

Clare took David's departure very badly. We'd all expected it, of course, but still . . .

On the first night of their separation, I was woken up by very cold, bony feet pushing their way into my bed.

'What're you up to, Clare? Go back to bed.'

'I can't. It's too quiet.'

'Of course it is, silly. It's meant to be. It's night time.'

'I can't sleep. No one's breathing with me.'

She pushed her face into the curve of my neck. I could feel long shudders running down her body, but her cheeks were dry.

'Oh, Clare love,' I put my arm around her and drew her tense little body under the covers, tucking them around her. 'It'll be Christmas before you know it and David'll be back. That's something for you both to look forward to.'

When the tears came, they were hot, hard and slow. They pooled in the hollow of my collarbone and soaked the flannelette of my nightdress. Clare cried silently, not like a child at all.

'But he won't be my David any more,' she whispered.

Long after she'd fallen into an exhausted sleep, I lay awake, staring into the dark, until the black shadows turned red with my rage.

How could they? How could they? Didn't they know what they had done to the twins by separating them? Didn't they care? Weren't parents supposed to love their children? If that was what love was all about – I wanted none of it.

That was the autumn Clare started her running-away fund. She was quite open about it. 'It's for when David runs away from school. He's going to need money to pay off the taxi.'

Olive exploded with laughter into her porridge. 'Arriving in state at the front door and waiting for you to run downstairs with your piggy bank, I suppose! No one runs away in a taxi, you goose! If David's really going to run away, he'd better make a good job of it. He'll have to disguise himself as a country boy and buy a train ticket, but you have to have enough money to buy those in advance.'

'Then I'll send him a postal order when he's ready to go.'

'And I suppose you imagine Mother and Pa are going to welcome him home like the prodigal son. You know they'll just send him back on the next train.'

'Then we'll have to run away together. So you see, I'm going to need even more money than I thought. D'you want your shoes polished, Anne? I'll do them for sixpence.'

'Mercenary little beast!'

'It's your turn to clean the hamster's cage this week. If you want to skive off it, it'll cost you another sixpence.'

Clare began to carry her little black account book everywhere with her and could be tripped over in odd corners, totting up her wealth.

Our pocket money then was always paid monthly and Clare's allowance was five shillings per month. We were always taken, by special arrangement, to Williams Deacon's Bank at 9 Pall Mall to collect it. The formality of the occasion was awesome and almost spoiled the pleasure of having money of our very own to hold in our hands. A solemn man in a black frock coat would ask us how we would like our money and would then shovel the chosen coins into little brown bags. Clare always used to ask for hers in silver threepenny bits, because they made her think of eating Christmas pudding. I was allowed a pound and, being very conscious of my seniority, would ask for eight half-crowns or sometimes even two ten-shilling notes.

Clare accounted for every penny spent and earned. The entries were brief: 'From Pa for ironing his newspaper – 1d' or 'Put in Box for Waifs and Strays – ½d'. On Friday nights, she would do her weekly accounts.

'It won't come right,' she said one Friday, throwing down her pencil.

'That's because you can't count.'

'It isn't, it isn't. The columns won't add up.'

'Let me look,' I said, holding out my hand. I added up the columns and wrote at the bottom of the right hand one 'Unaccounted for – 4¼d' and ruled two lines under it. 'There, that'll make it come out right.'

'That's all right, then,' answered a relieved Clare, glaring suspiciously at the totals.

'How far can you get on that?'

'Not even two half tickets to Southampton yet.'

'Whyever Southampton?'

'Because we're going to America, silly. Guess what? I've got a new pencil sharpener. I've only used it once. You can buy it from me if you like.'

In the end, Clare didn't need her running away fund. David came home from school for the Christmas holidays and never went back. He was very quiet that first night home, a little, silent waif who kissed his parents and his sisters dutifully, but wouldn't be cajoled into telling us all about the adventures of the term.

The thick, blue velvet curtains were drawn against rain that streamed down the windows. The fire had been lit first thing to warm up the room and its light reflected off the silver tea service. The trolley was loaded with scrumptious things. It was our favourite time of day, the time when we were allowed out of the rather

63

spartan nursery into the secret splendour of the grownup world. David sat on a leather pouffe with his feet right in the hearth, so close I swear I could see his slippers smoking. He had his back turned to the rest of us.

'But your letters didn't tell us anything at all, darling,' protested Mother, when we all had full cups and loaded plates, 'except that the food was awful, but then, it always is, otherwise what's the point of coming home? Cook's made your favourite brandy snaps especially for you. So do tell us, Clare's dying to know, all about your housemaster and rugger matches and things. Have you made lots of nice new chums?'

'They're all right,' David answered and couldn't be persuaded to say any more.

'Well, what a funny little chap you are,' said Mother and picked up her new copy of *Queen*.

Later, Nanny put it all down to tiredness.

'You're worn out, poor lamb,' she said, filling a stone hot water bottle for his bed and wrapping it in a towel before slipping it between the sheets. 'Never mind. Finish that hot milk now and into bed with you. A good night's sleep and you'll be as right as rain in the morning. You'll see.'

I heard her get up in the night and in the morning there was a mattress propped up against the guard of the nursery fire. Even with the window wide open for ventilation and a piercing wind blowing across our breakfast table, the ammonia smell of drying urine caught in our throats. David wouldn't walk past it. Hanging his head, he took the long route round the room rather than go anywhere near the symbol of his shame.

Nanny clucked and shook her head. 'A great, big boy like you . . .'

Next morning, the mattress was there again. It was

64

taken away after breakfast and a new one from the Army and Navy Stores was delivered, with a red mackintosh sheet.

Dr Holbrook came to see David that morning. David was still in his dressing gown and pyjamas, with a shawl wrapped around him, listlessly reading in front of the nursery fire. Clare had her account book open and was trying to interest him in the self-denial that her savings represented – she had her two half fares to Southampton by this time.

'And even enough to get us onto a boat, though only half way to the Isle of Wight, so far. But still, if we save up all our Christmas money . . . you won't ever have to go back to that place, David, not if I can help it.'

But anyone could see that David wasn't listening.

Dr Holbrook exuded bonhomie. His black coat and striped trousers, his bulging black Gladstone bag, were all designed to inspire confidence in his ability to magic away illness.

'Now, then young man,' he said, 'what's all this? Not feeling too chipper, I hear.'

Nanny shooed us out of the room, but we watched through the slightly-open door as the doctor took David's temperature, pulled up his eyelids, held down his tongue with a teaspoon and peered down his throat, and squinted into his ears with the aid of a tiny torch.

'Nothing too obviously wrong, there, Nanny. Probably just in need of a tonic. How does he seem to you?'

'Well, as I said, he's only just back home, Doctor, but he's been complaining of earache on and off for a long time. Not violent, or I'd have asked for you to be called much sooner, but enough to make him grizzly.'

Dr Holbrook moved behind David, took out his gold pocket watch and held it to David's right ear. 'Can you hear that, young fellow?'

65

'Yes, sir.'

'Can you hear it now?' The doctor held it to David's left ear.

'Yes.'

'And now?'

'Yes, sir.'

Ah, but Dr Holbrook had got him there. He was far too clever for David's tricks. He was standing behind David, so the boy hadn't been able to see that the watch had actually been put back into the pocket of his grey waistcoat. David thought he was clever – he said he could hear a watch that wasn't there at all – but the doctor was cleverer.

'Now then,' said the doctor, 'let's just have another little look in those ears.'

'I knew, I knew all along,' said Clare indignantly, 'but no one listened to me. No one ever does. David hasn't been able to hear properly since he had measles.'

'But he's not deaf,' said Olive, 'he can hear us talking to him.'

'Only if he knows you're going to say something and only if you're facing him. He won't hear you if you come up behind him, or if you're a long way away.'

'So he's really only a little bit deaf,' I consoled her.

'How would you like it, if you went to a new school and had a seat at the back of the class and you couldn't hear the teacher and everyone thought you were just stupid?'

'Well, I wouldn't like it, of course, but why didn't he just say he couldn't hear?'

'Because all the other boys thought he was soppy anyway, because he likes reading better than rugger, and they all teased him and called him names because he was new and had arrived late. They made apple pie beds for him and threw his pyjamas down the lavatory.

They were perfectly *beastly*. I wish I could get my hands on them. I'd make them sorry. I'd make them sorry they were ever born.'

It was hard not to laugh at her fierce little face, scarlet with fury, as she thumped her little fists on the plush tablecloth. But it was hard not to cry, too.

'I'll bet you would,' I said, 'but why didn't David tell the teachers and get a seat at the front of the class?'

'Because they'd already decided he was a dunce and they would just give him detention for not paying attention.'

'What a rotten place to send him. Do Mother and Pa know all this?'

'Not yet,' said Clare. 'But they will soon. I'm going to tell Pa this afternoon.'

'David won't like you interfering,' Olive warned.

'David never minds anything I do.'

So David was the first and last of our family to be sent to school. He didn't go back after Christmas. A new tutor was engaged and the day nursery became a proper schoolroom.

And I – I was left with nothing to fill my life for the four eventless years until I came out and was considered safe to be let loose in the world.

Oh, I was bored. No one could even guess how thoroughly, totally bored I was. Sometimes I used to wake up and wonder whatever was the point of getting out of bed. The mere act of swinging my leg over the side and onto the linoleum seemed utterly pointless. I wanted to pull the bed covers over my head and frowst all day in a hot, smelly little cave, where no one would bother me by asking if I'd 'been' that morning or tell me how lucky I was to have such a lovely home and that lots of poor young women would be only too glad to change places with me.

'Well, let them,' I'd mutter, trying to stick my head back under the covers.

But of course I didn't. Nanny would never have allowed it. She'd have said I was bilious and dosed me mercilessly with Kruschen Liver Salts.

Perhaps all young people are like that. I don't know. Sometimes on television I see great, hulking, spotty brutes complaining they've got 'nothing to do' and I think, I'd soon give you something to do, you idle lay-abouts. You never heard anyone complaining like that when I was young.

And you didn't, that's true. But perhaps only because we knew no one would listen. If I'd had an audience, if someone had stuck a microphone under my nose when I was fifteen or sixteen, I might well have complained bitterly of having 'nothing to do'. But there was no one to listen to my generation. No one dreamed of finding out whether we had anything worth saying. Young people today don't know how lucky they are.

If I'd been born into another class, of course, I'd have been at work, not very exciting work, perhaps, but enough to give me independence. It would have given me a goal, if only looking for another, less humdrum job. I might have been a post office clerk, or a typist. Or I might have been a telephonist – that could have been fun, with earphones and a speaking tube and a delightfully common little voice saying, 'Number please'.

As it was, the years when I was fifteen and sixteen were a desert: too old to be a child, too young to be a woman. Was there ever such an awkward age? All I had to look forward to was the brief glory of coming out.

Before too long, it was Olive's turn. She stood in the hall while the Daimler's engine ticked over outside and Pa fretted. Mother, slender as a shadow in her court dress of sapphire and silver brocade, and MacDowall fussed over the last, tiny details, tweaking here, primping there. The white gown, with its glittering, beaded train and three white feathers in the headdress, shimmered in the lamplight, but not as much as the bright threads of gold and russet in Olive's hair. I leaned over the banisters and blew her a kiss for luck. She caught it and smiled up at me. Then MacDowall gave the elbow-length kid gloves a final smoothing, adjusted the feather headdress minutely to the left and handed Olive a bouquet of gardenias, myrtle and rosebuds. Pa looked at his watch again and practically hauled her out into the car.

I kept my fingers crossed for Olive all evening. Don't let her lose her Card of Command or they won't let her in. Don't let her trip over her train.

When my sister came back, fortified by endless cups of black coffee, after the traditional late night photographic session, she was a woman and I was still a child.

Days and days and days with no point to them. Fox-trotting around the nursery to the music of the Savoy Orpheans with Clare press-ganged into winding the gramophone and Olive obligingly taking the lead. (Would it feel different with a man? How would a man feel different? Would he be clumsier, flatter, harder?) Practising the Charleston, supported by a dining chair, flicking my legs sideways at a ridiculous angle (I was jolly good at it. Ballet lessons turned one's toes out, but riding turned them in again – I'd always preferred horses to ballet.)

Then, as that longed-for summer came tantalisingly closer, learning from Madame Vacani in Brompton Road how to perform a court curtsy without falling on one's nose: 'Throw out your little chests and burst your little dresses!'

I would lay out endless games of patience, flicking

though the cards in their seven columns again, and again, mesmerised by the illogicality of chance.

If this comes out, I'll be allowed to stay up for Olive's dance.

If this comes out I'll meet my future husband at my very first dance.

If this comes out, I'll be married at eighteen.

If this comes out, I'll have red-haired twins.

It wasn't too much to ask, was it?

I didn't want a knight in shining armour to throw me across his saddle bow and gallop away to his castle. I didn't want a desert sheikh to bear me away to a billowing tent. If someone had clasped me in his arms and burst into song – 'Blue heaven and you and I, and sand kissing a moonlit sky' – I should just have burst into absolute hoots. I was much too prosaic for romance.

All I wanted was a nice, ordinary man who would allow me to be myself. I wanted him to take me away from my boring, pointless life, and give me something worthwhile in its place. I wanted a house of my own to organise exactly as I pleased. I wanted him to give me lots of beautiful babies. Oh yes, lots of those, squirming, pink, gurgling babies – six, maybe, three of each. I utterly adore them – little round faces and little chubby fists and those darling circles around their wrists and ankles where the fat folds over.

A man wouldn't necessarily have to love me to make babies – I knew enough about the world to realise that. In fact, it would probably be better for all concerned if he didn't love me. I didn't want my children to grow up lonely little orphans of love as my brother and sisters and I had done. I wasn't going to shut *my* children out of my life and make them feel that they were just a by-product of my relationship with their father. That's what love does for you.

No. My husband would have to be kind, of course, and gentle and sensible, but ordinary. And, above all, he wouldn't be required to love me.

Besides, Olive's love life was quite complicated enough for our generation. Her actions broke over the family, that summer I came out, like a cloudburst. I don't think we need to go into the details here. If she wants to talk about it, that's her business. She was the one who suffered in the end. Very silly.

Mother had not been presented when she was young. She used to dither over the reason, but I'm pretty certain it was because her family, although wealthy, was trade and didn't have the right connections. However, she had been presented on marriage, having by then found some impoverished countess or other willing to sponsor her – for a consideration. So Mother herself was able to sponsor Olive without difficulty. However, when it came to my turn, because I was only two years younger than Olive, the silly three year rule got in the way. For some extraordinary reason, a lady could only make a presentation every three years, so Mother suggested delaying my presentation for another year, when I would be eighteen – a quite normal suggestion.

But I screamed – literally screamed. Another year of that dismal half-life in the nursery would have driven me crazy. I'd run away to a nunnery, I threatened, or a brothel, or an Australian sheep farm. Even Mother could see that I meant it. So – again for a consideration – another impoverished lady, this time a baronet's wife, was lined up to sponsor me. I was presented at the first Court of 1928, on 8th May, a day when the weather was more like February, when the blossom in the parks and squares was pinched and ungenerous.

And suddenly, almost before I realized what had happened, I was standing in front of the cheval glass in white satin and chiffon velvet. Everything I had dreamed of had come true, so quickly that I scarcely had time to draw breath.

Two white dresses in one year, two veils: the first hanging from a debutante's headdress of Prince of Wales feathers, the second shielding my traditional bridal modesty. There I was, a virgin bride, anonymous as a Mohammedan, peering out through the folds of tulle that blotted out my face. She – the girl in the glass – was me!

Mother's tiara perched perilously on top of my long veil. The weight of the full-length beaded train dragged my short gown back over my shoulders, rucking the neckline and exposing my knees. Behind me stood Clare, pudgy in tiered pink crepe-de-soie, with a sheaf of gladioli in her hands and goose flesh all over her arms.

'You look lovely, darling,' Mother lied. 'The first of my little girls to be married – properly that is. I know you and Nicholas will be very, very happy.' She made a kissing motion towards my cheek.

'Oh, Mother, thank you – thank you for everything.' I gave my mother the first spontaneous hug of my life.

'Do be careful, darling, you'll crush my hat.' She stepped smartly backwards and gave the front of my gown a sharp tug downwards. 'And do try to keep your knees covered. They're not your best feature.'

Well, it was what I wanted, wasn't it?

The problem was that once I had met my nice, ordinary man, he fell in love with me. That was his misfortune. I suppose, in a way, it was mine too.

'I love you,' he said. 'I'd do anything – anything to make you happy. If only you'd tell me what you really want.'

But when I really wanted something – wanted something so badly I couldn't go on without it – he wouldn't give it to me. That proved how little his promises meant.

He would give me anything I wanted – except a divorce.

That proved he didn't really love me.

NICHOLAS

The Country Gentleman

I've been a lucky man. No one could say otherwise. Too young for the first war, just a little too old for the second (well, depending on how you look at it). A nice house, a handsome wife, four fine boys – didn't see too much of them, though, especially once they'd grown up. (Pity, but then I scarcely knew my father at all.) As much shooting as I wanted – can't see to do that much now, but I've brought down a good few brace in my time, I can tell you – always a good horse in the stable, a good dog at my heels and a good meal on the table. What more could a man ask?

Have I made it all sound a bed of roses? Didn't mean to. It wasn't, of course. Well, you tell me, whose life is, after all? We've had a few sticky moments, Anne and I. There was a time when I was afraid . . . no, that doesn't matter any more. I'm wrong. On the whole, it's not been bad. Not bad at all.

Pretty little thing, Anne, when I met her. All fluffy hair and big eyes and long lashes. Feminine, if you know what I mean, a real woman. Not like lots of the girls of her day – boys in disguise, if you ask me. Some smart alec said they were trying to make up for all the young chaps who died in the trenches. Sounds crazy, I know, but there might be something in it. My sister, Rose, wore a monocle. Not for long, though. I found a cracking new song recorded by Cyril Ramon Newton and the Savoy Havana Band and played it whenever poor Rose made an appearance.

> Masculine women, feminine men,
> Which is the rooster, which is the hen?
> It's hard to tell 'em apart today . . .

It drove her crazy. Soon all I had to do was whistle the chorus:

> Girls were girls and boys were boys when I was
> a tot
> Now we don't know who is who, or even what's
> what . . .

So, the monocle disappeared. It was only an affectation and she said it did frightful things to the skin around her eyes – turned it into a map of the Underground!

Anne wasn't like that. No bosom-binding brassière for her. She was round in all the right places. Dancing with most girls then was like dancing with a pair of fire tongs – and about as exciting – but not with Anne. Wonderful tits. They used to jostle against my shirt front, like marshmallows in a bag. When we foxtrotted sedately around the floor, I was tall enough to be able to look straight down her cleavage. She used to powder her chest to hide those adorable freckles and some of it always rubbed off on the silk lapels of my dress jacket.

A dead giveaway, that. It was obvious to anyone who cared to look that we'd been dancing much closer together than we ought. God, I used to be in a muck sweat by the time I escorted her back to her party.

I suppose I married Anne because I lusted after her. Don't look so po-faced. That's not such a bad reason, you know, and better than a good many. It's a damn

78

sight more natural than marrying for money or because one's ageing parents want to make absolutely certain of an heir before they die.

I've never been much good with girls. I've always liked them, of course, but never been . . . well . . . never been quite at ease in their company. It's a knack, of course, like most skills, but one I didn't seem able to pick up.

Girls always seemed to me to be a different species altogether. You know how it is – prep school, public school, Sandhurst, a couple of years with a regiment that never seemed to get off Salisbury Plain, a sister very much older than me – not much of a preparation for playing the gay Lothario. Now, I'm as red-blooded as the next man, of course, but no debutante's mother ever had to write on her list beside my name, NSIT – Not Safe In Taxis!

The barriers seemed so enormous. Between kissing a girl on the cheek and kissing her on the lips there was a hidden world of knowledge. Between kissing her on the lips and touching her body there was an unbridgeable chasm. Between touching her body and . . . anything else, well, the stars seemed more accessible than that.

Yet people surmounted those barriers, every minute of the day and night, even one's own parents, difficult though it may be to believe. As yet, I was on the far side of the chasm, but I dreamed . . . on hot, shameful nights, God, I dreamed.

Nice girls didn't. No really, I mean it. In those days, nice girls most certainly didn't. In fact, some of those little things just out of school had been so protected that they probably didn't know exactly what it was that nice girls didn't do, but whatever it was, they didn't!

And then there were the girls who did. The first generation of women to have sexual freedom and no need,

79

if you were clever enough, to worry about the consequences. Lucky them. Lucky me. Every man's dream.
We all knew who they were, of course. We knew who
could be enticed into the summer house. We knew who
would draw the line at waist level and who would go
the whole hog. The knowledge had done me no good,
I might add.

To tell you the truth, they rather scared me, those
smart, sharp girls with enamelled masks and nails like
bloodstained talons. They never seemed to be alone.
They hunted in groups – in bitch packs – one could hear
them giving tongue clear across a room. 'Gone away'
and off they'd dash on a long point after some poor,
unfortunate male, little sterns waving with excitement.
They wouldn't stop for wire or plough until they'd got
the poor bugger cornered for the kill.

I didn't much care for being the quarry. I'd go to
earth whenever I got the chance.

But you can't do that too often, can you? I mean to
say, if a hostess is good enough to ask you to her daughter's dance, even if you know you're only there to make
up numbers, you can't spend the whole evening smoking in the garden, can you? You get a free feed, free
champagne and in return you have to make sure that all
the girls – even the shyest and most gauche – have their
dance programmes full. (Although one girl I danced
with said it was like going for a long country walk
wearing someone else's gumboots.) And the laundry
bills, all those stiff shirts and collars, all those white
waistcoats, five or six a week sometimes. That nearly
broke the bank. Then someone always had the bright
idea of going on to a nightclub afterwards. So there
were taxis and tips and cover charges. One doesn't care
to be a wet blanket.

It was a high price to pay for free salmon and strawberries. But one can't avoid it every time. It's just not

on. You've got to play the game now and again. We all know the rules.

But I was, frankly, hiding when I met Anne. And the funny thing was – so was she.

I'd spied a jolly looking little arbour from the terrace, all covered with wistaria and stuff like that. It seemed quite impenetrable and looked just the spot. I could hide in there and still hear the music. That way I could show willing and appear for Sir Roger de Coverley and the Gay Gordons – they were generally pretty safe – but keep my head down for the smoochy stuff.

I did a careful recce first. The arbour might already have been in use. How frightful to barge in on some courting couple. I'd done it once and nearly got myself a black eye for it. Once bitten, twice shy. So I made doubly sure there was no one else around, before I slipped in and took out my cigarette case, with a sigh of relief.

I obviously hadn't checked carefully enough. When I flicked my Dunhill alight, I thought I heard a little squeak and I definitely spotted a movement out of the corner of my eye.

'I say,' I said, hastily extinguishing the light. 'I'm most awfully sorry. I thought the place was empty.'

It would never do to be thought some sort of nasty peeping Tom. There are chaps like that, you know, who enjoy hiding behind curtains and opening bedroom doors unexpectedly. They get some sort of thrill out of it, don't ask me what. I'm not like that, thank God.

I started to beat a hasty retreat. Serves me right, I thought, for trying to be too clever.

'It's all right,' a little voice said, 'you don't have to go.'

'I'd rather not intrude . . .'

'You're not. I'm just sitting, thinking.'

'Oh, well, in that case – I'll sit and think with you, if I may.'

She didn't sound like one of the harpies I was hiding from. She had a sweet, husky voice, rather low – the sort of voice that ought to belong to a pretty face, but it was pitch dark in the arbour and I couldn't see her at all.

'Nice party,' I observed.

'Mmm.'

'Bit hot inside, though. I thought I'd have a breather.'

'Good idea.'

'May I offer you a cigarette?'

'No, thank you. I don't smoke. No, please – do go ahead yourself.'

Now that I did like. Call it old-fashioned if you must, but I still hadn't become accustomed to the sight of a woman smoking. It wasn't the idea of smoking so much as the way they did it. I loathed the hungry way women sucked in the smoke – quite different from men – there was a horribly predatory satisfaction about it, much worse than just being not quite nice.

We sat quietly for a few moments. Funny, I'd never been able to do that with a woman before. I'd always had the impression that they needed to be entertained, that they thought you a very dull dog if you couldn't keep up a constant stream of witticisms. Their boredom threshold was all too easy to cross. This girl seemed quite different.

Somehow, sitting there with her was better than being alone. I'd come out to escape company, but sometimes that can be a bit lonely. One feels a little isolated, perhaps even a little peculiar, sitting alone in the dark, while other people, presumably, enjoy themselves. This time I wasn't alone. There was something very companionable about the sound of her breathing, the rustle of her dress as she changed position, the whisper of her silk stockings as she crossed or un-crossed her legs.

There was something erotic about it, too. I hadn't expected that, believe me. It was enticing, tantalising. Sitting in the perfumed darkness with a woman I couldn't see, who sounded as though she might be pretty, who was close to me, who was warm and breathing softly, excited me, suddenly and un-expectedly.

We were anonymous in the dark. We didn't have to wear the labels that everyone saw whenever they looked our way. That night, I wasn't long, gangling Nicholas Lockyer with the big feet. I was cool and sophisticated, a taller Jack Buchanan. She was – whatever I wanted her to be. Small, soft, clinging. Mary Pickford before she married Douglas Fairbanks. The idea sent a little frisson of surprise and delight down my spine.

'I suppose I'd better go in,' she said and I could hear the crackle of net as she rose. 'My mother is bound to be wondering where I've got to.'

'Don't go.' Without thinking, I put out a hand and somehow it connected in the darkness with hers. It was a very little hand. 'There's such a crush in there, no one could possibly notice we're missing. Why don't we take a stroll around the garden?'

'Perhaps.'

Instinctively, I chose the darkest paths, those that wound through the shrubbery. The air was heavy, drenched with the scent of lilac and mock orange. Wet leaves brushed against my face and dripped honeyed moisture on my lips. I didn't know where I was going. All I knew was that I didn't want to take this girl back into the light and certain disappointment.

And all the time, this strange sense of mystery and excitement was growing, until I was practically run-ning, pushing my way through the undergrowth. It was almost as though I knew where I was going – but I didn't.

I wasn't drunk – I don't think so, anyway – but I might as well have been.

There was a little willow pattern bridge entwined with greenery. I drew her across it onto an island where weeping willows made deep, dense caves. She didn't hang back. She didn't ask where we were going. Most girls would have done. She just laid her little, warm hand in mine, trustingly, and followed me. Her feet in their dancing sandals pattered behind me through the leaves.

I was laughing as I pulled her under the trees, laughing with triumph. I knew now where my mad race had been taking us. The world was full of girls, of modern girls, available girls, just waiting for some man to take them. If one of them had followed me down a darkened garden, she only had herself to blame. Girls like that all knew the form.

I caught her up against me, hard, stroking my hand down the long curve of her back, moulding her pliant body against mine. I felt her quiver once, as she realised – for the first time, perhaps – the heights of my excitement, then she melted against me, soft and yielding and very, very female. When I bent to her, her face was already turned up to mine, her lips parting just for me, breathless. The soft places of her mouth tasted of champagne.

My hand was trembling as I laid it on her breast. It was like nothing I had ever felt before, so soft, so malleable, with its little hardened centre that peaked beneath my probing fingers.

At last. At last. This was what I had been waiting for, for so long. This was what it was all about. I felt a surge of strength and joy roar through me like a tide. I felt . . . I felt such power. I felt like a real man at last.

84

Suddenly, we were both very still. My hand lay unmoving, heavy and quiet, where I had laid it. And I knew that she, like me, was standing on the brink of the unbridgeable chasm. She wasn't one of those bright, knowing girls who seem to have been born with all the weary wisdom of the world in their little heads.

My hand slid away and with it the sense of exultation. Instead, I suddenly felt very quiet and at peace. I wrapped my arms around her again, holding her close, and laid my cheek against the perfumed softness of her hair. At that moment, I would have defended the girl I had not yet even seen against the whole world.

I should have felt disappointed. It should have been an awful let-down. But it wasn't.

We seemed to stand there for a long time. As my pulse steadied and other parts subsided, I became aware again of the sounds of the night. There was a jazzy, bass thump of music still reaching us from the house, a burst or two of laughter, the sound of engines firing as the first guests began to leave. Closer at hand, a dawn breeze had begun to rustle the leaves around us and ruffle the water to lap against the sides of a wooden punt.

The punt was gently rocking. Then, slowly, the rocking increased. The lapping of the water became louder, with the creaking of wood and the grating of the blunt prow drawn up on the gravel. Out of the darkness came the long, rising moan of a woman riding the fierce flood-tide of orgasm.

I couldn't get the girl away fast enough. It didn't matter that I had just planned a similar activity with her on this enchanted island. It would have been an appalling thing to do. Thank God I hadn't. She wasn't the girl I had thought she was and now I felt immensely protective of her. I had no intention of exposing her to this too sudden carnal knowledge.

85

We didn't get across the little bridge in time. There was such torment in the man's voice, a long, aching cry of desolation, a soul abandoned in the dark. It made me shiver.

'Oh, God, oh, God, Olivia!'

'Olivia! Oh, God!'

My girl's voice echoed the cry, with the same empty grief in it. She pulled against my hand, hard, trying to run back, but I held her fast.

'Let me go. I must go to her.'

'Come away,' I soothed, 'come away. She won't want you. It's nothing to do with us.'

She pulled away again, then slumped against me and we walked slowly back to the house, stopping behind nearly every tree to kiss. The Japanese lanterns that had lit the garden all night looked pale and tawdry against the brightening sky. There was enough light now for me to see her, but only just. She had a sweet profile, with a little blunt nose and a tender mouth. As we reached the terrace, she made an ineffectual, fluffing gesture at her hair.

'I feel a fright. Am I fit to be seen?'

'Do you have to go in just yet? Can't we go on and have breakfast somewhere, just the two of us?'

'I'm afraid I must. It's my party, you see. Mother will murder me for being away so long.'

How strange. To think that I had greeted her in the reception line that evening and scarcely even noticed her. Just another dance. Just another debutante, another plump little girl in white satin. If anyone had asked me what Anne Northaw looked like, I'd have said, 'I don't know. Pretty much like all the others, I suppose.'

Now in the pearl and silver dawn, I looked at her again: wide, innocent eyes; English mouse hair adorably tousled; lips swollen and abraded by my early morning stubble; a body ripe and ready – for me.

I looked at her and I thought, that's what I've always wanted.

'Come on,' I said and grabbed her by the wrist. 'I can't let you go as soon as I've found you.' We ducked round the side of the house, giggling like children off on a prank, to where my motor car was parked on the gravel sweep at the front. No one had seen us.

We roared along, through lanes that lay under an eiderdown of mist, past hedges that smelled of honeysuckle, to a roadhouse on the Portsmouth road that I knew would be open. There I ordered two enormous breakfasts and lots of tea. Excitement always makes me hungry.

'What a relief to get that over with,' Anne said, mopping up the last of her egg yolk with a piece of toast. I like to see a hearty appetite. 'It's been such an ordeal – I can't tell you.'

'Aren't all girls supposed to enjoy their own dances?'

'That depends. There were thirty to dinner before the dance began – people I'd never seen in my life before, but Mother said they simply had to be asked. Half way through the evening, the butler (hired, of course) passed me a note from Mother. It read 'Talk, you fool'. After that, I couldn't get a single word out without tripping over my tongue.'

'Oh, I say. That's a bit stiff.'

'And what is there to say, anyway? 'Do you go to the theatre often?' 'Care for hunting?' I ask you! Then later, I was dancing with Reggie Leggat, he's at least six foot five, I only came half way up his chest. He made a fancy twirl that caught me wrong-footed. I snagged my nose on his shirt button and bled all over him.'

I made a sympathetic noise, but couldn't find space to squeeze in a word.

'That's why I was hiding when you found me.

Mother had sent me off to Nanny to clean myself up, but I'd given her the slip and crept off into the garden. And then you came along.'

'Poor darling! What a catalogue of disasters. We were obviously meant to find each other.'

'Nickie's in love,' hooted Rose, 'isn't it sweet, Mummy? Our little Nickie's in love!'

'Shut up,' I growled from behind the newspaper, but without much conviction, because I hadn't slept much in the last forty-eight hours and because the idea was really rather a pleasant one.

'I absolutely shrieked when Jassie told me.'

'If you heard it from Jassie Duncan-Grey,' observed Mother, dipping her egg into the little pile of salt on the edge of her plate, 'you'd be well advised to take the news with a pinch of salt. Anyway, how would she know what your brother's state of mind is?'

'She only saw him, that's all, coming in from the garden with Anne Northaw yesterday – at the absolute crack of dawn – and she said he looked utterly shell-shocked and she looked extremely rumpled. So work it out for yourself, darling.'

'Nicholas?' Mother said, in the same sharp, querying tone with which she used to interrogate me over my school reports. It left me feeling much the same now.

'I . . . er . . .'

'I hope you warned her what she's getting,' said Rose, swinging back on her chair legs, more like a gawky girl than a woman of thirty-odd. 'You're not exactly the answer to a maiden's prayer, you know. I was always afraid we'd have to auction you off in the end. I used to lie in bed writing the catalogue description – young man of good breeding, new and quite unused, plain but very serviceable, finances in urgent need of some restoration . . .'

'That's quite enough, Rose,' snapped Mother, who was always sensitive to the word auction, ever since the contents of the family pile, Greywell, had been publicly auctioned to pay double death duties on my grandfather and father at the end of the war.

'. . . Never mind,' continued irrepressible Rose. 'If you marry Anne Northaw, you'll never have to worry again. Her people are stinking rich – descended from a long line of Hebrew bankers, I shouldn't wonder. No, not really, don't look like that, Mother, but they're not exactly in the stud book, one might imagine. Don't fret. Just close your eyes and think of all that filthy lucre! Where does it really come from, by the way?'

'Oh, this and that,' I hedged. 'Generations of captains of industry, textiles, mines, shipping, you know.'

'Dark, satanic mills? Ooh, goodie, goodie. So secure. Much more use than land these days. There's no money in land. In fact, the more I think about it, the more I'm positive that you owe it to us to marry Anne Northaw and bale out Greywell. After all, I've given up all hope of marrying a rich man at this stage, so it's all up to you now, brother dear. Your poor, destitute mother and sister are depending on you.'

She blew twin columns of smoke down pinched nostrils. I thought of the sweet little girl in the garden, who didn't smoke, whose body was inviolate – unlike Rose's – and I knew that I was going to marry her. But not because Rose said so and not for her money. I was pretty certain that I'd have married Anne Northaw if she hadn't a decent rag to her back.

All the same, the fact that she was rich did make it all rather suitable.

Mother buttonholed me later, as I knew she would. I'd tried to keep out of her way all day, but a chap has to come home for dinner in the end. She gave a little, scratchy tap on my door and came in at the same moment, without waiting to be asked. I was struggling with my collar stud and squinting fearfully into the looking glass.

'Nicholas, darling, I couldn't be more delighted about your news, of course,' she began wistfully, 'but I wonder if you've thought carefully enough . . .'

'Good heavens, Mother, I only met the girl the night before last. I shouldn't take Rose's exaggerations too seriously. Everyone seems bent on rushing me to the altar.'

'But you do like her, don't you?'

'Yes,' I agreed cautiously. It was always as well to be cautious when admitting things to Mother. One never knew quite what she would do with the information.

'Is she . . . is she suitable?'

'Oh, yes!' And this time my enthusiasm must have shone from my face.

Mother twisted her pearls disingenuously. She cocked her head to one side, a bright brown bird, but with a very sharp beak. 'Only . . . do sit down, darling, it's so difficult to talk to you when you tower over me like that . . . only I wonder how much you know about the family?'

I stood. If once I sat down, the conversation – or interrogation – might go on all evening.

'Not very much. They're quite all right, I imagine. Everyone knows them.'

'Yes, but all the same, even buried here in the country, one does hear the odd little rumour. They do mix with a rather fast set.'

I snorted. Fast! What a marvellously old-fashioned word. But then Mother was a bit long in the tooth by the time she produced me, so she was rather older than most of my friends' mothers. I always had to make allowances for that.

'I say nothing against Anne, I'm sure she's charming,

90

but the eldest daughter is certainly not . . . no, not the sort of girl I should dream of having in the family. Running all over town, positively throwing herself at some young writer or other. Everyone knows about it. And if only half the things one hears about him are true . . . Well, I know young girls today have considerable freedom, but still . . . And the only son, I hear, is mentally defective.'

'Now that really is quite enough, Mother. That's a shocking thing to say. Don't you ever let me hear you spreading that frightful rumour. The poor boy is only deaf, that's all, slightly deaf after having measles.'

'Really? Anyway, he had to leave school – very suddenly, I hear.'

The head of my stud finally snapped off under the pressure. I threw it on the floor in irritation and scrabbled in my stud box for another.

'You're being very naughty. It's most unfair of you to listen to stories like that and it's even worse to pass them on.'

'Well, I'd be the last person to gossip, as you know, Nicholas. Far be it from me to probe too closely into another mother's anguish.' I'd finally inserted that devilish stud. Mother took my bow tie from my hand before it became hopelessly crumpled and tied it, neatly and efficiently, in a fraction of the time I'd have taken. She stood back and patted it into place with a little, possessive gesture. 'There! Why didn't you let me in the first place, silly boy – I always tied your father's tie. You seem to be very well informed, darling. Do I take it, from what you say, that you've been making your own enquiries?'

'I've just talked to one or two people, that's all.'

She gave my tie a final tweak and with relief, I watched her walk to the door. I thought I'd got off quite lightly. But she never could resist having the last word. She turned, 'I suppose I'll have to ask them all to lunch, or something. What a bore.'

She almost left the room, then popped back in again, catching me in the middle of a grimace. 'I only want you to be happy, Nicholas. That's all I've ever wanted for you and Rose. You do know that, don't you, darling?'

And we left it at that. But Mother had made her position perfectly clear.

It was an absolute disaster. I knew it would be. Mother ought to have asked Anne and her mother to tea, if she had to ask them so soon in our relationship at all. Or she might have included the father and asked them to dinner. That would have been reasonable. But to ask the complete family, brats and all, to luncheon was to give the whole thing unforgiveably suburban overtones. She might as well have served tinned salmon and Nestlé's cream and made a thorough job of it.

It was as if she were saying, I know you're filthy rich and have bought your way into society, but that doesn't matter a jot to someone like me. However, if my son must interest himself in your dowdy daughter, I must just resign myself to it and lower myself to your standards.

She did it magnificently, of course, as she did everything, no matter how unworthy.

Mother looked more like the late Queen Alexandra than ever, with her fringe of curls and high pearl choker, as she sat at the end of the dining table in a room that felt much colder than it should in that drizzly, mild September. Her manner was no warmer. She hadn't skimped on the linen or silver, in fact, I think every piece we possessed was propped up somewhere or other, but that wasn't saying much, since the auction had cleaned us out of all but the most basic. A Lyon's Corner House

92

could display nearly as much silver as we could at Greywell.

The meal was atrocious: steamed whiting, with their tails tucked into their mouths, eyeballs milky and staring; reform cutlets with creamed potatoes; creamed rice mould (with too much sugar) and stewed plums (with not enough sugar). Actually, it was what we might normally have had for luncheon as a family, but I was astonished to find it served to guests. Mother was making no concessions.

What was she playing at? Did she think Anne wasn't good enough for me? Who was? What sort of impression was she trying to give with her 'poor but proud aristocrat' playacting? If she was trying to persuade Anne's parents that I was desperate to marry her because we needed their money, she was going the right way about it. I know that's what Marjorie Northaw always thought, but it wasn't like that – honestly.

I'd been absolutely straight with her parents when I'd asked for Anne's hand in marriage.

'I'd be pulling a fast one,' I'd said, 'if I pretended to be a terrific catch for Anne. A wonderful girl like her could have anyone she wanted. Greywell's a fine family home, but it's not worth a row of beans these days and I know I'm not the best looking chap in the world. But she could do a lot worse, too . . .' What a way to propose oneself as a suitor! '. . . There are some absolute rotters on the lookout for a rich wife these days. I'd look after her and see she had everything she wanted and I really do . . . well, I do care for her rather a lot, as a matter of fact.'

But I'd guessed from the cynical expression on her face that Marjorie Northaw suspected I was one of the rotters on the lookout for a rich wife. And now Mother wasn't doing anything to change her opinion.

'Of course, Nicholas has always been a country boy

at heart,' said Mother. 'He's never been one for gadding up to town. No dances. No theatre. No jazz clubs.' She pronounced the word as though describing the ultimate sink of sin. 'It may seem frightfully provincial to a little townie like you, Anne dear.'

'We don't live in the town all the time. We live in Surrey,' Clare informed my mother.

'Oh, Surrey!' she replied dismissively. 'I understand one can catch an Underground train into Surrey these days. That scarcely counts as country. I hope you know how bleak Wiltshire can be in February, Anne? February Filldyke!' She gave a laugh that could have frozen a puddle. 'Still, I imagine he'll keep you busy, hunt breakfasts and shooting lunches and so on, and the nursery, of course,' she finished coyly.

'I . . .' began Anne, but her mother rushed to fill in the gaps for her.

'Anne's the hearty one of the family.' She laughed like a scratched record, making it sound a very dubious compliment. 'Always rushing around with her horses and her garden. Never out of her rotten old tweeds. If you knew the trouble I have to get her to the simplest dressmaker's fitting!'

No wonder, I thought, if that's the result. Anne's frock was most unfortunate. It was draped and ruched and gathered onto one hip with an artificial flower in a way that made her waist look as broad as her magnificent bosom. Only a very thin woman could have got away with wearing a frock like that, in such an unflattering shade of plum. What could her mother have been thinking of? Positioned between Olivia, who was a beauty – a fox-coloured girl with a piquant smile – and my sister Rose, a *jolie laide* wearing an eccentric, but not unattractive, homespun smock in bright orange, even I could see that Anne was not looking her best, to put it at its kindest.

94

'Of course, Nicholas's father was a great sportsman – Master of the Tedworth, after *his* father. Do you hunt, Mr Northaw?'

'Not any more,' he answered shortly.

'Oh, oh, of course not. Thoughtless of me.' Even Mother had the grace to look embarrassed at having asked a one-handed man if he hunted. 'My husband – he fell at St Mihiel . . .'

'I'm sorry,' grunted Arthur Northaw, looking steadfastly at his knife and fork.

'. . . shortly after his father's death – would turn in his grave if he could see the state of our own stables today . . .'

'If he had a grave to turn in,' whispered Rose.

'. . . desolate, quite, quite desolate. Several of our neighbours have been forced to sell up completely, to grocers or munitions factory owners or . . . or to Jews. We ourselves only have Home Farm left out of the whole estate. What with income tax and double death duties . . . Still, you haven't come all this way to listen to my complaints. One wonders, really, who won the war.'

'Precisely,' replied Anne's father, with more enthusiasm than he'd displayed all day. At last my mother and the Northaws seemed to have found something in common. 'While we were fighting the war to end all wars, someone else was stealing our markets. The trades unions were cutting our throats behind our backs' – Rose sniggered at the impossible image – 'and now we're forced to put up with those same trades unionists in the government, for God's sake! Why we don't go the whole hog and invite Stalin to run the country, I don't know.'

'Now, darling,' warned Marjorie Northaw, with an unbecoming, skittish smile – heaven knows, a woman of her age couldn't afford to be skittish – 'you mustn't

95

be boring. This isn't the time or place for politics.'

'That's the whole trouble with this country, it never is the time or place. What we need is a strong man, a strong man who can put the unions in their place and get the working men back to work.'

'Say what you like about Mussolini,' said Rose with her wicked, curving smile that only I realised meant she was just egging Anne's father on, 'he has got the trains running on time.'

'Exactly! That's the sort of chap we need here – without the comic opera uniforms, of course. We need someone who'll get these scroungers off the dole and back to work. Force them, if need be. I wouldn't give a penny to any man who didn't work for it, breaking stones, if nothing else.'

'But don't you think times are difficult all over Europe, Daddy? The Germans are having an awful time too, aren't they?' Clare asked.

'But they lost the war, dammit, and we won it. Although you'd scarcely notice the difference.'

'All the same,' she persevered, in a little voice that somehow could be heard right around the table, 'it can't be very nice for them, having to carry a suitcase of money to the shops just to buy a loaf.'

Anne had told me all about Clare's running away savings. I realised the subject of money must be a sensitive one with her. In her imagination, she would have needed whole trunks, whole attics full of banknotes to get to America if she and David had been little Germans. Anne had laughed as she told me the story, but I thought her devotion to her twin quite touching.

'We'll be doing the same here, before too long,' observed Mother.

To give him his due, Arthur Northaw did try to talk to his daughter as though she actually had a mind and was entitled to an opinion of her own, but he was too hasty a man to take time to explain properly (and who could, these days, explain the fast-moving politics of Europe?).

'It's not like that any longer, Clare. The Germans are doing very nicely out of that piece of muddle-headed American meddling called the Dawes Plan. They're actually falling over themselves to lend Germany money to pay off its war debt, for heaven's sake. It's as though – as though I were to go down the High Street and say to the baker, 'Look old chap, I can't pay my butcher's bill, but if you lend me some money I'll pop next door and pay him off – and in the meantime, may I have a loaf on tick?' Sheer lunacy!'

'How clever!'

'And in any case, the war reparations have been costed in marks, so the further the mark falls, the less they have to pay in real terms. They can't lose.'

'Well, I feel sorry for anyone who gets pushed around,' maintained Clare with more courage than commonsense.

I may not have agreed with her, but it took nerve to stick to her viewpoint. I wanted to leap up and shout 'Bravo!'. Rose gave a slow, ironical handclap.

'Good heavens, sweetie,' she said. 'I didn't realise you were old enough even to find Germany in a schoolroom atlas, let alone have an opinion about it.'

'When you're old enough to know what you're talking about, Clare,' her mother said acidly, 'we just might listen to you. Until then . . .'

Thank God one isn't obliged to like one's in-laws. With any luck one could get away with a few day's purgatory over Christmas, bite the bullet until it was over, and then avoid them for the rest of the year. I thought I might manage that, for Anne's sake.

I pushed the sweet, stodgy rice around my plate and looked across at Anne. The poor darling looked utterly

97

miserable. She was eating in a mechanical fashion, shovelling the food into her mouth with solid concentration, as though, if she stopped chewing for long enough to think, she would throw down her spoon and run away.

I winked and she managed a watery little smile. It was the best she could do and I didn't blame her. Mother thought her a plain little dowd, but then Mother didn't know what a darling Anne really was – I did.

She was a jolly good sport, too. If we met each other at a dance, we'd always manage to find a secluded corner behind a potted palm or something. She'd be so patient with me. She'd let me slip my sweaty hands – I knew they were, I couldn't help it – beneath the flimsy fabric of her gown, she'd let me tease and tweak and fondle until I was gasping. She didn't really enjoy it. I mean, women don't, do they? Not these furtive, hole-in-the-corner gropings. I knew all along she was only putting up with it because she wanted to please me. As I said, Anne was a jolly good sport.

Only if my hand went too high, if it strayed above her garters and probed around the loose legs of her French knickers, would she draw back, pushing my hand away.

'We can't, darling,' she'd whisper, 'not here, not yet.'

And the promise in those words 'not yet' would console me until next time.

Cautiously, I stretched out my leg, trying to reach Anne's foot – I only wanted to cheer her up, give her a bit of moral support – but it tangled with someone else's. On my right, Clare gave a tiny squeak and her face turned scarlet. I drew hastily back.

Mother always had a trick of closing and opening her eyes, very slowly, just once, followed by a slight quirk of the brows. It used to quell me as a boy. It still quelled me now.

'After luncheon, Nicholas,' announced Mother, 'I think you ought to take Olivia and the twins out to show them the garden. You might walk out to Home Farm and back, a little rain won't hurt. I'm so looking forward to having a nice chat with Mr and Mrs Northaw and dear Anne.'

Anne's face! I'd have laughed if it hadn't been so tragic. I felt an out and out rotter, leaving her to face Mother's 'nice chat', but an order is an order!

It was still drizzling as I took Olivia and the twins into the garden. We had found gumboots and mackintoshes to fit – more or less – in the gun room and set out. I whistled up the dogs and they went lolloping joyfully ahead of us.

'Look,' I said to the twins, delving into my pocket when we were out of sight of the house, 'here's sixpence each. Cut along down to the village and buy yourselves a sticky bun or something.'

'They've only just had lunch,' protested Olivia.

'If you could call it that. Go on, off with you, and don't come back until tea time.'

I had bent over to talk to them, as I always do when talking to children – sometimes I frighten them, being so tall – but these weren't children, not any more. I'd misjudged them badly and this time I'd overdone the 'jolly uncle' thing and found myself looking directly into Clare's eyes. She looked straight at me. Heavens, she looked straight through me. I had the oddest sensation of being impaled, as though I were wriggling on the end of a lance of blue light. I could feel myself struggling to break free, but I just couldn't do it. She was coolly assessing me and there wasn't a thing I could do about it.

'Why have you got those funny fluffy bits under your eyes?' she said finally.

It was such a relief to have the silence broken, that I

didn't tell her to push off, cheeky brat, as I ought to have done.

'I don't know – they just grew there.'

'May calls them bugger's grips.'

Good grief! I straightened suddenly, free at last. 'Who's May?' I asked, wondering what thoroughly unsuitable company these children had been exposed to.

'Our nursery maid. What's a bugger? Is it a sort of animal? And why would one want to grip you? Would it hurt? Mr Jarman at home has a bulldog that never lets go.'

What should I say? What could I say? I could feel myself blushing in a way I hadn't done since prep school discovering we all had to get in the bath together, with matron supervising (she called it!). I jingled the change in my pocket and cleared my throat, to give myself time.

'If you want to keep those sixpences, Clare, you're going the wrong way about it,' interrupted Olivia. She wasn't helping – her voice was quavering with suppressed giggles. Any moment now she'd burst out laughing. 'If you don't cut and run – now – Nicholas will ask for them back.'

'A gentleman would never ask a lady to return a gift,' Clare answered scornfully.

The frightful girl scampered off anyway – just in time, I was on the verge of giving her a clip round the ear and damn the consequences – but her brother lagged behind. She stopped, looked back, and waited. When they were level, she seemed to try to take his hand, but he kept both of them in his pockets. So she did the same and they trudged off together towards the village.

'Honestly – that girl.' The giggles won and Olivia burst into helpless laughter. 'She gets worse and worse,' she said, when she could draw breath. 'I'm so sorry. I shouldn't laugh, it only encourages her. She was only asking all those innocent questions for effect, you know, leading you on. She knew exactly what she was doing.'

'Oh, well, yes, I knew that, of course,' I said casually, scuffing up some weeds on the gravel with the toe of my shoe, 'that's why I didn't get too heavy-handed.' Heavy-handed? That child wants her bottom well spanked, I thought. I'd been itching to do it. Great heavens – what sort of family was I marrying into? 'Anyway, I've got my own back. The village is a good two miles away. By the time they get there and back, we shan't be bothered with them at least until tea time.'

'Oh Lord, are we expected to stay for tea? Sorry, it's your house and all that,' Olivia smiled placatingly, 'but lunch wasn't exactly a howling success, was it?'

'A bit sticky,' I agreed.

'It could have been worse, but not much. Gosh, I was glad to escape. I wouldn't be in Anne's shoes for anything.'

'Wouldn't you?'

'Certainly not. Oh dear, that sounds awfully rude. It's not what I mean at all . . . not really . . . I mean . . .'

'It's all right. You don't have to be polite to me. We're practically related.'

With one foot on a stile, Olivia stopped. In the flapping old mackintosh and clumsy boots, she still managed to be one of the most attractive women I had ever met. Drizzle beaded her lashes. The fox-red hair that peeped beneath her cloche hat didn't hang in rat's tails (like Anne's did in the wet) but frizzed into a bright cloud, insubstantial as mist. Her skin was pale and so clear I fancied I could see right through it. She seemed somehow to glow. She had that special something, the something that has men dangling on a string, nothing to do with the relationship to each other of two eyes, a nose and a mouth. In those days, we used to call it 'It' and Olivia most certainly had 'It'.

'I'm very glad, Nicholas,' she said softly, 'really, very glad. You and Anne'll be so good for each other. You're a very sweet man.'

'Doesn't make me sound very exciting,' I replied with a wry grin.

'That's why I like you. Anne needs someone like you – someone steady and stable and . . . and harmless.'

'I think that was probably a deadly insult, but I can't quite pin it down!'

'It was a compliment, believe me.'

Blushing again – oh God! I bent down and fondled Raider's soft, wet ears to disguise my embarrassment. 'There's a good lad. I'd do anything,' I said, my voice muffled, 'to make Anne happy. She deserves it. Off you go then, old chap.'

The dogs thrashed in and out of the hedgerows, their tails wagging furiously, and I encouraged them with whistles and hisses.

'Seek 'em out, boys, seek 'em out.'

I felt I was beginning to breathe again at last, long, relieved breaths, after the claustrophobic atmosphere of the dining room. Five minutes longer and I swear I'd have stifled. Poor Anne. What she must be going through.

We walked in single file for a while, where the foot-path narrowed. Then it widened a little and I came alongside Olivia.

'Do you think I might take your arm for a bit?' she asked. 'I'm not feeling quite the thing.'

'Of course. Do you want to sit down?'

'No, it's so wet. I'll be fine in a moment.'

But we hadn't gone much further when Olivia dashed behind a bush. There was a frightful noise of retching and choking, then silence. I wavered over what to do for the best, but had just decided to go after her when she came back out again. Her face was beaded with moisture and it wasn't just the rain. Her pale skin didn't glow any more, but had turned the colour of uncooked dough. The skirt of her mackintosh was soaked, where she had knelt on the grass, and there was a spray of vomit on her chin. I moistened my handkerchief on some large leaves and gently wiped her chin clean. A sour smell overlaid her scent.

'I'm so sorry,' she gasped.

'I wasn't too certain about that fish at lunch myself. I'll certainly ask Mother to speak to Cook about it. Look, do you think you can make it to Home Farm? It's just over the rise. Mrs Wilsher will make you comfortable, then I'll dash back for the motor.'

She just nodded.

I managed to get her over to the farm and Mrs Wilsher seemed delighted to have someone to cluck over. Then I sprinted home and came back with my Crossley tourer. I can't have been more than fifteen minutes, but Olivia was already looking as radiant as though nothing had happened. Mrs Wilsher saw her out to the car.

'Now you mind,' she said, 'it's the early days that's the dangerous ones. The little beggars need time to bed in, like, and don't care to be shook up. So you put your feet up when you get back to the house and don't go clambering over no more stiles.'

Oh, God, no. Poor Olivia.

I didn't like to look at her on the short drive home. I didn't dare to. She might have misunderstood my stare, might have taken it for prurience or censure. I don't seem to have the knack of doing the right thing at the right time. I wanted to say, 'I'm sorry'. I wanted to say, 'What a waste'. If I'd had the bastard who did it in front of me, I'd have knocked him for six. But whatever I said or did would be wrong. I just didn't have the right words to say to a beautiful girl in that position.

Olivia kept her gaze strictly to the front. From the

103

corner of my eye, I could just see her hands, folded in her lap, in gloves too big for her, with crumpled-over fingers.

I couldn't have known, of course. It had never even crossed my mind. Although, now I came to think about it, I had seen that look before occasionally, if the wife of a chum was expecting. A transparency and glow at the same time, eyes set in with a sooty finger. But I'd never have guessed . . .

'Do you really want to come back and face everyone?' I asked as we left the village, 'I could run you to the railway station – make some excuse or other.'

'No, no. It wouldn't be fair on Anne. Or you. I can't ask you to lie for me. Anyway, I'm fine now. Let's just go back and pretend nothing's happened.'

If only she could.

I drove round to the coach house and put the car away before anyone noticed it had even gone. When I had cut the engine, I leaped out and ran round to the other side to help Olivia out.

'I'm not going to break, you know,' she said. Then she put her hand in mine and smiled a smile that made me her devoted servant forever. 'Congratulations!' she laughed, 'you're the first to know.'

Olivia beat us to the altar, not surprisingly. Anne and I didn't have the same need to hurry. (Well, I was pretty keen, but not enough to rob Anne of all the little trifles that are so important to a girl when she marries.) When I say altar, I don't mean it literally. Olivia was married at the Register Office in Mount Street, practically across the road from her family house, in October 1928, with Anne as bridesmaid and only a few members of her family present to see her become Mrs Guy Tarver. No one came to support him at all.

I had expected such shabby little affair. After all, isn't

it supposed to be the crowning moment of a girl's life? Doesn't she have the right to walk into church on her father's arm, radiant in white tulle and orange blossom? And if one or two are forced to carry rather large bouquets to hide the growing bulge, that shouldn't detract from the fact that it's their own most important day. Call me a romantic, if you like.

Olivia's wedding seemed terribly hole-and-corner. Her mother had obviously been crying; she wore a veil that was nearly thick enough for mourning and she never raised it once – not even to kiss the bride or groom; her father looked as though he'd just left his horse whip propped up in the porch. Terribly melodramatic.

Actually, I blame them. It's a parent's duty to make sure a daughter isn't tampered with. If Anne had become involved with a different sort of chap from me, the same thing could have happened to her. She was so innocent and willing, so sweet. She'd have been quite incapable of saying 'no' to a really determined man. Her parents certainly wouldn't have noticed – not until the consequences were forced on their notice, anyway.

If I'd been lucky enough to be the father of a girl, I'd have made sure no whippersnapper laid a finger on her without a wedding ring in his other hand. I wasn't so hard on our boys. It's different for boys. Everyone knows that.

It was all very sad. At least, I thought so until Olivia appeared.

Radiant is an awfully over-used word. I can't think of another one. Suddenly, it didn't seem to matter that we were in a dreary room on a dreary autumn morning. It didn't matter at all that only a handful of people had come to celebrate her wedding with her. The one person who really mattered was there.

Guy stood up and waited for Olivia to make the short walk to his side. I wasn't watching him, so I never noticed his expression, although Anne, uncharacteristically acid, said later that he looked as though he was about to mount the scaffold.

'That's only natural,' I replied. 'Men are supposed to be nervous. It's traditional.'

'And women are supposed to be radiant. I know, I know. They're supposed to be late, too. Olive is the first bride I ever heard of to turn up early for her wedding. It was indecent. Pa had to make Cleeve go round and round until they could respectably arrive.'

I laughed and, drawing her to me, nuzzled her neck. 'When it's our turn, I won't care how early you arrive, darling. It can't come soon enough for me.'

'But until then you can just keep your hands to yourself, naughty boy. I've no intention of walking up the aisle in Olive's condition. That's definitely not traditional.'

She took my hands decisively off her breasts and tucked them safely away in my pockets. She was laughing as she did it, but I knew she meant what she said. Quite right, too. I respected her for it. But letting me go a little further wouldn't have done any harm. And it would have done me a lot of good!

If I have one abiding memory of Olivia's wedding, it's of her face as she walked to meet Guy. I thought of the bride in the Song of Solomon going to meet her beloved. I knew it well. We used to read the naughty bits in chapel at school, while pretending to follow the lesson being read. I was thrashed once for sniggering when we were supposed to be remembering the late Latin master in our prayers.

As the apple tree among the trees of the wood,
so is my beloved among the sons.
I sat down under his shadow with great delight,
and his fruit was sweet to my taste.

106

Lucky Olivia! Lucky Guy!

If we had been in church, thoughts like that might have earned me a stray thunderbolt. I'm not a fanciful man, yet it seemed to me that joy shone around Olivia like a halo.

There's a couple that deserves to live happily ever after, I thought.

It was only later that I wondered, with a little pang of disquiet, whether Anne would look like that on the day she married me. And even as I wondered, I already knew the answer.

'Why doesn't your mother like me?'

'Not like you, darling? Of course she does. What ideas you get in your silly little head!'

'Now, Nicholas, you're to stop humouring me at once. You know she can't stand the sight of me.'

'That's just because she doesn't know you properly yet.'

'Well, she jolly well ought to. I'll be her daughter-in-law in twenty-four hours time.'

'No, you'll be my wife in twenty-four hours time. You'll be Mrs Nicholas Lockyer.'

'Junior – as the Americans would say.'

Yes, that was part of the problem. I drew Anne's head down onto my shoulder and settled her comfortably with my arm around her. She snuggled down and stopped talking. But I didn't stop thinking.

Anne would be expected to be very much Mrs Nicholas Lockyer Junior. My mother would make sure of that. She had never had a rival for the position, as she had never had a mother-in-law, my father's mother having died before his marriage (just as well, or there really would have been fireworks). She wanted me to marry – of course she did, what mother wouldn't, and she'd absolutely dote on grandchildren – but I know the sort of girl she'd have chosen for me, the sort of girl I'd be unlikely to get much fun out of. (Why can't a girl be sexy enough for the husband and meek enough for the mother-in-law? Now, that would be a combination!) As long as Anne was prepared to accept that situation and be reasonably submissive to Mother's dictates, at least at first, all might still be well. If not . . .

'But why doesn't she like me?' Anne persisted.

'Perhaps because she feels a little . . . a little insecure. You know – possible rival for her son's affections and all that.' This modern, psychoanalytical claptrap made me feel that I was well out of my depth, but Rose had said something along those lines and a good deal more too, that I didn't even begin to understand.

'Insecure? Your mother?' Anne sat up and broke out of my embrace. 'She's about as insecure as the Rock of Gibraltar!'

'You really ought to try to make allowances. See it her way. My mother is rather older than most and it can't be easy for her, darling, seeing another mistress of Greywell coming into the house.'

'She ought to be grateful to me! I'd have thought she'd be delighted to see someone else take over the burden of running that dump!'

'Dump? Oh, I say . . . isn't that going a bit far?'

'Oh, for heaven's sake, open your eyes, sweetie. Greywell may have been a terrific place once – a long time ago – but living there today is like living in the ark. The first thing I'm going to do is have a great, big generator fitted in the old laundry and have the whole house wired for electricity. Then we can close up the old kitchen and scullery and convert the butler's pantry into a modern little kitchen – much more convenient for the dining room – might get some hot food for a change. And while we're on the subject of food, that gorgon of a cook will have to go. Then a telephone is an absolute must . . . Olive has had heaps of marvellous ideas. You'll love them. She's really frightfully clever about colours and things.'

'Steady on, darling.' I felt battered by the rush of words. This wasn't the cosy little cuddle I'd visualised when we'd sat down. 'I realise the old place isn't exactly the Ritz, but do we have to rush it like that? Your ideas sound grand, but maybe we ought to do it slowly. You know, save up the old pennies for a while.'

'Oh, don't worry about silly old pennies. Daddy's already agreed to pay for anything I want to do.'

'Oh.'

Well, what did I expect? I'd always known I was marrying a rich man's daughter. And hadn't that thought always added extra spice to our physical relationship (such as it was at the moment)? Sexy and rich. You lucky bastard, Nicholas.

So why quibble now? Why did her plans – just a little girl playing houses after all – make the hairs on the back of my neck rise? Trouble ahead.

'Darling, you're looking frightfully fierce. You're not cross with your little Anne, are you?'

'Cross with you? Of course not. Why should I be?'

'Well, I was going to talk to you about it first, but there never seemed to be time, what with dealing with dressmakers and milliners and photographers and all those boring people who will write to one as soon as an engagement is announced. And then Daddy asked what we would like for a wedding present and I said . . .'

'It's all right. Really. Greywell is going to be your home. You must do exactly as you like.'

'You're such a sweetie, Nickie. I don't deserve you.'

She began planting little, feathery kisses all over my face. She looked so sweet and submissive. How could

I be cross? Her kisses lingered. She put a hand on either side of my face and gently guided me down towards her. The sofa twanged under our weight and both our heads jerked guiltily towards the door.

Anne giggled. 'Only twenty-fours hours more and we won't have to worry ever again about someone walking in on us.'

I trailed my lips down her throat and into the low vee of her neckline. There was a mass of fiddly buttons all the way down her blouse and I couldn't steady my hands sufficiently to undo them. Coolly, Anne unfastened them for me. Her breasts, slithery under silk, slid sideways and apart, falling one each into my waiting hands. But her petticoat had no fastening at all and I couldn't . . . I couldn't . . . oh, damn!

The constriction was frightful. I wanted to butt and butt myself against her, to batter my way in. Anne laid her hand on me and gently massaged the bulge, but that did nothing to comfort me. If anything, it was worse.

'Only twenty-four hours more . . . no twenty-three. Oh God, darling, couldn't we . . . ?'

'No,' she said.

'Silly me,' Mother said, 'I was under the impression that you had only intended to marry Anne, but it appears you've married the entire Northaw family.'

Ignore her. That's always the best method with Mother when she's in one of her moods. I pretended not to have heard.

'What's five letters – "falsehood, for instance, about true subject" – beginning with M?'

'I have no wish to be inhospitable,' Mother persisted, 'but someone ought to tell me just how long those twins are expected to stay here. I am not running a refuge for unwanted members of the Northaw family.'

110

Rose leaned casually over the back of my chair. '*Liege*,' she said quickly, 'falsehood is a *lie*; for instance is *eg*.'

'But that makes the beginning M wrong,' I protested.

'Of course it does – the answer's *entrammel* – that gives you your beginning L.'

'But . . .'

'Oh, for goodness sake, Nicholas, you're hopeless. Give up. I don't know why you bother with that thing, anyway.'

I folded the newspaper up roughly and thrust it at her. 'Well, if you're so clever – you do it.'

'No need to get shirty. I always end up doing it for you anyway, or hadn't you noticed, silly? Mother, did you know it's the twins' birthday – or should it be 'birthdays' – tomorrow?'

'I have no need to know,' she replied, taking a paper knife to her morning post. She sat back to catch the light better and began to read a letter. Her glasses were no longer powerful enough so she held the sheet of paper at arm's length. For her, the subject was closed.

'Well, I do think someone ought to do something about it – after all, with their parents in Florence, it's not going to be a very exciting birthday, is it?'

'I didn't know. Anne never told me,' I said, feeling unreasonably aggrieved. After all, unwanted visitors they might have been, but I had no wish to be unkind to any of Anne's relatives.

'Anne's mind never rises above two-ply wool these days,' answered Rose with a sneer and then, with deadly accuracy, mimicked, "Pink or blue? Oh dear, white is boringly safe, and lemon's so common!" Have you seen her latest endeavour – a mangled mess of grubby wool that's supposed to be something called a matinée coat? Is she really considering taking your sprog to matinées as soon as it's born?'

111

'Don't ask me,' I replied, trying not to sound bitter, 'all I did was father it. My responsibilities quite clearly ended at that point.'

'Ah, but have you considered that 'it' might be 'they', after all, don't twins run in families?'

'Oh, don't!' I shuddered. The thought of having a pair like Clare and David running riot permanently around the house was too horrible. 'I'd run off and join the Foreign Legion!'

'I don't suppose Anne would even notice! Twins – or triplets, even – might be rather fun,' Rose said wistfully. 'If I'm really going to be a spinster aunt – and I wouldn't give long odds against it nowadays – you might as well provide me with a decent number to be aunt to.'

For a moment, behind the bright, snapping mockery of her smile, I saw a whole generation of young women deprived of future husbands and children by the ravening maw of the Western Front. Rose would have made an appalling mother – casual, absent-minded, utterly maddening – but her children would have adored her. Then Rose shrugged, put on her mask again and reached for another slice of toast.

'Anyway,' she said. 'I've decided what I'm going to give the twins for their joint birthday.'

'What?'

'Something they'll thank me for, for the rest of their lives.'

'I don't care for the sound of that, Rose dear,' said Mother firmly, 'there is no obligation on you to mark the occasion in any way, since their parents are so obviously uninterested.'

'Well, that seems a bit rough,' I said, 'I'll have to see what I can come up with. I do wish Anne had given me some warning, though. I haven't a clue what young people of their age might like. How old're they going to be – fourteen, fifteen? D'you suppose they'd be glad of some cash? The young are perpetually hard up, I seem to remember.'

'Very appropriate, Nickie dear, especially since it'll be Anne's father's cash you'll be handing out so generously to his children.'

'Steady on, Rose, that's uncalled for.'

Unfortunately, it wasn't – uncalled for, I mean. I scarcely had two pennies of my own to rub together. Anne never reproached me. She was an absolute darling about it. Nevertheless, there were times when I felt like a little boy having his pocket money doled out to him. Or Anne might buy me a hugely extravagant present – a monogrammed dressing case, or the great, raw-boned hunter (I named him Attila, he was a real Hun) that had been her wedding present to me, standing in newly renovated stables – and she'd pass it over with the casual air of one dropping coppers into a busker's outstretched cap.

We had our first (and only) real row when I bought her something in return, a pair of fashionable diamond clips. I'd ordered them specially from Garrards. Two curly A's, shaped to nestle either side of her neckline. They'd arrived one morning by registered post. I'd slit open the wax-sealed, blue-crayon-crossed package with wild excitement. Perfect. Just what I'd imagined. I could scarcely wait until the evening to give them to my wife.

She'd held them up briefly to the neckline of the dress she wore, turned her head from one side to the other to view them, then popped them back into the velvet-lined case.

'Very pretty, darling' she said and carried on outlining her lips as though I'd never even come into the room.

'Put them on again,' I said. 'I want to see you in them.'

Sighing, she took them out and clipped them back on.

'They don't look right on that – put on that black dinner gown thing, you know, the one I like.' I opened the door of her dressing room and looked around as though I expected the appropriate gown to jump out at me. 'Where is it? Put it on.'

'Don't be silly, Nicholas, there isn't time. We're due at the Bouchers any minute now. Besides, I've just finished my hair.'

Yes, I was being silly. No, I didn't want her to tell me so. I wanted to see her wearing something I had chosen. I wanted to see her wearing something for me – not for the Bouchers or the Duncan-Greys or whoever else we were seeing. I wanted my wife to make herself beautiful for my sake.

I rummaged along the rails of clothes and flung the black velvet gown across our bed. 'There – put it on. I want to see you.'

I came up behind her and began to undo the buttons down the back of her frock.

'Nicholas!' she squealed, 'what do you think you're doing? You'll make us late.'

'For once – for once do something for me.' The sound of my own voice shocked me. It had come out hoarse and demanding, breaking, squeaking on the last word as it hadn't done for fifteen years or more.

'I don't know why you're making such a fuss,' she complained, in a cool, dismissive voice, as though I were a tiresome little boy. 'After all, they didn't cost you anything.'

Not cost anything? I felt cruelly wounded by the jibe. They may not have cost *me* any money – it may have been her father, in the end, who paid for them – but it was grossly unfair to suggest that I had spent nothing on the damned clips. They had cost my concern that they should be right for her and anticipation of her pleasure and time and effort going up to town and choosing them. I had so badly wanted to please her.

Anne rose from her dressing table, clutching the unfastened frock about her shoulders as though she was in the presence of a ravisher, rather than her husband. In the triple mirror behind her, I could see the reflection of her back, three times repeated: sweet, perfumed flesh, white and freckled, soft and juicy as ripe fruit; on the nape of her neck, a little question mark of hair, soft as a baby's, escaped from her coiffure.

Desire shafted through me. I felt dizzy with it. I wanted to dress her like a queen, adorn her like a votive saint in a procession, strip her bare as a newborn child. I wanted to conquer her. I wanted to love her, there and then, and have her love me. I wanted her to be mine.

I shot my hand out and snatched at the slipping dress. With a ripping sound, it came away and left Anne defenceless in her petticoat, her arms still crossed over her bosom.

'Nicholas!' she cried out, scandalised. 'What do you think you're doing?

'I have a right, don't I? I have a right to see my own wife?'

Across the dressing table stool, I challenged her to say no. I challenged her to give me the excuse to exert my rights. Dammit, I wanted her to. One hesitation – that's all it would have taken. If she had denied me, I would have been within my rights to take that denial and break it into little pieces.

Into the silence, she said, 'Yes, of course. You have the right.'

She slipped down the straps of her petticoat and stepped out of it. She unhitched her stockings from her girdle and rolled them neatly off, pairing them before putting them down. She didn't hurry. She might have been undressing alone before the bath. Her knickers, her brassière followed, until she was naked before me. The triple mirror reflected the thin red lines around her back and waist, left by her foundation garments.

'The law gives you the right,' she said, 'to do anything you choose to me.'

She stood perfectly still before me, straight, not shielding herself, a sacrifice to married privilege. She waited to see what I would do next.

Clever Anne. She was always so much smarter than I. She knew – she knew that I could no more take her now than I could kick old Raider downstairs.

I picked up the purple morocco box and hurled it with all my strength across the room. It broke open as it hit the wall and spilled its glittering contents onto the carpet. If I could have reached them, I'd have trampled them then. Worthless, worthless. I sat down on the bed, on that stupid velvet gown which had started the whole horrible business, and sank my head into my hands. How had this ghastly scene grown out of nothing? She made me feel such a brute. I had been on the verge of forcing myself on a helpless woman. I was a monster.

All I had wanted to do was worship her. Yet, naked and defenceless, she had made herself untouchable.

There was a whisper of skin on skin, her pigeon-plump thighs rubbing together as she crossed the room to stand before me. Still sitting, without looking up at her, I threw my arms around her waist and buried my face in the alabaster mound of her belly. She entwined her fingers in my hair, tugging it, keeping me down in my place.

'Such a fuss,' Anne said softly, 'about a very little thing.'

'I'm sorry. I'm sorry. I just wanted you to be beautiful,' I murmured into her flesh.

'Kiss and make up and I'll tell you a secret. I wasn't going to tell you just yet, darling, but you've rather forced my hand. I can't put the silly old black dress on because it won't fasten round me any more.'

'Then breathe in,' I said, still determined, like a spoiled child, to get what I wanted in the end.

'It'll take more than that to get me in,' she replied with a litle giggle. 'In fact, I shall have to order some new, much bigger clothes before long.'

I raised my head, puzzled but now attentive to what she was saying.

'Oh, you are a goose!' Anne ruffled my hair even harder, hard enough to bring tears to my eyes. 'Do I have to spell it out in words of one syllable? You're going to be a father!'

It was like being punched in the solar-plexus. It was like riding for that big fence you knew you couldn't manage and flying over it with inches to spare. It was like downing a bottle of bubbly in one, just for a bet, like plunging naked into the Serpentine in January, like all the mad things one does when young.

No, it was better than any of those.

'You wonderful, wonderful, wonderful girl!'

I tugged at Anne's waist and toppled her over on top of me, while she squealed and giggled and feebly protested. Then I kissed her, very carefully, all over.

'If you haven't completely ruined my hairdo,' she said briskly, 'we might just get to the Bouchers before it's hopelessly late.'

'Must we? I want to celebrate. Must we really?'

'Yes, we must,' she said.

So I had postponed my private and personal celebration of impending fatherhood until later that night. It was worth waiting for. Afterwards, when Anne lay in the sheltering crook of my arm and the sweat on our bodies was drying and our breathing returning to

117

normal, I asked her, 'Do you love me, darling Anne?'

She kissed the tip of my nose. 'You silly boy,' she said sleepily.

'Happy birthday,' I said to the twins and slipped them a jingling envelope each.

'Gosh, thank you, Nicholas,' said Clare.

'We didn't think anyone had remembered,' continued David.

'Oh well, I'm sure your parents haven't forgotten,' I lied. 'I imagine the post from Italy is atrocious.'

'Bound to be,' agreed Clare flatly, with a, by now, customary let's-humour-the-grownup expression on her broad, grumpy face.

Poor little blighters, dumped by parents busy gadding around on a reluctant, heavily pregnant sister, wanted by nobody, never knowing when, if ever, they'd go home. One had to feel sorry for them. No wonder Clare was often surly and David never spoke to anyone unless he had to. I felt a sudden, unexpected surge of sympathy for them.

'I tell you what – why don't you both come out with the hunt for a treat tomorrow, to make up for any disappointment?'

'Yes, yes,' said Clare, 'the very thing I'd have chosen!' Strange how excitement seemed to lift her sullen, rather plain face. With her usual dour expression gone, she looked thinner, brighter, pretty even. That wasn't a word I'd normally have associated with Clare and I was surprised to discover that her pudding face, obstinate chin and blue-button eyes hid enormous potential for charm.

'I'd rather choose my own treat, if I may?' asked David.

Ungrateful little devil. 'Yes, I suppose so, if you must.'

'Please may I *not* hunt tomorrow?'

'Is that all? That's a harmless enough request, I suppose.'

Good heavens, what a pathetic specimen. Imagine any boy turning down an opportunity like that. What a pity he and his sister had not had their sexes reversed before birth.

'Then I won't go either,' announced Clare, with the stubborn set to her mouth that I was beginning to grow accustomed to.

'Make up your mind,' I growled. 'I'd just as soon you didn't come anyway.'

'You never do anything with me, now, David. You never want to be with me,' she wailed and I could sense that tears were not far away.

'You go, Clare. Enjoy yourself,' said David softly and touched her cheek in a gesture that was father, brother and lover all in one. 'I'm happy if you're happy.'

It was a perfect morning, mild and damp, with a bright sky over low-lying mist and the scent running breast high. I stood at the dining room window eating my porridge and thought that nothing could be so perfect as the anticipation of a good day's sport.

'Eat up,' I said to Clare, 'if the huntsmen did their job yesterday and stopped up all the earths, we shan't be back until dark.'

She pushed her plate away and took a long drink of coffee before answering. 'I'm too excited to eat.'

'A flask of cold tea and a few mutton sandwiches won't keep body and soul together. Can't have you falling off your horse in a faint.'

'I shan't be so feeble!'

I rather resented Clare's presence, even though it was I who had invited her in a moment of weakness! I'd always enjoyed the solitude of a hunting morning: rising

119

in the dark and throwing open my curtains to find a transparent shadow of a moon looking back at me; the cloud of breath I blew in the icy dining room, where the air was so still and cold it made my nose ache; the hiss of the spirit lamp keeping my sausages and coffee warm; the clatter of my boots across the black-and-white tiled hall; the howls of complaint from Raider and Glengarry, shut up in the gun room to stop them from following me; only one set of footprints tracking behind me through the dew across the lawns to the stables; the dung hill steaming under a white frosty coating. These were special things – private pleasures – and I didn't like to share them with Clare.

She looked very well, though, I must say. I like to see a girl well-mounted and well-turned out. She rode astride, but her coat was cut long enough to cover her bottom – nothing worse in a woman than a coat cut too short and a shapeless bottom bulging over the saddle. Her boots, breeches and gloves were immaculate, her hair well-netted and neat. Her bowler was set straight on her head, no nonsense, no rakish tilt some women fancy makes them look dashing, but only means that the hat will fall off at the first fence. What useless creatures they are, some of them, expecting gallantry on the hunting field. It's catch as catch can out there and no quarter given to man, woman or beast.

We hacked quietly over to the Crown at Everleigh. It gave me a chance to assess Clare's horsemanship. She'd do, I decided, and I introduced her to the Master without too many forebodings.

There's always a lot of waiting around before the off – time to smoke and have a gossip, time for a quick snort to keep out the cold. At last we clattered off down the old Salisbury to Marlborough road, closed by the army at the turn of the century, drawing the coverts of mixed hazel, beech and fir. We found almost at once by

Snail Clump. He was a goer, all right, and we shot off on a long, breathless point across the lines of prehistoric ditches towards Sidbury Hill.

I knew that Clare, on Blériot, would have her hands full. He may have been old, but I think his ancestors must have been at Crécy. At the first blast on the horn, he would tuck his chin into his chest and charge as though he carried a fully armoured knight into battle. My new hunter was a bit green, so I didn't have as much time as I'd have liked to keep an eye on Clare. She went flying past me and up to the head of the field.

Well, he's twenty years old, I thought. He won't keep up that pace for long. They'll have to drop back soon and then I'll be able to watch her, but Attila was fighting the bit and sidling sideways and generally making a nuisance of himself, so I soon lost sight of Clare. Up and over Sidbury Hill we flew, round the chalkpit and off towards Seven Barrows.

It's long, hard, galloping country hunted by the Tedworth, up and down the chalky sides of the plateau of Salisbury Plain. There's nothing much to get in the way, nothing much to stop for – no hedges to speak of, or fences or ploughland. You need a strong horse, not necessarily big, but with sound wind and a great heart.

You sit down, sit tight and go with the animal, leaning forward over his neck as he takes the steep slope out of the Bourne Valley. The flints fly back from the hooves in front of you, sparking as they're struck by metal shoes. The wind whistles past your ears and your breath whistles between your teeth. The tight-packed chalk track thrums beneath a hundred or more galloping hooves. And then you're at the top, spreading out across the close-cropped turf and the sound changes, becoming hollow and muffled, like a funeral drum.

Your fox dashes into a little, whale-backed copse of trees and you hang around outside, with time now to notice other things: the smell of sweat that hangs over horses and men; the visible pall of steam; the unexpected whiff of mothballs from some dowager's habit; the way the sun catches at cobwebs weighted down with beads of dew; the last rags of crimson on the spindle trees as the cerise fruit splits and reveals its orange seeds, in a gloriously clashing colour scheme no one would ever dare wear.

Perhaps you have a quick nip from your flask, while the huntsmen send in the hounds. You know the fox will be out before long, because the earths were all stopped the day before. And there he goes, belly to the earth, streaking off downhill with the hounds baying behind, and it's all to do again.

There's no feeling like it on God's earth.

Not every day is as good as that, of course. The army puts its spoke in the wheel now and again. You might take a well-known short cut through a copse and find it full of men digging holes where no holes ever were before. I once saw a frightful accident when a horse stepped into a tangle of left-over wire and severed all the tendons in both back legs, like a cheese sliced on a grocer's slab. Filthy mess. It was shot on the spot. Or some idiot from the aerodrome at Upavon might take his bloody machine down for a closer look and spook all the animals into fits. But on the whole, we all manage to exist amicably together and the Plain is big enough and old enough to take everything in its stride.

And then there are the days – few of them, thank God – when nothing goes right. Attila suited his name. But if I say that he wasn't an animal I'd have chosen myself as a hunter, I'm leaving myself open to accusations of looking a gift horse in the mouth. Anne's intentions had been of the best – but her choice had been based on Attila's flashy chestnut hide and nothing else. A horse can have a head like a coffin and a rump like a goose, but if his heart's in the right place, he'll go for you. Attila was a real cracker to look at, but he had a nasty squint in his eye that would have warned me off, if I'd seen it first. He had a way of rolling it at you, bloodshot and wicked, if you so much as attempted to lift a hand to his head. Turn your back and his teeth were snapping at your backside. But Anne had only wanted to please me.

After schooling him patiently for most of the season, taking it steady, not pushing him too fast, this was our first hunt meet together. 'Back to school again for the rest of the season after this,' I thought, as he napped at every little ditch, taking me right to the brink, then planting his forefeet just as I rose for the off. Time and again, we interfered with the horses behind, so in the end, I decided to hold right back and follow quietly on, just to give him some much-needed experience.

I missed what was going on at the head of the field, but it seemed to me that we were taking a peculiar line. From the little I could see, I guessed the hounds had lost our fox, (probably foxes, given the distance we'd covered) and had been sent in to draw the beech copses around Clarendon Hill. They came out in full cry – downhill, towards the barracks.

The hunt staff tried to turn them, whips snaking across their pied backs, but they were nose to ground. Down through the barracks we clattered, shod hooves skidding on the hard roads, past dreary, terraced married quarters – the Merthyr Tydfils – past soldiers' women who screamed and snatched their children away from the hooves, across the camp railway, straight over a parade square to cheers from the band, who laid down their instruments and hurled their caps in the air.

It was incredibly dangerous – incredibly exciting! John Gilpin on his ride had nothing on us. Struggling with my hard-mouthed brute to stay at the back, I still felt a wicked thrill as we broke every rule in the canon. Anyone with any sense would have pulled out and headed for home – but not many did! It was madness. It was wonderful.

The hounds weren't headed off until we reached the row of thatched cottages at Hampshire Cross. Or rather, they'd run out of steam by then and so had we. The horses were blowing and hanging their heads. The whippers-in were rounding up the last few, recalcitrant hounds and trying to count the waving sterns. All the urchins of Tidworth were mixed in with them, patting heads and being licked by dripping tongues. I wouldn't have cared to eavesdrop on the Master's language.

Oh God – Clare! I couldn't see her. Somewhere in that mad run, she and Blériot must – *must* have broken away and gone home. Please God. I'd promised Anne I'd look after her sister and then forgotten all about her. I'd failed, I'd failed them both. I thought about Blériot, old and weakening, stumbling and tossing Clare down among the trampling hooves. I thought about her lying in a ditch, her neck at an impossible angle. Don't be stupid. Someone would have seen her. People wouldn't just have ridden on and left her. But supposing . . .

I stood in my stirrups to get a better view over the crowd. And there she was – thank God – she had dismounted, and was running up Blériot's stirrups and slackening his girth. She gave me a wave and led her horse over.

'Oh Nickie,' she shouted, before she reached me, 'wasn't that tremendous!'

Her bowler was missing. Her coat and breeches were spattered with mud and sweat and foam. There was a raised weal across one cheek – she must have been caught by a whippy twig. Her eyes – I'd never noticed before how blue they were – blazed with cold fire, the light that hides in the depths of an iceberg. For the second time, I was taken by surprise, caught out by the change in her – something inside puddingy, surly Clare had caught alight and she was transformed. A thought snatched at my mind, worried it, and slipped away.

'All right?' I asked, sliding off, my knees buckling, rather than dismounting. I slackened Attila's girth and let him blow, his head hanging.

'Never better!'

And Clare flung her arms around me and kissed me full on the lips. She smelled of sweat. So did I. We were two of a kind.

'Jolly good,' I said, when I could speak again.

'We never thought it'd be so successful.'

There was more than elation in her smile – there was triumph. She had dared something and won. She looked around the still chaotic throng and laughed. Lots of people were laughing, shrill and high, now that the excitement and panic were over. They had been afraid and had conquered it and wasn't life wonderful. But something about Clare's laugh chilled me. I didn't know what it was, at first. She was entitled to be elated. She'd just been through something that she'd never – one hoped – go through again, and she had come out safely. But there was more to it than that. I was uneasy. She wasn't laughing *with* us, she was laughing *at* us. It was as though she knew something that no one else knew. She was challenging me to guess her secret.

'What do you mean,' I asked slowly, 'you never thought it would be so successful?'

'Oh, nothing,' Clare answered, looking quickly away, 'you know . . .'

I turned her back to me. 'No, I don't know. Tell me.'

One by one, the thoughts crossed her mind and I saw them, as clearly as though they'd been printed out on a Wall Street tickertape machine. She was running through her options. She could be evasive and pretend she didn't know what I was talking about. She could lie. But how much more fun it would be to tell the truth. When you've done something outrageous, there's no point in it unless you confess. What's the fun in being clever, if no one knows about it?

'Who'd have thought you'd be so perceptive – dull old Nickie, who never notices anything unless he falls over it,' she began, insolently, but I knew she was only trying to hurt me for effect. She didn't mean it – did she?

'Tell me, Clare,' I insisted.

'Oh, it was nothing really.' She shrugged. 'We just unstopped the earths.'

'You unstopped . . . ?' I began to shout, but quickly lowered my voice. 'Come over here – talk quietly. The Master'll lynch you if he hears. Are you telling me you unstopped the earths after the hunt staff had been round?'

She nodded. Dammit, she wasn't in the least ashamed. Her eyes burned brighter than ever.

'And that's not all,' I continued. 'There's more, isn't there?'

'Then we laid a trail for the hounds, all round the garrison. And it worked, didn't it? It was a roaring success! We did it!'

'We? Who's we? No, don't tell me – that namby-pamby twin of yours.'

Of course, she leaped to his defence straight away. 'It was my idea . . .'

'It would be!'

'But I couldn't manage it by myself, so I . . . persuaded David to help me.'

'What did you do? Put him in thumbscrews?'

'Don't be silly! I just told him what happens to foxes when they get caught by the hounds. I described them

126

being thrown to the pack and torn apart. I told him about the starving cubs waiting at home . . .'

'They don't have any cubs at this time of year, stupid girl.'

'*I* know that,' she said, indignantly, 'but David doesn't. He was nearly in tears by the time I'd finished describing the fox's last throes.'

'I can't think when you found the time . . .'

'We were out on our bikes all day yesterday – but I don't suppose anyone even noticed. If we cycled off one day and never came back, no one would miss us at all. And then last night . . .'

'You were out last night?'

'All night, laying the trail. We'd only just got back when you got up. I thought you were going to catch us sneaking upstairs. You nearly did, but we heard you coming and ducked into the linen room until you'd gone down. Just as well you've got such big feet. You made enough noise for a regiment.'

'My God, you deserve a good thrashing. And I'm mad enough to give it to you myself – here and now.'

'Oh, what fun!' she sneered.

I could have done, too. Looking at her twisted, triumphant face, I was so angry I could cheerfully have put her across my knee, there and then, and spanked her in front of everyone. There was something about the idea of Clare turned over my knee and her bottom in its tight breeches beneath my hand . . . I ran a filthy finger around my sweaty stock, where it was chafing my neck. I could feel myself changing colour. Clare – damn her – saw it, too. Quickly, I turned away and fiddled about a bit with Attila's girth.

'You know you'll have to apologise to the Master,' I told her sternly.

'What? Now?'

'Good lord, no, not now. I've too much respect for

my own position to force you to do it now. He'll be furious, of course. He'll certainly ban you from the hunt forever – serves you right – and probably me, too, for the rest of the season.'

'Sorry,' Clare mumbled. Now that the first elation had died away, she was beginning to see what a harum-scarum, downright irresponsible act it had been.

'For heaven's sake, what got into you? Why did you *do* it, Clare?'

'It was something to do.'

You could almost admire that sort of dedication to mischief – almost. There was a sort of perverted grandeur to it. Clare was too old for childish tricks like scrumping strawberries or shutting the gardener in the potting shed and hiding the handle in the manure heap (heavens, I was thrashed for that!). She had to do something bigger, better, wilder. And she'd certainly displayed all the qualities that instructors had tried to drum into us at Sandhurst – initiative, leadership, foresight. She'd planned the action, ensured an element of surprise, and carried it through. As a soldier, she'd go far.

But *why* had she done it?

There's something awfully daunting about the sight of pregnant women in a room together. Even just two feels like several. Such fecundity, it frightens the socks off me – even though, in this case, I was responsible for half of it. Anne and Olivia seemed to fill the little winter sitting room. After the brisk air outside, after all we'd just been through, after the speed and the fear and the anger, the room seemed overheated and soft. Its atmosphere was flabby and female.

'You're back early,' said Anne, raising her cheek, flushed from the fire, for my kiss, 'it isn't nearly time for tea yet.'

'Yes, we finished earlier than . . . than we'd expected to.'

'Good day, Clare?'

I shot her a warning look. Don't you dare . . .

'Er – yes, thank you. Very exciting.'

'Isn't this nice?' Anne went on. 'Olive's turned up out of the blue.'

'Very nice,' I agreed, not, I hoped, noticeably lacking enthusiasm – Lord, all I wanted was to put my feet up and have a nice, lazy evening, not to be forced to entertain Olivia and her smart set. 'Planning on a nice long stay?'

'A few days, if you'll have me.'

'Delighted. Guy here, too?'

'Yes. We motored down with a chum. Guy's just showing him about the place until tea's ready. To tell you the truth,' she giggled, 'I think they were frightened off by all our baby talk.'

'Goodness,' interrupted Clare, 'what a gathering of the clan. Why don't we wire Daddy and Mummy while we're about it – then poor Nickie can have the whole, blasted Northaw family clogging up his house.'

'Oh, don't mind Nickie,' Anne said, smiling up at me, warm, rosy and very, very plump. 'Nickie never minds anything – do you, sweetie?'

Like hell I do. One of these days I'm going to say it. I'd give anything to see their faces – Mother, Rose, Anne, Olivia – all of them. Nickie *does* mind. Minds like blazes. One day . . . one day I'll say it.

'No, of course not. Delighted.'

'Anyway, it's the twins' birthday – but I suppose you knew that already – and I'd have brought them a present if the shops hadn't been closed when I remembered – so I said to Guy, 'Let's just run down and give them all a surprise'. So we did.'

I flopped down in a chair near the fire and propped

my stockinged feet on the fender. 'You're looking well, Olivia.'

'I am well.'

Oh, small talk – very small talk indeed. But it oils the wheels of family relationships. I've never understood those families who fill the silences with intelligent and articulate discussion of current affairs. If one wants talk like that, one can go to one's club. Families aren't meant to challenge the intellect. They're meant to be as comfortable as old shoes.

'How d'you think Anne's looking,' I asked, 'blooming, eh?'

'Oh, yes, she's certainly that!'

When I said that Anne was heavily pregnant, I didn't actually mean that our baby was due at any moment. In fact, she had a good six months to go. But somehow, in a very short time, she'd just exploded in every direction. Her face was rounded, with only a little trace of a chin. Her shoulders and bosom seemed to merge. She was already wearing shapeless clothes. I'd never seen her look happier – a little, round fertility idol. I found her very desirable, looking like that. It's what women are for, after all.

I thought that was normal, until I saw her sister. Olivia, in contrast, looked the same as ever – except she had this grotesque bump in front. It looked indecent, as though she'd just stuffed a cushion up her frock for effect. There was her little, pointed face, then she went straight down, flat as a billiard table, and suddenly – boom!

How different the two sisters – no, I looked across at Clare – the three sisters were. One would scarcely imagine they were related at all. Clare was definitely nodding off. She was making a very determined effort to keep her eyes open, but was losing the battle. The cold air, followed by the heat of the fire, had turned her face quite pink. Blue eyes, gold hair, pink cheeks – she looked as innocent as a doll. Only I knew better.

At least she wasn't troubled by the runny nose I always suffered when I came in from the cold. I blew my nose thoroughly and Clare's eyes jerked open.

'Oh, you've woken her,' said Anne. 'Poor Clare. It's all been too much for her. She looks utterly exhausted. You've worn her out, Nickie. I told you not to.'

'I've . . . ?'

'It's not Nickie's fault,' put in Clare, 'I just didn't seem to be able to get to sleep last night.'

'Too excited, I expect,' said Anne, comfortably.

'Yes, I expect that's it,' answered Clare and gave me a contorted wink that must have been obvious to anyone whose mind wasn't totally obsessed with procreation.

It's the unexpected pain that hurts the most. One doesn't have time to prepare for it. Sitting in the dentist's chair, one is aware that at any moment the drill may slice into a nerve. So one is tense and ready for it, gripping the arms of the chair, willing oneself not to scream or kick out.

But imagine the agony, if one has not expected it.

I sat, toasting my toes, waiting for tea and hot buttered crumpets to appear. Already, the events of the day seemed less dramatic and more amusing. What a lark – those twins had nerve, if not too large a helping of common sense. I could laugh about it. I was warm and happy and at ease with myself and my wonderful wife.

I didn't know that, in a moment or two, Guy would walk into the room, bringing with him the death warrant of my marriage. If I had known, what would I have done, what could I have done? Barred the door? Flourished my horsewhip? Thrown him out into the gathering dusk?

131

And, because it was so very unexpected, it hurt so very much more.

'Nickie dear,' Olivia said, 'this is Christopher Berry. He's a terrible man, I warn you – the original Red under the bed! You'll probably long to throw him out on his ear before the night's out. But he's a sweetie, really. Aren't you, Chris?'

'You must take me as you find me,' he answered and his voice surprised me. His accent was more educated than I'd have guessed. Not one of us, by any means, but not uncouth, either.

Olivia – why did you do this to me? Why did you bring this man into my house?

I rose to greet him. I disliked him on the spot – a working class intellectual, too clever by half. He was everything I despised, in his green corduroy jacket and soft-collared shirt, his knitted tie, baggy flannels and brown suede brothel-creepers. But manners are manners, after all, and he was a visitor to my house. The hand I shook was wide with stubby fingers, yet well-kept, with short, clean nails, as though he'd left far behind the manual labour he'd been born into.

Such an insignificant little man, dark and square. What did she see in him? Oh Anne, why? Why?

I'd have done anything for Anne, to make her happy. Anything. But sometimes you have to be cruel to be kind. It would have been too easy to cave in, to play the white man and oblige her by providing evidence of my fake adultery in Brighton with some paid woman. I could never withstand a woman's tears, but I stood out against Anne's. It was for her own good.

What wrong had I ever done her to deserve this? All I did was love her.

Advice and sympathy (well-meaning and otherwise)

poured in from my female relatives. I could have done without most of it. What I really needed was another man to talk to, but there was only Anne's father and he wasn't likely to be much help. Besides, he was in New York. I wished I had a wise old uncle to lean on, but they're pretty rare birds.

Mother said, 'I told you so.' (She hadn't, but that didn't mean she hadn't thought it.) 'I sincerely hope you'll admit from now on that I know best. You're too much of a gentleman for your own good.'

Olivia said, 'Pregnant women aren't responsible for themselves (and I should know, Nickie dear). We're totally at the mercy of our hormones. She probably just got frightfully emotional over some silly thing, ran away to make you sorry, and now she doesn't know how to come back. Don't hold it against her. Try to make it easy for her to come home again.'

Rose said, 'Well done, Anne. So she's got some spunk, after all. I never thought she had it in her. Let her go, Nickie. You're well out of it. Jolly good luck to her, I say.'

Clare said, 'Of course she doesn't love him – how could she? She doesn't love anyone at all. Never has. Not even you. Now, don't look so hurt. I can't bear it when you look like a whipped puppy. You must have known. Obviously, you must refuse to divorce her, Nickie. It's your duty to stop her making a fool of herself.'

On the whole, I preferred Clare's advice, if only because she put into words what I really felt. Anne had been an ass. She'd be sorry for it, sooner or later. It was my duty to make sure she had a bolt hole to run to when she needed it.

So I gritted my teeth, stopped my ears to Anne's tearful telephone calls – and it broke my heart to listen to her – and waited for her to come home.

'Let me go, let me go,' she wept, her grief tinny and distorted along the miles of line, but real enough to rake me with remorse. 'If you loved me, you'd let me go.'

If? If I loved her? If I didn't love her, I wouldn't hold on like this. I'd let her go and good riddance. It was only because I loved her that I was prepared to hang on, to take back whatever leavings that bastard Berry could spare. The easy way out would have been to jettison her, like so much unwanted ballast, but I've always been stubborn.

There was some ancient Greek, I seem to remember from school classics lessons (ghastly!), who was doomed to push a stone up a hill for eternity and every time he got it to the top, it would roll back down again. Conversations with Anne were just like that.

I'd put my shoulder against the weight of her demands, shoving and straining to make some headway against her muddled, female logic. Then, just when I'd think we were getting somewhere, she'd burst into tears and back I'd go, tumbling down to the bottom again.

Up and down, round and round we'd go.

Bewildered and hurt, I'd say, again and again, 'How can I help you? Tell me what I can do to make things better.'

'You can let me go.'

'I can't do that. I love you.'

'So you say, but if you really loved me, you'd let me go.'

'Don't you want me to love you?'

'I never wanted that. It wasn't in the plan.'

'The plan? What plan? What did you marry me for, if not for love?'

'A woman has to marry. Children have to have a father.'

'And for that, you married me? To be a . . .' I couldn't say the word, not with the postmistress

134

probably listening, agog, on the line. 'Why me? Oh God, what did I do to deserve to be chosen?'

'Not just for that . . . Oh, Nickie, why do you make it all sound so sordid? It wasn't that at all. You were so nice to me. I liked you so much. I still like you.'

'Liked me enough to crucify me?' Now I was shouting and the whole village would know about it as soon as the receivers were replaced. 'If that's liking, I suppose I should be grateful you never loved me.'

There was a long silence on the line, but I knew she was still there. I could feel her, could almost see her, standing with her hand against her mouth, her eyes red, her face all blubbered. Poor little Anne. What had she got herself into? I decided to press home my advantage.

'You don't suppose *he* cares for you, do you?' I demanded, relentlessly. 'That type never does. You're just his little bit of high class skirt. But when he's finished with you, I'll still be here. Your home's still with me. Remember that.'

'It's not true . . . it's not true . . . Oh, I wish I could hate you.'

I could hear Anne crying now, in great, breathy gasps. I was back at the bottom again, bruised and defeated, with it all to do over again.

She'd come back to me, in the end. She'd come. I could afford to wait. Time was on my side. It wouldn't be long. She was bound to be back before the baby was born.

She'd thank me for it some day.

OLIVIA

The Seeker

Take what you want, God said, and pay for it. So, I took. And I paid. And in the end, you wonder if it was all worth it. Those desires, those passions that burned inside like white fire, that drifted away like ash on the wind, did they matter at all, in the end? You tear yourself apart and, in the doing of it, carelessly rend those you love – and for what?

I have Chloe. I have grandchildren. They are a constant joy. But I have paid for that joy – with interest that has been exacted at usurer's rates.

Poor, dear Nickie. Everyone loved him – except his wife. How could anyone not love Nickie? Just a glimpse of his fresh face, his sandy hair with that darling little pink spot at the back, his gangling arms and legs, brought out the maternal instinct in most women. They couldn't help adoring him. There was something so sweetly childlike about Nickie. He's the only person I've ever met whom one could literally take at face value. He was an innocent, untouched by the bitterness of war that seared so many men just a little older, untouched by the cynicism of peace that spoiled and blighted and destroyed so many hopes.

It was as though the story of Sleeping Beauty had been reversed. Somewhere in the wilds of Wiltshire, locked away with his horses, his guns and his dogs (and with his mother or by his mother, I wonder?) Nickie had slumbered all his adult life. The world passed him by and he was happy to let it. Why not? He had everything he wanted. What you've never had, you never miss, they say. Then one day, along came a plump little girl who kissed him awake. And suddenly, Nickie discovered all sorts of dark longings that he never knew existed. He found out what being a man was all about. But did that make him any happier . . . ?

What right had I to populate his house with my family and friends and friends of friends, behaving as though it were my own? All those amusing, witty people that I scarcely knew, treating them to a weekend in the country was a cheap way of entertaining them. Nickie never complained. He may have preferred a quiet dinner followed by a game of billiards, or to sit until bedtime by the fire with *Sorrell and Son*, rather than rolling up the carpet and dancing all night, but, being his own sweet self, he never dreamed of saying so. Instead, he always volunteered to man the gramophone.

'No, no,' he would urge, 'you go on – don't mind me.'

And so 'Don't mind Nickie' became a catchword and a habit.

He could have blamed me for bringing Christopher Berry to Greywell on that dull winter's day. But he never did. It's typical of Nickie that he never blamed anyone else for anything that happened. Like a dog that is beaten, not knowing the reason why and wagging his tail all the same, he just accepted Anne's madness as one of the inexplicable cruelties of life. It simply never occurred to him to fight it.

If he'd come out of his corner with his fists up, like a man, Anne would have crawled home and begged him to take her back. But Nickie just looked hurt and retired to Wiltshire to lick his wounds. Silly boy.

Either Anne had gone barking mad, or she was in

love. Personally, I thought madness would have been a lot easier to handle. But who was I to moralise?

I nearly told him so, when he came battering on the door of the flat Guy and I had rented on First Street.

'She's here, isn't she?' he demanded as he burst past me.

No need to ask who. 'No, she's not, Nickie. And next time you feel like slamming the door against the wall, please make sure I'm not standing behind it.'

'I'm sorry. I'm sorry. But Anne's gone and I don't know where she is. I'm almost demented.'

I tried to put an arm around his shoulders, but he was too tall for me, so I slipped it around his waist instead.

'Look, come and sit down. We can talk about it. You look as though you need a drink.'

'I've had more than one too many already,' he said, taking the whisky tumbler from my hand. He gulped the drink down in one, walked over to the fire and poked it, wandered over to the window and pulled back the curtains to stare out into the darkening street. The lamp lighter was making his way towards us. Pale pools of light followed him, but kept themselves to themselves and never mingled. They reminded me of our respectable neighbours in the surrounding flats.

'For heaven's sake, Nickie. I can't talk to you while you prowl around the room like the troops of Midian.'

'Sorry. Sorry.'

'You seem to be saying sorry rather a lot at the moment.'

'Sorry. I mean . . . yes, I do. Anne always used to tell me it's a bad habit. Oh, God . . . she's gone, Olivia. What am I going to do?'

'You can start by sitting down and telling me all about it.'

He plumped down on the sofa, all legs and arms, a

grasshopper in a tweed suit. 'I don't understand . . . didn't she have all she wanted . . . didn't she know I'd do anything to make her happy, anything at all?'

How could she? How could she do it to him? Poor, bewildered, well-meaning Nickie. Anne had taken his life and knocked it down. Like a toddler's tower of bricks, his marriage had teetered for a little while, long enough to make him proud and very happy, then crashed around his feet. The howls of outrage were only natural.

I felt like scratching her eyes out myself. Silly bitch! Didn't she know what she was throwing away? Didn't she know that Nickie was worth a dozen Chris Berrys and – yes, I had to admit it – a dozen Guy Tarvers, too?

'I was certain she'd come to you first. So where is she, Olivia? I promise I won't do anything silly. I only want to talk to her. Tell me,' he begged.

'I don't know, darling. If I knew, I'd tell you. Promise.'

'Even though she's your sister?'

'Especially since she's my sister.'

'She didn't even leave me a letter, you know,' he complained. 'She just . . . just went. I didn't know what to think. She has these dizzy spells, you know, since the baby. I thought she might have fallen somewhere, hurt herself, or worse. We wasted hours searching the countryside, until someone said she'd been seen getting on a train. Never a hint . . . If I'd thought – guessed – sooner I might have caught her up.'

He flopped back, leaning his head against the back of the sofa, and closed his eyes. His big, red, countryman's hands lay open and helpless in his lap. From under closed lids, a tear oozed, but he dashed it angrily away before it slid down his cheeks. I was glad he did that, because I'd had an awful urge to lean forward and kiss it away.

Anne had never loved him, not as he understood the word. It just wasn't in her to love anyone. She was much too self-contained, too . . . too orderly and love is such a disorderly emotion, disorganised and messy. When two people love each other, common sense is the first casualty. But she had liked him. You just don't do things like this to people you like. I'd never have believed Anne could be so cruel. Calculating, yes, frequently – but not downright cruel.

'I don't blame Anne at all, you know,' he said. 'It's not her fault. She's a woman, after all. She's been taken advantage of – she couldn't help it.'

I snorted inelegantly. Poor, deluded fool! 'I don't know quite what you think women are, Nickie, but we're not all the helpless victims of our hormones that you seem to imagine. Most of us are quite capable of making our own decisions – Anne as much as any.'

'But she's such a sweet little thing, so innocent. She's not responsible. Anything might happen.'

Heavens! Were we talking about the same Anne? My hardheaded sister who'd married this poor, besotted simpleton – the father of her child – without love as a reaction to our mother's cloying real-life romance? I felt I could cheerfully strangle her.

'I'm sorry, Nickie. I feel so guilty that Guy and I brought Chris Berry into your house.'

'Not your fault. All the same, Olivia. You and Guy do have some funny-peculiar friends. I don't know what you see in half of them. They're not – you know – proper types for you to know.'

'I think our friends are our own business,' I replied frostily.

'No, but – don't you see – this has made it my business, too. If you and Guy hadn't . . . no, sorry, sorry. You're quite right. None of my business.' He got up and walked over to the window again, twitching apart the curtains, staring down the street, as though he expected Anne to come tripping along after an unscheduled day's shopping. 'As for this Berry chap – I'll kill him. I swear I'll kill him, if I get my hands on him.'

'She's not with Chris. I can tell you that much. He's in Berlin and has been for three weeks.'

'Oh God, Olivia. Then where is she?'

In another two hours, I was able to answer Nickie's question.

When I opened the door, Anne was leaning against the lintel, looking grubby, tired and very, very permanent.

'I've been expecting you,' I said.

'But what's she doing here?' Guy demanded. His voice reached me across the dark divide that separated our beds – and, over the last few months, not just our beds.

'Shh. She'll hear you. The walls are like cardboard.'

'I don't care if she does hear. This is my house and I'm not going to whisper to please anyone. Why here, of all places?'

'Because she's left Nickie.'

'I'd worked that out. She dumped herself on the sofa with her bags like a roly-poly pudding surrounded by prunes.'

'That's typical – just the sort of reaction she expected from you. D'you know, she sat drinking gallons of tea in an ABC all afternoon because she was frightened you'd throw her out as soon as you saw her.'

'I'm surprised I didn't. What's she playing at?'

'I wish I knew. It's all so unlike her – she's always been so conventional . . .'

'You mean boring . . .'

'No, I don't mean that at all. Nickie's boring – bless him – but so sweet, you can't hold it against him.'

'A marriage made in heaven, I'd have thought.'

'We all thought that. I tried to get some sense out of her this afternoon. I didn't exactly ask her if she'd taken leave of her senses, but I dropped a few hints.'

'And?'

'She said something about being stifled, that there's no such thing as an equal marriage, that there's always one who loves and one who is loved, that being loved too much is worse than not at all . . .'

Guy groaned. 'Claptrap! How long is she staying, for heaven's sake?'

'Just a night or two; until Chris comes back from Berlin and then she'll move in with him – if he'll have her.'

'You mean, he doesn't know?' Guy gave a soft laugh. 'Well, well. I'd like to see Chris's face when he finds his family's doubled in size while he's been away. For all his wild talk, he's so awfully working-class conventional. He'll have a fit.'

'It's not funny, Guy. It's a tragedy for Nickie, for both of them.'

I heard Guy turning over in bed. I lay in the dark and traced his movements by their sound. There was something so sensuous about the rustle of the sheets as his naked limbs slid across them. Without even closing my eyes, I could picture the way he would be lying, sprawling loose-limbed, his arms behind his head. And in the morning, the covers would be tangled, the pillows on the floor. He'd be on his stomach, one leg lying free, the other drawn up. His thin face would be flushed, dark with stubble, and always, always beautiful.

Twin beds are made to divide married couples. Or perhaps they only formalise a division that has already taken place. I couldn't imagine my parents ever wanting to sleep with three feet of floor between them.

Perhaps if I crawled in with him now – he wouldn't, he couldn't turn his back. I'd curl round him, not demanding anything, just being there, soft and warm, the way he used to like me to be.

Sometimes, when we were first married, he used to say, 'I can't sleep. My brain won't let me relax, Olivia, it's too busy in there. Help me to sleep, darling.'

And I'd touch him in the way he'd taught me, in all the places he liked. A few strokes – long, firm strokes – and he'd give a shudder and a sigh and fall asleep. Leaving me awake.

It's for the baby, I'd think, he doesn't want to hurt the baby. He's just being considerate. But of course a man can't, well, you couldn't expect him not to, not for all these months.

He never thought of me, lying awake in the dark, aching.

And now – now if I crawled into bed beside him, he'd say 'There's not enough room for you, me and the bump in here. Go back to bed. I need to sleep.'

I could hear Guy's breathing now, altered, slowing as he slipped into sleep. Would he notice, would it matter if I crept in with him now? Just for a few minutes, for comfort. Just until I was ready to sleep myself. I felt so isolated, lying awake and listening to him. I pushed back the covers, swung my legs out of bed and then the baby kicked me in the bladder. I knew I'd have to go to the lavatory instead.

The door was locked. Anne had beaten me to it. I waited outside the door, hoping she wouldn't be long. Two pregnant women in the house put a lot of pressure on the plumbing. The linoleum was slippery and cold as fish skin beneath my feet. For some reason Anne seemed to be running water. It sounded as though she'd turned all the taps full on. There'd be no hot water in the morning if she carried on like that and Guy would sulk for hours if he had to shave in tepid water. I put my ear to the door and beneath the gush of the bath taps I thought I could hear the sound of sobbing.

'Anne? Anne?' I tapped on the door. 'Are you all right?'

'Who is it?'

'Olivia, silly. Who else could it be? Is there anything I can do?'

'Go away.'

'But Anne, darling . . .'

'Go away, I don't want you.'

So I padded back down the landing, the urgency in my bladder increased by knowing that I'd have to wait.

Guy stirred as I came back into the bedroom.

'Anne's crying,' I said. Dammit, if I was awake, why shouldn't he be?

'What?'

'She's sitting in the bathroom crying and I need a pee.'

Guy groped on the night table. He rattled the clock, my glass of water and then found the light switch. He sat up, blinking his beautiful, short-sighted eyes in the sudden glare. His hair was tousled and he pushed it back out of his way. I wanted him, I wanted him so badly. I wanted the comfort of his love.

'Is she all right? I mean, she's not going to lose the baby or anything . . . ?' Guy asked.

'Of course not. Don't be silly. I think she's just frightened. After all, maybe she's been a bit hasty. She's thrown one man away before actually getting her claws into the next one.'

'Good God – are all you Northaw women so voracious? Isn't one man enough for her?'

'One man seems to be quite enough for you,' I countered and I hated the voice I heard – sneering, bitchy. It seemed to be the only one I had left. I was becoming the thing that Guy already believed I was, the shrew, the virago. I was powerless to stop the change.

'Don't. Don't start that all over again. I married you, didn't I? What more do you want?'

'You – I want you.'

That's all I'd ever wanted.

I can hear my mother's voice now.

'Your father asked me to marry him when we were five years old – but of course we had to wait for a little while . . . love at first sight . . . happily ever after . . . never looked at another woman since . . .'

It was a litany and we children, the faithful, joined in the responses. Why should we not believe in it? We believed in God and Father Christmas; we believed that eating crusts made your hair curly and that hairs grew on the palms of your hands if you were going mad; we believed that if you didn't say your prayers every night, you'd be found dead in bed in the morning (until Clare quite deliberately skipped prayers one night and was still there, alive and well, for breakfast, but just in case, she said double next night – no point in tempting Providence); we knew that Nanny believed that all sorts of horrors could be kept at bay by being 'regular' and always having a clean handkerchief tucked up the leg of your knickers. And we believed implicitly in Mother's romance.

It was a lovely story, far more satisfying than anything in any of Andrew Lang's Blue or Pink or Violet *Fairy Books*.

I remember once when I had a bilious attack (it must have been during the war, because Mother came upstairs to see me and she'd never have bothered if Father had been at home). I'd been a little pig at a party and stuffed myself with strawberry ice cream and fairy cakes. Mother had laid her cool hand on my sweaty forehead and it felt wonderful.

148

'Tell me a story,' I begged. 'Tell me about when you and Pa were little.'

'Well,' she began, 'we'd been to a party, too, just like you today. I remember I wore green velvet . . .' And she recited the well-known, soothing phrases.

'Will someone love me just like that one day?' I asked when she'd finished. 'Will I be someone's princess?'

'Just like that,' she promised. 'You're my princess now and you'll be someone else's one day.'

'Promise?'

'Promise.'

And I was. For a little while.

'I'm going to sit beside . . . beside the handsomest man here.'

There was no contest. Amongst the sunburned, peeling noses and vacuous expressions, there was only Guy. I looked at them all, holding their tummies in, drooling at my long, brown legs, and I wanted to shout, 'Don't be silly – you surely don't believe I'm going to choose you, do you?'

When Guy turned his long-lashed grey eyes on me and tilted his head to one side, giving me his whole attention, listening as though I had something really important to tell him, I knew that I'd found a man to cherish me for the rest of my life. A new fairy tale was beginning, the magic was working, just as Mother had said it would. How was I to know that he only stared at me in that penetrating way because he was shortsighted?

Any one of those men, that summer in Provence, would have taken advantage of me, given half the encouragement I gave Guy. No better than a filly in her first season, I flaunted my short skirts and tanned body at him. He would notice me, he would want me – I would make him want me.

149

When other men, as old as my father, squeezed my thighs or patted my bottom, becoming less and less avuncular, I would dart away from their podgy paws. Like a moth before a flame, I circled Guy, enchanted by his beauty, enchanting him with my own.

We are so suitable, I thought, we deserve each other. Oh, I was right about that, we did deserve each other, but how right, I didn't know then.

Magic, magic summer. All I had to do was stretch out my hand and he was there, his limbs silky with coconut oil and cool from an early swim. Hot sea, hot sand, hot sky. And inside me, a fire that burned brighter and harder than the sun. I was consumed by it. Surely Guy, anyone, only had to touch me to feel the heat of it. And amongst all those men willing to touch me – more than touch, if I let them – only Guy stood apart.

That's how it should be, of course, I thought. The hero is only rewarded with the body of the princess at the end of the story, after he has passed all his tests. No one asks the princess how she feels about the wait.

Then Mother drew the line beyond which she would not allow me to step. She was taking us home and I was desperate – desperate enough to corner Guy at the bottom of the garden, far away from the house and from prying eyes.

'Don't you like me?' I demanded. 'Don't you think I'm beautiful?'

'I think you're the loveliest thing I've ever seen – and you know it, you little harlot.'

'Then why don't you touch me? Everyone else does. They can't keep their hands off me, whether I want it or not. They do this, and this.'

I took his hand and placed it on my breast. My silk frock was like another skin, transmitting the heat of his hand. Under his touch, my nipple peaked and hardened.

150

I gave a gasp of surprise – that had never happened before – and my gasp was echoed by Guy.

'Do you like that as much as I do?' I asked.

'It's . . . it's amazing . . .' There was wonder in his voice and a hushed awe.

He put his other hand on me, tentatively, as though I would bite, and then more positively. Flickers of fire, like summer lightning, licked up and down my thighs.

I put my arms around his neck. He was so tall that the action tightened the muscles across my chest and tilted my breasts upwards. He dug his fingers in, probes of iron, making me wince yet exciting me at the same time. When I laid my mouth on his, it felt right to open my lips to him, but Guy's mouth remained unmoved, cool and firm, beneath my own. I didn't know enough to wonder at that.

'Don't you understand?' I gasped, when lack of breath forced me to raise my head. 'We're going home. Mother is determined to separate us. Don't you care?'

'You're very young,' he answered, but it was no answer.

'I'm fifteen.'

'Exactly. And I've no ambition to spend the next few years in prison on your account.'

'But I won't always be young. I'll grow. I'm growing every day. And when I do, where will you be? How shall I ever find you again?' My eager voice quivered and broke. The shell of sophistication I'd adopted to impress Guy disintegrated. The bitter pain of rejection was a new experience to the child that was left.

He took my face between his hands. With his thumb, he stroked away the tears of anger and frustration that spilled down my cheeks. His smile was as sweet as ever, but the words – oh, the words were all wrong.

'Promise me you won't try too hard, Olivia,' he said.

★

151

I didn't see Guy again, not alone, anyway, until the night of Anne's coming out dance. By then, he wasn't just an up-and-coming young writer; *Imperial Echoes*, that savage satire on post-war society, had been published and everyone wanted to claim that 'of course, one had always known' – 'brilliant, my dear, quite brilliant'. People said that it was only a matter of time before he produced *the* twentieth-century novel. Mother was not averse to inviting the new literary lion to the dance.

'I think I may safely claim to have discovered him, oh, when he was just a scribbling hack, but the talent was always there. Your father and I always thought very highly of him. Fortunately,' she added, 'he is really very presentable.'

And that was when I decided I'd finished being too young and had grown enough to match him. Poor Guy, he didn't stand a chance. Against a moonlit night, a silvery lake and me, he had no defences. I took him to my secret island and there let him discover that under a sliver of silk velvet, I wore nothing, not a stitch.

Love was as sweet as I had dreamed – pierced and pierced again, invaded and invading, captor and captive – yet over so quickly that I was left still trembling and expectant, waiting, I didn't know for what. And as Guy cried out, I wrapped my legs around him and exulted. He's mine now. Nothing can come between us.

How had this led to twin beds separated by a river of darkness?

Sensible Anne can only cry for a specific length of time (her emotions are only skin deep, after all). After that, common sense reasserts itself and she realises that she's just making a fool of herself. The sound of running water stopped and I listened to her padding back to bed. Guy was asleep again, but tossing and turning as always.

I thought about getting up and making my long-delayed visit to the lavatory, but I realised that while I'd been waiting, my physical discomfort had undergone a subtle change.

I lay and listened to what my body was telling me. What a fool I should look if I started making a fuss about nothing. But it didn't feel like nothing. Fingers of pain encircled my belly and spread round to my back, tentatively at first, then gripping me with increased vigour.

Not now, not now, I thought, I'm not ready. But I was as ready as I was ever going to be.

I leaned over and woke Guy.

At some time during the blur of hours that followed, I can remember lashing out at Anne's worried face.

'No, of course I don't want a bloody hot water bottle,' I snapped. 'And I don't want any bloody tea either. All I want is for it to stop.'

Poor Anne. Looking at me, how could she have been feeling about the fate that was lying in wait for her in a few months time? I suspect it frightened the socks off her. Later, when I'd passed the stage of swearing at everybody, I can remember gripping her hands with bone-crunching force.

'Make it go away,' I moaned, 'oh, make it go away.'

'Now, now, Olive. You know you don't mean that,' she answered with a horribly brave smile (what had she to be brave about? It wasn't her tossing about on the bed – not fair, not fair – her turn next). 'Just think about the darling little baby at the end of it all. What do you want it to be?'

'The last!' I groaned and Anne gave a little smile to the nurse as if to say, 'She doesn't mean it really'. But I bloody did.

I know the nurse tried to keep Guy out, but he forced

his way in. Through the plastered-down strands of sweat-streaked hair that blurred my vision, I saw him push past her outstretched arm. He was in his shirt-sleeves, unshaven, and his hair stood up in ruffled crests.

'She's my wife and I'm going to make sure she's all right.'

'I rather think that's my job, sir.'

'Then call a bloody doctor, will you? I'll hold you personally responsible if anything goes wrong.'

'Mrs Tarver is going through a perfectly normal labour . . .'

'Normal!'

'Normal, if rather prolonged. I shall call Doctor when and if he is required and not a moment sooner. Now will you please leave the room?'

'Get out!' I screamed. 'Get out! I don't want you here. Go back to your fancy boy – go on.'

There was an awful silence in the room, thick enough to touch, not broken until I gave another scream.

I watched Guy through narrowed eyes. He was bending over the lace-trimmed crib that my mother, reverting to her Edwardian instincts, had thought appropriate to a modern baby. His long body was folded at an awkward angle beneath the canopy. His manner was furtive, as well it might be – if Nurse had caught him disturbing 'her' baby, she'd have given him what for. Fathers had no place in her scheme of things.

Still motionless, feigning sleep, I watched Guy lift his daughter out of the crib. He held her awkwardly, high against his chest, his beautiful eyes peering down into the face of the limp, jaundiced scrap I had laboured so long to produce. His long fingers, curiously gentle, absorbed the texture of her dark fuzz of hair, her crumpled, old-lady's skin. He delicately touched the puckered lips that turned to him, rooting and sucking.

There was such tenderness in his exploration of the fragile features. He saw what he had made and it was very good.

'Hello, Chloe,' he whispered.

I stirred then, as though turning in my sleep and Guy slipped his daughter back into the crib and came to stand over me. My lids were squeezed shut, probably not very convincingly. Guy stood silently for a moment and I tried to slow my breathing to sleeping rate. I felt his fingers push back a frond of hair from my face, then trail, soft as breath, down my cheek, but I never moved. I didn't move until I heard the door closing behind him.

One is a prisoner after a confinement, trapped for two weeks beneath starched sheets by a martinet in a winged cap and sensible shoes. She controls the timetable – time to eat, time to sleep, time to sit on the commode, time to renew the bandages that bind one's womb back into place. She controls the ebb and flow of visitors – not enough ebb and rather too much flow for my liking.

Mother and Pa came first, dashing back from Paris as soon as they received the wire, bringing with them some elaborate French baby gowns (as if Chloe didn't have more than enough already). They gooed over their first grandchild, but I noticed Mother didn't attempt to pick her up. A well-aimed projectile of vomit might have ruined the stand-up ocelot collar of her coat, which she had not removed. A flying visit indeed.

Nickie brought his mother and Rose. Nickie was carrying a bunch of daffodils to add to the vases that already stood on every available surface in the room and a ridiculous, pink, fluffy rabbit, bigger than Chloe. 'I say,' he said, giving me a smacking kiss, 'what a clever girl you are, Olivia. What a dear little thing.' And in the wistfulness of his voice I could hear the secret fear that his wife might never allow him to see his own child.

'A bit puny,' remarked Rose, characteristically,

then, bending lower over the crib, 'just like a skinned rabbit.'

David and Clare came in hand-in-hand, needing each other's support before either had the courage to face the messy secrets of birth.

'I thought it would be more cuddly,' remarked David. 'Are they always as skinny as that?'

'Come back next week. At the rate Nanny's pumping in the Cow and Gate, she'll be as fat as a whale by then.'

'What's it like, having a baby?' asked Clare.

'Hell,' I answered, truthfully.

'You didn't have to, you know, have a baby at all.'

'I didn't have much option, as I seem to remember.'

'Rose had me fixed up with a most amazing little gadget, jolly useful, to stop babies . . .'

'She did what . . . ?'

'It was a birthday present. Not that I've had any call to use it, so far. Still, you never know – might come in handy some day.'

Why won't they leave me alone?

New mothers are allowed to cry. More, they are expected to cry. People are completely indulgent of tears that they wouldn't put up with in any other circumstances.

'That's right, dear,' encouraged Nurse. 'Have a good cry. It'll do you good. Get it out your system.'

Get what out of my system? What are all these tears for? I don't know. They just come. They began the day I heard the door click behind my husband and the flood remained undammed.

'You'll feel better when you've had a good cry,' said Anne with all the firmness of an authority on the subject.

'How do you know?'

'Because Nurse says so.'

'How does she know – a dried-up virgin like her?'

'Well, she just does. She's seen lots of weepy new mothers.'

'How can it make me feel better?' I demanded. 'How can swollen eyes and a runny nose and sodden handkerchiefs make me feel better?'

'Oh, I've no patience with you, Olive. Here we all are, doing our best to jolly you along, telling you how clever you've been every minute of the day, and all you can do is wallow in self-pity. You won't talk to Guy. You won't feed Chloe. Snap out of it, for goodness sake.'

'Nurse can feed her better than I can.'

'How do you know? You've never even tried. Come along now,' she commanded briskly, 'it's time you did your duty.'

Anne marched over to the crib and dragged poor, sleeping Chloe out. She thrust her into my arms like a bundle of washing. The baby began to cry, a thin, keening wail of misery.

'That's all she ever does when I hold her,' I said and the ever-present tears began to fall again. 'She doesn't like me.'

'No wonder, if that's the way you hold her. Come on, now,' Anne coaxed. 'Pretend she's a puppy or a kitten, if it helps. She doesn't feel safe with you when your arms are all stiff and knobbly. You've got to make a comfy little nest for her. Look – like this.'

Anne took Chloe back from me and cradled her niece against the cushion of her bosom. Why couldn't I do that? It looked so right. Anne was so soft and ample, her face shining as she bent over.

'Who's my own little darling, then?' she asked, with a silly grin on her face.

She walked up and down the room making little jiggling motions and shushing noises, but still the baby

157

wailed and the noise crept under my skin and stuck needles all over me.

'She's hungry, the little pet,' Anne told me, knowledgeably.

'She can't be. Nurse feeds her every four hours on the dot and there's still more than an hour to go before six o'clock.'

'That's not enough. Don't you remember the fox cub that David found – we used to feed him with a dropper every two hours until he got bigger.'

'My daughter is not a fox.'

'But still . . . Oh, listen to her. I don't know how you can bear it.' Anne dropped her face and nuzzled Chloe, like an animal sniffing her young. 'I'd do it if I could. It makes my breasts tingle just to listen to her. Oh Olive – can't you? Won't you?'

I turned my face away and the tears slid down my nose and soaked the pillow.

Everyone, in their own way, asked me the same question – 'What's wrong with you?' If I could have brought myself to admit it, I'd have answered, 'My husband has a lover.'

It was downright embarrassing, watching Anne and Chris Berry together. Anyone would think they'd invented sex, the way they carried on. And Anne getting bigger by the day with her husband's legitimate offspring. So much for the girl who didn't believe in love. She ought to have realised that no one's immune. The French are right when they call it a thunderbolt.

But what a time to find out. Imagine waiting until you're four months married and four months pregnant into the bargain before you find out that love can knock common sense into a cocked hat anytime? I could have told her that. She only had to ask. But when had she ever listened to me?

158

Chris had come back from Berlin with a broken nose and a gap where his two front teeth had been. He came limping upstairs to our flat and lowered himself very cautiously into a chair.

'My God, Chris,' gasped Guy. 'What happened? Have you been in a motoring accident?'

'Half a dozen storm-troopers happened, that's what,' Chris answered with a wry grin that made us all wince. 'They didn't seem to care for my face as it was.'

Their rearrangement of Chris's features was certainly not an improvement. He'd never been a good-looking man and his new, lopsided nose, side by side with his old, wicked grin, made him look rather like an out-of-work pirate. Across both cheeks bruising flared green and yellow and mauve. Yet there was a sparkle in his eyes, a fierce, fighting spirit. Here was a man who would continue to proclaim what he thought was right, to shout it from the rooftops, no matter how many Nazi thugs tried to kick him senseless.

Anne had been coming through from the kitchen with a tray in her hands. She stood there still, rigid with shock at the sight of him. Chris didn't seem surprised to see her there. He levered himself out of his chair and took the tray from her hands.

'It's all right,' I heard him murmur, softly as though to a child woken suddenly from a nightmare. 'I'm here. It's all right.'

He dumped the tray on a table and took Anne by the hand, drawing her with him back to the chair. She knelt at his feet, her head on his knee, grotesque with her swollen belly and yet . . . and yet, some dark and nameless emotion stabbed at me as I watched them together. Softly, Chris laid his stubby hand on Anne's hair, smoothing and stroking, and she let it stay there.

'Didn't you make an official complaint?' I asked. 'Didn't the Embassy help you?'

159

'I got myself into it and, as far as the British authorities were concerned, I could get myself out of it again. I shouldn't have been involved in the first place, according to them. I was lucky. Fifteen people were killed in three days. The police shot anything that moved after curfew. So much for democracy.'

'I'm sorry, Chris, we ought to understand what you're talking about,' said Guy, 'but you know I never read the papers while I'm writing.'

Chris gave a short crack of a laugh. 'It depends on what you read. It was either a Bolshevik-inspired rising against the legitimate government, put down with necessary force or . . . or a forlorn attempt to stop the Weimar Republic sliding down the slope to fascism and repression.'

'I think I can guess what you'd call it,' I put in.

'It's all just words anyway, but they were three terrible days, three grand days. Marching arm-in-arm towards the Reichstag with banners flying and all the world cheering. And if the sun wasn't shining, it felt as though it was. Breaking glass and running feet and police whistles and dark alleys. Hacking out paving stones to throw at mounted police. Never knowing anyone in the crowd you're running with. The spasm of fear as you hear the sound of footsteps behind you in a dark, deserted street. It was . . . it was living.'

'Poppycock! I don't understand how you can possibly say that,' I interrupted, angrily. I couldn't bear the gleam in his swollen eyes. I couldn't bear the soppy, hero-worshipping look Anne gave him. 'They're no worse than you and you're no better than them. You're all hooligans. All you did was get involved in a riot, frighten the life out of ordinary, law-abiding people for three days and achieve nothing at all.'

'Those same law-abiding people will have a great deal more to be frightened of in the future. What do you know? You've got no idea, have you, in your cosy little Chelsea flat . . . If we don't make a stand against fascism now, this year, next year at the latest, it'll be too late. I got off lightly because I'm British. They just amused themselves with me – and you can see the result. 'A regrettable accident,' they said, strapping up my ribs, 'mistaken identity.' But there were men arrested with me who'll never be seen again.'

'Oh come on, now, Chris,' Guy butted in, 'that's coming on a bit strong. People just don't disappear in a properly run, civilised country.'

'You didn't hear the sounds coming from the nearby cells. You didn't see the smears of blood and vomit on the walls and floor. I'll never forget what I saw and heard there. Political prisoners are sneaked away by night from police custody and taken by the SA or SS to beating stations all over the city. They're . . .'

'Chris . . . don't,' I interrupted, glancing anxiously at Anne.

'No, you needn't worry. I won't say it. You wouldn't believe me anyway. It's too much for you. But you wait,' Chris warned. I heard fear, like a prowling beast, breathing in the dark. I looked at his battered face and knew that he meant every word.

'You wait until the streets of London are full of roaming, brown-shirted gangs looking for a spot of fun – then see if you still feel like pontificating about a civilised country.'

Anne moved in with Chris that day.

When I was on my own for the evening – not an uncommon event – it was too easy to take a taxi to Chris's flat above a pawnshop in Wapping. Guy was writing again and had shut himself up like a hermit in the pokey cupboard we called a study; I could hear his typewriter clacking away. Between the spasms of tapping, there were long hours of silence, but I wouldn't dare interrupt. Rather than tiptoe around my own house, I'd go off to see how Anne was enjoying living a life of sin.

Brave girl. She'd had the courage to reach out for what she wanted and grab it with both hands – to hell with the consequences. I'd certainly gone all out too, but at the last hurdle, I'd baulked and held out for the respectability of a wedding ring. Now I had to live with my mistake.

Those mean streets, where every other name on shop fronts was unpronounceable. They were alien. They frightened me.

Of course, I was too sensible to arrive looking as though I'd just been to the Ritz for tea. On my first visit to Anne, I dressed in a sensible little petrol blue costume trimmed only modestly at the collar and cuffs with Persian lamb. With it, I wore the plainest of hats, a matching beret tipped cheekily to one side, and brogues with stacked heels. It didn't look at all extravagant.

Yet when I stepped down from the taxi, into this frightening other world, I shrank from being seen. These people were not alien – I was. Out through the archway of a scrapyard, men were pushing barrel-organs on wobbly hand carts, on their way to the West End to catch the theatre queues. Above each one bobbed a sign saying 'Hire me – 6d a day'. A de luxe version bore the notice 'Cheap. Only 1/6d a day'. For a short, horrified moment, I thought it was the men who could be hired for such a trivial sum. Then I realised that they were advertising the hire of the instruments, as they trudged up the road in the silence of despair.

Up and down a short street, children were bowling each other in an old motor car tyre – boys with long shorts belted with string, girls in dresses with hems let down to the limit and bodices strained to breaking point under their arms. As I stared, they stopped playing and stared back. The weather was mild and yet the nose of the youngest dripped green mucus.

Rearing up at the end of the street, above the broken slates, above the smoking chimneys, were the masts of a great ship. The resiny smell of Swedish pine lay over the stink of drains. It was a surreal landscape, as foreign as the moon.

Even the colour of the pavements seemed to be different from the ones that I knew, that were swept and watered and manicured daily. The gutters were clogged with the detritus of the morning market: cabbage leaves, rotten oranges, fish heads. A woman was picking through the street traders' garbage, pouncing on a yellowed cabbage, some sprouting potatoes, a black banana. She put her finds into a crate on wheels that held her baby too – snotty, bare-bottomed, its mouth ringed with scabs.

A man was leaning against a lamppost – just leaning, doing nothing, but there was no policeman to move him on. The shop windows, behind tattered, fly-spotted advertisements for luxuries no one here could buy, displayed practically nothing. In the attics above, the refugees from a different type of persecution advertised their trades: Abramsky, Furrier; Moishe Aarons, Gentlemens' and Ladies' Bespoke Garments. Who were their customers? Not the stunted, hungry people who walked the streets below without even the energy to stare at me, as I picked my way up to my sister's lover's flat.

'But it's so squalid. How can you bear it?' I said during one visit.

Anne gave me a look that held both patronage and pity in it.

'There are a lot of people around here that live in far worse conditions than this.' She was even beginning to sound like Chris.

163

'Well, yes, of course, one knows that. But after all, they're born to it. They don't know any better, while you're used to something rather different. Don't you find it horribly depressing?'

'Yes, if I'm to be honest, of course I do. But it's worth it.' And she gave a sickly smile in Chris's direction. He was at the table, hogging the only light, which was turned to shine on his book.

'I wonder how long the novelty will last. Where do you wash and whatever do you eat? You've no kitchen or bathroom.'

'Neither has anyone else. There's a pie shop across the road and fish and chips round the corner. Or we can always take some meat and potatoes along to the baker's oven when he's finished the day's firing. We can make tea on the gas ring. And Chris likes a bottle of stout with his meal.'

'Pies, fish and chips . . .' I shuddered.

'As for washing – nothing wrong with a strip wash in the morning, or we use the public bath house, like everyone else.'

'Anne!' I squealed, really aghast this time. 'How can . . . you'll catch . . .'

'What?' she challenged.

'I don't know. Something. Nits, scabies . . . something ghastly. Nanny would have a fit.'

'Nanny doesn't have to do it.'

'I don't know what you're twitching your upper class little nose about,' said Chris, lifting his head from his book. 'She's well looked after. I don't stint her. Your sister's here because she wants to be. No one's forcing her. And when she's fed up with pies and chips and fed up with me, too – well, the door will be open. I'll not keep her.'

Without turning, he held out his hand. There was such confidence in the gesture. He knew, without needing to look, that he would not reach out to her in vain. Anne moved towards him, slipped her hand into his and stood there for a moment with her cheek against his hair. Together, they possessed a strength that I had looked for in my own marriage, but it had eluded me. I saw it and – nearly – understood what had driven Anne to abandon her husband and home. I saw Chris, still without looking at her, give her hand a squeeze that was a strange yet moving caress. I wanted to scoff, but the look on her face brought the tears that were always so close these days dangerously near to the surface.

'Well, of course I wouldn't dream . . . it's none of my business.'

'That's right,' snapped Anne, 'it's none of your business.'

I looked around at the dingy little room, with its piles of books everywhere – on the table, on chairs, on the floor. Anne had tried so hard to brighten it up with a cushion, a rug, one or two pictures. Somehow all she had managed to do was highlight its lack of comfort.

Whatever did she see in him – a prickly, aggressive, common little man with an abrupt way of speaking and a dangerous smile? Heaven knows. But then, someone asks that question about almost every relationship.

Chris was over-sexed, of course. The lower classes always are. That's why their wives are never seen without a clutter of snotty-nosed children around their feet. I can't imagine that Nickie had made too many physical demands on Anne (although he hadn't wasted any time in ensuring the future of the Lockyer line).

Next time I came round, I brought an Anglepoise lamp to try to lighten some of the stygian gloom. Chris tried not to look pleased, but couldn't help it. Of all things, he appreciated a gift that helped him to get on with his studies.

'But you obviously haven't noticed, as you're dying

to leave from the moment you set foot in the place, we've no electricity, only gas. So I'll have to say, thank you but no thank you. And no more,' he warned. 'I'm not having you traipsing round here every five minutes with your arms full of castoff luxuries, like Lady Bountiful. I know your type – "Oh, I bought too much of this or I was just going to throw away that".' His mimicry was deadly accurate. 'I won't have it. If you come at all, you come because you want to – and that's all.'

Stubborn little man. He was dragging my sister down to his own level and I couldn't stop him.

Chris ran a bookshop on Commercial Road, between a tailor and a Kosher butcher, with a wired–up window behind which he displayed dreary-looking tracts and pamphlets. I don't suppose that he sold many books, although the money for rent and pies and stout must have come from somewhere. At the back of the shop, next to a single gas ring, several dirty milk bottles and an overflowing ashtray, stood an ancient mimeograph on which he produced a so-called progressive magazine that opposed militarism and reaction and proclaimed the brotherhood of man in ringing tones. It seemed to spread as much ink on him as on the paper, purple ink on violet paper. He wanted it to be noticeable, he said. It was noticeable, all right – it was one of the nastiest looking pieces of paper that ever dropped onto a breakfast table.

Most of the time, his shop seemed to be a meeting place for men who looked just like him. The meetings were advertised by chalking on the pavement. One might trip over some fellow bending over and would think he was tying his bootlace, but actually he was chalking up the date, time and topic.

There would always be two or three in the shop, men with wild eyes, wild hair and knitted woollen ties. They talked in urgent voices about the same old thing: the capitalist menace; the march of the proletariat; industry in chains. Words, words, words and not a deed in sight. How they thought they would change the world by putting their heads together in smoke-filled rooms puzzled me.

They'd have been much better going out and doing something positive, like fumigating vermin-ridden buildings or lagging the stand-pipes in backcourts where hopeless women stood in line trying to draw water through frozen pipes. I might have had some admiration for these garrulous malcontents then.

The next time I visited Anne, she had a healing black eye, a tropical sunset of mauve, green and yellow.

'Anne!' I gasped. 'What has that man done to you?'

'Don't be so melodramatic. It wasn't Chris.'

'You would say that, wouldn't you.'

'No, really. Chris would never lay a finger on me – never. It was Mrs Grouting across the court. She elbowed me out of the way when I was going for water – said I ought to stand aside and let decently married women go first. And I said that everyone knew how long the coalman took to make deliveries to her. And she said . . . well, it just went on from there.'

'I hope you called a policeman and laid a charge.'

'Don't be silly. Policemen are as rare as hens' teeth around here. D'you think they bother to sort out every squabble in a slum court? Besides, I gave as good as I got! She's still got the bare patch on her scalp!'

'But the baby . . .'

Anne smoothed her hands down the wrap-around floral pinafore that made her almost indistinguishable from her neighbours. 'Still there, alive and kicking.'

I saw the faded roses and forget-me-nots, stretched tight as a drum, flutter and ripple under her touch, as the baby catapulted around. Anne laughed.

'Oh, you little blighter, lie still.'

I turned away, sickened, unable to watch.

'I know it was wrong,' Anne continued. 'Chris was so cross with me. But that woman has been goading me for weeks, calling me names, sticking out her broom as I walked by to trip me . . . she won't do it again.'

'Anne, you mustn't stay here any longer,' I urged. 'You don't fit in. You don't belong. No matter how you think you feel about Chris, it's wrong. These people are not our kind of people.'

'Is that their fault?' she challenged.

'Of course not. They can't help being what they are. They don't know any better. But fighting in the street . . . it's the absolute end.'

'Chris needs me,' she said simply.

'Needs you! Now I know you've gone quite dotty. Oh, I dare say you're useful enough to keep the draughts off his back at night, but you're secondary to his real life – his revolutionary cronies, his horrid little shop . . .'

'You don't understand,' said Anne, seizing on the last criticism to change a subject that was becoming much too personal for her liking. 'Chris's bookshop is all about educating the masses. Education is the tool of the common man. He must use it to pull down the edifices of privilege.'

'Privilege – poppycock! What pompous claptrap! You sound just like a gramophone recording of Lenin's favourite speeches,' I scoffed. 'For heaven's sake, Anne, you're an intelligent woman. How can you allow yourself to be hoodwinked by all that Bolshevik nonsense? And how many people round here can even read, let alone understand, what Chris and his cronies are trying to stuff down their throats?'

'More than you think. People who are denied education have a terrible thirst for it. Like me.'

'You?'

'Yes – me. We're two of a kind, Chris and me. D'you know that Chris educated himself by sitting up all night with whatever newspapers he could salvage from the gutter or wrapped round fish and chips? His mother was a widow who shelled peas in Covent Garden for tuppence a quart. Think of that, next time you gobble up a helping of fresh peas with mint and butter. Chris was collecting jam jars and bottles to sell back to grocers almost as soon as he could walk and running errands for bookies – that's how he learned to count. He never had the chance to go to school – neither did I.'

'Oh Anne, you've gone too far this time.' I felt battered by her flow of words, her phoney emotions, her upside-down logic. Her self-pity disgusted me. What did she have to feel sorry for herself about – she who'd had the best of everything?

'And you've got the nerve to call yourself the sensible one of the family? How dare you compare your childhood – your secure, comfortable, cushioned childhood – with that of some little guttersnipe who's dragged himself by his bootstraps out of the dirt?'

'I dare,' she answered arrogantly, 'I dare because Chris is the only person I've ever met who treats me as though I have a mind and opinions of my own. He's the only one who's ever listened to a word I say. Even you, even now – you've heard my words but you still haven't a clue what I'm talking about. No one has ever listened to me before.'

'Perhaps,' I said acidly, gathering up my hat and gloves – time to go, before we fell out completely – 'that's because you never say anything worth listening to.'

Such gross over-reaction. Imagine running away, breaking up a perfectly decent marriage, just because she thought no one had ever taken her seriously. I mean,

169

one can forgive a little fling – lots of people have them – as long as it hurts no one, but this . . .

'You don't understand,' said Anne again.

'And you do, I suppose?'

'Chris is trying to teach me.'

I absolutely hooted. 'You can learn all he has to teach you lying flat on your back. Or, given the size of your tummy now – perhaps he's the one flat on his back.'

'You're just jealous,' she flared, 'of something you can never have. Chris loves me and he's man enough to . . . to . . .'

'To do what . . . to prove it by rogering you? Poor, silly Anne. What an innocent you are. Didn't you know that you could have your cake and eat it? Lots of women do.'

'That's a shocking idea.'

'Shocking? More shocking than brawling in the street? More shocking than abandoning a nice, dull husband when you're carrying his child? More shocking than setting up a little love nest with a raving Bolshevik? No wonder you've got a black eye. You're an affront to the respectable poor.' I couldn't help a cynical little sneer. 'Don't fool yourself – you're only a woman after all, no better than the rest of us. You think it's a meeting of two minds, but all you really needed was a good . . .'

Oh, Lord, I couldn't say it, not when Anne was looking at me with the startled eyes of a virgin bride.

'It's not like that. I . . . I love him,' said Anne simply and I believed her.

'Then I'm sorry for you. You didn't have to bury yourself in a slum just because you fancied a spot of rough trade. That's not love. There's more to love than that. There's more than one way of loving someone.'

I found that I was quoting the words Guy had said to me only a few nights earlier. I still didn't believe them.

In his own way, Guy loved me, but his way was not my way. He had always enjoyed beautiful things. When he had the money, he'd never be able to resist some small, perfect object: an enamelled patch box; a Mogul miniature, translucent pigment barely staining a sliver of ivory; a wife. As long as I remained the prize piece in Guy's collection, I was happy. Why not? I didn't know any better. But since Christmas, I'd discovered that Guy had other needs, needs that I couldn't slake.

Guy and I had motored down to Bramleigh just before Christmas. Mother and Pa were at home for once and I wanted to show them that they had been wrong. I wanted to prove that Guy and I were – whatever dark misgivings they may have had, whatever veiled hints they had dropped before our marriage, hints that I still didn't understand – a normal, happily married young couple with a much-wanted (if rather too well-developed for supposed dates) baby on the way.

We were. We might still be, if it had not been for that ill-timed visit. Perhaps I'm deluding myself even now. If not then, it would have happened some other time. If not with him, then with some other.

We stopped at the garage in the village for petrol before going on to the house. I stayed in the car and Guy got out to stretch his legs while the garage hand filled the tank. There was a light sleet falling, stinging pin points that melted on the hot bonnet of the car, but eddied across the forecourt in wind-blown spirals, liquid as smoke. Guy's dark head and shoulders quickly whitened. He shrugged his collar higher and walked forward, caught by the beam of light that spilled from the open door of the tearoom adjoining the garage. Hearing customers, a man came running out to fill the car, cranking the handle of the pump by the feeble light

of the illuminated advertising lozenge at the top of the
pump.

Inside the dark car, secure, wrapped in furs, looking
forward to seeing my parents, I sat, listening to the
stirrings within me with the self-absorption of the
breeding woman. I had no inkling of what was happening outside my cocoon.

How did it happen? Was there a look, a sigh, a touch
even? How are these things managed?

Guy seemed to be a long time. The slurping of the
pump had stopped. I imagined there must be some
problem, perhaps with changing a note, or perhaps Guy
had asked for oil to be checked or tyres to be inflated.
I had never understood the arcane mysteries of the
motor car – sufficient to me that it moved. I leaned
over to the driver's seat to wind down the window and
looked out.

I had the oddest feeling that the two figures there in
the dark, standing apart now, had been closer when I
began to turn the window handle. The man began to
count change into Guy's hand.

'And a penny makes eight bob and two makes ten.
Thank you very much, sir.'

'Merry Christmas,' said Guy.

'And a Merry Christmas to you, sir.'

'Merry Christmas,' I called through the open
window.

'And to you, I'm sure, madam,' he replied, turning
towards me for the first time.

Another car turned in to the garage and its lights arced
across the man's face. In that instant I saw that he was
tall and well-set, bareheaded in the fast-falling sleet, that
his hair was the colour of new thatch and that he was
smiling. He saw me looking at him and smiled like an
old friend. Insolent.

Quickly, I wound the window back, telling myself

172

that the sleet was driving onto my face, and rapped on the glass to Guy to make him hurry.

Only later did I remember where and when I had last seen the smiling man. A boy, not a man then, and his face not smiling, but twisted with anger as he had threatened me with his fist. Yet he was not so very changed, after all. I put that memory firmly back in its place. I would never, never refer to it and I'd be very surprised indeed if he wanted to drag his ancient humiliation back into the light.

Guy says he loves me and I have to believe him, because he says it so often and because, if I didn't believe him, the earth's foundations would quiver beneath my feet. He says that there are many different ways to love, each one as valid as the next, but his way of loving is not mine.

He says that if I had paid any attention to my education (what education?), if I had bothered to read my history books, I would have discovered that his type of love was normal amongst the Greeks at the height of their great civilisation. And yet the Greeks didn't die out, so they must have been capable of sustaining what I call an unnatural love and what Guy calls a natural one, at the same time as marrying women and rearing families. He quotes Achilles and Patroclos, Alexander and Bucephalos (Wasn't that the horse? All these names sound the same to me.), Sophocles, Plato, Aristotle. Good heavens – can they all have been queer? All I know is that, even if I had scanned the small print of every history book I had ever owned, I should have found nothing of this.

Yet when I looked out from the car into the darkness beyond, I knew. Nothing had prepared me for it, yet I knew. The significant looks, the dark murmurings, quickly broken off, between Pa and Mother, all fell into place with kaleidoscopic suddenness. Sniggers, raised eyebrows, shrugs, the common currency of the parties I had been to with Guy, all told me the same thing, the thing I could not bear to hear. I looked out of the window and the darkness was split open.

On Christmas morning, we all went to church, for different reasons: Pa because it was the done thing; Mother because she adored the smell of the candles and fir branches lying heavy on the cold air; me because I could sing the old, traditional songs at the top of my voice; Clare and David because they were still young enough to wake before it was light and stretch their toes down to the bottom of the bed to test if that exciting, lumpy shape was hanging there.

Guy refused to come with us, preferring to go for a walk. He said that he didn't believe in mumbo-jumbo and had no intention of pretending that he did. I thought Pa was going to object, but at the last moment he changed his mind – 'You can take a horse to water,' I heard him mutter.

Clare and David decided to walk home after church. They asked me to go with them, but the lanes were slippery and I dared not risk a fall with my precious burden. So I went home in the Daimler with Mother and Pa, but we were beaten to it. The twins had taken the footpath across the fields and must have run all the way while we swept sedately along the road. As we turned into the drive, I saw them burst out from the shrubbery, scarlet-cheeked and breathing like horses after a long point, blowing white hoar. They were hand–in–hand. Hearing us coming, they turned and waved with their free hands, looking absurdly like those little clay figures from Provence that David had liked so much. So young. So untroubled. I envied them with an intensity that felt sharp as a knife.

The servants were invited into the hall for their traditional glass of mulled wine. Pa became very baronial and dispensed the drinks with a show of bonhomie that embarrassed the staff into silence. It was the same every year, but a tradition is a tradition. We stood around the great tree that towered up through the stairwell, so that walking downstairs felt like climbing down its branches, exchanging compliments of the season with awkward jollity. Then the family moved to the drawing room fire with fresh glasses and tried to fill in the gap until Guy should appear and we could all go in to lunch.

I stood at the window, shielded by the curtains, watching the drive, watching and waiting. I tried to tell myself that I didn't know where he had gone. Surely not . . . women do get funny ideas sometimes, especially breeding women. Surely not . . . but all the time I knew that I was only trying to shut my eyes and pretend that there wasn't a bogeyman behind the bedroom door.

Only when Cook sent her compliments and said that she was afraid the gravy would dry up completely if she had to keep it hot any longer did we give up the wait.

Guy came back when we'd reached the pudding stage. He wandered into the dining room with a mumbled apology. ''Fraid I got lost – one footpath looks much the same as another when it's covered with mud.'

He pushed aside the covered plate that was put in front of him and picked a tangerine from the dish in the centre of the table. I watched him across the table, my head lowered towards my plate, my lids lifted only just far enough to be able to see without being seen.

He had pushed his chair back and slouched sideways, one elbow on the table, as he peeled the tangerine. Was I the only one who could sense the suppressed excitement that rose from him? He smelled of deceit. With neat, nervous fingers, he stripped the skin from the fruit and dissected it, laying all the segments in a circle,

before tasting the first. I watched, fascinated. Everything he did was done with the grace and precision of
a cat. Nothing he could do was ugly. He even lied
beautifully.

Then Guy raised his head suddenly and caught me
watching him. He smiled that melting smile, the smile
that was only for me, and, at the same moment, a lump
of pudding dropped off the spoon into my lap.

I flapped at the sticky mass with my napkin. 'Oh,
how silly – it'll stain. I must go and change.'

'Hot water, dear,' advised Mother. 'The cloth must
be stretched over a bowl and have boiling water poured
through it from a height. Have MacDowall do it for
you.'

'I don't know why you're fussing,' commented Clare,
'you won't have to wear those great balloon frocks for
much longer. Just throw it away. Or give it to some
poor, wronged village maiden as a Christmas present,'
she shouted after me and hooted with laughter.

I was still in my petticoat when Guy came upstairs.

'Everyone's gone for a nap,' he said. 'It sounds like
a good idea.'

He came behind me and folded his arms round me.
Once – yesterday – I'd have leaned against his chest,
surprised, grateful for his attention. Today, almost sub-
consciously, my body resisted him. He was still tense,
taut as wire, and as he drew me back against him I could
feel his excitement. Light, exploring fingers trailed
down over my breasts and round my belly, pausing to
feel the waves of movement that rippled across it, as
the baby explored me, too.

It wasn't me who had excited my husband.

'Not now, Guy. I've got a headache.'

'I've got something for you that cures headaches,' he
whispered in my ear, then, suddenly, savagely, bit it.

I almost squealed. Not quite. Not now. 'I've had too

much to eat and far too much to drink. All I want is to have a good, long snooze.'

'But I want to open my Christmas present now,' he said, petulantly, slipping the straps of my petticoat down over my shoulders. His lips were against my skin as he murmured, 'It's so prettily wrapped. I can't wait to find out what's inside it.'

I jerked myself away from his grasp. 'No.'

He was still laughing, not angered, his mood heightened by my resistance. 'I don't seem to remember you saying that when you ought to have done. You wouldn't be the shape you are now, if you'd said 'No' at the right time. In fact,' he said, following me as I retreated across the room, 'I seem to remember that I was the one who said 'No' but you wouldn't take 'No' for an answer. You were like a cat on heat for me then. It's my turn now.'

'Why – wouldn't *he* give it to you?'

The words were said – and I'd have given anything for them to be unsaid. I'd have given anything to have no need to say them. All the disgust I felt was mirrored on Guy's face.

'How like a woman,' he said softly, sadly. 'Your view of the world seems to be limited to the little you can see from between your legs.'

I'd put the width of the bed between us, but I didn't feel safe. Guy was too tall, too quick, too agile.

'It's not me you want,' I spat, feeling the safety of the bathroom door handle poke into my back. 'But you'll make do with me, until something better comes along.'

I made a dash into the bathroom, but the bolt snagged and Guy shouldered the door open before I could secure it.

He used me, there on the bathroom floor, without love.

I didn't make a murmur. When it was over, Guy picked me up, awkwardly because of the roundness of me, and carried me over to the bed. He put me down gently and pulled the eiderdown over me and up to my shoulders. He brought a moistened flannel and wiped away the streaks of mascara that had run down my cheeks. He tidied up the smeared lipstick and combed my hair. He sat down on the edge of the bed.

'I love you, Olivia,' he whispered. 'You know that I love you – in my own way. Why do you make me do these things?'

I turned my face aside. My husband laid his face down on the mound of my belly and wept.

I'll fight for him. He's mine and no one else shall have him.

I had been trapped by my body, then, and now I was trapped again by the helpless creature my body had produced. Biology had made me into a dependent creature. I had thought that I was free. A modern woman who could go where she wanted, do what she wanted, have what she wanted. But modern women are just women after all – no better and no worse than their mothers or their grandmothers. And not a whit more free. It's all an illusion. Take away the cigarettes and the short skirts and the free love. Underneath is just a woman, tied to a man by the coils of tubing inside her. We wear our wombs like fetters. Convicts have been delivered of the ball and chain, but women still carry theirs around with them.

I would look into the crib and think, This time I will love her, this time I'll feel something – I must feel something. I'm her mother. Where is that glow I'm supposed to feel? Nothing. Nothing. I hate her. Oh God, no, are you listening? I didn't mean it. If I even so much as think it, something terrible will happen. She'll stop breathing before my very eyes and I'll know that I've killed her. I don't hate her . . . I don't . . . but I don't love her, either. She just is.

Who can I talk to? Not Mother – heavens, not Mother, still toting her perfect romance around, and a photo album filled with happy-family pictures; Anne, conventional little Anne who's had the courage to cut through her fetters and do what she wants to do – but she's still bound to a man. Worse, she's bound to two, her lover and the father of her child. She's worse off than I am, although she doesn't realise it yet. (She will, though.)

Nickie might understand. He knows what it's like to lose someone you love. Nickie listens. But he's still a man, with all the normal man's abhorrence of the love that dare not speak its name. He would feel obliged to do something about Guy. I don't want smirking policemen and grubby notebooks and smutty innuendo. 'Society author in illicit love scandal'; 'The writer and the garage hand'; 'Secrets of Chelsea love nest'. I don't want Guy pilloried and doing hard labour on Dartmoor or somewhere. I just want him for myself.

I shall have him for myself.

Anne has a son. She has a bawling, demanding son, as lusty as Chloe is puny. He popped out as quickly as one of Chris's mother's shelled peas. His name is Alastair and he weighed nearly as much at birth as Chloe at five months old. No, that's an exaggeration (though only a slight one), but the contrast between the two cousins is astounding. Perhaps babies are like plants and only thrive when they feel themselves to be loved.

Anne sits, fertile as a queen bee, dripping with milk and honey. Why not? Anne has enough milk for triplets, for quadruplets. Chloe wails with hunger, yet spews out the mathematical commercial formulae and cow's milk derivatives that are supposed to take the magic out of feeding a modern child, replacing it with science. (But it is magic – long-ago, secret, women's magic and I have not been initiated.)

The answer is there, in front of me. Well, why not, if Anne is willing?

Guy is outraged and calls me an unnatural mother. I shriek back that there is only one unnatural person within this marriage and it's not me. He tells me I'm not fit to be a mother and I retort that he knows nothing about decent women, that he doesn't have the moral right to father a child.

We're tearing each other apart and the shadow of Guy's lover stands and watches us.

I will not share him.

Nanny threatens to give notice if we can't conduct ourselves with more dignity in 'her' nursery. Chloe howls.

'There! Look what you've done!' I accuse and snatch her to my maternal bosom, but she only howls louder and I'm forced to hand her over to Nanny.

But in the end, Guy gives way, because he can't bear to see his daughter wither away day by day. I find him, with tears in his eyes, kneeling at her crib. I think, if he could, he'd feed her himself.

So now Anne has a child at each breast. She sits in a battered nursery chair, eating and drinking enough for three (milk stout?), while Chris sits at her feet, smoking filthy yellow French cigarettes and reading aloud to her his latest diatribes against capitalism. When he reaches the bottom of the page, he kneels up and lays his dark head on the bulging, blue-veined breasts. One of the babies, sated, drops off the nipple with its mouth open like a milky rose. The marvellously efficient pump that Anne has tucked away in her chest continues to work and her unoccupied breast spurts. Chris licks off the drips with a greedy, pointed tongue and, when he is not repulsed, fastens his mouth voraciously where the baby's has been. Anne smiles.

I walk in and Anne covers herself, but lazily, and not before she is quite certain that I have seen. She looks at me over Chris's dark head and smiles. Look, I must see how much she is needed and wanted, how much she is loved. The scene only lacked a caption beneath it to make it complete: Triumph. The plain sister has proved her worth and has everything she ever wanted, while the beautiful sister is a worn-out butterfly.

Chris gives a little, shamefaced laugh and gets to his feet, dusting off his knees in an effort to keep his face turned away from me. 'I'll . . . er . . . I'll put the kettle on, shall I?' When he comes back, he brings a tray neatly set, the milk in a jug, not a bottle, the tea pot covered by a cosy. My sister is taming the wild man and turning him into a suburban pussy cat.

Nickie still hasn't seen his son and is being egged on by his mother to do something desperate.

Guy is still in the cupboard, writing. He has a secretary now to keep his papers in order. His lover is no longer a shadow. He has a name – Raymond. He has taken human shape, like some frightful djinn in a fairy tale, and walks around my house, impertinent and bold, with an armful of typescript to give him authority.

I try not to talk to him. He looks at me from the corners of pale blue eyes. His expression says, 'I know what you are. You're nothing. You're trash. I could tell your husband things about you – if I chose.' Publicly he is scrupulously polite: yes, Mrs Tarver; no, Mrs Tarver. But I know what he's thinking. 'Make no trouble for me and I'll make none for you.'

Without husband or child to keep me, there's nothing

to stay for in London. I might as well go home. On the other hand, what is there to go home for? Where is home? Who needs me there? I drift, I hover. Inertia takes over and I do nothing.

I've had too much to drink. I thought it would be a nice feeling, but it's horrid. Those cocktails, deliciously coloured in their sugar-rimmed glasses, are now nauseating. I feel like a child who's eaten all the icing off a birthday cake, but now there's no Nanny to clean up the mess.

People are dancing, fox-trotting round the floor. There's a smell of powder and perfume, of Odo-ro-no and Veet, of banked flower-arrangements and something rank underneath it all. The singer's forehead is glistening with sweat.

> Oh, I want her to be nice and cuddly with me,
> But she don't wanna, she don't wanna
> Oh, I want her to pet, like the others I've met,
> But she don't wanna, she don't wanna . . .

Guy has disappeared. I haven't seen him since we arrived. He's a celebrity now. People compete to invite him to parties. It makes them feel important to write at the bottom of their invitations 'To meet Guy Tarver'. He could go to a party every night if he wanted to. He doesn't have to write any more. He can stay famous just by being famous.

> We could have so much fun, but it takes more
>   than one
> And she don't wanna, she don't wanna . . .

Who wants to work, when he'd rather be beautiful and witty? Who wants to work, when he can dine out at someone else's expense every night? Who wants to drag a wife around all the time, like a badly-stitched hem that's coming down?

'Dance? I'd love to. Whoops! Sorry.'

'A teeny bit squiffy? I know just the cure for that.'

It's cooler on the balcony. He's got nice eyes, but his teeth are crooked and they bump mine when he tries to kiss me.

'Now, now. Don't struggle. You'll like it, if you only let yourself.'

The balustrade is cutting into my buttocks. It prints a sooty line across the back of my gown. His hands are sweaty. They leave greasy prints on the front of my dress. I hate him, but not as much as I hate me.

'You're hurting! Let go!'

'Silly bitch. What makes you think you're so special? There's plenty more where you came from. Anyway – I don't like my women drunk.'

The powder room is crowded. It's presided over by a dried-up little woman in black, dispensing soap and threaded needles, who dares not say what she thinks of her bright young clients, but whose eyes have seen it all before. No place here to sit and weep. Why do women need to have company to go and pee? It's a ritual. Pick up the handbags, signal with the eyes and off they go to powder their pert little noses.

'Drat! My nose is shining like a beacon.'

Pink enamelled faces, pink enamelled backs gleaming in a fierce light.

'Just dust over my shoulder blades with the powder puff, will you, sweetie?'

'Anyone got a pin?'

'Would you believe it?' wails a voice from a cubicle. 'An unexpected visitor – tonight of all nights.'

I'm propping up the wall. No, the wall is propping me up. We need each other, the wall and I.

'Have you met him yet?'

'Oh divine, quite divine. He looked right through me with those marvellous eyes.'

'What d'you think of his wife, then? I suppose she is his wife?'

'Oh, yes. No doubt. That kind of man always needs a woman, to protect him against other women – like you, darling! So hands off! She serves her purpose, I suppose. What was she? His secretary? Typist?'

'Oh no, my dear. She's a lady. He has quite a different sort of secretary – in trousers!'

'Author's wives are generally odious. It's such a bore, having to remember to invite them.'

'Crashing!'

'They all seem to suffer from the delusion that being an interesting man's wife makes them interesting, too. Oh horror – my nail lacquer's chipped.'

After the stuffy femininity of the powder room, the corridor is black and chill.

I lean my forehead against the wall. I can feel the embossed pattern reproduce itself on my skin. Count how many times it repeats itself. Count how many stars there are in the sky. Anything. Just don't close your eyes. Because if you do, the pictures will begin again, there, on the backs of your eyelids, where it ought to be decently black.

Look, there's me. I'm walking along the corridor towards the bedroom I share with my husband. I've been shopping. I've bought a new hat, very smart, and a great bunch of sweet peas. The flowers are for our bedroom. I'm humming a little tuneless tune as I carry the vase of sweet peas to put on the low table that divides our beds.

I put my hand on the door handle. Don't. Don't. You're home early. You're not expected. Take the flowers back to the kitchen. Open cupboards. Bang about a bit. Sing louder. Just don't open the door yet.

Too late. The door is open. And two startled faces, one dark, one fair, are looking back at me. Drawn curtains. Slipping blankets. Pale, entwined limbs.

I'm walking back to the kitchen, taking great care not to slop the water from the vase. I vomit neatly into the sink and then again, less neatly, over the clean crockery on the draining board.

Count the patterns on the wallpaper. Count the stars in the sky. Just don't look at the pictures behind your eyes.

'Hey, steady on. Where d'you think you're going?'

'I don't know. Home. I'm tired.'

'Tired? Oh, I've got just the thing for that. Hold out your glass. There – get that down you like a good little girl – you'll feel like dancing all night.'

Powder that fizzes in the glass. Cold. Bubbles up my nose. Slipping down my throat like iced velvet. And lights. And music. My head in two halves, hatcheted down the middle.

He has a halo. Like a saint. Like God. Bright, bright eyes. Shirt studs that sparkle. Splinters of light. I could dance, I could sing, I could fly. I could perch on the banisters like a bird. I could swoop around the great brass hall lantern. I could peep in at the windows to find where Guy is hiding from me. I'd tap on the glass with my sharp little beak and say, 'You can't hide from me. You can't ever hide from me. I'll follow you to the sun and back.'

The man is so kind. 'I think you need a little rest,' he says. Oh, I do, I do. His arm cradles me. His chest is like the bark of a tree beneath my cheek. He's so kind. We stop on the half landing so that he can transfer me onto his other arm. I give him a kiss to say thank you. I couldn't have got up the stairs without him. When he opens the bedroom door, it looks so dark and peaceful inside. No lights. No music.

So kind. I try to say thank you. But when he closes the door, he's on the inside, not the outside. His halo has gone. It's only rumpled hair, after all. When he kisses me, he tastes of fish and quails' eggs and ice cream in a hideous jumble.

'You smell,' I say.

He pushes me against the closed door and leans against me, heavy as guilt. I give a feeble shove against his chest that only unbalances me. His leg is thrust between my thighs.

'I hope you're not going to be silly,' he says, pinching my cheek. 'I don't like prick teasers.'

Well, why not? What else is there to do?

Whatever happened to the girl who wanted so much – who wanted to be and do and have everything?

I miss her.

'Olivia, you're drunk,' Nickie said sternly.

'I am not.'

'Well, you're certainly not sober.'

'Just the teeniest, weeniest bit squiffy. Where's the harm in that?'

'But why? It's only three o'clock in the afternoon.'

'Because it makes the sun shine brighter. Because it makes the day seem shorter. Come and sit beside me, Nickie darling. You've no idea how long the days seem sometimes. Aeons and aeons to live through before I can take a lovely Veronal and go to sleep again.'

'I'm sorry,' he said, 'really sorry.'

'What for?'

'Well, because you're . . .' He finished with a gesture that took in the darkened room, the crumpled cushions, last night's glasses still on the table.

'What right have you got to be sorry for me?' I snapped, with the irritability of the permanently not-quite-sober. 'I'm perfectly happy. I've got everything I always wanted – everything I deserve. Anyway, you've made just as much mess of your life as I have of mine.'

Nickie sat down, carefully choosing a chair opposite mine. What did he think I was going to do – ravish him? If only he knew. I'd lost all interest in that sort of thing. It didn't even help me sleep any more.

Beyond the artificial evening of my drawn curtains, the temperature was well into the 'nineties and looked set to stay that way. Nickie's dear, gentle face was red and sweating, but he was far too conventional to make any concessions to the temperature. He still wore a waistcoat under his dark jacket and a regimental tie around his stiff collar.

'Heavens, it's stifling,' he said. 'I can't stand London when it's like this. No wonder people are dropping like flies. D'you know, a chap dropped down when I was crossing Jermyn Street this morning – dead, stone dead. Amazing. Not much better at home, though. Looks more like Africa than Salisbury Plain.'

'Have a little drinkie then, to cool you down.'

'Don't tempt me. I've a feeling I'm going to need to keep all my wits about me. Sure you won't come with me?'

'Absolutely. The last thing I feel like doing is trailing off to some dull old solicitor to face Anne's holier-than-thou sermons. Sorry, darling. No can do. She's all yours.'

At the door, he turned, his hat in hand, looking for all the world like a schoolboy summoned by the head-master. 'Please?' he asked.

It was too hot. The sun was too bright. It was all too much of an effort. Oh damn!

Nickie had had to get a court injunction before Anne

would let him see his son. And then she had thought up every reasonable and unreasonable excuse to delay complying with the injunction. The weather was too cold to take a baby out. It was too hot. Alastair was just getting over a cold. He was just about to catch another one. He was teething. He had nappy rash. She wasn't well enough herself to make a trip.

In the end, she had to surrender. Almost a year after his birth, Alastair and his father were about to meet.

The offices of Housden, Mintram & Elderton were situated in a narrow court off Portugal Street, up a steep flight of stairs, at the bottom of which had been left a large, very obviously second-hand, double perambulator. I panicked. Nickie had no right to expect me to face this, just for him. I wasn't going to. He couldn't make me.

'You don't want me involved with all this, Nickie. Why don't I just take a stroll until you're finished? Meet me in Lincoln's Inn gardens. Take your time.'

'You can't walk out on me now, Olivia.' He grabbed my wrist and then dropped it as though bitten. 'Please.'

Housden, Mintram & Elderton can have seen – or heard – nothing like it in a long and distinguished history. The baby sitting under the clerk's desk had emptied the waste paper basket and was tearing paper into shreds. Another stood in the middle of the room and wailed, a desolate, comfortless sound. Anne was trying to divert this one with a picture book – look, darling, look at the pretty rabbits. Chris stood at the window, smoking one of those filthy French cigarettes and pretending he had nothing to do with the squalid scene.

As though he could make no progress against the buffeting sound waves, Nickie stopped in the doorway. 'Which one is mine?' he hissed to me.

'The quiet one, I think.'

188

'Thank heaven for that!'

Then husband, wife and son were called through to Mr Mintram's office, leaving me alone with my daughter.

Alone in a space too empty for her, Chloe stood and cried. Her cry was bigger than I remembered, stronger, but still had the same capacity to make me feel as though I were being unjustly persecuted. Her stick-thin arms and legs were rigid with grief.

'Don't cry, Chloe,' I begged, 'please don't cry.'

My voice shocked her into silence. She stared back at me with Guy's great, grey eyes, red-rimmed and swimming with unhappiness. Then she ran over to the window and buried her face in the rough flannel of Chris's trousers.

'She doesn't like strangers,' he said. I looked for irony in his voice but couldn't find it. Chris picked my daughter up and held her easily against one shoulder. Chloe turned her face into the shelter of his neck.

I took out a cigarette and tapped its end hard against the case. My hand, the lighter, the faded Turkey-red carpet below, all blurred, but I blinked hard to clear my sight. Well, what had I expected? A touching reunion scene?

'No regrets,' I said brazenly and managed to light my cigarette without any visible trembling. 'Especially now.'

'I know. Anne told me. I'm sorry.'

'Oh, everyone knows. It's not even a talking point any more. Guy is even thinking about moving to a larger flat, now that we're such a cosy little *ménage à trois*!'

'And what will you do then?'

'Do? Why, what I'm doing now, I suppose.'

'Nothing?'

'I'm not doing nothing, Chris, believe me. I'm

189

surviving. I'm hanging on with my fingernails, because I know the fall will kill me.'

Chris shifted the child to his other shoulder before he answered. Chloe had her thumb in her mouth and was waggling the other fingers, watching the patterns they made in the air.

'That makes you a parasite, doesn't it? Latching on to something, leeching, feeding on it, growing round and through and into it, whether it wants you or not. Never standing up for yourself. Never being responsible for your own life.'

'He owes it to me,' I said stubbornly. 'He's ruined my life.'

'You mean he's given you a child – this child. Look at her, Olivia. Is this what you mean by ruining your life?'

'If it wasn't for her . . .'

'If it wasn't for her, if you hadn't become pregnant, you'd never have married Guy Tarver? That isn't the way Anne tells it.'

'Oh, Anne! What does she know? I suppose she told you all sorts of nonsense . . .'

'She told me how you trapped Guy into marriage, yes. That was silly, Olivia. It could only hurt both of you. He's not a man made for marriage. Didn't you know?'

'How should I have known? How *could* I have known? No one told me anything. Besides, I loved . . . I love him still.'

'So you'll hang round his neck like a millstone until he's frantic to get rid of you? Oh, I've no patience with you, Olivia. You're nothing, don't you realise that? Look at you, in your floaty summer frock and your silly little hat. What's the point of you?'

'No point at all – that's the whole point,' I answered brightly (but if I'd been close enough, I would have

scratched his eyes out). I took a long drag on my cigarette and dropped the butt into the dregs of cold tea that
stood on the desk. It hissed and went out. I stared at
the soggy, floating mess, stained at one end with the
crimson imprint of my lips. 'I just am – like it or lump
it. And, if we're going to be clever, what's the point of
you, for that matter, or Anne?'

'Anne rears your child. She does your job for you.
What're you for, Olivia?'

Chris turned back to the window, looking ostentatiously down into the shadowed court, anywhere rather
than at me.

When Anne and Nickie came out of Mr Mintram's
office, Anne's cheeks were as scarlet as though they'd
just been smartly slapped. She held Alastair so fiercely
against her that the poor child was struggling to free
himself. Nickie looked hot and unhappy. His collar had
wilted and he'd obviously run his fingers through his
hair in a gesture of despair. It stood up in comical peaks,
making him look a bit like a tall Stan Laurel.

'I take it the meeting hasn't been a success,' I said,
rather smugly.

'Well, what did you expect,' Anne rapped, 'that we'd
fall into each other's arms? Don't be so silly.'

'Well, I'd be quite happy to do that. I thought it went
jolly well, actually,' said Nickie. 'I'm to see Alastair as
often as I like, take him out and so forth, get to know
him. I'm to choose his school. I'd like him to go to
Rugby, one day. Otherwise . . .'

'. . . Otherwise, I shall be dragged through the
divorce courts as the guilty party.'

I couldn't see Nickie doing that. He was much too
much of the gentleman. But it didn't seem the right
time to say so. He had called his trump and it wasn't
for me to accuse him of bluffing. 'Why can't you do
the decent thing, Nickie, and take some little chorus

girl to Brighton?' Anne's voice dripped bitterness. 'It'd be so much more . . . more suitable.'

'If you really loved me,' Chris said, softly and sadly, 'you wouldn't care about that.'

'What's love got to do with anything?' She turned on him then, like a vixen. I had never before seen Chris deliberately avoid an argument – he always seemed to relish them – but this time he took a step backwards. His shoulders seemed to sag.

'I was under the impression that your discussions were over,' interrupted the solicitor smoothly. 'I was obviously wrong. Forgive me. Perhaps you would like to step back into my office. This is scarcely the place . . .'

'No. We're going home.'

Anne started to gather up the torn paper, bricks and picture books that littered the clerk's office. She dumped everything into a capacious bag that, when she picked it up, made her look like a tinker selling from door to door.

'Wait. Oh Chris, let me . . .'

I held out my hand to my daughter. Once, Chloe had grabbed my finger with the fierce reflex grip of the new-born. I'd scarcely touched her since. Now, she looked at my hand with its long scarlet nails and screamed.

'Sshh, sshh,' Chris murmured. 'It's all right, poppet. You're trying too hard, Olivia, don't force her,' he went on and I know I deserved the disdain in his voice. 'You don't have an automatic right to your child's love – no one has – you have to earn it.'

Chris wouldn't let Nickie pay for a taxi back to whatever lair they had come from. Nickie and I stood and watched them go, an oddly-assorted pair. Anne pushed the battered perambulator. Chris walked at her side, just slightly behind, his hand possessively on her shoulder.

Behind me, I heard Nickie sigh and the sound sliced through me, leaving me bleeding, as though from one of those unexpected cuts when an edge of paper catches your skin.

'Jolly little chap, Alastair. He smiles a lot, you know.'

'I feel like getting awfully drunk, Nickie. Shall we?'

'That doesn't sound like a terribly good idea to me. Besides, Mother's expecting me back tonight.'

'Oh Nickie – let Mother go hang for once! Be a man! What do you want to do?'

'Have a jolly night out with you, of course, but . . .'

'Look, if you don't stay and keep an eye on me tonight, Nickie, I shall do something simply frightful. I can feel it.'

'What?' he asked nervously.

'I don't know yet, but I'll think of something – knock a policeman's helmet off!'

'Oh, I say.' I could sense the relief in his laugh. I was only joking after all. Wasn't I?

'I want to laugh and dance and dance and laugh all night long.'

Well, what're friends for?

So Nickie booked into his club for the night and I kitted him out with Guy's evening clothes, since he hadn't brought any of his own. They were both much of a height, yet the clothes hung on Nickie like a string of wet washing.

'Won't Guy mind?' he asked anxiously. 'Won't he need these things himself tonight?'

'Guy's away,' I answered shortly. 'In France, soaking up some local colour – with Raymond.'

I wanted something gay, something colourful and noisy, to take my mind off things, so we went to see *Rio Rita* at the newly-opened Prince Edward. It was full of stamping feet and flirting dark eyes, with jolly songs like 'Eight Little Gringos' – just what I needed. Then we went on to the Café de Paris, in time for late supper and the cabaret, the Western Brothers – frightfully good chaps, as they described themselves. We danced to Jack Harris's band. As more diners arrived, more and more tables were squeezed onto the dance floor, until we were gently shuffling in each other's arms. It didn't matter that Nickie couldn't dance to save his life.

> Although he may not be the man that
> girls think of as handsome,
> To my heart he carries the key.

His arms were round me, his face in my hair and he hummed softly to the sweet, sentimental tune, in an off-key voice that was oddly comforting.

Oh Nickie, I thought, you're not the most exciting man in the world, but you're so nice. If the man I'd married had been half the man you are, my life would never have been such a mess. How could Anne treat you so badly? But she'll come back – I'm certain of it. If only I could be as certain of Guy.

> I'm a little lamb who's lost in the wood;
> I know I should always be good
> To one who'll watch over me.

A few years earlier and we'd have been able to go on to a club after the Café de Paris closed, but continual police raids had effectively closed down London's early morning night life – all except the real dives and Nickie wouldn't dream of taking me to one of those.

I tripped on the way up the curving staircase that led to street level. Nickie grabbed my arm, saving me from a tumble.

'Steady on, old girl,' he whispered. 'Hold on to me and no one'll notice.'

194

On the way back to Chelsea, I rapped on the glass dividing us from the taxi driver. 'Stop here,' I ordered, 'we'll walk back. It's a glorious night,' I answered Nickie's protests. 'Besides, what's the point of going home too early? There's nothing there I want to go back to.'

So we walked along the embankment – how romantic. There were stars in the sky and the river smelled surprisingly salty, clean. If Guy had had his arm around my shoulders like that, instead of Nickie, I'd have known how to act. I'd have had him on his knees for me, gasping for me – for me. I'd have blotted that man right out of his mind.

But it was Nickie's arm round me. Yet he was a man and tall and strong and comforting and, above all, there, while my husband was not. I snuggled closer, squirming my wicked little body right up against his, and felt Nickie respond.

'You're a marvellous girl, Olivia,' he said. 'Guy doesn't deserve you.'

And then he kissed me. I wanted the stars to explode, but, to be honest, they didn't. He wasn't very good at it. He kissed me respectfully and tentatively, in all the ways I didn't want. And when he'd finished, being Nickie, he apologised.

'Sorry, sorry,' he said. 'I don't know what came over me.'

'Moonlight came over you and loneliness. What's so wrong with that? I won't hold you to it,' I laughed.

'And you're not cross with me? We're still friends?'

'Still friends,' I promised. 'Come on.'

We linked arms and strode off down the embankment towards Chelsea. Every now and then, a bench would be occupied by a shapeless huddle of rags covered with old newspapers. I would turn my head away, trying not to look, trying not to wonder if the summer night felt colder to those who had no bed to look forward to.

'I'm ravenous,' declared Nickie as we turned for the long haul up Chelsea Bridge Road.

'You can't be. You had the most enormous dinner.'

'Fresh air and exercise, it always makes me hungry. Fancy a cuppa, duckie?' he asked in an horrific, mock-Cockney accent.

There was a tea stall at the next road junction. Nickie ordered great wads of ham sandwiches and thick, sweet tea in cream enamel mugs with chipped blue rims. We wolfed everything down as though we hadn't eaten in days.

'Oh, delicious.' I leaned forward and pinched a hanging scrap of ham from Nickie's sandwich, then licked my fingers, enjoying the sweet, fatty taste. 'You are clever, Nickie.'

'More? Open your mouth, then, little bird.' He broke a piece off his sandwich and popped it into my waiting mouth.

It was all so funny. I laughed and laughed and tried not to see the shadowy figures who stood with us under the canopy: mittened hands around a mug of tea that would have to last all night, sipping carefully, savouring every mouthful; blackened nails; old men's necks, scored with dirt, in relief like the mountains of the moon; young men's faces left empty when the hope drained away, leaving them dry as husks; heads still respectably covered, although boots had been mended with slivers of cardboard for soles.

They watched us steadily, without rancour – or so it seemed to me – as though we were bright beings from another planet, with no connection to their everyday world of shadows. We were oddities. We had curiosity value, but were of no practical use to people who scrounged in dustbins for crusts, or scoured the gutters

196

for fag ends. There was no purpose to us, no point.

Chris had said as much.

I looked down from the heights into the inhabited depths and the view gave me vertigo.

I shivered, conscious suddenly that my strappy dancing sandals had rubbed my heels raw. I didn't want to walk any more, didn't want to have anything more to do with these inimical, night-time streets.

'Take me home, Nickie, please – now.'

And then it seemed churlish to send Nickie away again, when he had come so far out of his way, without asking him if he'd like some coffee. There wasn't any coffee, so I poured us both a good slug of Guy's precious single malt.

'Pretend it's Russian tea,' I said, 'if it makes you feel any better. Anyway, it's Guy's fault. He should know better than to leave temptation in my way.'

We had another, because it tasted so good, and another, because the first two had made us thirsty. By then, it wasn't worth saving what was left in the bottle.

We sat together on the sofa and Nickie put his head on my shoulder. I smoothed the hair back from his forehead, the way Nanny used to do, when we nestled close to her, begging sympathy for a grazed knee or tummy ache.

'That's nice,' he whispered. 'That's awfully nice.'

And Nickie was still there – dear innocent – when the change of light outlining the curtains told me the night was long over. My arm was too dead to feel painful, but my neck was twisted at such an impossible angle that I could scarcely raise my head.

'Nickie. Nickie, wake up. Time to go home. It's morning.'

Watching him surface was like watching a caricature

of a waking man. If I'd seen an actor go through that pantomime of yawns and grimaces, I wouldn't have been impressed. Realisation dawned only slowly.

'Nickie, come on! My little woman will be here before you know it and she's such a prude. She'll be scandalised.'

'Olivia! We haven't . . . we didn't . . . I haven't been naughty, have I?'

I gave him my most enigmatic smile, Mona Lisa with twisted neck. 'Oh no. In fact, you were very, very good!'

Then I tottered off to put on the kettle and let the bath run, leaving Nickie to work out what I meant.

When he'd finally gone, I looked in the glass and a clown's face, smeared with yesterday's makeup, stared back at me. I shuddered.

What am I for? What's the point in me? My existence has no meaning. I just am.

I'm twenty-one years old.

I needed a holiday. Yes, that sounded a very good idea. Heaven knows when Guy and Raymond would be home. The last I'd heard, they were touring the Cevennes watching butterflies and following in the steps of Stevenson and his donkey. The Americans have a phrase – stir crazy – to describe the feelings of imprisonment that I suffered that summer. London was a cage. Everyone interesting was still in the country. I couldn't go home to my parents – they'd only say 'I told you so' and besides, I didn't know where they were. Anne was no comfort – too smug for words.

Nickie's suggestion of a week or two in Wiltshire was like a gift from the gods. No lounging around in bed allowed – so inconsiderate to the servants waiting to make one's bed and clean one's room. Mrs Lockyer's disapproval and Rose's healthy cynicism might be just what I needed.

'I'd like you to come,' Nickie said, 'because I'm worried about Clare. No, I mean, that sounds frightfully rude . . . Well, what I really mean is – I'd like you to come, anyway, of course, but if you can manage to sort out Clare as well, I'd be awfully grateful.'

'But whatever are they doing there?'

'Where else are they to go? Really, Olivia, I know it's not my place to make remarks about your family, but you do seem rather careless with each other. Your parents had an invitation at short notice to join a Mediterranean cruise on Tommy Brightling's yacht, you know – the banking Brightling. They could scarcely ask you to take the twins – not in, er, your state of health – and Anne wouldn't be at all suitable, so, well, they're at Greywell.'

It was with more than a twinge of conscience that I travelled down to Wiltshire. If Nickie and Anne had still been married (they were really, but you know what I mean – only in law), it would have been suitable, if a bit thoughtless to dump the twins, but, as things were, it seemed the height of bad manners to use Nickie's family as a convenient repository for stray children. Scarcely children. I did a quick calculation. Heavens – sixteen. Nearly proper people.

I was nervous, too. I'd not given them a thought all summer. Clare would be prickly, rude, would probably snub me, quite rightly. David – well, no one ever knew what David thought.

I was right to be nervous, as it turned out.

By the time I'd been shown upstairs, had a bath, changed and come down for tea, I still hadn't seen my brother and sister. You'd think they might have been on the steps to greet me, since we hadn't seen each other for so long. On second thoughts, that was probably the very reason why they weren't waiting on the steps.

They bowled up, late for tea, from different directions.

'Oh hello, Olive,' said David, throwing himself down in a chair and helping himself to a sandwich.

Clare didn't even say hello. She just flopped down and accepted the cup that was passed to her.

'Aren't you going to kiss your sister?' asked Mrs Lockyer.

'I've forgotten how,' she said and took an enormous bite out of a slice of cherry cake.

I'd remembered them both as children and, although I acknowledged that those years had passed, somehow I still expected them to look as my memory prompted. I expected rather taller versions of the children I'd last seen. I was shocked by the change.

David was a young man – a long, thin young man whose elbows and knees seemed to be more than usually pointed. His wrists stuck out below his shirt sleeves and led into fine, bony, long-fingered hands. His face was beaky, not quite finished, with a nose he had still to grow into, yet the foreshadowing of the man he would be was already there. His smile was still the same though, poignant, too watchful for a boy, too sweet for a man.

Oh dear – Clare! David's twin, once so like him that only their clothes visibly differentiated them, now less and less identical as their characters diverged. The same straight fair hair, but out of shape from lack of cutting, ragged on her collar. The same beaky nose, but lost in a pudgy, spotty parody of David's fine features; David's fragile smile mutated into a scowl, like a dog that wags its tail and snarls at the same time, longing to be patted yet certain that the outstretched hand will beat it. Bulges where bulges shouldn't be. Shapeless skirt and laddered stockings.

Someone ought to do something with her. I ought to do something with her.

I wrote to Guy, telling him where I was, care of poste restante at Alés, which was the last address I had, but that had been more than a fortnight ago. Still, I thought it best to remind him that he still had a devoted little wife awaiting his return. He might even have surprised me by coming home. Not very likely, admittedly.

I received no reply.

Nickie had been right. A holiday was just what I needed. Perhaps it was the fresh air or perhaps – probably – the enforced abstinence. Mrs Lockyer would countenance no more than one dry sherry before dinner and one glass of wine to accompany it. One was often more than enough – the best of her late husband's cellar had been sold to help to pay death duties and what was left was definitely the dregs. I must admit, I found the regime difficult at first.

On the third night, I'd had a terrible craving and crept down, holding my breath at every creak of the stairs, to the dining room, but everything was efficiently locked away. I rattled the sideboard cupboard doors, but they didn't move. I rattled them again, frantic. I shook the handle until the decanters inside rang like the bells of hell, but the doors stayed closed.

'Oh, God – just one, just one . . .'

I kneeled before the sideboard and leaned my head against it. The wooden beading pressed into my forehead. I leaned harder, letting the wood bite into my skin. Harder, harder. I wanted it to brand me permanently, to mark me so that all the world could see me and know what I'd become. The mark of the beast . . . look, look, here she comes, here comes the drunkard, the loose woman, the abandoned wife, the abandoning mother . . .

Suddenly, it was all so clear. This was what I had to do. Slowly, quite calmly, the frantic excitement dulled, I began to bang my head against the edge of the sideboard. The crystal inside tinkled until the first piece smashed and then the sound changed. It was breaking, breaking . . .

The light snapped on, blinding white. Through a veil of blood I flinched from its brightness and the faces that surrounded me, horrified, accusing, disgusted . . . Nickie, with his face of sorrow. I began to retch.

I'm told Mrs Lockyer sat by my side until the doctor's sedative wore off. She sat, doing her duty as she saw it, with a piece of mud-coloured canvas flung across her lap, filling its blankness with meticulous, darker mud-coloured stitches.

Someone had washed me and bandaged my forehead, but my lashes still felt sticky with blood. Some of them would not separate and I looked at Nickie's mother through stiffened spikes, as though made up for a Boris Karloff film.

'You had a fall, Olive,' said Mrs Lockyer, looking up briefly from her canvas work, 'on your way to the lavatory in the dark. The light switches are rather difficult to find.'

'Did I? I thought –'

'Yes,' she said firmly. 'You did.' She gathered up her hanks of wool and rolled them into the canvas. 'David and Clare will be glad to hear you're awake. I expect they'll come to see you, if you feel up to it, but not for long. You may sit up for an hour or two tomorrow and, perhaps, come down the day after that.'

'I'm sorry,' I whispered as she reached the door.

Mrs Lockyer paused with her hand on the door-handle. I think she was angered to be stopped, angered

202

to be forced to acknowledge the facts that she had so decently reorganised. She had covered my conduct as hurriedly and as completely as she would have covered my nakedness if I'd stood up in public and stripped off my clothes. These things are not to be talked about or even acknowledged. Not ever.

She looked back across the room at me with utter contempt and loathing. She looked at me as though I were something extremely nasty, as though she might have to call a housemaid to remove me with a pair of tongs.

'The day my son met your sister,' she said slowly, wearily, 'turned out to be the worst day in my life. If I had guessed, I would gladly have walled him up alive, rather than let the Northaws embroil this family in their nastiness.'

By the time the bruising faded, I could see that I looked better in the mornings than I had for a long time. That frightful puffy look about the eyes that used to make me shudder and reach for the mascara, seemed to have gone. I could face myself first thing. Days that had seemed too difficult to fill in London now bulged at the seams with activities – not very stimulating, but just right. I no longer needed to dose myself with Veronal before attempting to sleep. When the young abuse their bodies, they are able to recover so quickly. If I'd been over forty, no doubt I'd have taken longer to dry out.

Nickie and Rose were wonderful. They just let me take life at my own pace. If I wanted someone to walk with, that was fine. If I wanted to be alone, they'd let me. Sometimes, Nickie and I used to ride out before breakfast, before the sun grew too hot for the horses or the flies too troublesome. We'd arrive back with ferocious appetites, disgustingly healthy, as Rose would say.

Nickie was always the perfect host, the perfect gentleman. After that one small (tiny!) slip in London, he never again laid a hand on me. In fact, although we were constantly in each other's company, he always made sure that there was a seemly physical gap between us.

There were whole days when I scarcely gave Guy and his extended walking trip – or his companion – so much as a thought. I wish I'd been so easily able to dismiss the problems with the twins.

There was a problem and there wasn't, if you see what I mean. Nothing one could put one's finger on. David was studying hard, having been given holiday work by his tutor. He was destined for Oxford, but was drifting there in the way that young men climb mountains – more because it was there than because of any burning desire for the academic life. He worked hard because it was in his nature always to do his best, but even I could see his heart wasn't in it. He didn't seem to know what he wanted to do, or, if he did, he didn't confide in any of us at Greywell – not even Clare.

And Clare? Well, Clare was doing nothing but slouching around, getting into mischief. If I think of her as she was in those days, the French word *farouche* most nearly seems to describe her. She was a great, sulky lump with a ferocious glare and a walk like a ploughboy. It was like living with Brünnhilde.

Clare had always been well aware that her eyes could have a most disconcerting effect on people. As a child, she'd used her penetrating blue gaze most effectively when trying to wheedle something out of Mother. It always worked. Now she used it indiscriminately. At meal times, she'd pick some unfortunate person and treat him or her to an unwavering scowl. There was no rhyme or reason to it. She'd just do it. Rose would tell her sharply that if she didn't stop staring, her eyeballs would fall out on the plate and be fed to the pigs. Most of the rest of the family, with practice, managed to ignore her and carry on eating. Visitors were less fortunate. Once, the vicar's wife dropped her napkin to break the tension and, on bending to pick it up, dragged the table cloth with her and tipped cabinet pudding and custard everywhere. Clare just hooted with laughter.

There was a cruel streak – no that's not exactly right – there was a heartless streak to her humour that the rest of us didn't appreciate. Her pranks were the sort that might easily have been played by a ten year old, but with an unpleasant bite to them.

Once she shut the gardener in the greenhouse and took away the handle. Nothing unusual in that – it's a favourite childhood trick, one of the occupational hazards of being a gardener. On this occasion, it was nearly a tragedy. The man had just lit a fumigation cone to kill insects and barely managed to break the glass and get out before he was overcome by cyanide smoke.

Another time, she had been to the cinema in Amesbury with some young people from a neighbouring house. There was a showdown on the screen, with the goodie and the baddie facing each other along a deserted street. Clare suddenly took a pistol from her bag and 'shot' the goodie before he had time to draw. Only blanks, of course, but she caused a panic that might easily have become nasty. It took a certain amount of skilful diplomacy on Nickie's part to talk her out of that one. He and the Chief Constable were shooting chums, but even so, it was a near thing. From then on, Nickie carried the gun cabinet key with him wherever he went.

'I can't understand her,' I complained to Rose one day, as we did the flowers together. 'Nothing I can say seems to make any impression on her. I can rant and rave, I can reason with her, it makes no difference. She's completely impervious to emotion, logic or brute force.'

'Well, if I were a devotee of Freud – which I'm not, thank goodness,' answered Rose, shaking earwigs from some dahlias into the flower room sink and heartlessly turning the tap on them, 'I'd come up with all sorts of exciting reasons for Clare's behaviour – murky thoughts about what goes on in the parents' bedroom and all that. However – what d'you think of that? Should I stick some more foliage in at the back? It looks a bit mean to me.'

'There's a bit of a gap round this side. Go on. You were saying however . . .'

'However,' Rose said slowly, 'Clare does need special understanding. She's not simply bad, as my mother seems to think. Look at things from her viewpoint . . .'

'Does she have a viewpoint?' I asked acidly. 'I always think of her as a bit like a savage – acting from instinct rather than reason. Kick first – ask questions later.'

'Oh, you're right about that. She is rather primitive. If something hurts her, she hurts it back. Simple. If society isn't good to her, she lashes out at it. She won't conform. Ever.'

'We're not exactly a conformist sort of family. Is that necessarily a bad thing?'

'Not necessarily. But in this case, yes. You're all individuals, completely selfish, with no time to spare for anyone else, least of all your own family.'

I didn't have a clever, instant answer for that. I took my time over it, selecting flowers carefully, placing them in exactly the right spot. Dahlias, a little vulgar perhaps, and lurking within those gorgeous petals, earwigs with open pincers, ready to nip the unwary finger; chrysanthemums, gold and bronze, spicing the air with their special, funeral smell; late roses, blowsy, bursting out of their corsets. I picked one up and its petals fell all at once, in perfect rose shape, onto the wooden draining board.

The early sun slanted low, below the holland blinds, and gleamed on the egg-shell porcelain of old, beautiful vases: brilliant sang-de-boeuf K'ang Hsi and lucent celadon – chipped now, cracked with careless handling, but lovely still. It fell on Rose's clever, busy fingers as she sorted through the dripping bundle of foliage. She made no attempt to follow on after her comment. The next step was meant to be mine.

'I suppose Clare has been rather . . . rather left to grow, a bit like a healthy weed. But after all, she has David. She's never really wanted anyone else.'

'She *had* David, you mean,' said Rose carefully.

'Had?'

Rose took the clippers and stripped the stem of a rose of all its thorns in a quick, vicious movement. 'You really don't see anything until it's pushed right under your nose, do you? Clare has lost David and she doesn't know what to do about it.'

'But . . . but they're inseparable – always have been.'

'Clare is inseparable from David, certainly, but David is already separated from her. It's his deafness, you see. You do know that he's deaf, I imagine?' Rose asked sharply.

'Of course I do,' I snapped. 'I'm not totally insensitive. But only a little, surely. It's not serious.'

I was beginning to resent Rose's interference. This was my sister she was talking about, my brother. She was criticising my family from the lofty heights of condescension. Anyone would think her family was perfect in every way. Why, Nickie couldn't even manage to hang on to his wife and son. Oh God, that was an awful thing to think. He'd done so much – they'd all done so much for Clare and David. Of course I was grateful. That's what they all wanted, wasn't it? But dammit, there was no need to be so frightfully priggish about it. No one had forced them into taking in my difficult brother and sister.

Rose must have read my thoughts.

'We don't have to talk about this unless you want to,' she said briskly and picked up the newly arranged vase. The flowers wobbled alarmingly and then steadied. 'I'd be the last person to interfere.'

'Rose, I'm sorry.' I forced myself to be suitably contrite. 'You're so much cleverer than I am.'

'If you think about it, that's not really much of a compliment, is it?' She looked pleased, all the same. 'David's hearing is certainly better. We had to call the doctor some time ago because of some rather horrid discharge from his right ear. In fact, this seems to have been a good thing. Whatever had impaired his hearing after he had measles seems to have cleared itself at last.'

'So he's better now.'

'He can hear reasonably well in that ear now. The other is still muffled, but may spontaneously clear at any time, we've been told. The problem is that it's taken so long. His deafness cut him off from the world for quite some time, just at an age when he should have been making friends and having fun. He couldn't take part in smart chit-chat. Parties were a nightmare, because with background music, he couldn't hear a word anyone said. He's not terribly athletic, so tennis parties were out. He's naturally studious and when he couldn't hear, he used books as a defence from the world he couldn't join. His world and Clare's have just drifted apart.'

'Poor David.'

'Poor Clare, you mean. David may not be wildly happy, but he's not unhappy, either. Clare is utterly miserable. You see the result.'

208

'But what can I do? No, don't go yet. Rose, help me, please.'

Rose already had her answer thought out. 'It's obvious. Clare must go away, of course. She must be sent to Paris or Florence or Munich, with other girls of her own age. Perhaps if she is shown what a fascinating world is waiting for her, she won't feel David's defection quite so badly.'

Rose's idea had its merits. The more I thought about it, the better it sounded. Rose always had common sense. I wrote to our parents, suggesting that Clare ought to be 'finished'. In fact, far from needing to be finished, Clare hadn't even been started properly. Having her around the house was rather like having an overgrown prep schoolboy with a vicious streak. With one difference – one can beat some sense into a schoolboy.

I had a reply in a surprisingly short time, on paper headed The Grand Hotel, Cap Ferrat. Mother wrote that she thought Rose's idea was sensible and practical and that, since it was clearly impossible for her to supervise Clare's worldly debut herself, I was to make any arrangements I thought right. She finished by saying that she'd met Guy at the Villa Mauresque and that he'd introduced her to his friend. She put no inverted commas, real or imagined, around the word 'friend'. I found that quite incredible. Did Mother really live in such a sheltered world? She also said that Pa had refused to shake his hand and she'd been very cross with him.

So Clare and I were on our own. Oh, well. I didn't have anything else to do. It's not as though I'd really expected Mother to rush back to find out what was wrong with her youngest daughter. Not really.

Mrs Lockyer cast about amongst her friends to find a suitable establishment where Clare might be given a little Continental polish. (A bit like slapping veneer on a deal-framed cabinet, I privately thought, but didn't say so.) A few names were recommended, all of them mittel-Europäisch aristocrats whose fortunes had not survived the Great War. From this short list, we chose Baroness de Rutz, whose promise to introduce three or four young ladies to art, music, literature and spoken and written German in the healthy air of Bavaria seemed to be everything we were looking for.

Clare would have the rough edges rubbed off, be weaned gently from her childhood attachment to her twin, make some lifelong friends and be ready, when she came home in two years or so, to be presented and have her Season. By spring 1933, with a little bit of luck, she'd be fit to release on the world and, after that, she'd be someone else's responsibility. I was so grateful to Rose for her sensible suggestion. Why hadn't I thought of something like that?

In the meantime, we'd use the short time before departure to organise a simple wardrobe suitable for a young girl leaving home for the first time. Nothing too outrageous: some good English tweeds (no one but the English can cut tweeds properly); a clutch of smart afternoon frocks for luncheon parties and visiting art galleries; cocktail frocks wouldn't be appropriate at her age, but certainly a dinner gown or two, absolutely simple, for the opera or theatre. I had cast my eye in despair on Clare's lingerie. Plenty to worry about there! We could leave winter clothes, I thought, to be bought in Munich. Clare might look rather fetching in a swing-back loden coat and a little hat with a feather. With her blonde hair and bright blue eyes, I told her, she'd look a real Fräulein!

Flattered by all this unusual attention, Clare was surprisingly affable and our shopping expeditions were rather fun. We shopped in Salisbury for everyday items, but for important things like the dinner gowns, I took

Clare to Debenham & Freebody and Galeries Lafayette. We'd have lunch at the Berkeley and tea at Gunter's and talk girl talk, as the Americans say. Clare made an effort with her appearance. It was a pity about the spots, but at least her hair was clean and her stockings mended.

Goodness, I wished I'd taken the trouble to do this earlier. Clare was just aching for someone to notice her, someone to love her for herself. All our problems seemed to be well on the way to being solved.

There you are, I thought, so much for Rose's pseudo-Freudian babble. What rot. Rose is too clever for her own good, as Nanny would have said. All Clare needed was a little bit of attention and some pretty clothes.

If I had known, what would I have done, what could I have done? Perhaps it was better that the future was shielded from my sight.

One morning, Clare and I were coming downstairs together. Clare was in front and when she reached the half-landing, she stopped so suddenly that I cannoned into her back. I opened my mouth to complain, but something about her wary stillness silenced me. I stretched to see over her shoulder.

Anne was standing in the hall.

From this height, foreshortened, she looked like one of those dumpy slum wives who grow wider rather than taller on a diet of margarine, tea, chips and too much child-bearing. She wore a twin-set of unflattering beige, stained at the front. (Good heavens – she wasn't still feeding that great hulk of a child herself, surely?) Her tweed skirt had 'seated' badly and the hem was down at one side. At her feet, tied up in brown paper, were two bundles that contained all she possessed.

My clever, sharp-tongued, conventional sister – the most unlikely rebel imaginable – had returned both to her senses and to the fold. She was beaten. I looked down at the bedraggled woman and, unexpectedly, my heart ached for the briskness, the quick mind, the acid tongue. What a waste. In each arm, Anne carried a child.

Alastair was a huge, wriggling lump who suddenly folded over at the waist like a penknife, stretching out his arms towards the floor and letting out a series of sharp peacock screeches. Patiently, Anne hefted him up again, balancing him on her hip bone, with the immemorial stoicism of the poor. She swayed to one side, offsetting his weight.

In her other arm was a skinny child with a dirty face, dressed in faded dungarees, whose grip round Anne's neck must have been painful. She looked around the hall with wide, wondering eyes and then her face crumpled and she hid it against Anne's shoulder. If she made a sound, I couldn't hear it above Alastair's howls of frustration.

Chloe. My daughter. If I could say that my heart yearned for her, I would, but all I felt was a mule's kick of shock somewhere round the breast-bone.

The day was dull. Clare and I were in shadow. Anne couldn't have seen us. Clare made a movement to run down, but I grabbed her shoulder and shook my head. The library door had opened and Nickie, attracted by the noise, came out into the hall.

If we'd had any sensitivity at all, we should have tip-toed upstairs and stayed there for another ten minutes. It was not for us to watch a husband and wife come together after all that had separated them. But the ideal moment had passed. Our movements would have attracted attention, so we stayed and watched, but I wished I had not seen. The memory of their meeting, like a pain in the night would wake me, again and again. I would never be rid of it.

'Hello, Nickie,' Anne said softly.

Oh, she had courage. Nothing she would ever do in life again would take the courage of uttering those two words.

If Nickie said anything, I couldn't hear it. I saw him reach out, wondering, longing to believe, yet afraid to hope. He touched her hair, her eyes, her lips. Then he held out his hands in an unexpected gesture of welcome that made me catch my breath at its simplicity. In one arm, he cradled his son. With the other, he encircled his wife. He took them back and held them. Nothing would ever make him let them go again. He lent Anne his strength and still had some to spare. He asked no questions and demanded no answers.

Anne was home. There was nothing more to say.

The door banged and Rose appeared with the suddenness of a demon king.

'Good lord,' she shrieked, 'kill the fatted calf! The prodigal wife's come home!'

I could have picked up the hideous life-size statue of a negro boy that decorated the half-landing and – quite cheerfully – dropped it on Rose's head!

'Olive? Are you awake?'

The whispers and the scratching pierced my dreams, getting into them and muddling them up. The laughter still echoed. It had stolen my soul away with it and left a heartless changeling in its place.

I was in the old punt at home. I knew it had rotted two summers ago and settled into the mud, but somehow I was in it. I could feel it rocking beneath me. I could feel the pressure of its planks across my back through old, thin cushions. When I opened my eyes, the sunlight struck sparks through the flickering green filter of willow branches.

Looking down at me was the tow-headed boy. And I remembered that I had been able to make him cry, just by looking at him. If you want something very, very badly and you think you're going to be given it, then – at the last moment – it's snatched away, the tears you weep are real tears. I was sorry I had made him cry, but that's what happens. I couldn't help it.

Only this time, I knew how he felt, because I had had something snatched away from me, too. I knew how it felt to stretch out my hands and find that they're empty. I wanted to say, 'Don't cry. I understand. Don't cry.'

But the boy wasn't a boy any longer. He was a man who looked at me with the contempt I knew I deserved. I tried to speak his name, but when I said, 'Raymond,' the word came out like the hissing of a snake. He reared up above me and spat. The gobbet lay between my naked breasts and burned like a brand.

It was dark, nothing to see. I didn't know where I was or where I was going. But there were noises, people talking, glasses chinking. A party, then, somewhere, anywhere. Then above the noises came Guy's laugh – I knew it well – clear and joyous. He was happy and I was in the dark and alone.

I should have been glad that he was happy, but the empty place where my soul had been was filled with bitterness. If he had been sad, I could have comforted him. He would have needed me and turned to me. He would have wanted no one else. But because he was happy, I was turned out into the dark night, like a stray cur.

His sadness would have been so much easier to bear than his happiness. I could not endure that he might be happy without me.

My face was wet with tears, but they weren't mine. They belonged to Raymond.

The scratching and tapping hadn't gone away.

'Olive? Are you awake? It's Anne.'

I struggled upright, fumbling for the light switch, the dream still so vivid that I turned to the empty bed next to mine, half expecting to see the imprint of Guy's head on the pillow.

'I know it's late – well, early, really – but you're the only person I can talk to.' She plumped down on my bed and tucked her bare feet under the eiderdown. 'And if I don't talk to someone, I'll go mad. You've made a mess of things, too. You know what it's like. You'll understand.'

'Whatever are you doing, creeping around like this?'

'Nickie's so nice.' Her whisper was a tiny, intimate sound coming out of the darkness. 'I just can't bear it.'

'Lucky you. Not many women would complain about that. What did you want him to do – beat you into submission?'

'Yes! That might have made me feel better – no, of course not, don't be silly. That may be your idea of a reconciliation. But he makes me feel so wicked. No questions. No demands. He just kissed me goodnight and said that he'd sleep in his dressing room. And then I hated myself all over again because I felt so relieved. I'd been so afraid that he'd want to . . . that he'd try . . .'

'He should have! Most men would have put such a mark on you that you'd never dare go swanning off again. You don't deserve a man like that.'

'I know and that makes it so much worse. I wish Nickie was a brute and then I could be a martyr. I wish . . . oh, I don't know what I wish.'

'But why did you come back? Did you finally get tired of pretending to be something you're not? Did you fall out of love?'

'No . . . no, never that.' The thin whisper in the dark cracked and broke, then picked up strength again. 'I came back because of the children. Nothing else. There was an outbreak of diphtheria. It was the children or Chris. I had to choose.'

'That was no contest, knowing you.'

'You make it sound so simple,' she retorted bitterly, 'you in your nice, clean flat with a bathroom and lots of hot water and money to pay for a doctor to call at any time of day or night, if you so much as have a headache.'

'Did you wake me up because you wanted someone to talk to or someone to abuse?' I asked acidly, turning to plump up my pillow again.

'Have you ever seen diphtheria, Olive? No, of course not. You don't know what it's like. It's an evil web, thick and grey, that grows over their little throats. They can't snatch a breath. They suffocate. Have you ever heard it – the filthy noise of a child struggling to live? But in the end, they always lose. There were children that we knew, whole families . . .'

'Could nothing be done?'

'The children were taken away to isolation hospitals – and they never came back. Some mothers hid their sick children because they wanted them to die at home, not in some strange, faraway place. I took down all the curtains, took up the rugs, anywhere germs might lurk. And I scrubbed everything that could be scrubbed with lysol and disinfected the vegetables and boiled every drop of drinking water. I scrubbed until my hands were bleeding, but there was never enough water for cleaning. I was carrying buckets of it upstairs all day. And it's been such a long summer, no frosts at all yet. It'll die out when the winter comes, but in the meantime . . . I couldn't take the risk. I couldn't put my children in danger because of . . . because of Chris.'

My children, she had said, my children – but one of those children was my daughter.

Anne sagged forward. It was too dark to see her, but

216

I felt her weight shift on the mattress and I heard her take fierce gulps of breath in her fight to stay in control. I could sense that she wanted to throw herself on the ground and howl – I knew because I had wanted to do the same sometimes. But one doesn't. One hasn't been brought up that way. It hurts more to be civilised, so much more, and Anne had always been so horribly civilised.

I wanted to put out my arms and hug her. I wanted to rock her back and forth until she had cried herself out. I could have cried too and we'd have healed each other. But we'd never been close – no secrets, no whispers. We were just people who'd happened to be born in the same house. It would have been foreign, it would have been false to embrace her now. I couldn't do it.

But I put out my hand into the darkness and touched Anne's rough-cut hair, shaggy as a pony's. I felt her grief transmit itself along my arm, like an electric charge. It flowed into me, into my own private pool of misery, filling it almost to the brim. I put my arms around her then, and rocked her gently. My sister – I had never loved or understood her so well – nor ever would again.

'And Chris?' I asked softly when Anne's breathing had steadied.

'Do you remember? He always said that he'd never force me to stay. But oh, Olive – I can't bear it.'

But she did bear it, for in the morning, Anne was there, wearing a fresh and smiling mask, at the opposite end of the breakfast table to her husband.

I decided that Clare and I would drive together to Munich, travelling across northern France and Belgium: first, because it was something to do; secondly, because one or two friends had asked me to look out for sumptuous materials or tapestries on my travels. I had such an eye for colour, they said, so clever. And, of course, there'd be a useful little commission in it for me. It was all rather flattering.

So my nippy little Alvis Silver Eagle was horribly overloaded with the amount of luggage two women thought vital to a Continental tour. We travelled in easy stages across the flat fields of Flanders, staying a few nights in Brussels, where I ordered a pair of ornately carved armoires that would look simply wonderful after they'd been stripped and pickled. Away with gloomy, dark wood! Let there be light!

Clare couldn't understand my passion for haunting the *marchés aux puces* in larger towns as we travelled. 'Goodness knows what you could catch,' she would say, 'rummaging through piles of old clothes. I wouldn't touch them with a barge pole.'

'You sound just like Anne,' I'd scoff, 'and she sounds just like Nanny.'

Then I'd display some trophy I'd found at the bottom of a heap of rubbish – a bolt of old Lyons silk, frail as a cobweb and as strong, or a Flemish tapestry, huge, rotten with age, but perhaps with a central motif that could be cut down and used as a dramatic focus for a smaller modern room.

'Well, yes, quite nice, I suppose,' Clare would admit grudgingly, 'but what's it for?'

'Beautiful things don't have to be *for* anything,' I'd say. I felt a twinge of memory, of things past and forgotten and unpleasant. No, it was gone. 'It's enough that they're beautiful. One day, I'll realise what has to be done with them and then they'll be ready and waiting for me.'

I left little hoards stashed all over the place, waiting for me to pick up on my return journey, once Clare's luggage had been removed. I would travel home as fully laden as I'd come out.

On our last night in Belgium, we stayed in Spa, in a dignified old hotel with windows shaded by green and white striped blinds from the bustle of the town square. Clare was suffering from a headache, brought on by the strong autumn sun in an open car and by the usual reason, and had gone to bed with aspirins and a hot water bottle for her tummy. So I wandered idly around the hotel, admiring some old pictures of the town in its Edwardian heyday. The proprietress was a chatty person who encouraged my interest.

'If madame wishes,' she offered, 'I could ask my daughter to show you around the town.'

So, with nothing better to occupy myself, I went off with the daughter, an educated woman who had been a teacher before her marriage. We took the paths that led around the wooded rise above the town.

'From over there,' she said, pointing east, 'the German army came in the summer of 1914 and they set up their staff headquarters here, in these buildings. The Kaiser lived in the château and it was from here that he fled to sanctuary in Holland to avoid capture.

'There were German officers billeted in the hotel. I helped them pack. They were stunned by the need to go home before the war was won. 'No one defeated us,' they said. 'We have been betrayed by Bolsheviks and Jews. It is a conspiracy. The Jews have lost the war for us.' I was nine years old when the Germans arrived. I was thirteen when I stood here and watched them march away.'

'That was a long time ago,' I said, tactlessly.

'You would not say that, madame, if you had lived here then.' She flung her big, red hands in a wide circle. 'Everything you can see, the Germans took. They took and held every hill and field and tree of my country, except for one tiny corner, where you English stopped them. Yet from here, every day we can hear German

219

broadcasts moaning about their bleeding frontiers – but who first tore these frontiers apart? They weep about the Ruhr and the Rhine, but who clung on to what they had stolen for as long as they could? It took four years and half the world to move them out again. Do they think we have forgotten so soon?'

She was trembling and we sat down on a rock to allow her to regain her breath.

'My brother was fourteen. When our father went to war, he was the man of the family. The town was being stripped. The Germans told him to hand over the keys to the cellars and the stores. Silly boy, he refused. He was taken away and we never saw him again.

'I have a little boy of three,' she continued softly. 'I would give the world to think that he might live out his life in peace. But from over the border, we can hear the sound of marching feet again.'

Next morning, we drove up and over sparse hill-farming country, then dipped down to cross a moor golden with gorse towards the frontier. Here a Belgian in uniform stopped us. On land that had been German before the plebiscite of 1920, a Belgian regiment was training. The road was closed and we had the option of waiting until the shooting was over for the day, or taking a more complicated cross-country route. The Belgian climbed onto our running-board to see us safely on our way. His left sleeve swung empty.

'Lost at Namur,' he said. 'Listen . . .' The crackle of gunfire punctuated his voice with its unfamiliar Belgian-French accent, making him difficult to understand. '. . . That is the sound of money going off with a bang. We must practise to defend ourselves, but every shot blows away money we need in Belgium. It spends our taxes and wastes our time, but what else can we do?'

Our guide left us at the next crossroads and we followed a long wooded road, bordered by a tram track, that led to a red and white striped barrier, beyond which waved the black-red-gold banner of the Weimar Republic. The barrier was manned by an official in a green jacket, but, lounging against the wall of the customs shed, was a gang of Brownshirts. Remembering Chris's smashed face, I shuddered.

Trams from Belgium and Germany met at the barrier and exchanged passengers. The Brownshirts had decided to allow no one in who wasn't willing to hold up his right arm and shout 'Heil Hitler'. It was the first time I'd heard that greeting and it struck me as incredibly amusing. Imagine having to shout 'Hail MacDonald' before being allowed off the ferry at Dover! What extraordinary people – if they weren't so funny, they might have been taken more seriously.

All the tram passengers obliged, except one woman who wouldn't say anything but 'Bonjour'. She was bundled, not roughly but rudely, back where she'd come from.

I don't know what authority these young hooligans thought they had – probably none, it was just their way of amusing themselves on that particular day – to force ordinary people to salute a man who wasn't even a head of state. The Nazis may have swept up 107 seats in the September election, but they were still only the second party in the land. I didn't find their ridiculous greeting nearly so funny when I discovered that they intended me to say it too. What – salute a jumped-up little house painter called Schicklgruber with a funny walk and a Charlie Chaplin moustache? Not on your life!

'I'm an Englishwoman,' I said, rather pompously, 'my papers are in order and I require you to let me pass.'

That's the way to treat them. Pa always said the Germans couldn't stand up to anyone in authority – or who sounded as though they might be. 'Give them an order and they'll lick your boots in gratitude,' he'd say.

221

They examined our passports in detail, asked why we were travelling to Germany, searched our luggage, opened the bonnet of my car and compared the engine number with the international carnet, carefully copying it down – all with scrupulous but inflexible politeness – but, in the end, couldn't think of any reason not to let us through. It may have been only a tiny triumph, but it left me feeling elated out of all proportion.

The moment was completely spoiled by Clare, who leaped to her feet in the car as the barrier opened, stuck her right arm in the air and shouted, 'Heil Hitler!' at the top of her voice.

I could have murdered her.

JUDITH

The Jewess

Like sheep following a wolf pack, the crowd followed the Brownshirts. Through the market square, weaving around the stalls, up and down the principal streets, in and out of hotels, restaurants and cafés, they followed.

Some were baying, no better than the wolves themselves. Some were jostling for position – let's see, let's see, serve her right, the bitch – craning their necks and standing on each others' toes. Some, at the back, were following out of curiosity, as though they were following a brass band, just to find out what all the excitement was about. A few, silent and appalled, followed because to look the other way, to pass by on the other side would have been even worse.

They had stripped her to her petticoat. Rough handling had ripped the cheap art silk so that it scarcely held together around her. Her stubbly head, nicked in places by careless shears, was bowed, her face hidden, but still I could see the trickle of blood that ran from one nostril, a scarlet thread, shocking against the white mask of flour and water paste. That, and the big, blue eyes – china doll's eyes – bulging with fear.

When she stumbled, her bare feet bruised by the cobbles, the men in brown shirts hauled her to her feet. When the crowd yelled, 'Speech! Speech!', she was hoisted shoulder high to whistles and jeers. Her head lolled forward on the long, white neck. Diners banged the tables with their spoons.

Her mouse-brown plaits decorated a placard that hung around her neck. In careful, black, Gothic script, it read:

ICH HABE MICH EINEM JUDEN GEGEBEN.
I HAVE GIVEN MYSELF TO A JEW.

And when they had tired of their sport, they dropped her on the steps of the town hall, the *Rathaus*, and left her where she lay. The crowd melted away, back to their dinner tables, their childrens' bedtime stories, their evening prayers.

I crept up and laid my coat over her near-nakedness. But her mother was there too. She snatched off my coat and flung it down the steps. Then she led her silent, shivering daughter away.

The girl was Krista. She was my cousin's fiancée.

'We are Germans who happen to be Jews,' my father would sometimes say. Another time he might say, 'We are Jews who happen to be Germans.'

Both statements were true. Our Germanness and our Jewishness were opposite sides of the same coin. We couldn't be one without the other.

At home, we never spoke Yiddish, only pure German. Hebrew, the language of God, was for prayers; German was the language of the land we called home. And then there was English, taught to us all by Father, who had studied in London before the war. We didn't need anything else. Three languages seemed to be enough even for educated people.

My father had fought for his country from 1914 to 1918. Like Hitler, he had been gassed at Ypres; like Hitler he had been awarded the Iron Cross. Every year, on the fifth Sunday before Easter, the National Day of Mourning, wearing his medals, he had marched with the League of Jewish Veterans in remembrance of fallen

226

comrades, Jew or Gentile. He was a teacher, a respected man in the community. He never really believed that the country he had been born in, his homeland, his *Heimat*, would turn against him.

When, finally, he understood – it was too late.

If he had still been alive to do it, my father could have set an examination paper to be answered by his tormentors:

Time allowed: eternity.
Answer any three from four.
Either
Did thinking they were the Chosen People cut the Jews off from the outside world? Discuss.
or
Explain, in your own words, what was so offensive about our way of life that we should be murdered for it?
or
Explain, precisely, why you hated my family. (You must have hated them, or why kill them?) Examine how it was possible.
or
What did we do, or neglect to do? Give examples.

It wasn't always so. The nineteenth century pogroms of Russia and Poland were the products of uncivilised societies, of feudal societies. And Germany was so very civilised. Think of the music. Think of the great minds. Name the names: Bach, Beethoven, Brahms, Mendelssohn, Goëthe, Schiller, Mann, Kafka, Röntgen, Einstein, Gutenberg, Kepler, Luther, Holbein, Dürer . . . Lists are very tedious and this one could be longer. How could this civilised, free-thinking country descend into that new, dark age of barbarism?

But never forget that it was not always so.

★

From Monday to Friday, I felt no different from my school chums. A gaggle of us would set off for school together, chattering, giggling, dodging the cars, the bicycles, the farm carts in for the day, running up and down the double stone staircases fronting half-timbered houses with gable-ends sharp as needles. Along Brüderstrasse, never caring that we were passing the Gothic front of the oldest house in North Germany, through the market square, skirting the Domplatz and down Bäckerstrasse, past the gable carvings of bearded, naked men modestly clutching their private parts, down to the bridge that crossed the Weser, to the bright, modern *Gymnasium*, our grammar school. And when we passed the entrance to the narrow alley called Judengasse, it never occurred to me that my ancestors may have been crammed together in its scary dimness. This was today and I was just one of the girls. Then home again, as the Rathaus clock struck the hour. You could always tell who were visitors or country people. They were the ones who stopped to watch the circling angels with their trumpets and the two great blackamoors, each striking the bell in turn with knobbly cudgels.

But if it was Friday, then the strangeness, the aloofness began. We only had a frugal midday meal – *belegte Brötchen*, perhaps – in order to save ourselves for the evening feast. On Friday afternoons, the house would be scoured; floors scrubbed, rugs shaken, furniture polished. Our maid, Bertha, although a Christian, joined in the effort with enormous energy. The clockwork time-switches that worked the cooker and the electric lights would be set, so that we had no need to risk the temptation to touch them. By the time Mother lit the *Shabbat* candles, they would shine on a spotless lace tablecloth, gleaming silver, glistening furniture. And then the special time, the different time, would begin.

God gives us all a precious gift on the Sabbath. He gives us a second soul. It is this that makes us all feel so special. Everything slows down. The workaday world seems as unreal as a puppet show. I could watch my Christian friends going off to Saturday school and know that they were envying me my day off. We might see people going in and out of shops, climbing in and out of trams or cars, buying, selling, labouring, but they would have no substance.

We weren't what my father would call, with the nearest to a snort of disgust that gentle man ever came to, 'three day Jews' – Jews who would be seen in the synagogue on Yom Kippur and the two days of New Year but who would open their shops on a Saturday.

When father and brothers and uncles would walk to the synagogue, they didn't look like the same people. My father wasn't the thin, bespectacled, rather vague *Studienrat* who had irritated Mother by giving up his ambitions of being a headmaster. My brothers weren't the cheeky monkeys I knew they really were. Uncle Rudi, big and noisy, became heavily solemn and though his fingers would often stray towards his cigarette case, they never actually arrived there. I suppose I must have looked different to them.

Even perfectly familiar, everyday objects took on a new significance. They became *Mukze*. I don't think there is one word in English that means the same thing. Untouchable, set apart, unnecessary – all of those and something else, too: matches, scissors, writing materials, money (especially money), garden tools, any form of transport except legs, the coal shovel, electric switches. If the postman brought letters, Bertha would sort them into business and private: business letters were set aside, private ones she would open for us, pulling a vicious hairpin out of her brown braids to slit along the envelope.

After the synagogue, Uncle Rudi and Aunt Lotte, with their frightful boys Oskar and Leo, would come visiting, or we would go to them, or to other friends, for coffee and cakes, *Strüdel*, perhaps, lavishly spiced with cinnamon, or *Nusstorte*, topped with fluffy whipped cream, and all served on the best china, laid out on the finest cloth.

'Lili,' sighed Aunt Lotte every time, squirming herself more comfortably into her corsets (and she thought we never noticed!), 'wherever did you get such a hand for pastry – in heaven?'

I remember so well the evenings of chatting and stories and singing. Reluctant to surrender our second souls, we'd hold on to every last, precious minute of the Sabbath.

Perhaps we did think we were special. Was that very wrong? I don't know.

So when were the signs there to read? Long before, I seem to remember, the *Machtergreifung*, the seizing of power in 1933, we might, if we had been looking, have been given a glimpse of the future. Perhaps not. The future was so overwhelming, so beyond belief or comprehension. If we had seen, even then, we might have failed to have protected ourselves in time, because we could never have realized the magnitude of the coming horror.

If I had been asked to make a list of the great calamities that had befallen mankind, I'd have put in it – along with the Fall of Man, The Destruction of the Temple and The Thirty Years War – The Treaty of Versailles. It was a recurring topic at school and its iniquities were constantly underlined. If the subject was economics, the terms of the treaty would be blamed for the inflationary years of the early '20s. If the subject was geography, we would be reminded of Germany's old, imperial frontiers.

If we were in the middle of a science lesson, we'd be told about the coal and iron deposits of the Ruhr that had been annexed by the French. And biology lessons – well, what an opportunity to remember the people of German blood who now suffered under a foreign yoke. And so on . . . no chance was ever wasted.

And lying under it all, sometimes spoken out loud, but always there, secretly, was the feeling that it was all the fault of the Jews. The Jewish bankers had let us down, they'd sold out to the Bolsheviks, they'd stabbed us in the back in 1918. Blame the Jews for it all . . .

One Easter there was a late fall of snow. My brother, Max, only seven years old, was spreadeagled against a fence by a gang of boys and attacked with snowballs. And as they pelted, they chanted a playground rhyme:

'*Jude Itzig, Nase spitzig. Kinder eckig, Arschloch dreckig.*'
  'Jew Ikey, nose spikey. Children gawky, arsehole dirty.'

At last, Frau Hummel, whose turn it was to sweep the pavement outside her apartment clear of snow, went after the thugs with the broom and chased them away.

'Such a shame, such a nice little boy,' said Frau Hummel, delivering Max to my mother, 'and some of those snowballs had stones in them, too.' She squeezed Max against the great pillow of her bosom until he squirmed. 'But don't you worry, I know their names and I'll soon let their parents know what little brutes they're bringing up.'

'Please, don't do that,' begged Mother. 'Don't think I'm not grateful, Frau Hummel, but I don't want trouble to come looking for me and my children.'

'They said I killed Jesus,' sobbed Max as Mother blotted the blood and snot from his nose, 'but I didn't, *Mutti*, I didn't. I've never killed anyone. How could I?'

'Never you mind what they say,' answered Mother, giving him a hug, 'they're only common, silly boys. You just ignore them.'

Above Max's dark head, I saw that Mother's face was white and bleak.

After that, Willi was told he must always wait for his little brother after school and never, *never* leave him to go home alone. No fishing trips, no bicycle rides, until Max had been seen safely to the door. Willi scowled, but obeyed. No one was likely to tangle with a big lad like him.

The propaganda posters began to cover windows, walls and hoardings. German respect for tidiness and other people's property became submerged beneath masses of painted swastikas that appeared by night on school and on factory walls, on the doors of the synagogue. In the morning, people on their way to work would shake their heads and cluck '*Schrecklich, schrecklich,*' but no one ever *did* anything about it.

In Austria, I read, a few town mayors, braver than the rest, ordered known Nazis to scrub the offensive slogans off, but next day they were always back again.

And soon, people stopped shaking their heads but said, 'Well, maybe they are a bit rough, these Nazis, but they have the right ideas. Germany for the Germans and guaranteed employment for every family man. How can you quarrel with that?'

Four elections in one year. The torchlight and the music. The marching and the singing. Oskar beaten up for not saluting the swastika banners. Leo beaten up for saluting and so defiling them – *sauJuden* were not entitled to salute the flag. Rumours, rumours. So-and-so was in *Schutzhaft*, protective custody. No, hadn't you heard – he'd gone to America? No, you're both wrong, so-and-so's home again – without a tooth left in his head.

In the synagogue, there were endless debates about how and why to vote. Where three Jews are gathered together, they say, you get four opinions. Some said that anti-Semitism was a divine plan to make the Jews return to the faith of their fathers, that God would solve the Jewish question Himself. (Since when had we become a *question?*) Others said that the recent outburst of violence might be a good thing, in the end. Foreign governments would see and refuse to ally themselves with Hitler's riff-raff, who would, in consequence, be forced to become less anti-Semitic.

'It stands to reason. What else can they do, if they want to be friends with the Americans?'

Round and round the arguments went, yapping at each other's heels, like dogs in the park. The Central Union of German Citizens of the Jewish Faith and the League of Jewish Veterans both declared allegiance to Germany and said they wanted to solve the problems of anti-Semitism within a German context by proving themselves good German citizens. The Zionists believed that Jews could only live peacefully within their own state in a secular organisation.

The Veterans wore their medals proudly. The Zionists publicly destroyed theirs.

Outside the synagogue stood an ardent young man wearing a placard around his neck, stating 'Next year in Jerusalem. Vote List B'. *Next year in Jerusalem* – the age-old hope of Passover, read from the illuminated text of the Haggadah at the Seder before the dish of bitter herbs, the air rich with the smell of eggs, wine and chicken soup – was painted in black against a background of blue sky, date palms and a white, hill-top city.

Gentle, doddering Herr Kugelmann, who always had sweets in his pockets for children, suddenly screeched, 'All right. Go to Jerusalem. *Geh schon.* You're just making it worse for us who are Germans, with all your shouting about Zion and your silly nonsense. It's Jews like you who create anti-Semitism.'

He lifted up his stick and would have struck the young man across the shoulders if Uncle Rudi had not caught his arm.

'Now, Herr Kugelmann,' he said quietly, 'since when is it wrong for a young man to have an opinion? You didn't have opinions when you were twenty? And isn't it bad for your heart to be so angry? Be good to yourself.'

My father, and many other moderates, were inclined to vote for the Catholic Centre Party. 'They're not extremist,' said Father, 'and there are many good men amongst them.'

'Vote however you wish, vote for the Pope himself, if you must,' answered Mother, with that nipped, clipped voice she always used when she thought no one was paying any attention to her, 'it makes no difference. Nothing you do will make any difference now.'

On the morning of 31 January, 1933, the day after Adolf Hitler had been elected Reichskanzler, Arni the postman came in and raised his right arm high. 'Heil Hitler,' he snapped, then he looked carefully from side to side before whispering, 'that's how high we are in the shit!'

School was a tiny reflection of the state – the world seen through the wrong end of a telescope.

Those who had taken part in campaigns or marches during the elections demanded that their marks should be made up for any time they had missed in 'service'. A great lout of a boy in HitlerJugend uniform marched up to Herr *Studienrat* Havel's desk and slapped his history essay down in front of the teacher.

'That's not good enough,' he blustered.

'My feelings exactly,' Herr Havel answered calmly.

'Then make it better.'

'I'm afraid it's quite beyond my powers to make that nonsense any better. It's completely beyond redemption.'

'Don't be clever with me,' the boy snarled. Watched by us all, aghast at his impudence, he snatched Herr Havel's own pen up off the desk and altered the marks.

Herr Havel was a marked man. Two weeks later, he retired on grounds of poor health.

By the time we went back to school after the Easter holidays, half the boys were in HitlerJugend or Jungvolk uniform and a good proportion of the girls wore the heavy, long skirt, clumpy shoes and dark neck scarf of the *Bund deutscher Mädchen*, the German Girls' League. The bolder boys would snigger and nudge each other as they swapped naughty versions of the initials BdM – *Bund deutscher Milchkühe*, the German Milkcows' League, or *Bund deutscher Matratzen*, the German Mattresses' League, or, naughtier still, *Bedarfsartikel deutscher Männer*, Commodities for German Men. But the girls were all very solemn and, if they knew they were being mocked, they paid no attention as they marched off, singing, on a weekend's hike or camp.

Little boys in the playground stopped playing Cowboys and Indians. The game was still the same, but now it was called Aryans and Jews. Willi came home more than once with an unexplained black eye or split lip, but when Mother questioned him about it, he just shrugged. Sensible Willi. Why make Mother's life more difficult than it had to be? Besides, Willi could always give as good as he got.

Herr Havel's replacement, a little bird of a man called Kreuder, taught history as though the Hohenzollerns had never left but had just popped out for a quick game of dominoes. He wore SA uniform every day. It made him look, as he sat behind his desk, like a drab little nesting sparrow. Herr Willrich, who taught science, also turned up in uniform. The little boys whispered that he shone his glittering boots with polish made out of the cut-open worms from the dissecting lab!

Had we but known (oh God, had we but known so many things, then and later) thousands of decent people, in every walk of life, were being whittled away in the weeks following the *Machtergreifung*, to be replaced by Nazi party comrades: civil servants, lawyers, doctors, all the influential men of the community; And teachers – most of all, teachers. The battle for the minds of Germany's children was over so quickly.

Shortly after Herr Havel's sudden retirement, the headmaster also announced that he was forced to take retirement for health reasons. It was said that he and Herr Havel suffered from the same disease – decency! For three or four mornings, he had been heckled in assembly by great, hulking boys in uniform.

Stamp, stamp, stamp had gone a pair of bright, black boots.

'Whoever is making that noise, please see me after assembly,' the headmaster had snapped.

Stamp, stamp, stamp – a row of feet, echoing off the bare boards, the sound of anarchy.

'Stop that noise at once.'

Stamp, stamp, stamp – young voices raised to chant to the beat of their feet.

'*Deutsch – land er – wach – e! Ju – da ver – reck!*
  Germany awake! Perish Judah!'

'Stop it! D'you hear? Stop it!'

'*Deutsch – land er – wach – e! Ju – da ver – reck!*'

★

236

It was suggested that he was no longer fit enough to maintain discipline and ought, for the good of the school, to retire. The next day, he was gone.

Father came home that night looking grey with fatigue. For the first time, I realised how much weight he had lost in the past few months. His spectacles were misted with rain and when he took them off to clean them with a big, white handkerchief, I saw that his eyes were puffy and tired, no longer pin-bright.

Mother was frying fish for supper, but her busy hands stilled as she saw his expression.

'Not you, too?' she gasped.

'Not yet. We have President von Hindenburg's promise that the veterans will have immunity.'

'The promise of a man of eighty-four? You're relying on that? That he should live to be a hundred and twenty!'

'What else do we have?' Father stood in the middle of the kitchen. He hadn't removed his scarf or his overcoat. He hadn't replaced his hat with the *yarmulke* he normally wore in the house. He hadn't even acknowledged his children, clustered around the table trying to finish homework before supper. 'Lili, they martyred him. He was a good man and they drove him out. And all the rest of the staff stood by and watched it happen. I, too. Not one of us lifted a finger – not one. There's no respect any more – not for learning, not for age, nor for decency. The Goths and the Vandals are within the gate. They despoil while we sleep . . .'

I don't think Mother had a clue what her husband was talking about, but she left the fish to burn. '*Na schon, setzt doch,*' she soothed. 'Sit down, let me take your coat. You're so cold.'

'I met Ernst Havel today, you know. He was sitting in the park, in the rain. He told me a joke. Can you imagine? Ernst Havel telling a joke! What is the shortest recordable unit of time? Can you guess, little Maxi?'

Max, who loved riddles, knew that this joke was not a joke. He shook his head and stared back at Father with wide, scared eyes.

'It's easy,' Father said and began to laugh. 'The shortest recordable unit of time is the time it takes a teacher to change his political allegiance! Isn't that a good one?'

He laughed and laughed.

And now Herr Willrich was headmaster. Pictures of the Führer appeared in every classroom and a huge, coloured one hung above the podium in the assembly hall. Classes began and ended with teachers and pupils standing and chanting 'Heil Hitler'. Even Father Paul, who gave the Catholics religious instruction and always began and ended his lessons by making the sign of the cross, was only allowed to continue as long as his first and last action was to give the so-called German greeting.

In big letters, at the top of every blackboard, the exhortation was hung:

DEUTSCH SEI DEIN GRUSS.
LET THY GREETING BE GERMAN.

We Jews were exempt from giving and receiving the salute, of course. We were denied the 'privilege' of greeting our German comrades in the accepted manner, because we were *untermenschen*, less than human. We all had to stand at the back in assembly, sticking out like a dozen sore thumbs, or sit in the back row in class. Willi was a little short-sighted and his new position meant he couldn't read the blackboard.

Subtly and then not so subtly, subjects began to

change: handicrafts included building model aircraft; mathematical problems about filling baths and digging holes were altered to include the theory of artillery trajectories or budget deficits accrued by allowing hereditarily diseased families to multiply; boxing was introduced to the boys, along with throwing dummy grenades; sport became an examination subject for the school-leaving certificate. The games teacher was appointed deputy headmaster.

But it was in the science lessons that Herr Willrich really came into his own.

'Pappi,' asked Max one evening, 'what does *Entartung* mean?'

'Who teaches you these words?' Father asked sharply.

'I didn't know it was a bad word, Pappi. We were doing fruit flies in science this afternoon and Herr Willrich said –'

'That's easy,' Willi interrupted, 'it means racial degeneration. Its what will happen when Oskar marries Krista. Krista's pure, Aryan blood will be contaminated by marrying into a degenerate, diseased, parrot-nosed family like ours.'

'That I should hear such words at my own table!' gasped Mother.

'If that is a joke, Willi,' Father said, with that slow, sad glance of his that always made me feel guilty, even when I hadn't done anything, 'it's in very poor taste. If it's not a joke – may God forgive you.'

Willi leaped to his feet, upsetting his water glass and sending his chair toppling backwards. 'I don't want to be a Jew any longer,' he cried and suddenly he wasn't big, tough Willi, but a little boy crying in the dark. 'I don't see why I have to be, if I don't want to.'

Mother got up to follow him as he ran from the room, but Father motioned her back to her seat.

'Leave him, Lili,' Father said softly. 'He doesn't need you. He doesn't need me, either.'

Soon, we were all learning about genes and chromosomes. The breeding habits of fruit flies led on through tulips and cattle to men. We learned to classify racial types as Slav, Nordic, Mongoloid, etc. We spent jolly afternoons measuring each other's skulls and writing notes on our findings. I learned that Jews, no matter how fair, can always be detected by giveaway signs like the position of their earlobes and the shape of their nostrils.

'Funny, you don't look like a Jew,' said my friend Irmgard on the way home. 'You look more like – well, like one of us.'

'Well, take it from me, I am,' I flared. 'Does that make me a freak? So what're you going to do about it? Write me up in your notes? Stop walking home with me?'

'Don't be silly . . .'

'Well, good – maybe I don't want to walk home with you any more, either.'

And I flounced off, fuelled by outrage. Irmgard had been going to come home for tea with me, so of course I had to tell Mother why she didn't come. The table was set and the house smelled of all the good things Mother had been baking, of *Kugelhopf* and *Sandtorte*. I thought Mother would share my indignation, but for once, she surprised me.

'Don't be too hard on her, Judith. She's only a child.'

'She's the same age as me. Am I a child?'

'It's hard for her. It's hard for all of them. They hear these lies all the time, from people they are supposed to respect, from teachers and pastors. How are children to sort out what is true and what is a calumny? Even your own brother, even Willi half believes what he hears.

He sees all the other boys in uniform, all singing and marching in step. He would give his right arm to join them.'

'But Irmgard was my friend.'

'Then don't throw her away. Good friends are hard to come by these days. Some day soon – God forbid – you might need every friend you can get.'

Next morning, Irmgard was waiting for me on the corner where she always stood. I marched past, pretending not to notice her as I rummaged in my school case for a pen or something. But in the evening, I waited for her.

Very shortly after that, during a history lesson, we were all told that it might be interesting to spend an hour writing out our family trees, going as far back as we were able.

'The people are the nation,' declared Herr Kreuder. 'We are what our ancestors have made us, so we should honour them.'

We had to write out the full names and occupations of our parents, grandparents and as many great-grandparents as we could manage and add their town or country of origin. The names glared out at me from the white page, as cruelly as though they had been written in my own blood: Rachel Klein, Emmanuel Rosenheim – Bookseller, Rifka Mendel from Lithuania, Chaim Weitz – Rabbi. They rose from the grave to curse me as I wrote.

I raised my head and surreptitiously watched my classmates write. The tinkle of nibs in inkwells, the scratching of those nibs across rough paper, the sniffs and sighs and shuffles, the wooden clatter as a ruler was knocked off the desk by a moving arm – all these noises had been the same for as long as I could remember. But today was different. Today we were busy building a wall of paper that would divide the class forever. I looked at the bent heads, some blond, several darker than my own, but still Aryan – *Aryan* – from generation to generation, privileged and untouchable.

I remembered Rachel, my mother's mother – the rustle of black silk, her gnarled hands folded over the head of her stick, as yellow as the old ivory. I remembered Great-uncle Leo, with the voice of an angel at prayer and pockets stuffed full of treats for naughty children. I remembered Grandfather Weitz, who always looked surprised whenever he saw us, as though he'd just come back from visiting God and hadn't quite adjusted to the everyday world again.

I *will* not be ashamed of them, I vowed silently, I *will* not allow their memory to be defiled by scum like Kreuder.

When we had all finished, our teacher collected the damning documents. Most, he pinned to the wall. Mine and Bruno Sachs's, he slipped into the drawer of his desk. Then he locked the drawer and smiled across the classroom.

One by one, the Jewish children slipped away from school and no one asked or cared where they had gone. The new *numerus clausus* restricted the numbers of Jewish children in mixed-race schools to a token five per cent. It also froze the female (whether Aryan or Jewish) share of university places to ten per cent and reduced the proportion of girls in the equivalent of grammar school from thirty-five per cent to thirty per cent. Of the ten thousand girls who passed the *Abitur*, the university qualifying examination, only fifteen hundred were accepted. The future was closing in on me. My horizons were narrowing to the size of a pinpoint. To be a Jew in school was bad. To be a girl was bad. To be a Jewish girl – well . . . !

But once again, the children of war veterans were

exempt from expulsion. As long as Hindenburg lived, he threw the protection of his name and reputation around those who had worn *feldgrau* in defence of their country. Before long, my two brothers and I were the only Jewish children left in school.

The only good thing to come out of all this – and that depends on how you look at it – was that Father was much in demand for extra coaching. There was no Jewish school nearby, so those families that could afford it paid for private instruction for their children. Teachers were appallingly paid, little more than a skilled factory worker, and the extra tuition fees were very welcome. Those that couldn't afford the tuition, sent their children to relatives in the cities where they might go to Jewish schools, such as the *Gymnasium* in Siegmundshof in Berlin. For the rest, those without money or city relatives, every day became a holiday. But even holidays pall eventually, especially when you are forbidden to go into swimming pools, parks, cinemas or cafés.

All over town, all over Germany, the notices were going up.

JUDEN HIER UNERWÜNSCHT

The sounds coming from the *Sommerbad* were like a magnet to Max. The laughter and screams floated over the wall, hollow with that booming echo peculiar to swimming pools. He could hear the splashes. He could smell the whiff of chemicals, clean and medicinal, that made the river seem unappetising by contrast. Now and again, some braver soul would appear above the wall, poised on the highest diving board like a flightless bird. There'd be a twang and a splash. Applause or laughter would tell us how the dive had gone.

Max stood outside the booth, fingering the ten pfennig piece that would give him entry to heaven.

'Can't you read?' growled the *Bademeister*, jerking his head towards the notice above his seat.

JUDEN HIER UNERWÜNSCHT

Max scuffed his little brown feet in their sandals in the dust. He bent down to peer at something terribly small and interesting there, something that only he could see. Anything to pretend that he'd never intended – never really wanted – to go swimming at all.

'Never mind, Maxi,' I said, 'let's paddle in the river instead. There's practically no one there. We can have it all to ourselves.'

We splashed and made mud pies and built twig dams all afternoon, so successfully that I almost convinced myself that Max had forgotten all about the Sommerbad. But it wasn't really the same. Max's heart wasn't in it. And on the wind, faint and sweet, tempting as the bells of fairyland to a child, came the sound of laughter from the pool.

The pool was quieter by the time we made for home. No shrieks and splashes sounded over the wall. The Bademeister leaned out from his booth as we went by.

'*Na mensch, Knabe, geh' doch schon 'rein*,' he called gruffly. 'Go on in. I didn't put the stupid notice there, anyway.'

I saw him hesitate – there was still a whole hour before closing time – take out his ten pfennig piece, look at it, then, 'No, thank you,' Max said sweetly, 'I have to go home now.'

When did the anxiety turn to fear? I can't say.

It wasn't during the first boycott of Jewish shops. That was frightening for a while, but soon over. We knew we simply had to ride it out and then – surely then – things would be back to normal again.

244

It was broadcast that the boycott would begin on Saturday, April 1st at 10 am and would continue until all Jewish business life had been eradicated.

'I don't believe it,' sniffed Aunt Lotte. 'That's cutting off their noses to spite their faces.'

That the first day was the Sabbath, we thought, was a blessing. Orthodox shop owners would have closed their businesses anyway and non-orthodox Jews would probably quickly have their shutters up. In the event, the excitement whipped up by the announcements sparked off the boycott almost immediately in some places.

Mother had sent me to buy some clothespegs, but the shutters had been pulled down at Papiermeister's hardware store and daubed with dripping, yellow letters: JUDE. Two SA men in uniform lounged, one each side of the door, fingers hooked in their belts, turning away customers.

'Don't shop there, love,' advised one, grinning amiably as he took in my light brown hair and blue eyes. 'They're Jews. Shop in a German store.'

Should I have marched past him, spitting with disgust at his feet? But I was only seventeen. I hovered, wanting to go in, wanting to go home. My insides were hollow, tight as a drum, and I felt sick. I looked further down the street. There were SA men outside the Frankl's newspaper shop and I guessed they'd be round the corner, too, at the Sachs's shoe shop. I hoped that Bruno, who'd always been the biggest boy in the class, ready to take on all comers, hadn't done anything silly.

While I hesitated, Frau Papiermeister came out of the shop. She looked up at one of the men with a bewildered face that seemed to have aged in a night. Her chin was quivering and she put her hand up to her mouth to still it, but the fingers fluttered on.

'But, please, what have we done to you?' she pleaded.

He didn't look at her. He folded his arms, so that his clumsy fingers partly hid the red armband with the black swastika on the white field, and stared straight over her grey head. The other storm trooper stared impassively in the opposite direction.

While they were looking away, Frau Hummel slipped unseen behind them. Awkwardly, she took Frau Papiermeister's hand.

'*Es tut mir so leid, es tut mir so leid.* I'm so very sorry,' she said and then burst into tears. 'Your friends have nothing to do with this. I'm so ashamed! I don't know what to say!'

They stood in the doorway, one in and one out, comforting each other, crying together.

Uncle Rudi and Aunt Lotte came as usual on the Sabbath, but there wasn't the normal gossip and laughter over the coffee and cakes. Uncle Rudi's furniture factory had also been staked out by the SA, but they hadn't prevented customers coming in.

'Oh no,' raged Uncle Rudi, 'I had plenty of customers – too many. They held a sale – a sale of their very own. That fat fiend, Neumann, stuck posters on the gates: SONDERANGEBOT – special bargains. Then he invited all his SA cronies in and flogged off my stock to them at half price. The cheek of the man! He said he was there to protect me! What's more, he even said he was bringing in extra business, so why shouldn't I pay him a fat commission on top of it all? May he rot in hell!'

No, it wasn't then that we became afraid. Anxious, yes, and alarmed and angry, but not yet afraid.

Were we afraid when the books were burned?

This was not Berlin, or any other great university town. The books did not arrive by the pantechnicon-load. To offset the cost of the banners and the brass bands, some of the weightier sets of volumes, those too heavy to carry, had been sold to a pulping mill. In private cars, in wheelbarrows, on waggons, the spoil of public and private libraries was brought to an intellectual *auto-da-fé*.

The Domplatz had been strewn with sand and a great platform of logs had been built in front of the Cathedral, whose priceless Christian library had been plundered of any works suspected of Judaism, to swell the funeral pyre. The air reeked of the petrol used to soak the logs. The crowd was thinner than I'd expected. It was nearly midnight, drizzling and chilly for May. Anyone with any sense would be in bed. In his raincoat, wrapped in the scarf Mother had wound round him to keep out the damp, Father stood to watch the desecration of knowledge.

The echo of martial music bounced around the high houses in the narrow streets. We could hear the sound for a long time, sometimes seeming to come from here, sometimes from there. Then, out of the black mouth of the Rathaus arcade, the procession erupted, in a burst of sound and light that deafened the ears and dazzled the sight. The scarlet banners flapped and snapped voraciously.

I felt Father shiver, felt the knobbly pressure of his slight, bony body against me. I wasn't certain which of us was supporting the other. I'd have taken his hand, but I'd never done it before. It would have seemed like impertinence to do it then.

The *Bürgermeister*, the mayor, walked onto the platform set up on the very steps of the Cathedral. As the parade circled the fire, every other man flung his torch onto the petrol-soaked logs. With a whoof and a roar, with an explosion of blue flames and fumes like the uttermost pit, the fire blazed up, hell on earth, repeated and repeated across the land.

The column of smoke rose higher, paler, than the black smoke, reeking of tar and burning rag, that guttered from the torches held by a detachment of HitlerJugend at attention. Their eager faces were hawklike in the flickering light, avid, ardent.

'For the betrayal of our men in the trenches, I consign to the flames the writings of Erich Maria Remarque.'

The voice of the Bürgermeister, distorted by the megaphone, boomed out across the square. There was a ragged cheer as a copy of *All Quiet on the Western Front* was hurled into the waiting flames.

'For telling the truth,' whispered Father.

'For destroying the nobility of the soul, I consign to the flames the writings of Sigmund Freud.'

Another book. Another cheer.

'For activities contrary to the German spirit, I consign to the flames the writings of Emile Zola.'

'That was for writing *J'accuse* in defence of Dreyfus, ' Father hissed in my ear.

'Because Dreyfus was a Jew? All those years ago and in another country?'

'For promulgating the evils of Bolshevism,' declaimed the Bürgermeister, 'I consign to the flames the writings of Karl Marx.'

Einstein, Mann, Preuss, the author of the Weimar Constitution; Hemingway, Lenin, Jack London, (how did *The Call of the Wild* offend even the Nazis' extreme sensitivity?) Proust, Scott Fitzgerald and Heine. What had they in common? It was enough that they were seen as impure. Dr Goebbels called them the debris of the past cleaned up by the young that night in Berlin.

The Bürgermeister grew hoarse. The cheers grew fainter. As a crowd-pleasing spectacle, the burning quickly became boring and most people crept off home to bed. Yet the storm-troopers hurled books onto the fire with undiminished zeal – unnamed books now, boring, stodgy, makeweight books. Yet even if only one of them had added a worthwhile thought to the sum of human knowledge, it should have been enough to have bought mercy for them all.

I can smell it still – the reek of the bonfire, not blazing bright as one might have expected, but smouldering dully, suffocated by the pile of damp paper and musty leather, stifled by the weight of centuries of learning and human striving.

In the enthusiasm of the moment, it was easier to toss a book whole into the flames. If the pages had been torn from the bindings, they would have burned better but, thrown bodily onto the pyre, they smouldered sulkily in the drizzle. Dozens of pages, escaping from their confinement, rose in the column of hot air and fluttered, only just singed, above our heads, like a covey of game birds.

'They'll set the whole town on fire if they don't watch it,' someone behind me muttered, 'silly sods.'

And in the morning, charred pages, white on black, negative palimpsests, stirred in the wind and blew about our feet.

Father took my hand as we walked away and I tried to remember when he'd last done that. '"*Dort, wo man Bücher verbrennt,*"' he whispered, quoting Heine, '"*verbrennt man am Ende auch Menschen.*"' '"Wherever books are burned, men also, in the end, are burned."'

No, we didn't suddenly wake up one morning and feel afraid. It crept up on us, like a fatal disease. Each symptom, considered on its own, might possibly be innocuous, might even be curable. But taken together . . .

Now when the storm-troopers marched, Jewish shopkeepers shut their shops, boycott or no boycott. Broken windows were the least one could expect. The worst . . . well, it hadn't happened in our town yet, but such rumours . . .

And singing as they marched, always singing.

'*Wenns Judenblut vom Messer spritzt, geht uns nochmal so gut.*'

'When Jew-blood squirts from the knife, things go well for us again.'

We'd listen and shiver in the dark.

We couldn't afford a telephone, but Uncle Rudi had one. One day, Aunt Lotte complained that it wasn't working properly.

'There's such a funny echo,' she said, 'as though one were speaking down a mine shaft. And it makes such annoying clicks even when it's not in use. I've complained already to the telephone company and they sent an engineer, but it hasn't improved.'

Uncle Rudi went pale . . .

The next time I saw his telephone, it wore a very fetching padded tea cosy. The drapers were doing a roaring trade. You couldn't buy a tea cosy anywhere in town for love nor money.

Hess broadcast that 'Every Party and *Volk* comrade impelled by honest concern for the movement and the nation shall have access to the Führer or me without the risk of being taken to task'. The invitation to denounce the enemy loosed an avalanche of suspicion: who was a friend and who was not? Were new friends all they seemed to be? Were old friends still friends? Could anyone at all be trusted?

People developed a habit of looking carefully over each shoulder before making the most innocent remarks. It was called the '*deutsche Blick*', the German look. Denunciations were rife, even within families. It was amazing how much rancour had been harboured in secret and now came spewing out. We Germans have a word for it – '*Schadenfreude*' – the malicious pleasure to be taken in someone else's troubles. The word doesn't exist in English. Maybe the nearest is 'spite', but it's not the same. That frightful element, gloating is missing. It's like counting your blessings on one hand while counting your neighbour's misfortunes on the other.

If you didn't give enough to *Winterhilfe*, winter poor relief – denunciation would follow. If you made a remark that could be interpreted, however loosely, as anti-Nazi – denunciation. If a farmer tried to sell a pig for more than the controlled price – denunciation. For fare-dodging – denunciation. For bosses passing over underlings for promotion – denunciation.

HitlerJugend members, cocky adolescents, reported their fathers for adverse comments over the morning paper. Lusty husbands might report their wives for refusing to have more children – reluctance to increase the German race was a quick and easy route to divorce. An innocent child might say to a teacher, 'My Daddy doesn't think all Jews are beasts,' and lose his father to protective custody camp for a short, sharp lesson.

The rumours were so terrible, reason told us that they couldn't possibly be true. What exactly was a *Konzentrationslager*? Was it for political prisoners, for hardened criminals . . . for people like us? How could people simply disappear and never be heard of again? How could a letter simply be returned to sender marked *Adressat Unbekannt* – Addressee Unknown? Someone must know.

How could these things happen in a civilised, European country in the twentieth century?

And a zealous brother might accuse his sister of giving herself to a Jew . . .

★

Poor Krista. Poor, poor Oskar.

They had been so sweet, so innocent. They walked together through the park beyond the town walls, around the old moat that was now almost hidden in shrubbery, dense enough to shield young lovers from prying eyes. They strolled hand in hand by the river, or watched the barges being lofted up by lock onto the overhead canal that crossed the river. And they did nothing more than snatch a kiss in the moonlight. Krista was a good girl, a sweet girl. And first love had sobered Oskar. He stopped gadding around and began to pay attention to the details of his father's business.

Oskar brought her to one of the *Shabbat* tea parties. Krista must have been braver than she looked to face Oskar's family on their own ground. Only a girl very much in love could have sat opposite Aunt Lotte in her sable stole that she had never, to my knowledge, removed in someone's else's house.

Krista was dressed smartly, but modestly, in a neat, light summer costume. She had hard-working hands (I saw Mother glance at them with approval) and wore sensible shoes. She spoke up well for herself in a clear voice, but was never pert. And oh, the touching way she'd look across at Oskar whenever she was asked a question about their future, as though to say, 'Is it all right? May I answer this?'

She was so pretty, with her soft, golden-brown hair, her wide, blue eyes, her little, pointed face. And good, too. No wonder Oskar was mad about her.

The meeting was a success on the surface, but the undercurrents swirled around the couple. I hope they were too much in love to notice.

'A nice girl,' commented Uncle Rudi afterwards.

'A nice girl, but to marry out?' exclaimed Mother.

'Such a thing!' moaned Aunt Lotte. 'You should put your foot down, Rudi.'

'He's a grown man.'

'A boy, a boy only and snared by a pretty face.' Aunt Lotte pressed on, sensing that her husband was weakening. She held out appealing hands, heavy with rings, to my father. 'Speak to your brother. Tell him no one in this family has ever married out before and his son isn't going to be the first. Go on. Tell him.'

'We've all heard of anti-Semitism,' remarked Father mildly, 'but this is the first time I've met anti-Gentilism. You should listen to yourselves.'

'What do you have against her?' I asked nervously, knowing the answer already.

'She's a *shicksa*, what else?'

'And a brother in the *Jungvolk*, too. No good will come of it,' Mother asserted.

'If he marries that girl, he's no son of mine,' declared Aunt Lotte, passionately. 'I swear his family will sit *Shiva* for him and never mention his name again.'

It was Aunt Lotte's Lithuanian blood speaking. German Jews had been integrated for generations, but under Russian rule Jews had been forced in self-defence to close ranks. Excluded from Gentile society, they had become exclusive themselves.

In the end, Krista's brother solved the problem for both families.

I looked into Krista's face, smeared with snot and blood. I looked at the scarred, stubbled head, the half-naked body, scarcely more developed than that of a girl of twelve. I looked at the obscenity of that pretty hair dangling from a placard and knew that my family had been right. No good had come of it.

Oh, Krista, I would have helped you if I could. I would have welcomed you into our family as a sister. I would have loved you. But the time for loving had passed. It was 1933.

Her mother hawked up a gobbet of viscous, evil spit and let it fly, to land right between my breasts. It stuck to the middle button of my blouse.

'Out of my way, Jew-bitch,' she snarled.

That night, Oskar, desperate to see for himself that Krista wasn't badly hurt, was caught in the street by a gang of storm-troopers. When they had knocked him to the ground, they jumped on him, every single one, with both, booted feet.

Ten hours later, his body was found, huddled at the dark entrance to Judengasse. Oskar had died of internal bleeding from his ruptured organs.

Now, we were afraid.

President von Hindenburg's protection failed us in the end, though not by his own volition. He was an old man, failing daily, and, by contrast, the power of the *Reichskanzler* grew day by day, like a monstrous tumour. When a politician's first act is to extract emergency powers (never relinquished) to prohibit free speech, to deny the right of privacy by letter or telephone, to give to the state the rights of house search and property confiscation, democracy is finished. When his second act is to induce the elected house of government to pass an 'Enabling Act', so that he may institute further legislation without seeking prior approval, that elected assembly may as well pack its bags and go home.

So what's so important about the promise to protect a few Jewish veterans?

Jews were only back room boys in the War, they said. They all had a nice, cushy billet well behind the lines, counting socks or packing parcels. They don't deserve protection. While our boys were fighting, the rear-echelon Jews were lapping up Bolshevik propaganda. We stabbed them in the back. So they said.

Men like my father, who fought in the front-line trenches for four years and had the Iron Cross to prove it, finally lost the frail protection against tyranny that had shielded them until then.

My father came home at the usual time, hung up his coat and hat, put on his yarmulke, went to wash and ready himself for supper. He didn't say a word, but then he was a quiet man.

When the meal was over, he said, 'I'll mend that loose hinge tomorrow – the one you've been telling me about for so long.'

'A miracle!' Mother cast her eyes up to heaven. 'It's only been loose for two years!'

Willi was very pale. He'd only picked at his plate before pushing it away. '*Bitte, darf ich aufstehen?*' he asked. 'Please, may I leave?'

'Are you sick?' asked Mother. 'That you're not eating is not like you.'

'I'm a bit tired.'

'Go on, son,' said Father, gently. 'Go and rest. Take Max with you.'

'But I'm not tired,' Max protested.

'Go with your brother. Go.' Father waited until we heard the sound of the boys closing their shared bedroom door. 'Willi can have a good rest tomorrow. He won't be going back to school.'

Mother opened her mouth to protest, then closed it again firmly. Of course she knew what was coming. Hadn't she been preparing for it for months?

'You might say I've been lucky,' Father went on. 'I've had a job longer than most. And there's the private coaching still needed – we won't starve.' He took off his spectacles and massaged the red pressure marks on each side of his nose with finger and thumb. One of the legs had been bound up with brown gummed paper. I hadn't noticed that at breakfast. 'Think of all the jobs I promised I'd do for you when I had the time. Well, I've plenty of time now.'

Mother got up and stood behind Father's chair, laying both hands tenderly on his shoulders. He leaned back in his chair so that his head rested against her. I slipped out and no one saw me go. They didn't need me.

In the corridor, I could hear the sound of sobbing. I wasn't really ever welcome in the boys' bedroom, but I couldn't ignore the muffled sound of my brother's grief.

Willi's face was buried in his pillow. He was doing his best to stifle the noise he was making, but long, shuddering breaths racked his whole body. Max sat cross-legged on his half of the big bed, staring, his eyes wide and inky-black.

'Willi, what is it?' I asked. 'Have you a pain in your head? Does your tummy hurt?' He shook his head, but didn't lift his face from the pillow. 'Such a row. Is it because you have to leave school? All your friends have gone already – Heinie, Norbert . . . Anyway, I didn't think you liked it all that much. You're always moaning about having to go . . .' I perched on the end of the bed and stroked his hair. Only the day before he'd have shaken his head free of my hand. 'How can I help you if you won't talk to me, Willi?'

'It's Pappi . . .' I thought I heard him say. 'It's Pappi . . .'

'Pappi? What about him?'

'They slapped his face . . . they hurt him, Judith.'

Oh, dear God . . . My hand stilled on Willi's head.

Willi's voice was still broken by grief, distorted by his tears. He was dragging in air with great gulps, but I could understand what he said. I wished I couldn't.

'It was in the English lesson this afternoon. Pappi was teaching . . . he was telling us about Shakespeare and his plays . . . he was telling us the story of The Merchant of Venice, d'you know it?'

'Yes, I know it.'

'We'd got to the bit where Shylock has a speech about how Jews are just like everyone else . . . 'If you prick us, do we not bleed? If you tickle us, do we not laugh?', d'you know it? I didn't understand it all, none of us did, but Pappi reads so beautifully, it's nice just to listen. Then Herr Willrich came in. He does sometimes. He listens to Pappi's lessons. But this time he had all the big boys with him and they were all in uniform.'

How like him, I thought, lacking the courage to come on his own, needing to be bolstered by a show of power. 'Go on,' I prompted softly.

'Pappi didn't pay any attention to him. He just looked up and looked back at the book again. Then Pappi said that when that play was written, a long time ago, every-one was prejudiced against Jews, but that today most countries had come to their senses. He said that in all the rest of the play, Shylock was a caricature, but that if we understood that one, sympathetic speech, we'd understand more than most adults in Germany today. Then . . . then Herr Willrich hit him.'

My soothing hand tensed in Willi's hair.

'Oh, Judith . . . he called Pappi a filthy liar. He said he corrupted the young, that he wasn't fit to have decent German children in his charge, then he hit him again, and again . . . Pappi's glasses fell off and his head flopped backwards and forwards . . . Oh, Judith, I didn't help him. I should have got up and punched that beast and kicked him and slapped him,' Willi savagely punched his pillow over and over again, 'for hurting my father. But I was frightened, Judith, I was frightened of the big boys and I didn't help Pappi.'

'Shhh, shhh,' I soothed. 'You did the right thing. It would have been much worse if you'd joined in. Pappi's all right. He isn't hurt. But Willi, promise . . . don't tell Mutti, you must promise.'

Father never did mend that hinge or put up the kitchen shelf as he'd promised. Our parents must have sat up all night talking. By the time I came down in the morning, having lain awake all night but pretending, for Mother's sake, to have had a good night, a lot of decisions had been made. Our little town, the place where we children had been born, was to be left without a backward look. My parents were going to Berlin with the two boys.

'Things will be better there,' said Mother. 'Here there are so few of us, but in Berlin there's a big Jewish community. They can't treat us all so badly. We'll find somewhere to rent where there's a good synagogue nearby. The boys will be able to go to school – a Jewish school, Adass-Isröel *Gymnasium*, maybe – with no one to torment them. Your father will maybe find a teaching position in one of these schools – they must be crying out for a man of his calibre . . .'

Suddenly I felt older than my mother. I listened to her bright description of the life she'd mapped out during the night, all the little consolations of a good synagogue, a friendly community.

Don't you know, Mutti, I thought, don't you understand? It doesn't matter how far or how fast you run. There's nowhere to go.

'And if not, there will be so many people in Berlin, wealthy people, who'll be glad to engage a tutor like your father. Not like here, little shopkeepers who only want their children to be able to write out a bill of sale and add up an account. In Berlin, there are still cultured people. And . . .'

'And me?' I asked.

'Darling, your father thinks it's for the best. You're the brains of the family. Willi will never win the Nobel

258

Prize, not if he goes to school until he's a hundred years old, and Max is still so young, but you've passed your *Abitur* . . .'

'Much good that has done. What university will take a Jewess these days?'

'An English one.'

With a generous loan from Uncle Rudi, kisses and wails and more kisses from Aunt Lotte, a kick on the shins from Leo to Max, promises to write, to phone, to visit, my family went to Berlin.

Aunt Lotte couldn't understand why I wasn't going too. 'A girl,' she said, over and over again, in the few days before departure, 'a girl needs all that education? She needs to go to university to learn how to nurse her children?'

'Her father says that she must have as much of a chance as the boys,' answered Mother.

'If my father had said that about me, my mother would have thought he'd gone mad.'

'If he'd said it about you, Lotte,' Mother snapped with unusual asperity, 'he *would* have been mad.'

In fact, I think I owe it to Aunt Lotte that Mother let me go. If it hadn't been for her carping, Mother would probably have resisted Father, tooth and nail, and never let me out of her sight. All father's patient reasoning didn't have the effect of a few of Aunt Lotte's back-handed compliments.

'In my day, it didn't matter if a girl was pretty or not,' she remarked, lifting a lock of my hair and letting it fall with a sigh. 'A good matchmaker could make any girl sound like a worthwhile catch. Nowadays . . . well, perhaps education is a useful thing. A teacher is a teacher, after all.'

I didn't even know that I was going to be a teacher – I didn't know what I wanted to be! But minds had been made up in the long nights spent talking quietly so as not to wake the children (as though the children were sleeping anyway!). Everyone else seemed to know what I was going to be, but me!

'Are you telling me Judith is plain?' queried Mother, with a devastating lift of her eyebrow.

'Of course not – and it doesn't matter anyway. A girl who is going to be a teacher like her father doesn't need to look like Greta Garbo. And she doesn't need to have a light hand for *strüdl* pastry, either, which is a good thing, thank God.'

CLARE

The Fascist

Well, why not? Why not anything, if it comes to it?

I did it because it was something to do. Because Olivia had looked so insufferably priggish, sitting there in the car with her best 'Made in the British Empire' expression on. I did it because it was a way to get back at them all.

I just did it. That's all.

Both my sisters fell into the arms (or into the beds – it's pretty much the same thing) of the first men who smiled at them. They were nothing, my sisters, but the usual collection of female attributes, arranged in the same order, if not having the same obvious impact. Just teeth, eyes, breasts – damn them. No character, no mind, no independence. I think that's what angered me most. They only existed through the eyes of someone else. I am looked at – therefore I am. They weren't real people at all.

What shall we do with poor Clare? Bundle her off to Germany out of the way. Send her to be finished, as though she were a thread dangling from a loose button. She might come home transformed – if we're lucky. And if she doesn't, if she's still the same great hulk of a Valkyrie who went away, we'll have had a couple of years without bothering about her. Anyway, some man might be persuaded to take her off our hands, for a fee. For goodness sake, take her away, Olivia, and do something – anything – with her.

Some people said I had been spoiled, and maybe I

had, but not in the way they meant. Love has nothing to do with how many toys and pretty clothes you're given. Love isn't an indulgence. No child could be ruined by being loved – it's neglect that spoils.

I did it because it made people look at me and talk about me – even if only to say I was bad – or mad. Why shouldn't I like being noticed? Most of the time, people noticed me about as much as a cabbage in the kitchen garden. If they spoke to me at all, it was 'Cut off and find something useful to do.' or 'Haven't you got anything better to do on a day like this?'

Run along. Run along. Whatever you do, don't bother us. Whatever you do.

Nickie was nice, though. Nickie tried to talk to me. He treated me like a person. It wasn't his fault. What? Well, everything. Afterwards. You know.

I stood up in the car and saluted. Oh, it was glorious. The wind from the accelerating car streaming through my hair, the stunned expressions on the faces of those darling *stürmers*, the way they snapped to attention in response. Olivia hauled at my skirt with one hand and hissed, 'Sit down, you ass!' It was like being Boadicea and Brünnhilde rolled into one. Glorious.

Olivia didn't speak to me for the rest of that day. She pretended to be disgusted with me, but I know she wasn't really. A little bit embarrassed, maybe, but who cares? So we both went along with our noses in the air, too proud to be the first to speak.

The roads in Germany were much better than those in Belgium, of course. We crossed the fertile uplands of the Eifel. They were patchworked with small fields, pale after the harvest, unexpectedly brightened here and there by crops of pumpkins or tomatoes growing on dunghills and by the scarlet spill of geraniums, brilliant beneath every windowsill. Children stared as we roared through the villages – clean, attractive children who smiled and waved at the *Ausländerinnen*. The littlest boys wore gingham aprons, nicely cross-stitched, over their shirts and shorts.

Then suddenly we were over the lip of the plateau and running down the twisting slopes of the Mosel valley, past vineyards where the grapes still hung heavy, distilling the autumn sunshine into luscious, syrupy sweetness. We left the sun behind us on the high ground and turned down to meet the evening, blue and smoky in the valley, with the river a silver thread appliqued along the bottom.

Olivia had the anxious look of the traveller who is beginning to think about somewhere to stay. 'I think we might stop in the town ahead,' she said, the first words she'd addressed to me since crossing the border. 'I don't much care to travel in the dark.'

As we drove in, we passed under a banner stretched across the road.

MEIN LIEBES DEUTSCHES VOLK, VERGISS NICHT DEINE VERWANDTEN IM SAARLAND.

'I wonder what that means,' Olivia said.

'I wonder,' I replied. But soon I'd be able to translate it – and to understand why that banner was hanging there at all.

We stopped at the sort of simple, comfortable *Gasthaus* one could find anywhere in Germany – dark rooms panelled in wood, enticing smells coming from the kitchen, ferociously clean, with the softest and whitest beds. The welcome and the view from the window restored our good humour and we were friends again before going down to a dinner of *Himmel und Erde*, which turned out to be a combination of black pudding, apples, onions and mashed potatoes that completely defeated Olivia's appetite!

After dinner we wandered, arms linked, around the little town and finished in a brightly lit café, attracted by the singing that filtered into the street. The café was full, but the owner found us a little table far from the door and explained that the singing club was enjoying its Saturday night relaxation.

They were middle-aged people, neatly dressed in holiday clothes, with red faces and red hands, who took turns to sing the verses and joined together in the choruses – sweet, sentimental songs that were strange to me then, but were to become so familiar. Their voices blended in heart-rending simplicity. I can still sing some of the songs that I heard that night.

> *Gold und Silber lieb ich sehr, kann's auch gut gebrauchen,*
> *Sei's des Mondes Silberschein, sei's das Gold der Sterne.*

Oh dear, my voice is awfully rusty now, but it was pretty once.

That night, before climbing into the big double bed with Olivia, I leaned out of the window. Under a sky snapping with early frost, the little square of half-timbered houses was still. No one else seemed awake. The moonlight silvered pointed gables, rooftops at crazy angles, tall platforms where white storks, unlikely household pets, would build their nests in the spring.

'Oh Olivia,' I breathed, 'it's like a fairy tale.'

'Some fairy tale,' Olivia groaned in the morning. 'Sleeping Beauty never had to contend with a row like that.'

She pulled the *Bettkissen* over her ears, but I jumped out to see who the early singers might be.

Out of the darkness of a narrow street, came a column of thirty-two young men, marching in double file, sun-

266

burned and wind-reddened – such fine specimens – in freshly-pressed grey uniforms and heavy knee boots. They looked neither to the right nor the left. Their feet hit the cobbles in unison. Their voices were like the crack of a whip, bouncing back off buildings that seemed to lean forward to watch them pass.

> 'Deutschland, Du wirst leuchtend stehen, mögen wir
>   auch untergehen,
> Vorwärts! Vorwärts! Schmettern die Heldenfanfaren,
> Vorwärts! Vorwärts!'

They looked so purposeful. They knew where they were going. They knew what living was for. And when they were gone, the square looked so empty.

'Labour corps,' explained our landlady, as she set our breakfast table with coffee, dark rye bread and slices of cheese. 'Fine strapping fellows. They rebuilt the castle on the hill with their own hands and now it's a hostel for young people from the cities – fresh air and good food – just what they need. Could you fancy a boiled egg, now?'

'Does no one in this country think of anything else but eating?' commented Olivia sourly as we drove out of town, under a bridge painted with the slogan:

HITLER – ARBEIT UND BROT.

Munich – München – hasn't changed, they tell me. Well, of course, I know that it has. I know that the war left it a ruin. In the Frauenkirche, imprinted in a slab on the floor, was the cloven hoof, the footprint of the devil. The builder of the church had wagered with Satan that he could build a church without any windows. Plant your foot into the devil's imprint, it was said, and from that spot you wouldn't be able to see a single window. When the war was over, the legend became

267

terrible truth. All around, as far as you could see, were blackened, windowless ruins.

They have done their best, I suppose, to rebuild the past, but to say it hasn't changed, well, that's nonsense. I could still find my way around, I dare say . . . No, of course I wouldn't go back. I couldn't. Anne wouldn't let me.

What a lot of young English girls there were in Munich in those years. It was a city as gracious, in its way, as Paris or Florence, but, given the preferential exchange rate, much, much cheaper. I need never have wanted for company. On any afternoon, one might see an impoverished *Gräfin* or two striding across the Englischer Garten followed by a gaggle of gawky English virgins, on their way to a lesson in artistic appreciation at the Alte Pinakothek. Giggling, gossiping, these girls were guarded with the ferocity of eunuchs by their aristocratic landladies.

Baroness de Rutz's town house was in Königinstrasse with a fine view of the park. Her family had a *Schloss* near Bamberg that had been the subject of a painting by Dürer, but she hadn't the money to keep it up any more. Before deciding to take in English girls – all of them from old family friends or friends of friends – she'd been reduced to accepting food parcels from some distressed gentlefolk's association and to doing *schaffende Arbeit*, handicrafts that she sold to more affluent friends. She had a beastly little French bulldog with bad breath. The girls all swore that she was having an affair with the vet, to save on bills.

'*Meine letzte Liebe*,' we'd sigh if we saw him on his way to the Baroness's rooms, 'my last love!'

She 'kept' six English girls, aged between sixteen and nineteen. Four of them – Caroline, Fiona, Marjorie and Barbara – were quite indistinguishable from each other, schoolroom misses on the verge of becoming debutantes. (I suppose I was too, but I didn't feel the same). They were very childish and very, very boring. When the older ones went home, half-way through my stay, and were replaced by two younger ones, I scarcely noticed the difference.

I did have a special chum. Her name was Jane – Jane Coxhill. We had a lot in common, Jane and I, including staying behind when the other girls went home for holidays. Jane was an orphan being brought up by a dashingly fashionable aunt and I – well, I might as well have been one too. There didn't seem much point in making the tedious journey back to England. Who was waiting for me? We were both rather naughty, too, always ducking lessons, but nobody seemed to mind.

The baroness, of course, never came down to breakfast. We wouldn't see her until well into the morning. After breakfast, Fräulein Kapell would come and we'd spend the first part of the morning all together, learning German conversation and studying German literature. Some writers were frowned on by Fräulein Kapell for ideological reasons – no Heine, no Thomas Mann – but since we hadn't heard of them anyway, it didn't seem to matter too much.

Fräulein Kapell taught us German history as well as literature. She taught it with a passion that made long-ago, dull deeds catch alight. But when she talked about the Treaty of Versailles, she was nearly consumed with emotion.

'A crime . . . a crime . . .' she'd lament. 'Chancellor Scheidemann cried out, "May the hand wither that signs this treaty". The French call themselves a civilised nation, yet they have ground our faces into the dirt and not one other government has had the courage to call 'Stop'. Of course, we were betrayed into losing the war – betrayed by communists and Jews.'

On the wall of the schoolroom, which had been the

Baroness's boudoir in more prosperous days, hung a coloured triple portrait, incongruous on faded flowered walls, of Frederick II, Bismarck and Adolf Hitler. They glared down on our lessons with hypnotic intensity.

'There is the man,' Fräulein Kapell told us, pointing towards Herr Hitler in his Brownshirt uniform, 'there is the man who holds out to the German people his model of the future. Only he can give us back what is rightfully ours.'

After formal lessons, we'd separate into piano, singing, painting, and flower arranging classes. If one was missed in a class, the assumption was that one was attending another. Easy. Jane and I could have been very wicked indeed and no one would have noticed. Of course, we weren't – wicked, I mean. I think we were protected, not so much by our purity, but by sublime ignorance. We didn't know how to go off the rails. We didn't know how one went about being debauched. So we spent a lot of time cycling around, just enjoying the extraordinary feeling of being free.

No one asked us if we'd spent our time usefully. There was no nanny hiding behind the door to reproach us or to warn us that the devil always found work for idle hands. If we wanted to spend half a morning at the Café Heck, sipping coffee and eating *Prinzregententorte*, watching the world go by, who was to stop us? It was a healthy sort of neglect – not the nursery kind that fenced one in with strictures, but the adult kind that said 'I'm perfectly satisfied that you know how to behave, now off you go and live'.

As long as we attended the morning German lessons and could give an amusing and instructive account (in German) of our day over dinner, everyone was satisfied. There was only one firm rule laid down by the baroness. If we saw anything in the streets like a scrimmage or if windows were being broken, we were to cross quickly to the other side and turn off the street at the first opportunity. Staying to watch was strictly forbidden.

We used to queue at the Opera House every Sunday for our three or four evenings' tickets. We'd see Wagner and Mozart, more Wagner, some Beethoven, but no Hindemith or Stravinsky, no Mendelssohn or Mahler – no Jews or degenerates, even then.

Like penniless students with rucksacks, we'd chug about by train, but although Jane was awfully keen on architecture – and there's an awful lot of architecture in Bavaria to be keen on – I always thought if you'd seen one baroque *Kirche*, you'd seen the lot. All that gold and those swags and swirls and little bare, pink babies. Wieskirche gave me galloping indigestion. Only one thing amused me and that was the little table in Schloss Linderhof that sank through the floor and returned fully laden, because King Ludwig II was rather keen on his privacy. It was called the *Tischlein-deck'-dich* – 'little-table-cover-yourself' – from the Grimm story of the tailor's three sons.

'You're the most frightful philistine, Clare,' Jane commented, rather in a huff because I'd dragged her out of some gloomy *Kloster* or other.

'I can't help it. No one bothered to educate me. Now, if I'd had your advantages . . . Come on. I could kill for a cup of coffee.'

On fine days during the holidays, even in the winter, Jane and I would cycle or catch a bus into the countryside. We'd walk in the mountains, puffing up and up until we were above the tree-line, sometimes making a long traverse across the bare, white faces of several mountains, sometimes making for a peak with views that could still your chatter and silence the hammering of your heart. Far below, the grass would be too green to believe, a bolt of velvet flung out for our inspection.

Often we'd meet groups of other young people, healthy and neat, who sang as they walked, and perhaps join them for part of the way. We'd always be made welcome.

We'd stop at a farm for fresh milk or for a bowl of *Bauernsuppe* and dark bread, coming down from the mountains in the evening, leaving the peaks still blazing behind us. My accent, so carefully instilled by Fräulein Kapell, became corrupted by the strangled vowels of the Bavarian peasant. We grew slim and brown. My hair was bleached straw-white by the sun and I began to wear it longer.

On wet days, we'd explore Munich and, somehow or other, I'd contrive that we end up at the Osteria Bavaria in Schellingstrasse around lunchtime. If it was a Friday, perhaps he'd be there.

He always came late, after most people had finished lunching, perhaps around two o'clock, sometimes even three. He'd bring his dog and his driver and a few friends – dear Putzi, perhaps, such a gentleman, or Hess, or Ernst Röhm. I was always a bit scared of Röhm with his scarred face, an overblown bladder. An atmosphere hung around him, almost visible, of violence, barely curbed. One always felt that he was on the verge of careering out of control. Future events showed how right my instinct had been. What a shock it must have been to Herr Hitler to find that his closest friend – the only man who ever used the familiar form '*du*' in public – was a pervert and a traitor.

But I wasn't afraid of the Führer. Not then, not ever. Oh, no.

You'd think a man like that would have surrounded himself with pomp and circumstance, but he was always so unassuming. The great displays, the trumpets, the uniforms, he saved for when it mattered. At times like that he was representing his country, he was Germany and the adulation was for the Reich. In private, he dressed modestly, even, perhaps, rather drably, in a plain brown suit covered with a mackintosh. He and his friends would slip into the Osteria Bavaria without any fanfare and eat a simple meal, the same as everyone, except that Hitler had become a vegetarian after the suicide of his niece, Geli. (Oh, I had cried when the news of that lovely young woman's death was made public – for her and for the Führer's loss.)

But he wasn't ordinary. You could see that he was a great man, all the same. He just couldn't hide it under a mackintosh. It shone from him. He had the look, you see. Those eyes – he could hold a whole table spellbound with them. He would push his plate aside and talk and talk. Everyone forgot about eating – I know I did. No one could have uttered a word. Hitler would bring his great mind to bear, like a battery of guns, on the problems of Germany and her place in Europe. He knew so much about politics and international banking and Marxism and the Jewish stranglehold on business. What could we do but sit in his shadow and listen, silent and amazed?

Jane was mortified. 'I thought we were friends,' she complained once. 'Friends are supposed to enjoy each other's company. You only want me here to keep you amused until your precious Führer arrives and then I might as well vanish.'

'You're just jealous.'

'Jealous? Of him? You're potty.'

Jane flounced out and we didn't make up for three days. She could be very childish.

I'm going too fast. He never spoke to me then. That came later. He noticed me, of course. Oh, yes. I used to see him looking at me sometimes, across the room, and the keenness of his eyes was almost more than I could bear. After I'd been noticed a few times, he sent an aide across to ask my name.

'You're English?' the man said with surprise.

'Of course,' I answered, with the same unconscious pride that Olivia had displayed when she'd been stopped at the frontier.

On the way out that afternoon, the Führer gave me a little bow as he passed, a brisk nod and a click of the heels. I inclined my head in reply, trying to be dignified. After that, he always nodded to me on the way to his table and on the way out again.

Munich was the most exciting place in the world.

Germany was a sewer, a political cesspit, governed by ancient men and bolstered by Jewish corruption. As my grasp of German improved and I began to be able to read the newspapers with intelligence, I read of five million breadwinners unemployed, of farmers unable to meet mortgage payments, of food queues in the major cities, of the government paralysed under an eighty-four-year-old president sinking into senility, uncertain from day to day as to which time-server was leading which faction.

Like the inhabitants of a scattered ant heap, politicians were scurrying here and there, leaderless, biting each other in their rage and fear. The business of governing the country was reduced to *Kuhhandel* – cattle trading – with each party (ten in the election of 1930 were big enough to poll over a million votes each) bargaining for special consideration for the interest group which had elected it and to hell with national interests.

Brüning for Chancellor, ruling by presidential decree, the 'Hunger Chancellor', clamping down on wages as well as prices, half-heartedly hankering after a return of the monarchy. Gröner for Defence, diabetic, victim of smears, rumoured Marxist and pacifist, father of a son born five months after his parents' marriage and so nick-named Nurmi, after the Finnish Olympic runner! No, now Gröner was down, but Brüning was struggling on, buoyed up by President von Hindenburg. Honest Brüning, making an enemy of the one man who could save him by suggesting that bankrupt East Prussian estates – including Hindenburg's own – should be broken up and given to landless peasants. Nothing could keep him in power now.

A lesser man followed him, von Papen, overthrown by a neat exploitation of parliamentary procedure. Brandishing the signed order for the dissolution of the Reichstag, he was ignored by Parliamentary president Goering, until a vote of no confidence in the government had been passed, when the dissolution order was automatically invalid, being counter-signed by a man just voted out of office. Brilliant!

Behind von Papen was a lesser man still – von Schleicher, arch-schemer. 'I stayed in power only fifty-seven days,' he once said, 'and on each and every one of them I was betrayed fifty-seven times.' He who had plotted and counter-plotted for years was not cunning enough to save himself. The reward for his deviousness, following the Night of the Long Knives, was a bullet for himself and one for his wife, too.

We were watching the death throes of the Weimar Republic.

Watching, too, waiting for his moment, was the one man who could pull Germany out of this political morass. The strong man, the leader.

Four elections in one year – in March, April, July and November; endless wireless broadcasts of encouraging speeches blaring out; every fence, every tree plastered with posters urging voters to declare for any one of umpteen parties; *Arbeiter Erwacht*, Worker Awake – a stalwart labourer, naked to the waist, towers over a cringing mob of usurers and parasites – Vote List 2, National Socialist; for the first time in Germany, the cinema is used to reach electors who think they can hide from their democratic responsibility in the darkness of picture houses; everyone must have an opinion, everyone must listen; gramophone records of speeches and martial music crash forth from loudspeakers on trucks; sound recordists lying flat on their stomachs on the road relay the sound of marching feet across the land.

To be honest, perhaps people became a little tired of the exhortations and shouting. For me, a foreigner, it was fascinating and exciting. Besides, the fate of the Führer hung in the balance with every vote that was cast. I pored over the lists of results, trying to analyse each swing of opinion, frustrated that I could not vote myself. The majority of Germans seemed to lack my stamina. In April, one million fewer votes were cast than in March.

Herr Hitler was not often at his favourite table in the Osteria Bavaria that summer. In a three-Mercedes column, he roared around the countryside, riding in the first next to driver Julius Schreck, with his valet Schaub and bodyguard Brückner in the back. In the second car travelled a troop of the *Stürm Abteilung* and behind them Putzi Hanfstängl with assorted photographers and guests. In Nuremberg, a bomb was hurled at them from the rooftops. In Bamberg, the caravan was raked by bullets.

He chartered an aeroplane from Lufthansa, a Ju 57, and flew around the country, making speeches to larger and larger adoring crowds. Frankfurt, Darmstadt, Ludwigshafen, into the communist strongholds of Kiel and Hamburg. On one day, 27 July, he spoke to sixty thousand people in Brandenburg, to as many in Potsdam and, in the evening, to 120,000 in the Grünewald Stadium in Berlin, with his voice being relayed to another 100,000 outside.

His stamina was phenomenal. He left his staff gasping. In between these energetic tours, he liked to recoup his energy at his house, Wachenfeld, in the Obersalzberg, drawing new strength from the sparkling air as blotting paper absorbs ink.

By 1st August 1932, the National Socialists were the largest party in the Reichstag, with 203 seats out of 608. Although they were to stagger back a pace or two in November, they were firmly set on the path towards the establishment of a *Dritte* Reich.

The table in the Osteria Bavaria remained empty. No one else was allowed to sit there.

Great joy. In the middle of all this political excitement, David, who was down for the summer, came out to see me. I arrived at the station much too early and, when his train finally pulled in, I stood on tiptoe, scanning the strange faces, terrified that after all this time, I might not recognise my brother.

It was impossible to miss him. He stood, blond and beautiful, head and shoulders above the stocky, dark Bavarians. For a moment, just for a moment, when I first saw him stepping down from the train, looking so very English with his good tweeds and his mackintosh over his arm, I felt an awful rush of homesickness. I realised for the first time that I'd been away for nearly two years.

What home? What was there to be sick for? Only David and, now he was here with me, everything was perfect.

'Goodness, how you've changed,' he exclaimed, holding me by the shoulders at arm's length. 'You're you – and yet, you're not you. What's different?'

'You are,' I laughed. 'And since I'm like you, then I have changed too.'

We laughed again and kissed and it was wonderful to see him after so long. I couldn't stop looking, couldn't stop touching.

It was astounding. In the two years we'd been separated, we'd grown more alike in appearance than at any time in our lives. I'd lost the pudginess that had blurred my features, leaving them a nearly perfect copy of David's. His hair had become as blond as mine and his skin as brown.

'I've been fruit picking all summer,' he explained, 'trying to make some money. Trying to make ends meet, you know. Students are notoriously poor.'

'I'm sure you only have to ask Pa,' I answered. 'He's very generous to me.' Only with money, I thought, but didn't say it.

'I don't want . . . it's not right . . . why should I be able to swan through my degree course without a care in the world, when other chaps – brighter than I am – don't know if they're going to be able to stay long enough to take their exams?'

'Why shouldn't you? Why should it make their lives any easier if you don't have any money?'

'That's not the point.'

'If that isn't, I don't know what is.'

'Practical Clare – always capable of making sixpence go further than a shilling.'

'One of us has to be practical – and it certainly isn't you. There have always been rich people and poor people and there always will. Your swanning around, picking a few strawberries in the sunshine and fooling yourself that you're working, isn't going to alter anything.'

'It's the principle of the thing.'

'Oh, principles . . .'

The girls at Baroness de Rutz's were wild about David – too handsome for words, where have you been hiding him, you selfish beast! I suspect the baroness herself developed a very soft spot for him. Throughout his visit, her corrugated curls were never out of place, set in concrete, and her lips were always perfectly outlined, without the usual smear on her front teeth that made me want to giggle. She seemed to have regressed suddenly into girlhood. She twinkled around on little, plump feet, wearing shoes too small for her, whenever David was expected for tea and she laughed a lot, a high, girlish laugh that curdled my blood.

Fräulein Kapell nearly fell down the steps the first time David met her at the door and held it open for her.

She managed to croak out, 'Heil Hitler'.

David deflected her straight arm salute by holding out his hand to shake hers and murmuring in his very English way, 'How do you do? I've heard so much about you, Fräulein.'

I could see now much deeper changes in David than the physical signs I'd spotted on the first day. His painful shyness had matured into something very attractive. There was a stillness at the core of him, a bright, central fire that burned with a steady flame. He listened, really listened, when people talked to him, with his head turned slightly to one side, taking advantage of his improved hearing in one ear. He didn't talk very much. He didn't smile very often either, but when he did – for me, at least – the sun came out.

David discovered changes in me, too. To be honest, I don't think he liked all of them.

I wanted to show David everything. Every day we'd meet and I'd link arms with him and we'd walk and walk. Jane tried to tag along for the first day or two, but I soon let her know that there was no room for her.

No one was as happy, no one as beautiful as we were

that summer. People turned in the street to stare as we went by. They looked at us and something made them feel unexpectedly happy. Our joy in each other shone out and embraced the streets and everybody in them.

There was so much that was old to show him, the relics of Bavaria's royal past, but so much that was new and exciting, too. The latest technology could be seen in the Deutsches Museum, a glorification of glass and steel and power. At the bottom of the Englischer Garten, plans were in progress for the replacement of a glass pavilion burned down the year before with a monumental museum of German art, the Haus der Deutschen Kunst. The Königsplatz had become a parade square and was neatly paved with granite slabs. Oh, you should have seen the parades – the flags, the torches, the marching, the music . . . Munich was being tranformed with energy and farsightedness into the capital city of the Movement.

We climbed up to the eyes of the statue of Bavaria to enjoy the views of the city, looking across the Theresienwiese and far beyond, to the mountains that are white, winter and summer.

We sat under the shade of chestnut trees in the Biergarten by the Chinese Tower, drinking *Russe*, a mixture of beer and lemonade introduced by the Munich Red Guards in 1918, and eating *Weisswurst* with pretzels and mustard.

'Better eat up,' I laughed. 'The sausages aren't supposed to hear the chimes of midday.' I licked my fingers, then leaned over and pinched a piece from David's plate.

I took David on one of the twice-daily tours of the Braune Haus on Briennerstrasse, the headquarters of the Movement, remodelled from a palace at a cost of 750,000 marks. It was easily recognisable by the giant scarlet banner emblazoned with a swastika that billowed from the rooftop, and by the smart young sentries on duty outside. The old ballrooms and reception rooms had been turned into offices for propaganda, member-ship and culture. They were elegantly decorated with cream-coloured walls, teak panelling and brass fittings. From the lobby, a great staircase rose to the Party Senate Chamber, with its double row of forty-two red leather chairs set in a semi-circle facing the Führer's seat. Herr Hitler had a suite in the corner of the building, but of course we weren't allowed in there.

I pointed out the Führer's nine room apartment in one of the best districts in the city, the Prinzregenten-strasse, to David. I marched him past the Feldherren-halle, with its monument to those brave men who fell in the putsch of 1923.

I shot out my arm in salute to their memory.

'I say,' murmured David, 'isn't that a bit excessive?'

'Everyone does it.'

'No, they don't. Those people didn't.'

'Oh, but they're just Jews.'

David stopped. I'd gone on a few paces before I realised he wasn't with me and had to come back again.

'Clare,' he said urgently, 'we've got to talk.'

'We talk all the time.'

'No, I mean . . . we chat, we don't ever talk.'

'There's no time for that. That's the difference between you and me, David. I live life, you just talk about it.'

The next day was Friday and I organised our activities around lunch at the Osteria Bavaria in the hope that Herr Hitler would be there. David and I were drinking coffee when the man I'd been waiting for came in, so I ordered more coffee and waited a bit longer.

All through his meal, I was conscious of Hitler's

eyes on David and me. When he'd finished, Herr Deutelmoser, the restaurant proprietor, came over to our table.

'The Führer asks you both to join him at his table.'

Two extra chairs were organised and we were invited to sit. Röhm was there, picking his teeth, and Goering, and Streicher, who betrayed his vulgar origins with every uncouth movement of his knife and fork.

'I don't think I have ever seen,' said Hitler, looking at us, but speaking over us, 'more perfect Aryan specimens. They are living proof of the superiority of pure breeding.' David kicked my ankle and I knew he wanted a translation, but I didn't dare interrupt. 'The Aryan is the Prometheus of mankind, from whose shining brow the divine spark of genius has sprung at all times. But the Aryan gave up the purity of his blood and, therefore, lost his sojourn in the paradise which he had made for himself.' Goering nodded. David cleared his throat and shifted in his chair. The Führer looked at us one by one as he spoke, holding us all spellbound with his fascinating eyes. I'd always thought that they were blue. Now I saw that the blue was tinged with grey. 'Blood mixture and the resultant drop in the racial level is the sole cause of the dying out of old cultures. All who are not of good race in this world are chaff.'

I looked at David's face. It was closed, tight and shuttered, with that stubborn look I remembered so well – his oyster face, Anne used to call it. When he wore that expression, nothing and no one could make the slightest impact on him.

'Is your father a Lord?' the Führer asked suddenly.

Startled at being directly spoken to at last, I stammered, 'Oh no. No, he's not a lord.'

'A Sir, then?'

'Well, not exactly, not quite.'

'The English are known to be modest. It's quite clear

that you are of good family. We must have another talk some time.'

The Führer got to his feet and left, followed by his party. David and I were dismissed.

David grabbed my hand and practically hauled me out of the Osteria. 'My God, I can't breathe. What was he saying? No, don't tell me, I don't need to know. It was like being shut in a cage with a pack of jackals.'

'That's very rude. You don't seem to realise what an honour that was. Almost no-one gets invited to the Führer's own table.'

'Lucky everyone else, then. I'd swap places any time.'

'You don't understand . . .'

'I'm afraid that I do.'

We were walking under the pillared arcades of the Hofgarten. Light then shade, light then shade, but David's face was all in shadow. David took me by the wrist and drew me off the busy street into the quiet of the garden.

'Clare, come home,' he begged.

My almost automatic response was one of refusal. The urgency in his face made me hesitate, but not change my mind.

'Not yet. It's not time yet.'

'You must. Can't you see what danger you're in?'

'Danger? Don't be silly. How can I be in danger?'

'I've never been so scared. I wish to God you'd been scared too. This man you worship . . . all his people . . . they're evil. You mustn't be caught up by them.'

I struggled to free my hand, but David's grip only tightened.

'You're wrong. They're . . . they're . . .' What? What were they? I couldn't find the word. I floundered, unable to share with my twin the magic of *his* presence. Didn't he know? Couldn't he sense it? '. . . they're saviours.'

283

'No, Clare, no. Look past the glamour. Look past the marching and the music and the banners. Something terrible is happening, something so wicked that we can only guess at it.' Dear David – always so sincere, but so misguided. 'One day we'll all have to choose between the darkness and the light. No one will be able to stay neutral. But you have to choose *now*. '

'You're just jealous. '

'I'm leaving tomorrow. I can book you a seat this afternoon. We can go together.'

'Such a silly fuss. I'm not ready to go home yet.'

'Clare, I beg you, come home with me – now, before it's too late.'

I turned my face away. I couldn't bear to see him like this. He was so dear to me . . . so wrong . . .

David took both my hands in his and brought them up to his chest. 'Please – for me . . .'

He was forcing me to choose – to choose my brother or my Führer. They were the most important people in my life and David wouldn't let me have both of them. Why couldn't I? I shouldn't have to choose. No one should be forced to make a decision like that. David or the Führer. It wasn't fair. David, how could you do this to me?

'No.'

He bowed his head over our clasped hands, holding me as though he'd never let me go. We stood like lovers in the cool of the garden. No, not like lovers. Lovers were never so close. We were one person but the rift that was opening between us would never heal. It was an ulcer on our love.

The following morning, David left for England. I didn't go to say goodbye. I didn't watch his train steam out of the station.

I had lost my twin.

★

Whatever David said to our parents, it seemed to have a drastic effect – certainly, far worse than I'd expected. A week later, my father was in Munich. Suddenly, there he was on the doorstep, with a face like thunder, uncharmed by the delights of the city, unimpressed by the mountains, still behaving as though all Germans were the Huns who had robbed him of his hand. By the next day my luggage was packed. The day after that, I was on my way back to England. I promised to write to the baroness and to Jane and they promised to write to me, but it all seemed too unreal to make any proper plans. I could scarcely see from the carriage window as the train pulled slowly out of the Hauptbahnhof.

It was raining when we arrived back at Mount Street. Nothing seemed to have changed. There was a new maid to open the door, but she was such a pale and puny copy of the last one that I scarcely noticed the difference. London and everyone in it looked so finicky, so prim, so . . . so *constipated*. I couldn't bear it.

'Where is Mrs Northaw, Hilda?' Pa asked the maid.

'It's madam's bridge afternoon, sir. She asked me to tell you that she'd be home in time for cocktails and she said to remind you that you're going to Mr and Mrs Dutton-Hall's for dinner.'

Pa sighed. 'Yes, Hilda. Thank you. Well,' he said, turning to me, 'since your mother isn't here to welcome you home, perhaps you'd like to lie down for a little while. You must be tired.'

No, I wasn't and I wouldn't, but it didn't seem the time to say so.

Dismissed, like a naughty child banished to the nursery, I prowled around my room all afternoon, picking things up and putting them down again. Nothing seemed familiar at all. The books and little childish ornaments that I'd collected over the years were completely unintelligible to me. The room, the objects belonged to someone who had left and had not come back again. It was a stage set, arranged according to someone's else's ideas. Nothing to do with me. I felt unbalanced, dislocated, out of all time or place.

Below, the front door banged. I could hear my mother's voice, high and clear, coming upstairs and my father's lower tones, answering. I heard my own name. I braced myself, but it was Mother's own bedroom door that I heard opening and closing.

The evening drew on. It was still light, but the sun had dropped behind the houses. Time to go down for cocktails. Well, I hadn't actually been sent to my room in disgrace. Pa hadn't thundered, 'Go to your room,' as he had after one of my childhood escapades, 'until you're ready to apologise'. All he'd suggested was that perhaps I needed a rest. I'd had one. Now I was ready to face the family.

Slowly, I peeled off everything that I was wearing and stood in front of the long looking-glass. Here was something else that had changed, but at least I recognised the girl in the reflection.

Two years older, two inches taller, two stone thinner – I had come home, but I was not the same.

From a suitcase I took out a black skirt, a black shirt and a wide, black, leather belt. I put them on and cinched the belt as tightly around my new waist as I could. I swept up my longer hair onto the top of my head and it made me look even taller. I wavered over the black gauntlet gloves – one couldn't wear them indoors, but they seemed indispensible – in the end, I compromised and shoved them through my belt. Still in front of the glass, I saluted my image with a straight right arm.

From the rising sound as I came downstairs, I guessed

that the whole family had arrived to witness my return in disgrace. I'd show them . . . I'd show them that, far from disgraced, I'd come home in triumph.

I pushed open the drawing room door and stood for a long moment in the doorway, neither in nor out. The chatter died away. It was a great entrance. Garbo couldn't have handled it better. Mother, Pa, Olivia, Anne, Nickie – even Guy – they were all there. And David.

Well, well.' Guy broke the silence, sneering and flippant. 'Enter the wicked Fairy Carabos – stage centre.'

The talk started up again, all directed at me, but the only thing I cared about was David's face, white and shocked, staring back at me.

Joining the British Union of Fascists was the most grownup thing I'd ever done – the most grownup and the most scary. There was plenty of choice at that time. I could have joined any number of groups with loosely the same aims: the Imperial Fascist League; the British Fascists (but they were just Conservatives with knobs on and were being dragged down by their alcoholic founder Rotha Lintorn Orman); the Britons' Society (frightfully middle class – what Mother would sometimes call 'rather MIF (milk in first) darling'!; the Nordics; the White Knights of Great Britain (could a girl really be a White Knight – if not, why not? – anyway, I didn't care for the hoods they wore, too American by half, or the silly ceremonies); the United Empire Fascist Party . . .

Oh, the list is a long one, longer than anyone would like to admit to, in this dull, sanctimonious, horribly *worthy* age. Where are they now, the people who filled the membership rolls of these societies? Dead? Reformed? Respectable? Embarrassed? Am I really the only one left? Or am I just the only one left who's prepared to admit to it, the only one with any guts? All those new leaves turned over – can you hear them rustling still, in a veritable forest?

I thought long and carefully about my next move. It seemed to me that there was only any point in joining a movement that had a chance of influencing society, a movement with a leader who had a future, who could attract intelligent people to his banner and keep them there them with an exciting personal style. The National Socialist Movement in Germany was proof of how a party could stand or fall by the strength of its leader. It would be nothing without the Führer. Given this, my only choice was the British Union of Fascists.

I turned up on the doorstep of 12 Lower Grosvenor Crescent as soon as it opened at 7.30 in the morning. I'd got used to early rising in Germany. There's something very degenerate about being in bed after the sun has risen.

The office looked much as one might imagine a military orderly room, not at all sinister, merely functional. There were maps on the walls, an official-looking notice board, lists, lists, and more lists. Behind a desk, freshly shaved and spruce despite the hour, was a serious young man in Blackshirt uniform. His hair was shorn right up the back of his head and what remained of it was heavily brilliantined. His long legs poked out beneath the desk and I could see that his shoes were brilliantly polished. A junior NCO, in all but title.

'I've come to join up,' I said.

Well, if I hadn't quite expected the red carpet, at least I'd imagined I'd be given some sort of welcome. I wasn't a house maid applying for a post, after all. I was shown upstairs to the offices of the women's section, where one of Lady Makgill's secretaries grilled me as though I'd come to steal the Crown jewels. She looked at my uniform with an early-morning, jaundiced expression.

'I don't think,' she began primly, 'that you're entitled to wear a uniform until your application for membership has actually been accepted.'

I could have *died*.

Why did I want to join? Because I'd read *The Greater Britain* and had been impressed by Oswald Mosley's logic. Any other reason? Because I felt that the parliamentary system was dominated by old men who had failed their country; because only a government of strength could deal with red terrorism.

Yes, I'd been doing a lot of reading since I'd come home from Munich. I'd discovered that my education had the most astounding gaps in it. I didn't know *anything*, but I'd buckled down to do something about it.

'I feel it's my duty to point out to you –' The woman turned rather red and blew her nose. '– that a number of girls have made attempts to join the movement for . . . shall we say, *social* reasons.'

'I don't understand.'

'They imagine that their social lives will be greatly improved by belonging to an association where women are heavily out-numbered by men – young men. I hope you're not suffering from that delusion.'

'At this time in the morning?'

She laughed a whinnying little laugh and began to look more human. 'Certainly, I don't think any of the good-time girls have ever been on the doorstep when the doors opened.'

'Anyway,' I blurted, desperate to improve my standing in her eyes, 'I'm a great friend of Herr Adolf Hitler.'

'Really?' She raised an eyebrow and managed to look both unimpressed and highly suspicious.

'Yes. I've lunched with him – well, nearly – and once we had tea together.'

'At Gunter's, I suppose,' she said with heavy sarcasm.

'Oh no, at the Carlton.'

'The Carlton?' she squeaked. 'Now, honestly!'

'Oh no, not that Carlton, not in London,' I blundered, 'the Carlton Tea Rooms. In Munich. He's awfully fond of cream cakes. And films. He's frightfully keen on films. He adores Marlene Dietrich. He's seen *The Blue Angel* over and over again. And we talked about Jeannette MacDonald. He says to keep an eye open for her – she'll be a star one day . . .'

My voice died away. What an awful bloomer. I was stumbling around, sinking deeper and deeper in the mire. And all because I'd tried to impress some boring little secretary.

She must have been so confused, as my conversation skipped around from parliamentary democracy through cream cakes to the cinema, that she put up no further resistance to my joing the BUF. I was allowed to sign the pledge and pay my first monthly contribution. From each according to his means . . . who said that? I promised five shillings a month. She didn't look very impressed, but I didn't dare pledge more. I wasn't even certain of being able to spare that much. Pa was so angry with me that he'd cut my allowance to the bone. I spared enough to buy, in the shop downstairs on my way out, a little badge of the fasces – the axe and bundle of sticks – which I pinned to my collar.

I walked out of the door a fully paid-up member of the British Union of Fascists and entitled at last to wear the uniform I'd been wearing for weeks.

1933. What an incredible year. I can't think of it, can't say it, even now, without a tingle of excitement.

I devoured the newspaper reports of President von Hindenburg's request to the Führer to become Chancellor on 30th January. At last. At last.

Expectant crowds had been filling the streets around the president's palace for hours. Shortly before noon, the man they had been waiting for appeared, to a roar of exultation. His guards had to clear a path for him to get into the Kaiserhof Hotel where he had permanent rooms. Everyone – the hall porters and maids, every-one – crowded around to salute and to shake his hand.

That night, there were torchlight parades through Berlin. The SA in brown, the SS in black, the veterans' organisations in grey, all marched through the Tier-garten to the Brandenburger Tor, then south along Wilhelmstrasse, past the British Embassy to the Reich-skanzlei. They surged across the invisible barrier of the Bannmeile – the central government area where political parades or demonstrations were not permitted – with bands blaring and flickering torches turning ordinary men into heroes and heroes into giants.

One giant, white haired and ponderous, stood behind a closed window of the Chancellory. President von Hindenburg raised a hand in recognition of the crowds, but no more than that.

Fifty yards further on, standing at an open window in spite of the bitter January air, silhouetted against the bright light behind him, stood the new Reichskanzler, wearing evening dress. He leaned out and saluted the crowds with the familiar outstretched right arm.

The crowd roared, as once they had in salute to their Kaiser. '*Hoch. Hoch. Hoch.*' The sound rippled and echoed right across Germany.

And I was not there. I *should* have been there.

I was not there when the Reichstag burned down. They say that the new Chancellor was dining with the Goebbels at their house. They were listening to music and chatting when a telephone call broke the news. It was a crime, a communist crime designed to strike fear into the hearts of the loyal people. Communist documents seized next day proved without doubt that the burning of the Reichstag was to be a signal for the start of bloody insurrection and civil war.

I could not be with him, but I did my bit, as people used to say during the war.

I sold the BUF newspaper, the *Blackshirt* on street corners. We did a roaring trade in the East End. I was given training in public speaking and was allowed to harangue the mobs, accompanied by one or two of the boys, the 'Biff Boys', for protection. I was cheered in Bethnal Green and stoned in Stepney.

I bought a dog to protect me, a wolfhound – Corsair – over six feet tall when he placed his front paws on my shoulders. A darling. He'd lick my face with great, slobbery kisses, but heaven help anyone who stood between him and me. He had to be put down when I had . . . you know . . . my accident. I was on a stretcher all the way back to England and no one else could do anything with him. I miss him still . . .

I kept my body fit and supple, ready for anything, by going regularly to meetings of the Women's League of Health and Beauty in Great Portland Place. One must be prepared. (Anyway, I rather fancied myself in the white satin sleeveless blouse and black satin knickers.) I attended rallies where Oswald Mosley held multitudes transfixed by his vision of the future.

The tide that had swept across Germany was gathering on the shores of England and when it rushed over us, nothing would stand in its way.

Heil Hitler! God save the King!

And this was the summer I should have been a debutante!

In April, I was one of seven attacked in Piccadilly Circus by a crowd of six thousand – six *thousand*. We were doing nothing illegal. We were going about our lawful business, offering pamphlets to passers-by. Of course, the police protected us against the mob – it was obvious where their sympathies lay. I got off lightly with a few bruises, nothing much, honourable scars. I was proud of them. But I don't mind admitting I was scared. This was London, for heaven's sake, a civilised capital city, where people have a right to express their opinions freely, without interference or molestation. Now, if it had been Moscow . . .

The result was a rash of anti-German posters that broke out all over the Jewish shops dominating the East End. The police soon put a stop to *those*.

In June, a thousand Blackshirts marched through London and I was with them. Corsair, on a short lead, stepped gracefully beside me, a hero of a hound. We started from Eaton Square and demonstrated our strength and solidarity through all the important streets of London. In black instead of in white, I brought up the rear, in the same position that my height would have placed me for the Queen Charlotte's Ball procession. Just so, I'd have swept down the staircase to the strains of 'Judas Maccabeus', with just this military precision, and curtsied to a cake! Good Lord! The English *are* mad, after all. And as we marched, so disciplined, so proud, I found the words of the 'Horst Wessel Lied' going round and round in my head, so insistently that it was difficult not to burst into song.

'Die Fahnen hoch! Die Reihen dicht geschlossen,
SA marschiert mit ruhig, festem Schritt.
Raise high the flags! Stand rank on rank together,
Storm troopers march with silent, steady tread.'

I was still humming and whistling when I let myself into the house at Mount Street late that night. The light was still on in Pa's study. I popped my head round the door to say goodnight.

Pa was just sitting, doing nothing, with an almost empty whisky decanter on the low table by his chair. His head was tipped back and he looked asleep, but I could see his eyes glittering in the light of the lamp.

'Are you all right, Pa?'

'Yes. Why shouldn't I be?'

'I just thought . . . it's late . . .'

'Oh, it's all right for my daughter to be out, gallivanting around the town with a gang of thugs, but too late for an old fellow like me to be out of bed? Is that it, eh?'

'I only meant . . .'

He leaned over and poured the last of the whisky into his glass, then gulped it down like a greedy child.

'Send me to bed, then. Go on. I count for nothing in this house any more. I can't even control my own children. One daughter has a shotgun wedding to a pansy and is talking about running a shop. Another runs off with a Bolshevik and lives in sin in a slum. My baby, my darling girl –' he started to snivel, felt in his pocket for a handkerchief, couldn't find one and gave a messy sniff '– is a Hun-lover. And my son, my only son, has thrown up his education to be a hack scribbler with a tinpot little newspaper. Dear God . . . tell me, tell me where I went wrong.'

I stood appalled, silenced by the fury of his impotence. What more did he want? He was middle-aged and his day was over. A stallion doesn't expect to rule the herd forever. He knows he has to give way to the coming generation. It was a rule of nature. Pa was only hurt because he wouldn't recognise it.

'Leave me. Leave me alone. At least let me choose when to go to bed. Leave me some pride, between you.'

His head drooped and the glass fell from his

slackening fingers. I tiptoed away. No point in trying to console him. In the mood he was in, anything I said would be wrong.

Pa had a point. His family did seem to have disintegrated. But it wasn't his fault. I don't think he could have done anything to prevent it.

Anne, admittedly, had been brought to heel and made to see how stupid she had been. Since she had come back, Nickie had done his damnedest to keep her busy and out of mischief. Richard had been born exactly nine months after she came home. Then, in October 1932, he'd been followed by Hugo. Now, if my eyes did not deceive me (and it was pretty hard to tell, as Anne's tummy had a permanent bulge these days), another little Lockyer was on the way. Bully for Nickie! That's the way to keep the little woman off the streets!

I wondered what Anne thought – really thought – about the speed with which her family had increased. She had greater need than I for the little gadget that Rose had given me on my fifteenth birthday. It still lay, crumbling and perished, in its dainty, floral-patterned tin.

On the other hand, it was a woman's clear duty to increase the Aryan race, as a response to the prolific birth rate of lesser types, the *Untermenschen*, who, given the chance, would fill the world with copies of themselves. Anne was certainly doing her best to counteract that trend. But not me. Not just yet, anyway.

Poor Anne. What a *hausfrau* she'd become. Twenty-two years old and the mother of three-and-a-bit children (four-and-a-bit, if you counted that little stick insect Chloe who still lived with her aunt and uncle). But perhaps it was arrogant of me to pity her. When had she ever wanted anything else but a comfortable, *gemütlich* family life? She was made for domesticity. Her flight with Chris had been an aberration – everyone said so. When it came to a choice between her children and her lover, the children had a head start. But oh, how boring she'd become.

And Olivia had turned shopkeeper. What a lark! Trade to trade in three generations. All that dabbling with fabrics and furniture she used to amuse herself with had turned into a productive little business. She'd been invited by friends (sorry for her, no doubt – 'Poor Olivia, married to that beastly pansy, we must do something for her') to do up a bedroom here, a study there. Bit by bit, her commissions increased, although still the cachet of having 'done' a whole house eluded her. After all, it's not what you know but who you know that counts and Olivia, by her marriage into arty circles, notoriously penniless, had rather cut herself off from the sort of people who would have been useful to her.

Guy had burned his boats. As long as he lived in London and kept his unnatural proclivities to himself, he could be accepted, even lionised by society for his savage, natural talent. He was clever, handsome, witty. His books were selling in their thousands and, after all, what people do in their own bedrooms is their own affair, as long as the door is locked. (Although the Führer classed homosexuals in the same group as the mentally ill and genetically undesirable.) But Raymond's party manners left a great deal to be desired. He'd been rather a naughty boy in a public lavatory in the Strand one night and had kept one step ahead of the law only by hopping on the next cross-Channel ferry. Silly, besotted Guy had followed him.

What a shock to Olivia's pride. I wonder if she'd even guessed what Guy had been up to. Yes, she must have done, but, between guessing that something's wrong and discovering that your husband has fled the country with another man, lie long, long nights of staring into the darkness.

Guy rented a villa in Normandy, a little back from the coast, between Deauville and Honfleur and there he and Raymond lived, ostensibly as writer and secretary, but everyone knew. That's what hurt Olivia most.

'He's awfully useful to Guy,' she said one dingy afternoon when summer had almost given up trying to make an appearance, as we were amusing ourselves by sorting through snaps and sticking them into an album. 'He does all that tedious research and keeps the papers in order and all the things that Guy's never been very good at.'

She picked up a picture of Guy and Raymond together and neatly clipped Raymond out of it. Guy was left alone, with just a disembodied hand lying on his sleeve. Without the other figure, the object of his love, Guy's smile, which had looked boyish and captivating, simply looked fatuous.

'So why keep a wife and a secretary,' she said, with bitter logic, 'when you can have both conveniently rolled into one? So much more efficient! So economical!'

Olivia picked up the discarded Raymond and chopped him into very tiny pieces.

She relieved her hurt pride by throwing all her energies into the only thing she did well – making other people's houses pleasanter places to live in.

There are all sorts of stories now about how Olivia first came to dabble in interior decoration, but I know the real one. I was there.

Anne had some garden furniture that she'd resurrected from an outhouse at Greywell. It was very simple, very sparse, quite unlike the ferny, lily-pondy Victorian furniture in the garden. It was also very rusty, so Anne was going to throw it out.

'Give it to me,' said Olivia.

'Whatever for?'

'Oh, I just have a little idea or two . . .'

Olivia rubbed it down herself, painted it white and sold it for a (very) small fortune. And that was the start.

From then on, little pieces of furniture were always on the move in and out. One never knew, sitting on a chair or putting a cup down on a table, if there might be a price label swinging off it somewhere. Nothing stood still for long.

'Chair today and gone tomorrow, eh?' as Nickie punned frightfully.

We'd have tea from ravishing porcelain – just to christen it properly – then Olivia'd rush off to wash it and take it round to some silly woman who'd pay well over the odds for something she could have found herself if only she'd taken the time and trouble.

'Don't mock. Busy women are my bread and butter,' Olivia laughed. 'The busier they are, the more they need me. Where would I be if they realised how simple it all is?'

Simple maybe, but jolly hard work. She was up before it was light, combing Caledonian Market by torchlight, picking over undesirable-looking heaps with busy fingers, never disgusted, eyes alight with the thrill of a bargain sought and a bargain found. She'd hop over to Paris every other Sunday, taking the night train to arrive at six o'clock, then dashing to the flea market to spend all day buying up carpets and tapestries. Stall-holders began to know her, to keep back interesting pieces she might like.

During the day, one would never guess that the elegant young woman, simply dressed in a Mainbocher coat and dress or a Worth afternoon frock, who could make such amusing little suggestions about one's curtains or lighting, had been up since dawn, in a shirt and slacks with her hair tied in a bandeau, rummaging through someone else's leavings. Nor did they guess that the Mainbocher, the Worth, the Paquin garments had been run up, working from magazine illustrations, by a clever little woman round the corner in Marylebone.

'It's all an illusion, you see, Clare,' Olivia would explain. 'The whole thing's just a clever trick – the mirrors, the lighting, a wave of the hands and Abracadabra – a transformation scene, just like a pantomime. The kitchen becomes the palace ballroom. The dark forest becomes nursery rhyme land. No one knows how it's done. They don't have to know, just believe. The way I look is part of the illusion. That's all.'

People began to say, 'Oh, I always go to that clever young woman, Olivia Tarver – you know – *that* Tarver. She has such witty ideas. You *must* try her.'

Clever Olivia. She had a nose, something inherited from Pa's trading ancestors, no doubt.

'Blood will out,' she'd declare. 'One of Pa's great-grandmothers must have been a rag-picker!'

Rather her than me. I felt sorry for her, really. It was obvious that she was simply trying to put Guy out of her mind. She had such passions, such enthusiasms, they had to find an outlet. Once, all her devotion had been consumed by her husband. When he failed her, she just transferred her energy to something else. Poor Olivia.

Despite Pa's disgust, his sniffs at the idea of buying and selling, it was a ladylike occupation. There were long established decorators like the New Yorker Elsie de Wolfe Mendl, who was known as the 'Chintz Queen', and Dorothy Draper. In England, the famous names were Sybil Colefax and Syrie Maugham. They were pioneers, explorers in a new dimension. Behind them, young and enthusiastic, treading on their corns, came Olivia.

She worked from an old furniture repository in Baker Street. Inside, it smelled of lacquer, turpentine and beeswax, sawdust, of acid from a huge, bubbling vat and, beneath the clean smells, the rancid, never-to-be-mistaken, street-market smell of old clothes.

After a while, Olivia needed to spend more time with clients and less rummaging around, so she hired two clever little Yids, brothers, who did much of her bargain-hunting for her, like a pair of thieving magpies. 'My Baker Street Irregulars,' she called them, quoting Sherlock Holmes.

In late 1933, Olivia put up her first shop sign over a little converted greengrocer's near the repository in Baker Street.

'D'you like it?' she asked. Her hands were clasped together like a little girl's at a pantomime when the curtain first goes up and all the lights and the music spill out into the dark.

LIVIA the sign read, in classically austere capital letters, black on a sparkling white ground.

'Not another change of name,' I groaned.

'It's more aesthetic, don't you think? More pleasing. It trips more easily off the tongue.'

'That's just an excuse. It was Guy who first started calling you Olivia.'

She shrugged, a flippant gesture, but though her face was hidden from me, she seemed to droop. The sparkle dimmed. 'One can't stand still.'

'A rose by any other name . . .'

'How frightfully hackneyed.'

Suddenly, she flung her arms around me and gave me the sort of hug I hadn't had from her in years. 'Not even you can make me cross today, Clare. You'll see – this is just the beginning.'

★

And David. Ah well, it was David who nearly broke Pa's heart.

Sometime, in between reading classics and history, rowing and picking strawberries for pocket money, he decided that he could only live with his conscience if he did something positive to earn a living. The fact that, within a year or two, he could have walked – with the double first his tutors predicted – into a good junior diplomatic post seemed to make no impression on his newly-found social (or socialist) conscience.

The fact that he, who had no need to be employed, might be taking a job away from someone who desperately needed it – practically whipping the crusts out of the mouths of babes – made no impression on him either. That's masculine logic for you. Men are so busy looking into the blue distance, they never see what's right under their noses.

'It's a girl,' soothed Mother, 'bound to be. Some pretty, little shop girl. He's just the age for a hopeless affair. We simply have to be patient until he gets her out of his system. He'll see reason in no time at all.'

'I don't think so,' I warned her. 'This is serious.'

'Oh, all you young people are far too serious these days. Does no one have any fun any more? When I was young, one worried about whether one's bosom was sufficiently developed, or, I suppose, one's moustache. We neither knew nor cared who ran the country. It was none of our business – and a good thing, too. Oh well, I suppose it could be worse.'

'Could it?' said Pa, gloomily.

'Oh much, darling, believe me. It could have been religion.'

They underestimated David. It was religion – of a sort.

Chris was at the bottom of it, of course. Without

Chris's encouragement or, even more importantly, the use of his spare bed, David would have lasted about twenty-four hours in the East End before being found in a gutter with his pocket picked.

No, I wrong my brother. That was just the impression he gave. Behind his long, slight figure and shy smile was a strength of purpose – a stubbornness, if you like, there's very little difference – that was both unexpected and unshakeable.

Apparently, David just turned up on Chris's doorstep (he didn't actually have one, but you know what I mean) one evening, saying that he'd nowhere else to stay and cadging a bed for one night. That was just the beginning. Of course, we didn't know that at home immediately. The first news that came to Mount Street was in a letter from the Master of David's college, asking what had become of him. David had packed a small bag and had simply vanished.

'You must call the police, Arthur,' Mother had insisted.

'Wait and see,' I said. 'He's up to something.'

Sure enough, David eventually wrote to our parents and told them that he'd secured a job, through Chris's influence, as a very lowly factotum on the staff of the *Daily Herald,* '– That communist rag!' exploded Pa. 'I wouldn't even let the servants read it –' that he didn't mean to cause the family any distress, but that he had no intention of giving it up, so would we please not try to persuade him.

The letter was typical of David: placatory, inoffensive, absolutely immoveable.

David's job was even humbler than our parents imagined. He did an awful lot of tea making, cup washing, waste paper basket emptying. Now and again he was allowed out, as one of an army of fifty thousand employed by all the popular newspapers, to canvass

302

households. A saucepan, a fountain pen, a place setting of (cheap) cutlery was your reward for allowing some persuasive young man to register you as a reader. If you were really crafty, you'd get something even better the next day from a rival canvasser. Then, as the stakes were upped, a mammoth one guinea copy of 'Universal Home Doctor' for two and six; a complete set of Dickens in leatherette covers; free insurance against a married couple being mown down by a runaway brewer's dray on the second Sunday in March in a leap year when the moon was full – all if you would agree to read the right newspaper.

Oh David, how could you?

I met him once for tea at Gunter's. Goodness, how shabby he'd become. You could see he was a gentleman, of course, his coat and trousers were immaculately cut, but the trousers bagged at the knee for want of a pressing, his shirt collar was frayed and his cuffs spattered with that dreadful purple ink Chris used for his tatty little newssheet. His face had hollowed, marked below the eyes with the translucent blue stains of late nights and poor nourishment, but his eyes blazed with a pure, bright fervour. He reminded me of some of the paintings I'd been dragged to see in Munich: St Sebastian, his eyes rolling piously heavenwards, stuck as full of arrows as a hedgehog with quills; St John the Baptist striding out of the desert to tell the world exactly what he thought of it.

His greeting was scarcely saint-like. 'Gosh, those look good,' he said, giving me a brotherly kiss, but spying over my shoulder the famous Gunter's brown-bread ices I'd ordered.

He polished off his own, then most of mine. The little, tempting sandwiches garnished with water cress were gone in no time. The pretty iced cakes topped with crystallised petals, rose and violet, didn't stand a chance. I felt like a maiden aunt treating a famished prep schoolboy to a slap-up tea.

'Sorry – made a bit of a pig of myself!'

'Yes, you did rather. Can't you even afford to eat?'

'Oh yes – well, almost. It's just that – well, I'd no idea how many things need to be paid for. It's all money out and not much in. I give Chris something for rent, of course – he's awfully decent to me – then there's laundry and shoe repairs – I go through shoe leather like nobody's business when I'm knocking on doors – and fuel and books and baths and what's left we use on food. Trouble is, I'm on commission and it's such a poor area that no one can afford to subscribe to a newspaper at all.'

'Poor darling!'

'Chris doesn't seem to notice. He gets by on next to nothing, but I must confess, sometimes I lie in bed at night and dream of treacle puddings – great big ones, steaming hot, with lashings of custard!'

'David, for goodness sake, you must let me . . .' I snapped open the catch of my bag and fumbled for some banknotes.

'No!'

'But –'

'Do you realise, people raise their children on the sort of money I spend on myself? Look at me, I'm strong and healthy and my teeth aren't loose in my gums and my legs aren't bowed with rickets. I'm not really hungry. I just think I am. The government offers people just enough money to keep them alive, but not enough to keep them in the sort of health they need to work. Whole families are brought up on tea with condensed milk, bread and margarine. No fresh milk, no fruit, no vegetables, no butter, no . . .'

'That's scarcely your fault.'

'But it is my fault. It's all our faults. It's the fault of the system.'

'You're beginning to sound just like Chris,' I scoffed. 'I hope you're not going to turn into another starry-eyed idealist.'

'Why not? We – all right, you – have probably spent as much on this tea as a family of six on the dole has to spend for a whole day – and that includes rent.'

'Surely not?'

'I'm perfectly serious.'

'Well, but . . .' I tried a casual shrug, but it didn't come off. '. . . their needs are very simple and food is quite cheap I hear.'

'Yes, if you have time to shop around for bargains, if you have money enough to take advantage of special offers. But these people never have enough money in their hands at one time. A tin of corned beef only costs eight pence, but they have to buy it at a penny a slice. The poorest even buy their bread at a halfpenny a slice. Imagine – never having the price of a whole loaf at one time. And these are the people who are called feckless because they'd rather spend their last threepence on a fish supper than on soap. What's the point of buying a good meaty bone for a penny when there isn't any fuel to turn it into soup? Clare – they're *hungry*.'

'I didn't notice you wrapping your tea up in grease-proof paper and carrying it off to distribute it through-out Mile End. Didn't it choke you?'

'No,' he answered simply, 'but it does now.'

'Oh, David . . .' I sighed. 'Still the same. Won't you come home?'

'I can't. If I'm lucky, I'm going to be allowed out on a few reporting jobs soon. Nothing spectacular – just jot-ting down names at union meetings and following fire engines, that sort of thing, but it's a start. And I've writ-ten a few book reviews for the *Daily Worker* – I think they'll print them. I hope so. The circulation war seems to be over for now and the canvassing's been dropped.'

'You can do it all from home. Pa won't mind – you'll see. I can talk him round. We'll all support you. Please come home.'

'I can't. It wouldn't be right. Besides, I've met some-one . . . a girl . . .'

'Oh?'

He blushed like a schoolboy. It was that, the innocent joy of it, more than his words, that entered my soul like iron.

'She's lovely. Her name's Judith.'

Judith? Judith! Judith!

'You'll like her. I know you will.'

'And when . . .' I asked calmly, 'are we going to be allowed to meet . . . Judith?'

'Soon.'

I can't bear it. I can't bear it. He had smiled that shy, sweet smile that had always belonged to me and said, 'You'll like her'.

I hate her. Just the sound of her name makes me want to scream out my rage. If only my thoughts could be poisoned arrows, showers of them, blackening the sky, aimed right at her – a hail of death. I'd scrawl obsceni-ties on her door. *JUDEN HIER UNERWÜNSCHT.* I'd . . .

How dare she? She has raised herself from the gutter where she belongs and battened on my gentle, beautiful brother like a leech. He's too innocent, too unworldly. He's only a boy. He doesn't realise what she is. He'll be dragged down to her level, down into the filth, into the piggery with her. He'll be degraded, defiled.

Who is this Judith?

I can't bear it. Oh, God . . .

Who was it who was supposed to have 'a lean and hungry look'? I can't remember.

Anne would know. She always had her nose in a book. I'd have asked her, but it wouldn't have been fair. I don't suppose she could even reach the library shelves any more, with eight little hands dragging at her skirt and her arms full of the biggest and noisiest baby yet.

Another boy – Edward – and the last, Anne said, with a grimace that was half-smile, half-shudder. Instead of popping out like a greased piglet, as his brothers had done, Edward brought most of her insides with him. I can't bear it – even to talk about it, even now, brings me out in shivers.

Anne looked dreadful. She'd lost that plump, rosy look that men (two, at any rate) had found so attractive. Everything seemed to sag. Gravity seemed to exert its forces more strongly on Anne's bosom and stomach than anywhere else on earth. Her skin was doughy, her eyes set like currants. She was an uncooked gingerbread woman.

Yet her arms would still open wide enough and her lap was big enough for all the children, her own four and Olivia's puny little Chloe. They'd all climb on somehow, sticky, dribbly, sometimes a bit smelly, and all the tears and squabbles of the day would be kissed away.

Once I caught Nickie looking at his brood. He watched them with the puzzled pride of a stallion standing at stud. You could almost see the cartoon bubble coming out of his head. 'Did I really do all that? What a splendid fellow I must be!' Then he looked at Anne. It's to his credit that he crept away shamefaced when he saw what he'd done to her.

His mother, in one of those excruciatingly delicate conversations, where no one says what they mean, told Nickie that Anne would probably perk up once her insides had been properly shoved back into place and she didn't have to run to the lavatory every five minutes. Well, not in so many words, of course. She was much too much of her generation to call a spade a spade. She pussyfooted around for a good half hour, using polite euphemisms that no one else understood, but that's what she meant.

'Oh, jolly good,' mumbled Nickie, with a wide-eyed innocent look that meant he hadn't a clue what she was talking about.

'What Mother's trying to say,' interrupted Rose, 'and making an awful hash of it, is that you'll have to keep your hands – and other unmentionable parts – to your-self for the foreseeable future, young Nickie.'

'Rose!' Her mother was aghast.

'What – you mean not ever . . . ?' His expression was as horror-struck as his mother's, but for a different reason.

'No, silly. I don't mean not ever – but no more babies, not if you want Anne to be able to walk upright ever again. You love her, don't you?'

'Need you ask?' Nickie replied indignantly.

'Then, for her sake, go and talk to a doctor.'

Nickie looked so relieved at being offered an accept-able alternative to celibacy. Personally, I'd have let him stew in his own juice for a while longer. He deserved it. His rampant physical demands had as good as clapped a ball and chain on his wife.

Anyway – who was it that had that 'lean and hungry look'? Someone in Shakespeare probably – that always seems to be the answer.

Otto von Darmheim had it too.

I've always thought it's important for a man to be taller than a woman and since I'm nearly six feet tall, height had always been a bit of a problem for me when I was young. I'd rather not dance at all, than dance with some little roly-poly, peering down onto his bald patch while he breathes into my cleavage, both of us looking and feeling ridiculous. The first thing I noticed about Otto was his height. He made me feel just right.

The next thing I noticed was the pattern of duelling scars slashed across his face. What a cliché. All the Prussians in Bulldog Drummond's rollicking adventures have duelling scars, don't they? That's how you spot the spy when he's trying to pose as an English gentleman! Simple.

But Otto really had them. Well, two, actually. One slanted across his chin, southeast to northwest, catching the lower lip, though only just. The other vertically split his right cheek. They were much uglier than the neat seams one might imagine – puckered, ham-fistedly sewn, horrid.

And there was a stiffness, a formality about him, that told everyone he was a foreigner, in spite of the immaculate tailoring, the colloquially perfect English. His manners were impeccable, but they didn't have the relaxed, 'silly ass' perfection of the English public schoolboy. Thank goodness!

We met, of all places, at the house of Jane Coxhill's guardians. As promised, I'd written once I'd left Baroness de Rutz's, but only in a half-hearted fashion. Jane had been a much better correspondent. She'd come home a year after I'd been dragged back and, like a good little girl, was waiting on the springboard, ready to dive in (or be pushed). In the early spring of 1934, mothers and other sponsors were holding little lunch and tea parties in order to break in their young for the real thing – dipping in a toe to test the water – and to compare lists of dates and guests.

A mother needed a memory like an elephant and the organising capacity of a regimental sergeant-major in order to make sure that her daughter reached August having had the maximum enjoyment and minimum sleep.

During January or February, lists of suitable young men and women would be exchanged by sponsors. Dates would be chosen for one's own ball, but the difficulties of finding a suitable evening were very real: not the night before or after a particularly splendid ball, for fear of comparisons; not too late in July, unless one was frightfully grand, in case people thought it wasn't worth staying in town for; if it was to be in the country, not during Ascot, Goodwood, Henley or whatever, because the travel would be so difficult. It was a wonder anything was ever arranged.

Jane was already in a state. Having been away so long in Munich (while her guardian aunt shrugged off one husband and donned another), she was at a disadvantage. She may have spoken perfect German and been able to tell the difference between Schiller, Schubert and Schopenhauer, but of what practical use was that when she knew scarcely anyone who mattered? (Neither did I, but I didn't give a tuppenny damn). Her only intimate friend (and that showed just how desperate she was) was me.

So I was invited to one of the girls' tea parties arranged to enlarge Jane's social circle before the real season began. There they all were, the pretty, well-bred girls, from families one ought to know, in their new spring costumes: prissy ice cream colours, with hats, bags and gloves that matched. There were the vases of hothouse mimosa, the tiny, triangular sandwiches, the feather-light sponge cakes. China or Indian? Milk or lemon?

There was I, in my uniform with the fasces collar badge, a black kite among the turtle doves.

And there was Otto.

It was most unusual to find a man invited to a girls' party. Men were neither necessary nor wanted. The whole point was to make sure that girls who were bound to see so much of each other became friends first, without the distraction of male company. But Jane's brother, Gerald, a cavalry subaltern stationed somewhere out in the sticks beyond Windsor (and anywhere beyond Windsor is as distant as Darkest Africa to a cavalryman), had turned up on a surprise visit, bringing with him a chap he'd met at some house party.

Oh, what a fluttering in the dovecote!

None of the half dozen girls there had ever come across anything quite like Otto von Darmheim. He wasn't at all like the cousins and older brothers and older brothers' friends that made up the whole of their experience of men. After all, a brother was only a brother and a friend not all that different. They were awkward young men, inclined to turn pink when spoken to directly, who leaped up when one's father appeared and called him 'Sir', young men who would only dance under duress and whose whole conversation revolved around horses and hunting, or their regiments or colleges. What was worse, they had known one since one was in pigtails and short socks. With the exception of one or two 'taxi tigers', they were so *safe* – younger versions of Nickie, I suppose.

Otto was a different species altogether. To start with, he was a man, as different from the chaps we were used to as a wolfhound is from a spaniel puppy. Then there was his accent – deliciously different, not gutteral at all, but with just enough strangeness in the way he pronounced 'a' or 'v' to add spice. And those scars – terrifying, repellent, exciting.

'Otto's something at the German Embassy,' Jane's brother explained, 'but I'm not sure what.'

'A spy,' I teased.

'An attaché,' said Otto.

'Exactly – a spy. After all, what does attaché mean? Just that you're attached to the embassy in some unspecified capacity. It allows you to travel around, with diplomatic immunity, to meet people – like today – to find out what we think of Germany and the Germans.'

'And what shall I report to my masters about today?' he queried, with a sort of half-smile twisting his damaged lip, making the scar on his chin pucker suddenly.

For some extraordinary reason, I wanted to reach out and touch it, smooth it, stroke it away.

'Tell them,' I answered proudly, 'tell them that today you met the Führer's greatest admirer in this country. Tell them that the English and the Germans must always be friends because we're too alike to be enemies.'

'Oh, you don't change, do you, Clare?' laughed Jane – a little, tittering laugh that scarcely camouflaged the gasps of horror from those silly, overbred, overdressed, dull . . . Well, I didn't have to like them, did I? I was required to have tea with them, nothing more.

'Clare was quite the little Fräulein when we were in Munich,' Jane continued patronisingly (what had *she* to be patronising about?). 'She practically worshipped the ground Herr Schicklgruber walked on.'

'What a card you are, Miss Northaw,' Gerald sniggered.

'Not at all. I'm just a firm believer in speaking the truth. I understand that's a rare trait these days.'

'It's certainly an unusual one in diplomatic circles, Miss Northaw,' added Otto. 'What an extraordinary young woman you are.'

If he'd said sweet, or funny, or even pretty, I'd have felt justly aggrieved. The witless girls all around me were pretty. But extraordinary – I liked that. I was extraordinary and I meant to stay that way.

'You will go far, I prophesy,' he went on, 'or else you will be put up against a wall early one morning and shot!'

'I'd consider it an honour to die for my country.'

'An honour I'd prefer to forgo. I hope I'm more useful alive.'

'Of course. Dead spies are no use at all.'

'Of course.'

Ignoring the empty seat next to Jane, Otto perched himself on the arm of my chair. He stretched his right arm out across the back of it. I felt the movement stir the hairs on the back of my head. He smelled of soap and freshly ironed linen. I wanted to slip backwards into the crook of his arm, to turn my face into his chest. I'd never felt this way before. It was unexpected, exciting, confusing.

'Tell me,' he said, 'how you have come to know Germany so well.'

I talked and talked. I told him all about Munich, about my wanderings in the mountains, about my meetings with the Führer, the music, the marching, the excitement. As I talked, I felt the room grow quiet around me, but I couldn't stop. No one had ever been interested before.

At the end, I gave an embarrassed little laugh. 'Oh dear, I seem to have talked far too much.'

'Yes,' said Jane.

'Would you permit me,' Otto asked quietly, with a stilted, old-fashioned courtesy I found fascinating, 'to introduce myself to your parents?'

Next day, Otto called formally on my family. He arrived with flowers for my mother (how un-English) and intelligent conversation (how unusual) for my father. Olivia was just passing through the hall as he arrived.

'*Who* is that?' she asked, grabbing me before I followed him.

'A German spy,' I whispered.

'You know,' Olivia laughed, 'for some reason, I'm rather inclined to believe you!'

'*And* he's a baron – Baron Paul Otto Kamenz von Darmheim.'

'Aren't they all, darling? Every other German one meets is a baron. Just think of all those romantic ruins on the Rhine.'

'You're just jealous.'

Either Otto had impressed my parents with his absolute trustworthiness, or they'd already (quite probably) given me up as a bad job – at any rate, no one tried to stop us as we roared around the countryside that spring and summer in Otto's Maybach DS8 Zeppelin. It was a black monster of a vehicle, three tons of it, with eight forward gears and four reverse. It took a strong man to handle it at a hundred miles per hour up the Great North Road on our way to BUF rallies in Liverpool or Leicester.

Otto never seemed to have any work. He never seemed to have any duties at the embassy. He was at my disposal whenever I wanted him.

Eager to prove that England was not lagging behind where Germany led, I took Otto to the new BUF headquarters at Black House in the King's Road, the old Whitelands Teacher Training College, next to the Duke of York's Barracks. I had to admit, as a headquarters, it was nowhere near as imposing as Munich's Braune Haus. It was the best we could do, but it was still obviously a red-brick, Victorian Gothic school. The posters on either side of the door:

FASCISM
FOR
KING
AND
EMPIRE

FASCISM
IS
PRACTICAL
PATRIOTISM

did nothing to alter its scholastic appearance.

Inside, however, it resembled a barracks, not a school. There were offices, rest rooms and rows and rows of iron bedsteads with the bedding neatly boxed on top of the mattresses. Yet when I introduced Otto to a few of the hundred-odd 'boys' living there under military discipline, he seemed unimpressed.

'They are not an elite,' he sniffed, 'they just would like to be, like our Brownshirts – unbelievably vulgar.'

'But . . . I don't understand. Don't you *believe* in all this . . . in the Führer?'

'Of course I do. I believe in the Greater Germany. I believe that a nation must choose to be either the anvil or the hammer. I believe that the soil exists for the people who possess the force to take it. I believe that our destiny lies in the east, that the new Reich must set itself along the road of the Teutonic knights of old, to obtain, by the German sword, earth for the German plough and daily bread for the *Volk*.'

I looked at his lean, scarred face and felt the force of his creed pass over and through me like the Pentecostal wind. I felt as though I stood facing the altar, listening to the unshakeable beliefs of the saints and martyrs. He was Parsifal with the Holy Grail in his sight.

'The alternative is communism,' Otto continued, 'and that's unthinkable – chaos and collapse, the new Dark Ages. The SA is little better – they are brigands. There must be discipline; there must be order. The

Führer must impose order or he will fail. The SA must be curbed.'

'But they have been faithful to him from the very beginning. How can he turn on them now? It wouldn't be fair.'

'Fair? When Germany is at stake? Not cricket? Did you not study Goethe when you were in Munich? Do you not remember what he said about order? "I would rather commit an injustice than endure disorder". The SA or the army, thugs or a true elite, the Führer must choose. Even he cannot have both.'

All spring and summer, we roared in the great, black car up and down the empty, open roads of England. The sun seemed always to shine on our faces and the wind blow through our hair. Birmingham, Bristol, Northampton, Newcastle. Town halls and school halls. Football grounds and market squares. The British Union of Fascists marched in step with shining black boots and, as we marched, the ragged-arsed children pranced alongside, chanting in time to our steps, 'The Yids. The Yids. We've got to get rid of the Yids.'

In Edinburgh, three hundred Blackshirts on their way to the Usher Hall had to be shielded by mounted police. A horde of young, fanatical communists – hooligans, rather, to my way of thinking – shrieked abuse and waved placards.

NATIONAL GOVERNMENT MEANS
FASCISM MEANS
WAR

BAA, BAA, BLACKSHIRT
MOSLEY'S LITTLE LAMBS

Otto looked at the messages with a puzzled expression. 'I thought that I understood English very well, but I don't understand what is this "Baa, Baa"?'

'It's a rhyme, a childrens' rhyme – "Baa, Baa, black sheep, have you any wool?" Black sheep – black shirt. You see?'

'Is it a joke?' he asked.

I looked at his serious face and laughed with delight. 'Yes, it's a joke – a very English joke.'

Otto laughed then, too. He put his arm around me and, almost absent-mindedly, brushed his lips against my hair. I shivered at the unexpected contact, as though he had touched a secret, very sensitive nerve.

'You must stay beside me then, all the time, to explain English jokes to me. It will be a very long time, I think, before I understand the English sense of humour.'

He had chosen me – *me* – gawky, gauche Clare. Of all the pretty, well-bred, sugar-and-spice girls he could have chosen from, any one of whom would have been thrilled to be seen with him, he had picked me. He wanted me to be with him all the time. There was nothing I wanted more.

The knowledge gave me a new poise. On the night he asked me (and my parents, worse luck, but Otto was a stickler for the formalities) to go with him to Covent Garden, I didn't, for once, throw on the first thing that came out of my wardrobe and rush downstairs, still tying and buttoning, with two minutes to spare.

When I stood at the curve of the stairs, for the first time in my life consciously coquettish, and saw Otto's expression, all the primping and powdering seemed worthwhile. I'd purloined a gown of Olivia's, more grown-up than anything I'd worn before – a bias-cut tube of heavy, black silk jersey that flowed over my hips like a waterfall and flared out like a flower around my feet. The neck was high and the back very, very bare. My hair, uncut since I left Munich, was piled and plaited around my head in a golden coronet.

Otto took my hand and kissed it with a little, simultaneous click of his heels. An Englishman might have looked ridiculous, but Otto was the Student Prince and Rupert of Hentzau rolled into one.

'Will you permit me . . . ?' he murmured and pinned a pale orchid corsage to my left shoulder. The fact that my mother was wearing an identical one didn't dim my excitement one little bit.

It was the last night of the German season at Covent Garden – *Die Meistersinger*, conducted by Thomas Beecham, with Rudolf Bockelmann, and the incomparable Lotte Lehmann as Eva. In our box, I sat back a little in the shadow and closed my eyes, letting the glorious sound wash over me. I could have been back in Munich or at Bayreuth.

'Whoever wants to understand National Socialist Germany must know Wagner,' the Führer used to say.

I sat, still and silent, until the sound of applause jerked me back to reality. When I opened my eyes, I was almost surprised not to see the scarlet swastika banners draping the stage and boxes. The audience was on its feet and, from behind the curtain, came the sound of returned applause as the cast said its goodbyes to England.

On our return to Mount Street, my parents were very discreet and hurried into the library, leaving Otto and me alone in the dimly lit hall. His shirt front was a blazing patch of white, but the rest of him was dark – hair, eyes, evening clothes – a dark angel with a flawed face. Some sort of magnetism made me sway towards him. I thought he was going to kiss me. Oh, I ached, I *ached*. Instead, he took my left hand and carried it to his lips. He kissed my fingers, then turned my hand

318

over and kissed the palm. His lips were dry and very hot.

Meetings grew noisier and more dangerous. Our speakers were heckled by organised communists wherever we went. Sometimes, stones were thrown. In sheer self-defence, it became necessary to have the meetings stewarded, to keep out the rabble. It was our democratic right to speak. They had no right to silence us. Anyone who tried was thrown out and if we were sometimes a little rough, that was no more than they deserved. The red revolutionaries had had it their own way for too long, but not any more.

But I stood in the long, dark shadow of Otto von Darmheim and nothing could harm me.

And everywhere we went, I would scan the heckling crowd for a face identical to my own. Sometime, somewhere, David and I would meet. I knew it. One evening, I would look across a crowded hall and I would see my own face looking back at me, my other half, my alter-ego. Beside him, would be a face as yet unknown, a dark face I had glimpsed, only dimly, in my dreams – Judith.

There was going to be trouble. That was obvious, long before we reached Olympia. We edged our way down Kensington High Street, but Otto couldn't force the motor car any further. Three mounted policemen were trying to keep the road open, edging back the crowd with the great, gleaming shoulders of their horses, but, as fast as they cleared the road, behind them the crowd spilled off the pavements again.

The junction of Holland Road and Warwick Road was packed with young people, hundreds of them, making their way in loose groups towards Olympia. They were a rabble, ill-disciplined, ill-dressed: students, clerks and shop assistants, labourers, serious young men with spectacles and long college scarves, plain, blue-stocking girls without hats, older people who ought to have known better, dangerous-looking men, certain of where they were going and why, who seemed to be organising the chaos – men like Chris Berry. Otto made a few random turns and parked his Maybach in Edwardes Square.

'Here – take this,' he said, tossing his Burberry across the seat to me.

'Why?'

'Do you want to go to the meeting?'

'Of course.'

'And do you think you're going to get through the crowd dressed like that?'

'I'm proud of this uniform.'

'No doubt you are, but there are people out there tonight who might be only too pleased to tear it off your back.'

We joined the stream heading towards Hammersmith Road. There would have been no choice, even if we'd been intending to go somewhere else entirely.

The banners were serious, held high in the air, shaken under the noses of steady police horses – no jokes this time about 'Baa, Baa, Blackshirt.'

Someone started a ragged chant that was taken up by other voices, until hundreds of people were yelling their hate and abuse.

'One, two, three, four – what are fascists for?
Lechery, treachery, hunger and war,
Two, three, four, five – we want Mosley,
Dead or alive.'

Nearer the single, open entrance to Olympia, we joined other, larger groups of Blackshirts going to the meeting, along with respectable people, middle-aged and middle-class, of no obvious affiliation, who were going out of curiosity. I felt sufficiently safe to take off Otto's coat. The press through the door was terrible. For half an hour we filtered slowly through as every ticket was checked, while the crowd behind trod on our heels and the Reds screamed abuse at us.

They might as well have let us all straight in. The checking was a farce. Tickets had been on sale for as little as one shilling and there had been two thousand free seats available on the day to anyone who would fill in a postcard saying 'Why I like the Blackshirts'. It was as good as an invitation to agitators. Things were managed better in Germany.

'We shall miss the beginning. We shall miss the Leader's entrance.' I said anxiously.

'They won't start yet,' Otto consoled me. 'There's practically no one inside so far.'

And they didn't start, not until every one of the fifteen thousand seats was taken.

During the wait, a band was playing brisk English folk tunes or sea shanties, mingled with patriotic marches. In compliment to our foreign fascist brothers, they played 'Giovinezza' and the 'Horst Wessel *Lied*'. I sang the words as loudly as I could, one of the few who could sing in German. Otto sang too, in a cracked, off-key baritone that soon dragged me down, so that I ended up singing flat too. I burst into giggles and dug him in the ribs to silence him.

It got later and later. Whenever the band stopped, we could hear the sounds of riot in the streets outside, the screams and the hackneyed slogans. Then the band began to play the Blackshirt anthem 'Mosley' and I knew we hadn't long to wait.

'Mosley: leader of thousands!
Hope of our manhood, we proudly hail thee!
Raise we this song of allegiance,
For we are sworn and shall not fail thee.'

I wasn't going to sing *that*. Committed fascist I may
have been, but nothing was going to make me sing
that excruciating twaddle. Why couldn't someone have
written a decent marching song?

There was silence and a spasm of tension, painful as
cramp, gripped the audience. I could hear fifteen thousand people holding their breath and letting it out with
a long hiss of relief. The spotlights swung to the
entrance and there was the Leader, all in black, flanked
by four tall, blond young men. He marched down the
steps to a frantic cheer that drowned the band and cut
off the yells outside.

'Hail Mosley! Hail Mosley!'

A ripple of black ran round the stadium and grew
into a swamping wave of blackshirted arms, saluting
the Leader. Looking neither to right nor left, with his
left hand hooked in his belt and his right raised in
acknowledgement, Mosley strode across the arena
through a double rank of chosen men. Behind him a
platoon of banners bobbed and fluttered, the Union Flag
and the Fasces flying together, a proud and invincible
combination.

On reaching the platform, Sir Oswald turned
smartly, like the soldier he had been, and stood at salute
while the cheers died away into a silence of expectation.
The house lights dimmed. A spotlight lit the tall, thin,
black figure of the Man of Destiny.

I couldn't help comparing him to the Führer. The
music, the lights, the banners were all designed to rouse
the audience to a peak of expectation. Herr Hitler could
have cradled us all in the palm of his hand. He could

have taken our emotions and wrung them out to dry. With a whisper, he could move a crowd of 100,000 to tears of joy. With a shout, he could set a nation on the march. But the man in front of us was a pale imitation. I had witnessed the real thing and I was not deceived.

They let him begin, just about. Three minutes or so into his speech, the first heckling began and was quickly dealt with. Then a voice came from somewhere else, then another from the opposite site of the arena.

'Fascism means murder.'

'Mosley out, Mosley out.'

'Smash Fascism.'

The Blackshirt stewards, picked for their size and strength, split into groups and ran up the aisles, half a dozen towards each heckler, and dragged them out. Mosley's amplified voice rose effortlessly above the hubbub.

'We are very grateful to those few people who are interrupting. They illustrate how necessary a Fascist defence force is to defend free speech in Great Britain.'

All at once, there were yells and screams from every direction. Organised groups of men and women were on their feet, waving banners, throwing eggs. Each group was silenced eventually by stewards, some of them women who dealt with the female protestors.

'It is typical of the red cowards,' cried Sir Oswald in a thunderous voice, 'to send a woman to do the job they dare not do themselves.'

Otto gripped my wrist. 'I'd take you out of this if I could,' he said, 'but we'd never get through the crowd.'

'Why?' I countered. 'No one else is leaving. I think it's the most exciting thing I've ever seen.'

'I hope you still think that by the end of the evening.'

The arc lights played on each dissenting group,

picking out the ringleaders for the searching stewards. If they met resistance, the stewards got rougher. Well, why not? This was a democracy, after all. Were Englishmen supposed to let some little slum kike thumb his nose at them? No wonder they gave the odd kick as they threw someone through the door.

There were people above us, running along the girder catwalk that supported the glass roof. How they got there, I can't imagine, but from that height, they had the meeting at their mercy. Eggs and tomatoes don't hurt much, but potatoes stuffed with razor blades and stockings filled with broken glass are meant to do damage. I felt no sympathy for them as they were silhouetted by the searchlights and hunted down by stewards.

Cat and mouse, they hunted along the beams, far above the arena, above the howls of encouragement and execration. There was nowhere for the scum to hide. The powerful lights could pick out the smallest huddled figure. I never saw what happened after they had been cornered, but I cheered along with everyone else.

And still the Leader carried on with his speech, refusing to allow himself to be intimidated by thugs. 'These people have succeeded in breaking up meeting after meeting in this land. Today their power over English audiences has come to an end. The interrupters go out as you have seen them go out tonight. If there are any more of them, they will go out as well. The simple fact is that they cannot meet our case by reason. They cannot beat us by reason and argument so they think they can beat us by shouting, but they are making the biggest mistake of their lives.'

There was a sound of breaking glass and violence broke out all over the hall. Directly behind me, people were shouting, two men's voices and a woman's.

'Smash Fascism. Fascism means murder. No concentration camps here.'

There were stewards running up the steps towards them, but still the voices, to my surprise educated voices, ranted on.

'No Blackshirt thugs in England. Nazis out.'

I turned, curious to get a closer look at people who were prepared to go to such lengths to break up a peaceful meeting.

David didn't recognise me. I turned and looked straight into his face, four rows behind, but he never even saw me. His mouth was wide open, contorted with anger, and he was waving a clenched right fist in the air. Placid, harmless David, who wouldn't step on a beetle if he could help it. It was an astounding sight.

Chris knew me, though. He gave me a giant wink, then opened his mouth to roar, 'Mosley out. Mosley out.'

The searching beam sliced through the shadows, blinding me, so that I didn't see the first rush of the stewards – six men and two women. I heard the rattle of their boots up the steps and the yells of defiance turning to grunts as the first blows landed.

When I could see again, David and Chris had already been hauled out of their seats. They'd made a mistake, sitting at the end of a row. They'd have been safer tucked away in the middle, shielded by respectable citizens. The women were dragging a slender girl up the steps. One arm had been twisted behind her back. Her head had been savagely jerked to one side. A woman had her hands fastened fiercely in the girl's long, brown hair.

'Let her go . . .' David panted and gave a frantic jerk and a kick to free himself.

I saw the dull gleam of a knuckle-duster, then David was down, blood spilling from his lip. As he lay, stunned, a thickset man put in two short, hard kicks, one to each kneecap. The sight of David's blood freed me from the inertia that had held me. Dear God, they were hurting him . . . they were hurting David . . . I wanted to hit back, to smash them for what they were doing to my brother. I would scratch that man's eyes out, if he stood still long enough. I lunged forward, screaming, but Otto held my arms in a grip I couldn't break.

'David . . . David . . .' I screeched, striking out at Otto's face and missing. No one – no one – could stand between me and David. 'Let me go . . . he's my brother . . . let me go.'

It was a diversion. The sight of my uniform and the noise I made halted the charging stewards for a precious moment. I think they must have imagined I was being attacked.

Chris jerked his head towards David and the girl. 'Out!' he commanded. Then he settled his back against a pillar and the lights glittered suddenly along the honed blade of a kitchen knife. He knew what he was doing. He balanced the blade easily and crouched slightly in the confident stance of a street-fighter. His piratical smile was wide and dangerous. 'Right then . . . come and get me . . .'

For a moment, they hesitated, then they came on in a solid phalanx of black. There would have been murder that night. But that moment's hesitation was long enough to allow Otto to disentangle himself from me and step out into the aisle.

'I think that is enough, gentlemen,' he said quietly, putting himself between Chris and the Blackshirts, between the knife and the knuckle-dusters. Two steps above the Blackshirts, he towered over them, impressive and calm. Chris, two steps higher yet, didn't match Otto's height. 'I cannot allow this to continue.'

The Blackshirts stopped. Chris had been their prey, and anyone else like him – red riff-raff, agitators, communist agents. Now they were faced by a quiet man with a cool air of authority, a gentleman. To reach Chris they had to get past this man and they had no orders to take on an opponent like this. Baulked of Chris, they clattered off towards the next disturbance.

Otto and I followed Chris out of the building. In the foyer, knots of struggling people staggered and bounced off the walls. I saw a man carried by his arms and legs and flung out the door. A Blackshirt ran out after him and gave him a parting kick in the kidneys.

'Fascist bastards!' Chris had muttered and, for a moment, I thought he was going to turn back. He wavered, then went on.

On the steps, a man leaned against the wall, trying to staunch his bleeding nose with a red, sodden handkerchief. Outside the gates, the shrieking crowd had thinned into diehard huddles who taunted the hard-pressed police, calling them 'Fascist lackeys' and singing 'The Internationale' in half-a-dozen keys.

Chris seemed to know where he was going. I guessed that he and David had agreed a meeting place in case they were split up. At any rate, he ducked off down Maclise Road and we followed.

'Look after them,' said Chris. 'Make sure they get home safely.'

And then he was gone, back the way we'd come, back to the struggling crowd in Hammersmith Road, where the police were trying to keep an open route, fearing that the Blackshirts might decide to march home in formation.

Otto and I were left in charge of my dazed brother and a woman I could happily have thrown to the wolves, if it would have saved David from the tiniest scratch.

There were David and his little Jewess, a slim, fairish,

English-looking girl, huddled in a doorway. She had moistened her handkerchief and was trying to staunch the trickle of blood that still oozed from David's split lip.

'Don't fuss, Judith,' I heard him say thickly, through his swollen mouth. 'Worse things happen at sea.'

Judith gave a little cry and flung her arms around his neck. 'I was so afraid for you,' I heard her say and the rest of her words were muffled by the pressure of David's lips on hers.

'I don't think we are needed,' said Otto quietly and he drew me away.

How dare she? How dare she? My brother needed help and she had come between him and me. Who had sat all night by his bed when he'd been hit by the taxi in Paris? Who had held his hand and soothed him when the pain in his ears kept him awake at night? Who had petted and cossetted and loved him all his life?

And now she stood between us.

Next morning, the newspapers were full of accounts of Fascist violence and not a word – not a single word – of the serious provocation and indignities we had suffered. And this country boasts of its free press!

At West London Police Court, Chris was fined forty shillings for using offensive words and sentenced to one month's imprisonment on a charge of assaulting the police and possessing an offensive weapon with intent to commit a felony. He had plenty of company. At a special sitting of the court, nineteen men and two women appeared on charges arising out of the disturbances.

It seemed that Chris had used his knife to cut the girth straps on a police horse's saddle – down had come policeman, saddle and all. In his defence, he'd claimed that his coat had become entangled with the horse's tack and that he'd used the knife as a last resort, to protect himself from injury. (Who'd believe a word of it!) That lessened the sentence he might have received, but didn't prevent him being found guilty on all charges.

'It may be,' said Sir Gervais Rentoul to the assembled accused at the end of the sitting, 'that altogether excessive and indefensible violence was used in ejecting people from Olympia. I do not know. It may well be that you may have witnessed something that raised your sympathy and your indignation, but you should know that it is quite impossible to allow individuals to take the law into their own hands.'

Bigoted old fool! They should all have gone to prison for a good, long time. They should have been set to breaking stones. Things were managed better in Germany. There, enemies of the Reich found themselves in Dachau in double-quick time. Chris would be back on the streets as soon as the prison door opened.

David and I watched Chris being led away.

'I've let him down,' said David. 'I've failed him.'

'What nonsense. Chris has only himself to blame. He's a menace to orderly society.'

'He's made of the stuff of martyrs and I'm afraid I'm not – not yet.'

'Not ever, I hope,' I said briskly. When David was in this moping mood, he always needed to be snapped smartly out of it. 'Now listen, David. It's time you gave up all this socialist nonsense and came home. You're upsetting Mother and embarrassing Pa. You're just being selfish.'

'It's not for me. It's for Chris and for Judith. It's for her parents still in Germany. It's for all the people who can't stand up for themselves.'

'David, you're no hero.' (Well, you have to be cruel to be kind, they say.) 'You're not cut out for this. Your little Jewess and her friends are more than capable of standing up for themselves. Her sort always have been. She's just using you . . . can't you see?'

David just shook his head and turned away. We stood in the drab, green-and-cream corridor barely two feet apart, but there might as well have been a wall of glass between us.

'David – how can you be so *wrong*? Is there *nothing* I can do?' I begged.

'Well, yes, there is, actually,' he answered, brightening. 'You can lend me the money to pay Chris's fine!'

Damn Chris. Damn Anne for going off with him. Damn Olivia for introducing them. Damn . . .

To my mind, if there was a hero of that ridiculous débâcle, it was Otto. He had stood unarmed between Chris's knife and a group of men angered beyond logic by Chris's defiance. Without fuss, without histrionics, Otto had defused an ugly situation and, in doing so, allowed David to make his escape. I would be forever in his debt for that one act alone.

When I tried to thank him, he just shrugged. 'That sort of violence achieves nothing. It is without a meaning. So I do not like to see it.'

'You don't object to violence, then?'

'Not at all – when it has a purpose. Violence can serve the state, but it must be controlled. That is the difference between authority and anarchy. We Germans, as a rule, worship authority, but detest anarchy. That is our strength and our weakness.'

'Gosh – I don't think I'm clever enough to understand that.'

Anne asked me down to Greywell. When I dropped a hint, she invited Otto too. We found the house in

uproar. She'd invited Olivia – now known profession-
ally by everyone as Livia ('Such a clever little thing, my
dear, so amusing.') – to modernise that solidly Victorian
house.

'But I like it as it is,' Nicholas protested weakly.
'Don't you like it, Otto?'

'I think it is rather fine – nicely English. My family has
lived in the same *Schloss* since the time of Barbarossa, I
think. Certainly, you would not think it had been mod-
ernised since then. The bedrooms are in little pepperpot
turrets at the top of winding stone staircases and there is
no plumbing. Imagine – the work for the servants! And
in the winter we always have wolf skins on the beds.'

'Where is this, Otto?'

'It seems, since 1918, to be in a strange new country
called Czechoslovakia, but when I was a boy, it was in
Sudetenland, then part of the Hapsburg Empire and it
will rightly be part of Greater Germany one day. My
parents left when my two older brothers were killed on
the Somme on the same day and now they live in our
hunting lodge outside Berlin.'

Nicholas cleared his throat, seeming uncertain
whether he ought to offer his condolences or to carry
the conversation on to its logical conclusion. Otto was
so matter-of-fact about it all.

'Well, at least there's nothing much one can do to
change a castle. You ought to be jolly grateful. Anne
seems intent on letting her sister rip the middle out of
this place. My mother's abso-bally-lutely livid.'

Anne was completely unrepentant. 'I have to live
here. I have to bring up five children here. Do you
realise this house used to have an indoor staff of fourteen? Now there's just Nanny and Cook living in and
we have to make do with ignorant little girls coming
in from the village every day. We offer the best wages
– one pound a week for a housemaid, if you can believe

it, all found – and still can't get staff to stay here for love nor money. So let's be done with all these draperies and open fires and hot water cans. I want light and air and running hot water and wholesome food for my children. Is that really too much to ask?'

'I'm with you all the way, darling. The idea of a hot bath whenever one wants it is absolute blissikins,' Rose drawled, 'but I think you'll find Mother a tougher nut to crack.'

'I can handle my mother-in-law.'

Anne had grown so hard. She was tough – there was no other word for it. It was as though she'd bricked up everything that was soft and malleable in her. What can't be touched, can't be hurt. Only with her children, in that nursery full of brawling boys, did she let down her defences. With them, she was as spineless as a rag doll. As a result, they were the most undisciplined little horrors one could imagine.

Edward, still only six months old, seemed to be permanently attached to his mother, like a suckling familiar spirit, because Anne believed in the bizarre idea of feeding on demand. In fact, she believed in just about everything on demand: sleeping, eating, screaming, fighting. Out of the window went Nanny's careful timetables for meals, bedtimes and potty training. 'His bowels will respond when they're ready, Nanny, and not a moment sooner. So if I hear once more that you've made Richard – or any of them – sit for two hours on a potty, I'm afraid I shall have to ask you to look for other employment.'

'But it's the only way to achieve correct habits, Mrs Lockyer, and correct habits last a lifetime, I always say – start as you mean to go on. The child must be put on the potty after every meal and not allowed to rise until he's performed. Richard is three years old. All my other babies were using the potty well before twelve months.'

'Then I expect they'll all grow up constipated and that will be entirely your fault. A sluggish system is the root of so much ill-health. Why do you think the newspapers are full of advertisements for Bile Beans and Fynnon Salts? The nation lives on laxatives and I'm very much afraid that ideas like yours are to blame.'

'I'm very sorry that I don't appear to give satisfaction, madam,' Nanny said stiffly. You could see from her expression that she wasn't sorry in the slightest, but deeply offended. 'In the circumstances, you leave me no option . . .'

'Oh, nonsense, Nanny. Now don't be so stuffy. How could you possibly dream of leaving all these sweet babies?'

Anne shifted Edward to her other side. Hugo had been sitting on the bare linoleum (no rugs, germs – Anne's children weren't going to be constipated, but they'd probably all have piles!) trying to stuff Marmite soldiers into his ears. Now he lost interest in these and began to climb onto Anne's lap, hauling himself up her skirt, leaving brown fingerprints on the cream linen. Once there, he slapped Edward's face so violently that the baby's mouth fell off the nipple and a stream of regurgitated milk dribbled down Anne's blouse.

'Hugo, that was very naughty,' scolded Nanny. 'Tell Mummy how sorry you are – at once – or you shall have no jam for tea.'

'Just a little sibling rivalry, Nanny,' Anne explained, with infuriatingly saintlike patience, 'perfectly natural. Now listen, darling, little Edward doesn't have nice, big teeth like you. He has to have a drink from Mummy because he can't eat those delicious Marmite soldiers. Poor Edward! Now, why don't you show Aunt Clare what a big, clever boy you are and scoff them all up?'

Hugo opened his mouth and gave three short, sharp screams.

I looked away, my fingers itching to grab Hugo and shake his sibling rivalry right out of him. My goodness, I'd certainly make those nice, big teeth rattle! Behind me, Richard was standing in a puddle – again.

Behind him stood Chloe, the oldest in the nursery, timid and sickly compared to those ghastly bouncing boys. She was clutching a filthy piece of rag, a strip of satin binding from a cot blanket, and sucking it with noisy relish.

Blast you Olive, or Olivia, or Livia, or whatever you call yourself today. If I had my way, you'd be first in the queue – even in front of Hugo – for teeth rattling!

Surprisingly, Otto was marvellous with the children. He'd often be found there around tea-time, sprawled on that horrid, bare floor, building fiendishly complicated brick castles, sometimes even whole villages. And as he worked, he'd tell tales of the people who lived in the houses – clever Grethel who ate her master's chickens and blamed the dinner guest or young Dummling who brought back the golden goose, the landlord's three daughters, the parson, the clerk and the two wood-cutters all stuck together and following on behind, so that the princess who never laughed burst into giggles at the sight.

I stood silently and listened to one of his tales.

'. . . so they killed the poor horse Falada and hung her head over the arch . . .'

'Why?'

'Because the horse knew that the real princess had been turned into a goose girl.'

'Why?'

'Because she'd dropped the three magic drops of blood that were supposed to protect her into the water.'

'Why?'

'Because . . .'

'I'm afraid they're all much too young to understand your stories, sir,' Nanny said briskly. 'Up you all jump now – bath time.'

Otto watched them all being rounded up. His thin face was in shadow and the yearning in it was unexpected, painful as a blow. This self-contained man was suddenly vulnerable and I didn't know what to do about it. He watched the children and, with the same hunger, I watched him. I knew how he felt. I knew what it was to *want*.

'Fine children,' he said softly.

'Little savages, every single one.'

'Nicholas is a lucky man – a devoted wife and all these little ones.'

'How funny. I've never thought of Nickie as lucky. We all seem to call him "poor Nickie" – I don't know why.'

'He has so much . . . such blessings . . .'

Blessings! A visit to the nursery, offered by Anne as a rare treat, was the nearest thing I could imagine to eternal torment. Anne had very advanced ideas. She was extremely firm on the necessity for schooling, but equally convinced that children ought to be allowed to find their own levels, to 'assess their human potential for right or wrong', as she put it, with minimum interference from adults. So she'd put their names down for Summerhill in Suffolk (a good long way from Wiltshire, I noted!), a school where the only rules were made by the pupils and where, by all accounts, the little brutes ran around in the buff and took catapult shots at each other.

Roll on the day!

'I've seen Chris,' I whispered to Anne on the way downstairs from one of these harrowing visits. Rightly or

335

wrongly, I felt she had the right to know. I couldn't just pretend he didn't exist.

Anne stopped. Her fingers clutching the banister rail were white across the knuckles. The new Anne, the hard Anne, was stripped right away, leaving her soft, vulnerable and bleeding. Was I right to speak? Should I have kept silent?

'Where . . . when . . . ?' she whispered back, afraid to speak too loudly, as though, by naming him aloud, she would raise him up in front of us in a puff of smoke, like conjuring a demon.

'At Olympia, raising hell as usual. And now he's in prison.'

'Prison? Oh God – was he hurt?'

'Oh no, not Chris. His kind is never hurt. It's only silly, deluded simpletons like David – the followers, Trotsky's cannon fodder – who get themselves hurt. Chris is hauling him to hell on a handcart!'

She smiled, a far-away, painful smile. 'Chris can be like that. He's very . . . persuasive. Did he . . . did he mention me at all?'

'No,' I said firmly. 'You'll have to face facts, Anne. He's forgotten you.'

Well, it could have been true. It was probably true, wasn't it? And wasn't it kinder to Anne to say so? It would do her no good at all to hanker after a man like that.

We walked into the library and caught the beginning of the mother and father of all rows.

The library was one of Livia's latest adventures. Her attacks on the fabric of Greywell had been becoming more and more daring. Like Goethe on his death bed, Anne had demanded 'More light!' and Livia had obliged.

The Victorian bays with their sashed windows had

been, one by one, knocked out. Their replacements consisted entirely of glass. Imagine funnels, pillars of glass, running the height of the house, windows that began on the ground floor, where one could look straight in on the occupants like looking at reptiles in glass cases at London Zoo, carrying on upwards, supported only by a shining spider's web of steel, past the bedrooms where we were all exposed naked as frogs, up to the eaves. Then all the knobs and twiddles, the key-stoned arches, the porches, the curly barge-boards of Victorian Gothickry had been removed, leaving the exterior plain and surprisingly modern, ready to be rendered over and painted.

Nickie had ventured a faint protest. 'I say, I hope you know what you're doing. It looks like a liner about to sail off across Salisbury Plain.'

'I'm only remodelling,' explained Livia patiently. 'Every generation does it. This was a Tudor house once, but your great-great-something-grandfather, Nickie, took out all those diamond-paned windows with their shimmering green glass and gave it a symmetrical Georgian brick facade and sixteen-pane sash windows. Your great-grandfather changed the windows yet again, slapped pointed Gothic arches all over the place and put those unbelievable dragon's head finials on the roof. You can't see the original brick and flint anywhere except around the coal shed. What am I doing that's any different – or worse – than that?'

'Well, it's all a bit drastic,' Nickie had mumbled.

'No one's asking you to pay for it,' snapped Anne.

Poor Nickie.

'By the time I've finished,' Livia consoled him, 'you'll love it.'

'And Livia, of course,' I added, a little maliciously, 'will have a whole house to show off – a sort of gigantic portfolio for potential clients. Her name will be made – or mud! She'll probably make you open up to the public at sixpence a time. Your mother could serve trippers' teas!'

Nickie gave a great snort of a laugh and changed the subject.

Then Livia had turned her attention to the inside.

She wasn't awfully interested in the kitchens. She was an artist, not an artisan. Anyway, food wasn't as important to her as it was to Anne. So the redesign of the kitchens was relegated to a minion. But the library – now there was a challenge . . .

It was panelled in dark oak from floor to ceiling, although little of this would once have been seen when the shelves were filled with heavyweight leather tomes. Since the Greywell auction in the early twenties, the shelves had been rather less thickly stacked. The choice works had been sold, leaving only volumes of sermons by eighteenth-century clerics and a series of poetry, bound in violet suede, by some ancient Pre-Raphaelite great-aunt of Nickie's. The curtains were maroon velvet that gobbled up what little light dared enter. The only thing the room was good for was as Nickie's bolt-hole for his after-lunch snooze. Now, Anne wanted a garden room.

'No, of course not,' Livia was saying as Anne and I came in. 'I've no intention of stripping out the panelling – simply stripping it. I'll bleach the colour out and pickle it. It should turn a lovely creamy colour.'

'Not while I have any say in the matter . . .' declaimed Mrs Lockyer.

'It's an experiment, you see,' Livia said, as though no one had interrupted her. 'I wonder what the room will look like in variations of one colour. Cream, buttermilk, ivory, oatmeal, vanilla, honey – what delicious words, good enough to eat.'

She drifted about the room, touching this, touching that. Her frock was of gossamer silk, leaf green, fine enough to see through and, when the sun shone and she twirled past the window, one had the uncanny feeling that one could see right through Livia too. She picked up a chair and moved it first to one side, then the other. Then, in a burst of energy, tugging and shoving with those narrow little hands on one of whose fingers she still wore Guy's wedding ring, she began piling the furniture into a corner.

'There's altogether too much in here,' she panted. 'Can't you see it?: the sunlight filtering through sheer muslin curtains; the walls bleached pale as driftwood; the floor – yes, the floor too – why not?; just a few chairs with stark hopsack covers . . . all that light . . . can't you see it?'

Her audience looked at her in voiceless amazement. Mrs Lockyer seized on the one word she had understood.

'Sacking!'

'Sackcloth and ashes – oh, you've chucked it away now, Livia,' chuckled Rose. 'There shall be weeping and gnashing of teeth.'

'Not sacking,' Livia explained patiently, using the sort of voice one might use to an idiot child, 'hopsack. It's a kind of sackcloth, certainly, but . . .'

'It's exactly what I want,' Anne interrupted briskly.

'And you always get exactly what you want . . .' hissed Mrs Lockyer.

Suddenly we were all standing on the brink of a pit filled with all sorts of unmentionable things, an evil broth of emotion. All the enmity and tensions of the past came bubbling up like scum.

It wasn't too late – not quite – we could turn back and pretend we hadn't seen. We could continue to exist in the old, uneasy, scrupulously polite way. And then the moment for turning back was past. We all had to go on whether we wanted to or not.

Mrs Lockyer the elder or Mrs Lockyer the younger. Mother or wife. There was no room for both. Nickie wouldn't – couldn't – choose. After this, he wouldn't have to.

'I loathe you.' Mrs Lockyer's face was distorted with venom. 'I loathe you and your squalid little family and all your sordid goings-on.'

'Steady on, Mother,' warned Rose. 'We've all got to live together after this, you know.'

'I've sat back all these years and never said a word, because Nickie's happiness was important to me, and, for some reason I shall never fathom, he seemed to care for you. I should have had him committed, rather than let him marry you. And I've hated you, Anne, since the moment you first set foot in this house, dragging your unwelcome brothers and sisters behind you. Your family seems to think it can drop its responsibilities at my feet whenever it suits – your communist brother, your fascist sister, that poor, unwanted child in the nursery, let them all come along – Nazis and pansies and sluts, it's Liberty Hall at Greywell . . . the more the merrier . . .'

The words were shocking enough, but coming from that stiffly-corseted, upright woman, with her iron-grey permanent waves and her beautifully-shod feet, they were horrifying, like the first symptoms of a disease for which there is no cure.

I had to admire Anne. No shouting back. No washer-women-over-a-garden-fence behaviour for her. She wasn't about to demean herself. Besides, she was winning, we could all see that. She only had to stay silent and wait until her mother-in-law's rage juddered to a halt. Anne strolled over to an easy chair, sat down, crossed her legs, and began to flip through a copy of

Horse and Hound. Normally she wouldn't touch it – too full of people who look like their horses – but today it served its purpose.

Mrs Lockyer gave a laugh that rattled like old bones. 'I've waited years to say this, Anne. I can't tell you how good it makes me feel. I want my son free of you. I want you out of this house, every one of you, today – now.'

Rose crossed the room in three quick strides. She took her mother by both arms, gripping her at the elbows, and gave her a couple of short, sharp shakes.

'Mother, you're ill,' she said firmly.

'Don't be silly, Rose, I'm not ill. In fact, I've never felt better.'

'You're not at all well,' Rose insisted. I could feel the power of her suggestion. I could feel the force of her will fighting her mother's, subduing her, winning. 'You're over-tired.'

Mrs Lockyer made a despairing effort to shake off her daughter. She jerked backwards, caught her heel in the Tabriz rug, priceless and worn, and staggered against Nickie's monstrous desk. With a splintering crash, the photograph that stood there, the photograph of Anne, painfully young, with all her illusions still intact, hit the floor. There was a tiny silence and then the glass tinkled out of its frame.

Nickie's mother sagged against her daughter. 'I'm not well,' she whispered. 'I haven't been sleeping properly . . .'

'Of course you haven't,' soothed Rose, her voice like honey.

'I've been under a strain . . .'

'You need a rest.'

'Yes, yes, I do.'

It was as though some invisible hand had laced her corsets more tightly. All the unpleasantness that had

341

spilled over, uncontrolled, was gathered in again and decently hidden from view. But then, to her generation appearances are all, whether one is talking about extra flesh or emotions.

She looked round at us all with a thin, perfect hostess's smile. Her voice was tremulous. 'I think I'll lie down until dinner. I have a tiny headache. I do hope you understand . . . please, make yourselves at home . . .'

Anne didn't raise her eyes from the magazine.

'The Führer must impose order or he will fail. The SA must be curbed.'

I remembered Otto's words when the news came through of Röhm's death, along with so many of the SA leaders, on 30th June. It was called the Night of the Long Knives by some journalist with a talent for headlines. The SA was purged of Röhm, Heines, Schneidhuber and their perverted gang, who had plotted, all of them, to bring down the *Dritte* Reich.

The Führer and his most faithful followers had roared out of Munich before dawn on their way to the Hanslbauer Hotel on the edge of the Tegernsee. There the Führer had faced the terrible, scar-faced Röhm alone in his hotel room and confronted him with evidence of his treason, before ordering his detention in Stadelheim prison. Heines and a young man were dragged from their shared bed and shot.

The imprisoned Röhm was given the opportunity to take his own life. Following tradition, he was left alone with a pistol. But when, after fifteen minutes without the sound of a shot, the door was opened again, the pistol was still on the table. 'If I am to be killed, let Adolf do it himself,' he was reported to have said. He was shot by two SS officers. Friendship was not allowed to stand in the way of the greater good of Germany.

Through the mountains of Bavaria, through the forests of Silesia, through the streets of Berlin, the Brownshirts were hunted. Across the land, the power of the SA was broken forever.

I twiddled the dial of the wireless set, hunting the needle round and round, frantically trying to pick up any German station. The crackling and whining of static allowed me only tantalising snatches.

'*He throws his anger into their pale faces and tears off their identification labels.*'

'*In this hour I was responsible for the fate of the German people and thereby I became the supreme judge of the German people.*'

'*He lives only for Germany. He is our father and our mother, keeping us safe from all harm.*'

Nickie came in and twisted savagely at the wireless knob. He banged the cabinet doors closed and sat down with his newspaper, shaking it out noisily, his glare defying me to open the doors again. How unlike him. He must have had another row with Anne.

'Did I not tell you that this would happen – must happen?' Otto said later. 'The vulgarians have been removed. The nation has been made pure again. The National Socialists rule Germany and the old families will rule the National Socialists. There will be no more need for excesses. You'll see. My dear Clare, it is time for me to go home.'

'Home?' I echoed stupidly.

'My work here is finished. I am needed now in Germany. There is so much to do.'

Going? Then what should I do? Where should I go? I looked into a future without Otto's sardonic smile and it was empty.

'Then take me,' I begged. 'Take me with you.'

'My dear . . .' Otto put out a wondering hand and

stroked back the hair that had fallen over my eyes. 'My dear, I am married.'

I held my breath. If I held it long enough, perhaps I'd never have to breathe again. I wanted to scream and shout and stamp. I wanted to throw myself on my knees before him. Look at me, I'd have said, what does your wife have that I cannot give you? I'm yours. Don't you want me?

But, being English, I did none of these things.

'I'm so sorry . . . how frightfully stupid of me . . . I should have thought . . .' My lips were frozen. The words came out in little, stiff spurts of sound that made no sense to me. But, oh, my manners were beautiful. Mother would have been proud of me. I was every inch a lady. 'Yes, of course, you must be terribly busy – so much for you to do. When do you leave?' I gave him a bright, interested smile that set like gelatine across my face.

'I never wanted to hurt you,' he said softly.

'Then why did you make me love you?' I wailed and my defensive wall of good manners crumbled to dust.

I was in his arms and his tweed coat was rough beneath my cheek. The tears that trickled into my open mouth were bitter. I couldn't breathe, but now I wanted to breathe, to live. I dragged air into my lungs in painful gulps. He was kissing my hair, my forehead, my swollen eyes. I lifted my face and intercepted his lips. They were thin and cold, but I made him open to me, I demanded that he answer me.

Then his mouth was hungry for me, teeth sharp as a wolf's, hands like claws. He hurt me and I exulted in it. We were mates, matched in our fury. All the rage, all the hurt I hadn't spoken, I spent on that kiss. I wanted to bruise his mouth, to leave him bleeding, so he would know what he'd done to me. Instead, he met my anger and joined in it.

Corsair growled, softly at first then with a deepening rumble, and rose from his place on the rug. On stiff legs, he stalked towards us, hackles raised.

'Good boy. It's all right. Down, Corsair,' I said and laughed unsteadily. 'He thinks you're going to hurt me.'

'I'm afraid that I've done that already.'

Then, so gently, he took me in his arms, as though all that anger had never happened. I don't know how long we stood, very quietly. I didn't hear the door open, but I heard it close with a sharp snap. Otto looked up.

'Come with me,' he said. 'There are too many people in this house.'

We walked away from the smell of paint and plaster, from the rubble and mess and the prying eyes. The garden was dusty and dry, the flowers wilted, hanging their heads. If we stood very still, I thought, we'd hear their roots scrabbling through the earth, stretching out for any drop of water. The light drained the garden of colour, leaving it painfully white. It hurt my eyes. The breeze, never still, that blew in from the plain, felt hot enough to shrivel my lungs. It brought with it the tang of burning grass and a sound that was more felt than heard, a sound that crept up through the soles of my shoes, through my legs and into my belly – the rumble of guns on the Larkhill artillery ranges. The earth and the air trembled together.

I was breathing in short, panicky gulps.

'When?' I asked.

'Tomorrow.'

So soon. So soon.

We left the garden by the little green gate in the wall that was the short cut to the village, but we turned instead towards the plain, where the road trickled away into a tight-packed, chalky track, a sheep track, that led on and up, over the downs to the Salisbury Drove Road, closed by the army. We startled a lark from its scrape in the nibbled turf. It rose high, high, until its song was a thread of sound, stretched so finely I thought it must break and then the bird would come tumbling to the earth.

We were two separate people who happened to be going in the same direction. After that cataclysmic kiss, we did not dare touch each other any more. There was a decent distance between us, too far for an outstretched hand to bridge.

'I have not been fair to you, Clare,' he said softly.

'No.'

'There are things I should have told you, but they are difficult things.'

'I'm not a child.' I was trying so hard to be civilised, but my voice was a quavering wail. I kept on walking, harder, faster, up and up.

'My wife is half-Jewish.'

Then I stopped and turned to face him. I had expected many things, but not that.

'It was a mistake. I was young, my brothers both dead, my parents anxious to settle into retirement in Berlin. Leona was – is – beautiful and I hurried into something when I should have stopped to think. It's not an unusual story and I'm not proud of it.'

The pause was just long enough to offer me a glimpse of heaven. The gates opened. The blinding beauty of paradise dazzled my sight. Then Otto spoke again and I was shut out in the dark once more.

'I could divorce her – mixed marriages are so easy to dissolve in Germany now – but I shall not. Her heart is not strong. She needs my care. We no longer live together, but I shall try to protect her for as long as I can. I don't know how long that will be. It will not be easy.'

I didn't want to know, but I needed to know. 'Do you . . . do you have children?'

'No.' We walked on for a while. I thought that was all he wanted to say. I thought the silence was his way of telling me to mind my own business. Then, very quietly, he went on. 'Leona was never strong enough. It's better that way. The SS demands racial purity and the higher the rank, the purer the strain must be. SS officers must produce proof of untainted Aryan blood at least as far back as 1750. I am only allowed to stay married to Leona because I have a certain amount of influence in the right places and because I have put her away. Children would be out of the question. Racially impure children would never be forgiven by the Reichsführer-SS.'

Poor Leona, I thought and was caught unawares by the unexpectedness of my reaction. Of all people in the world, why should I feel sorry for this woman who stood between me and everything I wanted? Poor Leona – cast aside, childless and alone. But what else could he do? He was an honourable man and no one ever said the path of duty was an easy one.

And suddenly I knew exactly what I had to do.

I had expected Otto's room to be dark, but it wasn't. The curtains were pulled back and the window was wide open. The moonlight was bright enough to read by. It lay in great, pale pools across the floor and over his bed. I could see the sleeping shape of him, long and limp, but his head was in shadow. I began to panic. Suppose he wasn't asleep? Suppose he had been lying awake and was now watching me, wondering? I wanted it to be decently dark.

As though I were ashamed? But I wasn't. I had done all my thinking. My mind was quite clear. I would give him a gift, the most perfect gift I had to offer. I was proud that it was mine to give.

I closed the door softly. As I walked across the room,

Otto stirred and sat up into the moonlight. His eyes were heavy with sleep and his hair was tousled. The scars on his face were black, black slashes on white.

I pulled back the straps of my nightgown and let it whisper down over my hips onto the floor. I stood naked in the moonlight and I knew that I was beautiful. Otto's breath hissed out, scarcely louder than the rustle of silk.

All my life I had been waiting, waiting . . . and I never knew the reason. Now, the waiting was over. Now, at last, I knew what it had all been for.

'I will give you a child,' I said proudly. 'I will give you a child – a gift for Germany and for the Führer.'

DAVID AND JUDITH

The Idealists

I stayed with Uncle Rudi and Aunt Lotte until arrangements had been made for me to go to England. I'd wanted to stay with my parents, but accommodation was so difficult to find in Berlin that even one extra person might have made it impossible for them to get anywhere at all. We had postcards regularly from Father, saying that they were all well and staying for a few days here or a few days there, but that there was no point in our replying, because by the time a letter reached them, they'd probably have moved on.

He managed to make it sound an amusing, rather Bohemian way of life: a room above a shop in old Spandau one day; a garrett in a courtyard in Moabit the next. I wasn't taken in by his brave words. My mother was never going to be allowed to unpack her carefully-stored boxes of linen, china and glass. From being a respectable, respected schoolmaster's family in a prosperous market town, my parents had sunk to being wandering Jews.

Why hadn't they stayed put? Why couldn't I be with them? Why had they abandoned me?

That's how I saw it anyway, may God forgive me. But I was young. Let that be my excuse. My Father was doing his best for his family, but his best wasn't good enough. No one should have told him that. It wasn't his fault.

Meanwhile, letters went backwards and forwards between the Jewish Committees in Berlin and London, trying to find me a training place and somewhere to stay. Later, when the committees in both countries were flooded with requests and refugees, all of them emergency cases – they wouldn't have been able to spare the time to pay attention to one, solitary girl who still had a family to care for her. Perhaps my father was wiser than I thought. Perhaps he'd foreseen that if I were to get away at all, it had to be at once, or never.

Later, when I arrived in London, I read the pathetic advertisements in English newspapers and was filled with shame that I had been hawked around like that.

Kind home wanted for eleven-year-old girl, intelligent, speaks good English, Jewish.

Will some generous person please take care of my son, Karl? He is thirteen years old and very bright. He is all I have left. Please save him. Jewish home desirable but not essential.

Is there a kind family who will give a home to my quiet, well-behaved little ones, Eva and Mimi, three and six years old? Their parents love them, but can no longer care for them in safety. They must live together, please.

With every month that passed, the advertisements became more numerous and appealed more frantically. People who had money could still find a way to escape to a friendlier country, even if it meant forfeiting most of that money for bribes. The mark wasn't worth much outside Germany, but there were a few, complicated loopholes in the currency regulations. If you were caught tranferring money illegally . . . well, the lucky ones were shot trying to escape.

'We don't want you. Get out!' said the Nazis and then

made it impossible for anyone to go. It was a cruel and cynical trap.

Those who had nothing, or who were already under suspicion, could only make despairing attempts to get their children away. The embassies and consulates of friendly countries were besieged by long lines of frantic people. Rumours multiplied like disease. The Bolivians are taking one hundred – get in the queue quickly. No, it's not the Bolivians, it's Brazil and only engineers need apply. Canada, Chile, Denmark, Panama, Holland. Quick. Quick.

How could these parents bear, I thought, to give away their children to strangers? What sort of parents were they? Later, I knew better.

I was found a room with a respectable Jewish widow in Shadwell. At such a late date, however, neither a university nor a teacher training college could be found to offer me a place. So I was offered an assistant's post at St George's School in Cable Street, where two-thirds of the pupils were Jewish. I hadn't a clue where Shadwell was or Cable Street. Even if I'd been able to lay my hands on a street map of London, it wouldn't have meant a thing. Anyway, it *was* England. It was the best I could expect and I was urged to accept quickly.

Armed with more kisses from Aunt Lotte, a packet of egg sandwiches, enough for four, an even bigger package of home-baked cakes, my tickets and ten Reichsmarks, the maximum amount of currency I was allowed to take out of the country, I boarded the train that would take me to freedom.

When I bit into the sandwiches, a couple of hours through the journey, I discovered that Aunt Lotte had interleaved the bread with banknotes.

'Not hungry, dear?' asked the old woman in the

opposite seat when I quickly wrapped the sandwiches back in their waxed paper.

'Not really. Perhaps I'll wait a bit. It's a long journey, so I'd better not eat everything at once.'

Not until I'd safely crossed the border, I meant. And although the border guards shook out the pages of the few books I'd brought, ripped down the linings of my coat and checked my suitcase for a false bottom, they left my picnic untouched. Thanks to my uncle and aunt, I wouldn't arrive in a strange country a complete pauper.

Krefeld. Change for Kleve. Nijmegen. Hook of Holland. Harwich. London.

And there I met David.

I think my new landlady, Mrs Lipkin, thought she'd got more than she bargained for when I turned up on her doorstep in Solander Street, behind the soot-stained bulk of St George in the East.

She and her late husband had arrived from Poland some time in the 1880s, but they had brought the old country along with them to their new home. Solander Street was known locally as Polish Street, with good reason. It would have been difficult to find anyone whose native tongue was English along the whole length of the street and its neighbours.

Mr and Mrs Lipkin, fleeing from yet another pogrom, had left their Polish *stetlach* in the back of beyond and sold everything they had, even their gold teeth, for two tickets to America. The boat went as far as London and stopped.

They got off the boat and just stayed put, along with several of their fellow townsmen, their *landsleit*, and created a little Poland, but one where they didn't have to tremble at the sound of strange men's voices in the street at night.

Approached to take a Jewish refugee, I suspect that Mrs Lipkin had been looking forward to a good, Yiddish-speaking girl whom she could mother and feed on *lokshen* and chicken soup, yellow and rich with *schmaltz*. She got a bit of a shock when she found she'd got someone who looked more like a German, who didn't speak Yiddish, only high German and the English she'd never learned herself, and was obviously a thoroughly modern young woman.

And I saw a little woman who seemed to have got stuck in the wrong century. Her dress was ankle length, dark grey, and completely unornamented. If I'd been able to see any hair, it would probably have been white, but not a scrap was uncovered. She had probably shaved her head on marriage, so that other men would not be tempted by the beauty of her hair. A good husband would love and take care of his wife, whether or not she was bald. I realised that I'd come into a very Orthodox household.

'*Shalom aleichem*,' I said in Hebrew and Mrs Lipkin's anxious face crumpled into a smile.

Despite our differences, there was something very homelike about that tiny terraced house in Solander Street. From the moment I stood on the doorstep and saw the little case holding the *mezuzah*, the sacred parchment, inscribed with passages from Deuteronomy, nailed to the right-hand doorpost, I knew that I would be safe there. No Jews in Germany dared advertise themselves so obviously any longer. Hanging up a *mezuzah* there was as good as going down on your knees and begging to have your windows broken and your door daubed with paint. And Yiddish wasn't so different from German after all, almost a dialect, so Mrs Lipkin and I could communicate without too much difficulty.

'My lodger, the teacher,' Mrs Lipkin used to call me.

But I wasn't. I don't know what I was. Neither flesh, fowl, nor good red herring. I wasn't a schoolgirl any longer. I hadn't even begun to be a student. And the job I had was so loosely defined that even after I'd been doing it for several months, I wasn't exactly sure what I could call myself. Still, beggars can't be choosers. It was work and they even paid me (just).

But what was I doing there, separated from my family, scarcely knowing if they were alive or dead? I should have been with them. They had no right to cast me out. From the day Herr Willrich had hit my father, a peculiar activity had taken hold of us. We had whirled into motion, as though to stand still, to stop and *think*, was to lay ourselves open to further attack.

Decisions had been made that night and by morning they might as well have been written on tablets of stone. Even my father, with his quiet, analytical mind, hadn't taken time to wonder if he might be allowing his wife's emotions to rule his head.

Move. Keep moving. Go. Go. They can't hurt you if they can't find you. The traditional Jewish reaction to threats.

Yet I would stand looking out the window of Mrs Lipkin's front bedroom, the 'best' (strictly speaking, the better) bedroom, and wonder how on earth I'd got there. I'd look down into the cobbled street that was never quiet, night or day, and try to conjure up the cleanliness and order, the well-scrubbed steps of Ritterstrasse: Frau Hummel sweeping the pavement, Herr Liebig watering the scarlet geraniums in his window boxes. And when I couldn't do it – I wept.

St George's School was so close that even if I'd stayed in bed until I could hear the bell ringing, I still wouldn't have been late. Not that I ever tried! Each morning I'd scuttle into school and I just couldn't help the knot of anxiety in my stomach that made me feel as though I were about to vomit. It had been there for so long, I had grown used to it. To me, school meant watching, listening, being always on one's guard for the false word, the sidelong look. It meant always being on the defensive, never knowing where the next blow was coming from.

I just couldn't get used to the fact that these boys in green blazers paid no attention to each other's religious beliefs. There were plenty of fights – sure – plenty of times a boy would come into class with a bloody handkerchief held to his nose or with grazed knuckles and a triumphant smile. But these were fights between *boys*, not between Christians and Jews.

So I pinned up maps and drew posters and ran off messy, purple-inked mimeographs. I listened to the younger children read and cleaned up the art room. I washed up the tea cups and milk bottles in the staff room. I put out the chairs and music stands for orchestra practice. I counted piles of hymn books, boxes of pencils, heaps of bean bags. In fact, I became so good at counting things, that I was put in charge of the stationery cupboard. An honour, indeed.

And all the time, I knew that my employment was just charity. Well, what did I want – as Mrs Lipkin said – that someone should be waiting with a gown and mortar board for me as I stepped off the ferry?

And I waited for the letter from my family that never came.

No one could eat three meals a day with Mrs Lipkin and still do up the waist button of her skirt, but I didn't have the heart to tell her so. So sometimes, I'd plead pressure of work and spend lunchtime in the library, only a short walk along Cable Street. It had a wonderful staircase, that made you feel you'd arrived somewhere important. (And of course, you had, because what is more important than making the written word freely available to everyone who cares to climb the stairs?) There, in the warm, panelled room, with inviting, green-shaded lamps, I could make myself comfortable for an hour. Perhaps in the summer I might be tempted to explore my surroundings, but in that wicked winter nothing would have made me wander around, through pea-green river fog, over cobbles slippery with rime and oil and other things I'd rather not enquire into.

The reading room was always busy. People who didn't have books at home, or who didn't have the leisure to read in the evening or the money to spend on gas for lights could spend some time there. Whether they read *Das Kapital* or *The Shakespeare Murders* didn't matter a jot.

I went to read the newspapers – all of them. I was hungry for news. My parents had vanished as completely as though they had never existed. In her letters, Aunt Lotte veered, sometimes in the same sentence, between little domestic snippets about the price of butter and veiled (for fear of censorship) rebukes to Heaven about the injustice of life.

Uncle Rudi's factory had been appropriated for the good of the people.

'Your uncle's life's work has been Aryanised,' she wrote. 'That we should live to see the day. That – (here she inked through the word so vigorously that the page was torn) Neumann was no longer content with the fat commission he was being paid for protection. He organised half a dozen small businessmen each to put up a percentage to buy your uncle's factory. Buy, I say! Did your uncle have a choice, when a band of storm troopers headed by Neumann arrived in his office one morning? He could say no? Now Neumann is the new manager and Rudi was paid a fraction of what his business was worth and was glad to get anything. Your uncle is a broken man. His life he spent in building that business and now we have nothing. But why should we worry? Who can even spend money when German shops don't allow us any more to pass through their doors? We can live on air, they think. But what can you do? You remember Bertha? She's very good to us. Her sister has a farm and sometimes she brings us eggs. She is a treasure, a heart of pure gold. But our Hildegard has gone. She has gone to a better job, she says. She means a job not with a Jewish family. Ten years living with us, since a child, not a day when she wasn't well fed, and now this. May God forgive her but I never will.'

I laid my head down on the table. Reading the letter had been like hearing Aunt Lotte's voice in my ear. And what she hadn't said seemed to be more important than what she *had* said. She hadn't mentioned my parents once. She hadn't mentioned them for more than a month.

I could feel the edge of the table cutting into my cheek, but it seemed just too difficult to lift my head. For weeks, my thoughts and prayers had been spinning off into empty air. I could feel them flying away, like Noah's raven, but there was no place for them to land. They had been forced to circle and circle until they came back to me or until they died. Beyond Mrs Lipkin's little house there was nothing – just a great, hollow emptiness. My feeling of loneliness was absolute. I had been cast into the outer darkness. There was no one in the world who had any need of me. Or was it my family who had been tossed away – used up, spent and finished? Worthless in the society they had been born into?

'I say, are you all right?' A hand touched me, soft on my hair, a gentle hand. I sat up suddenly and the hand was snatched back as though I'd bitten it. 'Sorry – awfully sorry – I thought perhaps you were feeling faint.'

I looked up into bright blue eyes that seemed immensely far away, as far away as the stars and as unapproachable.

'I hope you don't think I was being impertinent,' the young man said. His voice was like none I had heard since I had come to England – soft, but very clear, carrying right across the library, although he wasn't shouting. It had none of the heavy accent of Solander Street or the rattle and patter of the Londoners that I found so difficult to get used to.

'I'm quite all right, thank you,' I answered. 'I was just . . . just . . .' Well, what was I just . . . ? Weeping inside. Grieving. Mourning. Whose business was that but mine?

The feeling had come back into my cheek. The groove left by the edge of the table throbbed painfully and I knew that it would be all white and red. Tomorrow, it might be blue.

'I'm quite all right,' I repeated more firmly. 'Now, please excuse me, I must go back to work.'

I folded up my letter with a great show of decisiveness. I put the newspaper I'd been trying to read back in the rack. I buttoned up my coat and pulled on my gloves. I straightened my hat. And he was still there.

He was looking straight at me, at my lips, in a most unnerving way, as though he was able to read my very words before they left my mouth. I felt as though every thought in my head was open to his enquiring gaze.

He's picking me up, I thought with sudden shock. What a nerve! Then I looked again at his sweet smile. There was a purity about it, a rare innocence. Something in his face touched me very deeply, so suddenly and unexpectedly that I wanted to tell him everything. I wanted him to hold out his hand and assure me that I wasn't alone.

How stupid!

'Forgive me,' he said, 'it's just that I've seen you here often before and you always look so sad . . .'

'Well, I'm not,' I snapped. 'I'm wildly happy, of course – just like everyone else! What do you think? And if you don't stop blocking the door I'll be late back for work.'

He held the door wide for me and I tip-tapped past him, my shoes making angry little marks on the polished floor. I wouldn't dare go back to the library again – well, not for a long time. My grief was private. It was nothing to do with anyone else. Least of all with a tall, blond, blue-eyed *goy*. (Blast! Now I was beginning to pick up Yiddish words from Mrs Lipkin.) What could he possibly know about anything?

Was I being, in my own way, as racially discriminating as the Nazis?

I nearly sprinted along Cable Street back to school. I climbed the few steps to the door and looked back along the street. He might have followed me, I thought, and my heart hammered at the idea. But he hadn't.

Living in London was like living in Germany ten – maybe fewer – years before, when the Nazis were trying to prove to everyone that they were a responsible, serious political party with great plans for the people. Earnest, perhaps even reasonable men had stood on street corners then and had harangued the passing crowds. So-called 'popular' demonstrations had been arranged to encourage the people to display their natural feelings. The will of the people, expressed through the mob, was paramount.

Des Volkes Stimme ist Gottes Stimme.
The voice of the people is the voice of God.

And now it was happening again, in London, and from what I read, all over Britain, too. The men in black shirts had the potential to be every bit as frightening, every bit as sinister as the storm troopers in their brown. That they weren't – quite – was no consolation. Who knew what they would do tomorrow?

I tried to tell people, but no one would listen, or if they did, they thought I was exaggerating.

'It can't happen here,' they would say smugly in the staff room during break. 'The British wouldn't stand for it.'

'Ten years ago, the Nazis were thought of as harmless cranks,' I warned.

'Ah, but you'll find that we're different from the Germans, dear,' the music mistress soothed, looking up from arranging a piece for the recorder ensemble, 'if you don't mind my saying so.'

'We British are individuals, you see – all a bit odd, if you like,' continued the history master, between irritatingly slow draws on his pipe. 'We don't care to follow the band the way the Huns do – oh, sorry, no offence . . .'

'I hope you're right. I pray that you're right.'

'You'll see . . .'

What I saw were doors daubed with paint. I saw fences plastered with posters advertising meetings and counter-meetings. I saw the swastika and the hammer and sickle sharing the same sooty, brick walls. I saw serious young women selling the *Blackshirt* outside Shadwell station and people were buying it (a few, anyway).

I saw a man on a soapbox haranguing the stallholders in Watney Street market. He had stationed himself just outside Sainsbury's, so that everyone who went into the store had to squeeze past him. The naptha flares that lighted the market stalls glittered on the high polish

362

of his cross-belt and boots and turned his face into a black-and-white caricature.

And there were the gestures, the frenzy, the lies.

'International Jewry is a conspiracy to keep the British working man down . . .'

I'd seen and heard it all before.

With one difference – when the man had been speaking for five minutes, the manager of Sainsbury's came out and asked him to move on.

'You're offending my customers and we don't want any trouble, do we?'

In Germany, that manager would have had his face smashed in. But this was England, so the orator picked up his soapbox and moved on. Perhaps there was hope, after all.

But it was early, yet.

'. . . we don't care to follow the band the way the Huns do . . .'

Children do. Children are the same everywhere.

It was only a small band, but it made a lot of noise. The beat of the drums echoed along the walkways of the tenement blocks and the children came running, cheering.

I felt sick. They were playing an English tune, a rousing march I didn't know, but booming and banging off the high dockyard wall, the tune they played could well have been the 'Horst Wessel *Lied*'. Behind the band, black boots striking the cobbles in unison, came the Blackshirts. They swung along The Highway at a fine pace, looking clean and spruce and proud. Past the queue of men waiting for casual work at the West Gardens gate they marched, to Eastern Dock. The contrast between the two groups made me realise, for a moment, why people chose to follow the waving banners. There were the Blackshirts, well-dressed, well-fed, oozing

363

self-satisfaction. There were the casual labourers, muf-
flers wrapped tightly around hollow chests, broken
boots patched with cardboard, passing around a precious cigarette end that had been speared on a pin so
that none might be wasted, turning their faces politely
aside to cough before they took a drag.

The shining boots and the band called out to them,
'Follow us. We will give you work. We will give you
food for your children. We will give you back your
self-respect. England for the English.'

Who was I to blame those hopeless men because they
followed?

Thank God, this was England – not all followed.

The children capered alongside the parade: sockless
boots and baggy shorts; shorn heads and scabs; gawky
big girls with babies hefted on their hips. And as they
ran to keep up, they chanted to the beat of the band,
'The Yids, the Yids – we've gotta get rid of the
Yids.'

I stood still, watching them pass, and the hollow
where my heart should have been was filled with ice.

And when I turned to go, my feet had taken on a life
of their own. They marched to a terrible beat and nothing I could do would make them change their tune.

'The Yids, the Yids – we've gotta get rid of the Yids.'

I changed step, walked quicker, walked slower, and
still my feet pounded out the rhythm of hate. I was
half-running, half-skipping in a demented dance. The
chant still dogged my steps.

'The Yids, the Yids – we've gotta get rid of the Yids.'

And then there was a slower beat, a beat that drew
alongside me, that steadied me and stopped my head-
long flight.

'It's very difficult to break, isn't it?'

At last I found I could stop. I was panting as though
I'd been running a race and losing it.

'What . . . ?'

'It's a catchy rhythm. They could make a fortune as a dance band. Pity they don't, perhaps – better for everyone, all round.'

And there was the blue-eyed young man with the smile of a saint.

'How did you know . . . ?'

'I've found myself hopping like a demented bunny rabbit before now. There's something horribly compulsive about that beat. It stops people thinking clearly. It stops them thinking at all.'

'I feel very silly . . .'

'Don't. The devil has all the best tunes, they say.'

We'd reached the corner of Dellow Street, a convenient place for me to break away. I couldn't stand there, in the open street, staring at someone I'd only met once before and even then by chance. Aunt Lotte would have had a fit and Mrs Lipkin would have been close behind.

'Well . . .' I started to say and didn't get any further.

'Well . . .' he answered.

Like gudgeons on a bent pin, we gaped.

'I say, do you think you'd like a cup of tea or something? Coffee, maybe? They do a decent cup in here – much better than the usual English dish-water.'

'Oh, I couldn't.'

'Good for shock – or something. Doctor David's orders!'

He hustled me through a door into the City of Dublin Dining Rooms on the corner of Dellow Street. I'd often passed the window emblazoned A Good Pull-up for Carmen, but never imagined myself inside. It was much cleaner and trimmer than I'd feared, very respectable. David wanted a window seat, but I crept away to a darker corner.

Who did I expect might spy on me? And God could

see into that corner, anyway, no matter if I crept under the table!

It was the first time I'd eaten or drunk in a public place. It was the first time I'd been faced with the possibility of eating or drinking from utensils that might have been used for both meat and milk. At home, we'd only gone to each other's houses except for bar mitzvahs or weddings, when we went to the Rifkind's hotel. Mrs Lipkin always made sure that I took my own cup and a filled thermos flask to school every day.

'No one's going to have put meat in a cup,' I'd protested on the first day.

'Who knows?' she said, darkly, and shuddered. 'Bovril, maybe.'

Oh dear, did Carmen (whatever they were?) drink Bovril?

'I hope you don't think I was being impertinent,' he said quietly.

'Didn't you say that last time we met?'

'Did I? Oh, dear. But if I hadn't hurried you in here, you'd have gone. You see, if I don't do things in a hurry, before I've really thought about them, then I don't do them at all. I mean, once I start thinking, I see everyone else's point of view and then it all gets so difficult, I end up doing nothing. So I tend to do things on impulse, before the thinking sets in.'

'That's as good an excuse for kidnapping as I've heard, anyway.'

'Yes, isn't it?'

He laughed and the worried crease between his brows disappeared. I'd only ever seen him looking anxious before. The difference was startling. Heavens, he was beautiful in the way I'd never imagined a man could be. Blond and blue-eyed, but not in the muscular, Siegfried mould that was so much admired in Germany. Everything about him was finely made, slender but with a strand of toughness running through, like the wire armature that underlies a sculpture, giving it strength and form.

I realised that I was staring. I dropped my eyes to the two cups of coffee that had been ordered.

'Cream?' he asked.

'No . . . no, I'll have it black, please.' At least I could try to minimise that awful, possible clash between milk and Bovril. But when I tried to put the cup to my lips, I couldn't. I put it down again, untasted.

'Is something wrong? Too hot? Would you like sugar?'

'No . . . no . . .' Oh, this was awful. Whatever I did was going to be wrong. I closed my eyes and took a sip, then another. I listened for the rumble of an approaching thunderbolt, even a tiny one, but nothing happened.

'Heavens, you're worried about whether it's Kosher, aren't you? How stupid of me.'

'What makes you say that?' I snapped, suddenly, illogically fearful. 'You've been examining my earlobes, or something? I've got a hooked nose, maybe, that you hadn't noticed before? A forked tail?'

He jerked backwards, making the chair rock, away from the venom in my voice. I could have spat in his eye. I was a nice girl, he thought, maybe, until he discovered I was Jewish.

Nothing changes.

I looked fearfully across at the counter, half expecting to see the sign there reading JUDEN HIER UNER-WÜNSCHT. Thank God, this was England – but for all I knew I might still be thrown out the door. For two pins I'd have tossed the coffee over him and thrown the cup after it.

'Look,' he said, placatingly, 'I didn't mean to pry. I've seen you so often and you always look so sad – too sad for a girl of your age. Then that day in the library

– I couldn't help seeing that your letter was in German. I put two and two together. And I just wanted to say . . .' He leaned forward again and stretched out his hands until they almost – not quite – touched my clenched fists. '. . . I had to tell you . . . I'm so very sorry . . . about it, about all of it . . .'

He was staring again, intent on my face, watching my expression, the shape of my lips as I talked, the meaning that lay behind my words.

The young men who loafed on street corners stared, too, but not like this. They gave the girls sidelong glances, passing remarks out of the corners of their mouths, letting their eyes slide over, top to bottom. They didn't look at me very often. The girls they liked – blonde hair, pert little hats – walked about in twos or threes, arms linked, blocking the pavements. They'd toss their heads at the young men, then whisper together and giggle and maybe look back over their shoulders, bold and coy at the same time, and giggle again.

But this man's stare wasn't offensive or assessing. It was too intense for comfort. He watched my lips shape each word and then read it as though it had been written in a bubble. And he didn't just read the words. He read the thoughts that formed them.

Then he smiled and I found myself smiling back. How could I resist that combination of angel and small boy? I felt so ashamed of my outburst. I'd brought my paranoia with me when I crossed the North Sea and now it was becoming a burden.

'Besides,' he went on, 'I happen to know that the owner of this place is Jewish anyway. Does that make you feel any better?'

'You're right,' I forced myself to say, 'it's very good coffee.'

And suddenly it was.

After that, there didn't seem to be anything to say. The young man – I knew he was David, and I knew that David wasn't exclusively a Jewish name in England, but David what? – seemed to have run out of the burst of energy that had made him propel me into the City of Dublin Dining Rooms. He was stirring his coffee in a monotonous way that made me want to snatch the spoon out of his fingers. And I – what had I to say to an unknown young man to whom I hadn't even been introduced? Mother had always been so strict about proper introductions.

I stared through the coffee-shop window. Across the street, the stable gates of Meredith & Drew's biscuit factory opened to allow out a waggon pulled by a pair of heavy grey van horses. The driver tapped the right hand horse on the shoulder with his whip and the pair turned right. The iron wheel rims set up such a rattle that I wasn't surprised that grocers usually had a tub of mixed broken biscuits for sale at half-price to children.

Perhaps I bored him? Perhaps I was just a dull little foreigner? Perhaps he was wondering how he could get away from me without seeming too rude?

His worried frown was back.

'Are you thinking again?' I teased, but shyly.

'Yes, yes, I am, actually. I'm thinking that you must be awfully bored sitting here with me.'

'I must be? It's an order?'

'Usually. I expect you're wondering how you can get away from me without seeming rude.'

How silly it all seems now. Like children we were. We were children, but how quickly we grew up.

David would wait for me after school. I'd come down the steps and there he'd be, barely visible in the poison-ous glow of a pea-souper, sheltering in a shop doorway

369

with his collar turned up while the rain streamed off his hat brim, standing bareheaded with the sun gleaming off his golden hair, the brightest and most beautiful thing in all beautiful London.

And we'd walk. We couldn't afford to do anything else. We'd walk along the riverside to Tower Bridge to watch it being raised for the great ships in the Pool of London. We'd sit on the grass at the Tower and watch the ravens squabble over our crusts. We'd walk up to St Paul's and David would tell me about old St Paul's, about the Great Plague and the Fire and Sir Christopher Wren. He was so clever. He knew so much.

I'd never been inside a Christian church before, but once again, the thunderbolts failed to strike me. I expect God was occupied elsewhere. He had so much to do. I hoped He was taking care of my parents for me and Willi and little Max – wherever they were.

And when I came back to Solander Street, Mrs Lipkin's shrivelled face would be tight with disapproval.

'You needn't have waited up, Mrs Lipkin,' I'd say.

'How are you to get in? You'll climb through the window like a thief in the night?'

'Perhaps I could have a key?'

'A key? For so young a girl? Your mother wouldn't thank me if I give you a key so that you can stay out all night with a pretty *goy*. Yes, you can look ashamed. You think I didn't know? I tell you, everyone in the street knows that you are a disgrace to your family.'

'But we're not doing anything wrong. We're just friends.'

'There's wrong and there's wrong – who knows what you do. There's friends and then there's friends. I thank God every day that you're not my daughter.'

How could David, whose smile was the only thing that stood between me and engulfing loneliness, be a source of disgrace?

And I thought about Krista with the placard around her neck.

ICH HABE MICH EINEM JUDEN GEGEBEN.

What made the Nazis' attitude any different from Mrs Lipkin's? Only that their violence was physical and hers verbal. It was the Nazis who coined the word *Rassensc hande*, racial violation, but Mrs Lipkin knew exactly what it meant.

So we talked and we talked, David and I, and we walked and we walked through a world that was so very much wiser than we were. And never once did David touch me in a way that would have made me ashamed.

David lived in an upstairs room in one of those streets, narrow as a gangplank, that finish in steps to the river. He shared it with a broken-nosed Bolshevik called Chris, an unlikely friend, who nevertheless managed to keep David out of trouble on those mean streets. Or did God do that? David was the nearest thing to a holy innocent I'd ever met.

On the other hand, Chris got David into a lot of trouble, too. It was no coincidence that David and I met on the route of a Blackshirt march. David had been handing out anti-Nazi leaflets at the assembly point and was on his way to heckle at the finish, but I had diverted him.

As the summer progressed and the British Union of Fascists grew stronger and more threatening in the East End, Chris egged David on to more and more violent opposition. The two of them were fined for breaking windows at a school where the BUF were holding a meeting. They were shoved and hustled at the fringe of an outdoor rally in Poplar, but they gave as good as they got and the speaker had a hard time of it. They made lightning raids in the middle of the night on blank walls with pots of red paint, leaving daubs all over the East End: SMASH THE FASCIST SCUM.

To Chris, it seemed like a game, a gigantic game of goodies and baddies, but as the summer became hotter and dryer, as the precious green space around St George in the East became brittle and brown and tempers rose with the thermometer, I felt that David was becoming too involved.

He didn't smile very often, now, and I missed that bright blaze more than I'd have guessed. He was thinner, too, and often tetchy, though never with me, impatient with the government and with a democracy that took its own impartiality so seriously that it would allow pure evil to have an equal say with good. And he was too intense to appreciate the illogicality of his feelings.

The clashes grew sharper and fiercer. I don't know who was the first to escalate the struggle from bare fists to knuckle-dusters. Each side blamed the other and I dare say there was blame on both sides. All I cared about was that next time David met me he would still be in one piece.

They took their message to the smarter parts of London, too. Chris was a regular speaker (or shouter, rather) in Hyde Park. With his quick wit and brisk repartee, he could whip up quite a crowd on a good day, getting his message across with vehemence and courage. On a wet day, he might as well have talked to himself and stayed warm in bed.

I've made it sound as though they were the only two who stood between Britain and Fascism. Of course, that's not true. There were plenty of people, some communists, some moderate but far-seeing, who realised that their country could easily go the same way as Italy and Germany.

But Chris and David were the only two that I knew. David was the only one that I loved.

'This is going to be big,' Chris informed us. 'Bigger than anything that's gone before. It's our chance – perhaps our last chance – to show the country what these buggers are made of.'

His words were as heavy as guilt around my shoulders. I was frying fish on the little gas ring in Chris's flat (Chris had asked for sausages, but I hadn't fallen as far as that – yet). The fat spat up at me. The tiny, airless room was hazy with the smoke of cooking and Chris's cigarettes. I could feel my hair grow lank with sweat. It had grown during the summer and its weight was like a damp cloth laid across the back of my neck.

If Mother could see me now, I thought. She'd say, 'Is it for this I let my daughter study when she could have been at home helping her mother? Is it for this that I let her travel to a strange country away from her family? That she should become a skivvy to a pair of communists?'

I couldn't help smiling as I imagined her aggrieved voice. Then the smile crumpled. I'd give anything – anything – to hear her voice, no matter how angry she might be. I had had no news of my parents for months. The last letter from Aunt Lotte had been in April and now it was June. My last letter to her had been returned. Stamped across it were the words *Adressat Unbekannt* – Addressee Unknown.

Unknown? The Weitz's were unknown in the town they had been born in? When Arni the postman used to sit in the kitchen every morning to drink coffee?

Slow, heavy tears gathered and fell into the frying pan. They sizzled and flashed up in the hot fat. My hands were stung and spattered, dappled with tiny, angry burns.

Maybe Chris was right. Maybe it took violence to counter violence. How could a family just disappear? How could they be sitting down to eat together one day and the next be just a rubber stamp across an envelope? *Adressat Unbekannt*. What a polite way to inform me that I had no one left in the world to care for!

Except David.

It was too late for Germany, but at least we could try to prevent the same thing happening here.

I had to push aside a pile of papers to place three plates on Chris's stained table. Some of the papers fell off the other side onto the floor. Chris barely looked up. He was poring over a ground plan of some sort of public building, an auditorium, maybe, or a theatre.

'We're going to split up into small groups, twos or threes, and spread out all over the hall. Maximum noise. Maximum disruption. Mosley's not to get a moment to spread his foul lies. It's heckle, heckle, heckle all night. There'll be men in the roof – that should be quite a diversion – and voices coming from every direction. The aim is to provoke the Blackshirts into the most extreme reaction. The more they knock us about, the more we'll have public opinion on our side. People are going to get hurt, but –' he shrugged, ' – that's the cost.'

'Yes,' I said fiercely and both men looked at me in surprise. 'Then take me with you.'

'You?' Chris almost laughed, then he looked at my expression and changed his mind. 'We'll be glad to have you.'

'No,' said David, flatly. 'She doesn't come. Not if it's dangerous.'

'It's all right for you to be hurt and not me?' I hissed. 'It's your family and not mine that's maybe in a *Konzentrationslager*? I have stood by and watched you for a long

374

time. I couldn't make up my mind if you were right or wrong – but now I know. I'm coming.'

Chris took out a long-bladed knife and laid it on the table. The light shimmered along its wicked edge and I shivered.

'I don't care what we have to do,' Chris said, 'but this time I'm out to show those bastards up for what they really are.'

The violence at the BUF meeting at Olympia was fully reported in every newspaper. Despite letters of protest from articulate BUF members who swore that they'd behaved impeccably and had been hideously provoked by a communist rabble, the blame for the many injuries was squarely placed on the fascists. Chris had been right.

From that day, public opinion swung away from the Blackshirts and although they enjoyed a brief spurt in membership – misfits excited by the idea of a good fight – more and more of the middle-class support (who provided the funds) fell away. The decline had already begun by the time Chris came out of prison.

The other result of the Olympia meeting was that David and I got married.

I had never kissed his mouth before. I had felt the pressure of his lips on my cheek – hot and dry or cool with rain – but I had never turned my mouth to his when we had parted each night at the end of Solander Street and he, dear David, had never taken what I would not willingly give.

Now his mouth tasted of blood. It was swollen beneath my own. His pain was my pain.

He had stood between me and the Blackshirt stewards and I had watched him go down beneath their assault. I had kicked and screamed and bitten. I had felt my teeth sink into the fat arm of one of the women who held me. She tasted of black cotton and sweat and sour skin and it was bliss to hurt her. My head still ached where my hair had been yanked back.

I hadn't needed David – but he had thought that I did. I heard the crack of their boots on his knees. My legs ached for him. I felt my skin split and my bone crunch for him.

Then I had taken his face in my hands and had tasted his mouth, bruised as a ripe plum. His blood had a metallic tang that set my teeth on edge, but underneath he tasted of honey. His sweat was acrid in my nostrils, but underneath he smelled of sunshine.

With a little cry, deep in his throat, David had gathered me into his arms, pulling me hard against the long, lean length of him, pulling me up and off my feet. I could feel the strange pulsing of his man's body. It scared and excited me. He was so beautiful.

When he paused for breath, he laid his cheek against mine, in a gesture of perfect peace. I looked over his shoulder and into the eyes of a woman in black. Blue eyes, as blue as David's and hair as cornfield bright. She looked at me with such malevolence that I felt her shadow pass over us, black as the devil's cape.

Then she was gone.

Mrs David Northaw.

With Chris and an unknown typist from the Register Office as witnesses (Mrs Lipkin's reply when I had asked her to join us had been that she would pack my suitcase and leave it on the doorstep), David had made me his wife as soon as the law would allow. In the drab office, sparkling dust motes showered over us, as dazzling as confetti of gold. The registrar's face had sweated like a boiled pudding and his collar had turned his shaven neck purple, but he had woven magic that day.

376

Then leaving the poor typist (how could I do anything but pity her – she hadn't just married David Northaw) the three of us walked from Cable Street Town Hall to lunch in the City of Dublin Dining Rooms. I looked at myself in the shop windows as we passed.

The girl in the glass only looked like me. She was smallish and fairish, just like me, with a wide-eyed, breathless look, which was just how I felt. And her arm was linked with that of the most beautiful man in the world. Lucky girl! She wasn't me, though. Under the blue, flowered cotton dress and the little, tilted straw hat, Judith Weitz had been transformed.

I had walked into the Register Office an alien. I walked out a British citizen.

Chris left us at the door to his flat, after a long, late lunch. 'I've got plans of my own for the rest of the day, if you don't mind – but I can change them if you like! Sure you won't miss me?' he chuckled, with a wicked grin.

David blushed.

His narrow little bed had been made with starched white sheets with the corner turned back invitingly. The window was open to the noises of the street, but the curtains had been drawn, so that the air was cool. The twilight room smelled of the roses and lilies and stocks, great bundles of them, in vases and jugs and jamjars, that stood on the chest, the chair, the floor.

I laughed in delight. 'David! You must have raided a market stall!'

'A dawn raid,' he agreed. 'Well, I didn't do much sleeping last night! Would you like a cup of tea first? Gosh, that sounds . . . I mean, before you unpack . . . or shall I . . .' His voice broke. '. . . Would you like me to leave you for a little while . . . ?'

When he came back, I was safely tucked up in bed, with the covers pulled up to my chin. David decently turned his back to undress, then slid quickly under the bedclothes. He was warm and smooth and bony. The hair on his arms and legs felt oddly rough. How strange, how shocking it felt to be beside another human being in a bed – and naked!

I could hear my own breathing, shallow and quick, like a frightened animal. My skin shrank from contact with his, but there was nowhere to go. The bed was too narrow.

'Would you . . . I do understand . . . would you rather not just yet?' David whispered.

That worried frown was back. He looked so anxious and so young. He had been up so early and shaved so long ago, that his chin was freckled with gold-dust, just like the motes that had showered us as we had made our promises that morning. This was David, not a stranger. This was my husband. He wouldn't hurt me.

I shook my head. 'Now, David, please – if you don't mind.'

'Mind!' He gave a little, strangled laugh that softened into a sigh.

Hark! my beloved is knocking.
'Open to me, my sister, my love,
my dove, my perfect one.'
My beloved put his hand to the latch,
and my heart was thrilled within me.

David leaned on his elbow, rearing above me and looking down on my drowsy face.

'Judith Northaw,' he whispered. 'I've waited such a long time for you.' His fingers touched my lips and trailed slowly down my throat, coming to rest on my right breast. My skin tingled where he had touched. 'But you're worth a lifetime of waiting.'

★

378

'Sorry there's no honeymoon, darling,' David said. 'I can't afford one – well, I could if I let my father pay for one, but that's something I'd rather not do . . . unless you really want . . . then, of course . . .'

I shook my head and dreamily traced the shape of his nose and jaw with one finger.

David made an unexpected spelling error on his upright, black typewriter. 'Gosh, if you carry on doing that, I'll never get this article finished!' David caught my finger and nipped it between his teeth. 'But my people are all dying to meet you. We're going to have to do a grand tour of them all some time. So that'll be a sort of honeymoon, won't it? Is that enough for you, darling? I'd give you the world if I could – or if I weren't so damned stubborn, as Clare says.'

I thought about all David's unknown relatives – as numerous as the sands of the desert, he made them sound, and as friendly as a plague of locusts. How silly! I came from a big family myself. I realised that not everyone could be friends at the same time all the time. We're all human, after all. It should be give and take.

Yet the thought of being paraded around grand houses as the latest acquisition filled me with dread. David's little mistake – his heathen bride. Poor David. Still . . .

Why can't we just stay as we are, I thought. We're happy now. Why should we do anything to change it?

In the end, it was worse than I'd ever imagined.

Whispers are like daggers. They stab you between the shoulder blades when you're not looking.

'Such a sweet, little thing, my dear, and absolutely devoted to David. Yes, a Jewess, I'm afraid, darling, but still – you'd scarcely notice . . .'

What a relief to find that I'm quite presentable, after

all. No horns, nor forked tail. And to think I'd always been afraid!

'Yes, quite the little bluestocking. From one of those frightfully intellectual families – music, languages, you know. Can't play a round of golf to save her life! Ha, ha! Ideal for poor David, of course, with his disability . . .'

'No, not dark at all, no moustache, thank goodness. Quite English-looking, really. Though one hears they have an awful tendency to run to fat at about twenty-five . . . Anyway, we've all decided to be frightfully modern and make the best of it . . .'

Never let it be said that the English are not anti-Semitic. They are, as much as any German, with this difference: they are polite enough to try (not always successfully) to disguise it. Of course, if your name happens to be Rothschild, your ancestry doesn't matter. With a bank balance like that, you could be a Martian and still be accepted in society. If, on the other hand, your name used to be Weitz . . .

At dinner with his parents in their fine house in Mount Street, waiting for the men to join us after dinner; spending Saturday to Monday at Bramleigh Court while the jangle of the gramophone silenced the birds; suffering a few days with his hard-as-nails sister Anne and her cowed husband in Wiltshire, I grew attuned to the whispers.

Sensitive as a medium, I could spot the little bubble of thought that ballooned above peoples' heads – the silent bubble that contained the words no one would put into writing in this democratic country: *JUDEN HIER UNERWÜNSCHT*.

Or was I just being extra-sensitive, waiting for – almost longing for – the insult that was never intended? Yes, yes, I know, Jews are often accused of that, too. I was like a snail robbed of its shell by a marauding thrush. Does anyone blame the snail for feeling itself threatened?

And David – my darling David – hawked me around his relatives with that loving, innocent smile on his face. Did he really not hear? One never knew how much David heard. He loved me. He was proud of me. And to hell with everyone else.

What more did I want?

'You'll like Olive,' David said, not altogether convincingly. 'She's different from the others.'

'Different isn't always better,' I said with a little, strained laugh.

'In this case – it is.' David turned round, slipping his arm under my neck and drawing my head onto his shoulder. 'Darling, I know what you've been going through. Don't think I haven't noticed. They'll love you as much as I do when they get to know you. It's just . . .'

'Just the shock, you mean,' I said, acidly.

'Yes. No, no, I don't mean that. You're putting words into my mouth. It's just that they're old and stuffy and stupid and . . . and soon they'll realise that you're the best thing that could ever have happened to me.'

He drew me closer, his hand slipping softly down my spine, splaying out over my buttocks, tucking me against him. How could I argue?

And he was right. Olive was different.

I scarcely know what to call her. Olive, Olivia, Livia. She was Livia to the world when I met her and I suppose that is what she'll always be.

Livia had bought a 'little place' in Normandy, one of those plain, stone buildings with long, peeling, grey shutters and a slate mansard roof with an *oeuil-de-boeuf* window in the centre. It stood at the end of a long drive of poplars, beautiful as an impressionist painting, beautiful enough to make you feel that nature would be impoverished without it.

'Don't you dare muck around with this,' David greeted his sister, before he'd even taken time to kiss her. He looked around the square, flagged hall to the plain staircase that rose and divided harmoniously around the square. An aqueous light filtered down through the *oeuil-de-boeuf* onto a pale, stone floor and walls only a little darker.

'Do you know,' answered Livia lightly, 'I don't feel the slightest urge to alter it. Isn't that strange?'

David's sister was so slight that she gave the impression of having floated in on the breeze that blew between the open front and back doors. Her fox-bright hair was the only colourful thing about her. The rest was subtly muted: beige linen and feather-light, pale cashmere, long and lean, with white tennis shoes to finish bare, honey-gold legs. She had the sort of clotted-cream complexion, freckle-free, that all redheads imagine they deserve, but so few actually achieve. In my little-shop-round-the-corner cotton, I felt like her maiden aunt.

'Darling Judith,' she said, giving me a hug and a kiss, 'I've heard so much about you.'

I'll bet you have, I thought, grimly.

She looked at me as though she'd intercepted the thought. Her dry-sherry eyes were clear and honest, her smile a little quizzical grin that seemed, I suddenly imagined, to hide a hurt as great as my own. I realised, with relief, that I'd found an ally at last.

But all she said was, 'Come on up, you two, and I'll show you your room.' She hefted up my suitcase before I could bend to it and set off up the stairs. 'Of course,' she said, looking back over her shoulder, 'Guy is simply fizzing that I've moved in so close to his little love nest. We see each other quite often in the market and he pretends to be fascinated by the price of artichokes. I might as well be a shadow. It's an absolute hoot!'

She showed us to a room where sunshine filtered through slits in the shutters, dappling the wall with light and shade and throwing bright patches across a huge, white muslin-draped bed. I flicked back my sweaty hair and sighed with contentment.

Behind me, David blew softly on the back of my neck. 'I told you I'd bring you on honeymoon one day,' he whispered.

I accuse myself now, sometimes, when I'm feeling very low, of wasting time during those precious days that slipped by as easily as cream across a cat's tongue. You are guilty, I say, of being happy when you had no right to be. You are guilty of going to sleep each night in the arms of your lover and of waking up in the morning with a smile. You are guilty of snatching at joy as it passed and holding on to it, no matter how hard it tried to escape.

And in my defence I plead that we only had such a little while. We didn't know it then, but we were enjoying all the happiness that we would ever be allowed.

If Livia was trying to get her husband back, she was going about it in a very strange way. David had told me as much as he knew about them, but that wasn't very much. He'd never been very observant. I worked out the rest for myself.

Livia never wasted an opportunity to thrust herself into his notice. They were often in the market, as she'd told us, at the same time and once she snatched the melon he was thinking of buying right from under his nose.

'Sorry, darling,' she laughed, 'but I have a terrible craving for melon. Do you think I could be in an interesting condition?'

They would be at tables at opposite ends of the same restaurant and she'd give a little, finger-twiddling wave across the room, then for the rest of the evening be jolly in a frantic, look-at-me sort of way that just irritated the other customers.

Somehow or other (did she have a paid spy on his staff?) she seemed to know or sense when he'd be going down to the beach.

'I have the most awful urge for a picnic and a swim,' she'd announce. 'Are you two love birds coming?'

Not taking no for an answer, she'd bundle us and a hamper into her tiny car and roar off to some windswept, sandy cove. David and I would try to place ourselves in an inconspicuous position, but there was a gruesome fascination in watching Livia spread out her deck chair and sunshade as close to her husband as she could get without actually sitting on his lap. He'd be reading, or perhaps making notes, pages and pages of dense scribbles, and Livia would potter around busily looking for fossils – such a marvellous coast for ammonites, my dears – with a great display of arms and legs in the first two-piece bathing costume I'd seen. Such a flat, brown midriff. (Would David like me in one, I wondered. I didn't mind him seeing my tummy, but I'd no intention of showing it to anyone else. Did he think his sister a show-off or his wife a prude? Or did he not notice at all?)

And Guy's lover would be there, too. A great bruiser of a man, younger than Guy, blond and muscular, he'd lie sulkily face down on the sand, or snatch away Guy's notes and lie on them, so that Guy would have to tussle with him to get them back. They'd roll together in the sand, a tangle of arms and legs, fair and dark, scratching and punching. I'd look away. There was something wrong about it, but I didn't know what. Sometimes he'd swim furiously, splashy and showy, towards the horizon, so far that Guy would get up and stand at the water's edge, nervously biting his nails.

Then Livia would stop her manic pottering and watch him. The expression on her face often brought tears to my eyes.

'He's written nothing, you know,' Livia would declare, 'nothing worth reading since he came to hibernate here. Guy needs lights and people and noise to stimulate him. Here he spends so much time trying to keep his pretty boy – poor wretch – amused, he hasn't time to work. It's such a waste and I never could abide waste.'

'I don't really think that's any of your business any longer, Olive,' David warned.

'Oh, but it is, my dear. People will forget him, unless he produces something soon. The public memory is so short. And Guy will just die if no one reads him. So it's up to me to rescue him. You could even say it's my duty.'

'Don't meddle, you'll do more harm than good.'

'Oh, I don't think so,' Livia said airily and blew her brother a kiss. 'You're becoming so cautious, darling. Don't say you're growing up at last.'

It was a relief when one morning Livia suggested that perhaps David and I might like to amuse ourselves for the day.

'You've been very sweet and done everything I've asked, but I've decided to stop being selfish. So you two go and have fun. I've got a date!'

'Anyone we know?' asked David with an indulgent smile. 'Clark Gable, perhaps? Or Cary Grant?'

'Someone much handsomer than that! Guess!' Livia held her breath, an expectant smile making her look about sixteen years old. 'No, you never will. It's my husband!'

I don't think Livia saw the look of alarm that David shot towards me. 'Guy?' he said, incredulously.

'Yes – Guy! We're meeting for lunch and then – who knows – perhaps a walk or perhaps . . .' She winked and the effect was startlingly lewd, as though a nun had shown her stocking tops. Livia was frequently naughty, but I'd never known that she could be coarse.

'I suppose you know what you're doing?'

'Oh yes, darling. I know *exactly* what I'm doing.'

Livia looked ravishing. David and I were sunning ourselves on the terrace when she popped over to say goodbye. She wore a very simple frock, crisp and white, buttoning down one side, where the straight skirt flared into half a dozen strict pleats. It was tightly cinched with a striped straw belt in Breton red and white that matched the buttons.

'Goodness,' I exclaimed. 'You look good enough to eat.'

'I do hope so – what a sweetie you are. Now I don't expect to be back early, so you two do whatever you want.'

Whatever we wanted turned out to be not very much. Livia had so regimented our days, that it was a luxury just to lie in the sun, talking and reading. During the hottest part of the day, we slipped inside for a siesta and, what with one thing and another, it was early evening before we appeared again.

Livia was sitting on the terrace, sipping a virulently coloured cocktail. She was wearing sunglasses and a huge straw hat.

'Oh, goodie,' she cried when she saw us, 'here you are. Drinking alone is so bad for the morale, don't you think?'

'It sounds to me as though you haven't let that stop you,' remarked David in a schoolmasterish tone.

'Well, maybe I've had one or two . . . no harm in that. Pour me another, darling, won't you?'

'How was your day?' I asked, slipping into one of the chairs beside her.

'Oh . . . you know . . .'

'Fun?'

'Tremendous,' she agreed, with a little shake in her voice.

'Guy well?' asked David, handing his sister back her refilled glass.

'In cracking form.' She put the glass to her lips. It clicked off her teeth and the brightly-coloured liquid slopped over her white skirt. 'Oh damn . . . oh damn . . . do you have a hankie?' Livia dabbed ineffectively at the stain. 'Oh damn . . .'

Her voice cracked and broke. She put down the glass carefully and, for just a moment, laid her head down on her knees. Then she stood up, unfolding abruptly.

'I suppose you might as well know – can't go into purdah forever.' She took off the hat and glasses. Her left eye was grossly swollen, almost closed, with a sunburst of colours beginning to develop. Across the bridge of her nose was a small cut, the kind that might have been made by a heavy, embossed ring. 'It's not what you think,' she said, holding her head high with impressive dignity. 'He does love me . . . he must love me . . . he wouldn't do this to me if he didn't care . . . No, stay there.' She made a gesture to stop me getting up. 'I don't want to be any trouble . . .'

'But what are you going to do?' I asked, naively.

387

'Nothing, of course. What else? He'll come back to me in the end. He has to.'

She put the glasses back on and went into the house with a heartbreakingly jaunty stride.

'She should bathe that eye,' I said.

'She will. Just leave her for a while. It's better for her. She doesn't want either of us. People often used to think that I was simple,' David said softly, 'but there are times when I thank God I'm not as complicated as the rest of my family.'

'How wonderful,' Livia announced over one breakfast, 'Clare's coming to visit on one of her dashes backwards and forwards to Germany.' She tossed a letter across to David. It landed with one corner in a dish of *confiture de mirabelles*. David sucked it clean, then read it. His little frown was back. 'Isn't that tremendous?' Livia continued. 'I don't suppose you've seen Clare for ages. Won't it be fun to be all together again? Why don't I invite Anne and Nickie, too? We could have an enormous house party.'

'I don't really think that'd be an awfully good idea,' David said slowly.

'Now, don't be such a spoilsport. It's about time Judith met Clare, anyway. How can she really know you without knowing your other half? You're two sides of the same coin. It's like bread without butter, Fred without Ginger, Laurel without Hardy . . .'

'That's what I mean,' he answered.

Nothing that David could say would put Livia off her plan. She had a rather touching vision of one, big, happy family laughing, picnicking, swimming and playing tennis together.

'We're all grown up now,' she said and even I thought she was being a bit optimistic. 'Quite old enough to be friends.'

So guest bedrooms, untouched probably since 1914 or even before, were refurbished in a flurry of excitement. Extra staff were hired – the cook and one housemaid who looked after Livia couldn't possibly cope. Another car was hired.

'Such fun,' Livia announced as though no one could possibly disagree with her. 'I can't wait until they all arrive.'

Nondescript Nickie, with his coarsely-veined red cheeks, gave me a rather sloppy kiss on the mouth. 'Marvellous to see you again, my dear. You're looking so well. Marriage obviously suits you. This young devil looking after you properly, eh? You just let me know if he doesn't and I'll soon sort him out!'

Cool Anne. Another kiss, brisk and businesslike. As though to say, 'Well, she's my sister-in-law and there's nothing I can do about it, so I'll jolly well make the best of things.' Then her attention was distracted by a crash from the drawing room, where a litter of enormous children seemed to be dismembering the furniture.

'Darlings, is that really a good idea?' she wailed.

'Told you we should never have brought them,' Nickie muttered rebelliously. 'Don't know anyone else who travels with their brats.'

And all the time, I felt David vibrating like a bowstring. He was looking out the window, peering down the drive a thousand times a day. His face was expressionless, but his tension was almost audible. Even I didn't know whether he was excited by or dreaded the coming meeting.

And then, at last, he was caught out. The huge, black car crunched to a halt before the steps and there was no one there in greeting. Livia had kidnapped us all for a game of beach quoits that lasted until long after we should have been changing for dinner.

We all trooped in through the garden door, brown and salt-water-stained, with hair anyhow and bare, sandy legs.

'Gosh, I'm exhausted,' groaned Livia. 'Isn't having fun just too tiring? Let's all be sluts tonight – shall we? – and have dinner off a tray. Who's for a martini?'

And there she was. Clare. David stopped so suddenly that Nickie cannoned into him.

She sat in a chair by the window with the evening light behind her, so that she was all in shadow. Her legs were languidly crossed, her hands hanging loosely over the arms of the chair. But I had the impression that her calm was all a careful pose. I could feel a tight ripple of emotion run through her that mirrored David's. Behind her stood a long, black shadow of a man.

'Darling, how lovely!' Livia swooped towards her. I thought she was going to kiss her sister, but she stopped short suddenly. 'How beastly of us not to be here when you arrived. I hope you made yourselves comfy. Now, introduce us all to this devastating man.'

'I hope,' said Clare coolly, 'that you're not turning into one of those boring society women who call everyone darling and never mean it. Anyway, you all know Otto –' She swept us all with a smile that never went further than her teeth. '– except Judith, of course. Otto, this is Judith Northaw née Weitz. Judith, this is SS-Untergruppenführer Otto von Darmheim.'

Guilty of being happy. Guilty of snatching at passing joy. Guilty of forgetting.

I'd look at Clare's lover – oh, yes, we all knew they were lovers, they made no secret of it – and think of the letters (a fat bundle now) returned marked *Adressat Unbekannt*. I'd think of the last time I saw my parents: my mother filling in that awful waiting time at the station by repeating, like a charm, how much better things would be in Berlin; my father silent and – yes – weak, giving in to the urgings of his wife, against his better judgement, but unable to think of a credible alternative.

Move. Keep moving. They can't catch us if we move fast enough and far enough. Berlin had been nowhere near far enough.

Otto von Darmheim was smooth, charming, even to me – my mother, in a different world, would have adored him – but if I had not been a guest in Livia's house, I'd have taken one of the delicate, pearl-handled fruit knives and carved up his face a little more.

Clare's baleful glare was always turned on me. Whenever I looked up from my plate, whenever I looked incautiously across the room, or passed her on the stairs, I'd feel her eyes, fire and ice, that branded me with a mark only she could see. She called me to my face '*die kleine Judin*' – the little Jewess – with a contemptuous sneer, but only when David was absent. Not even Clare dared taunt her twin to that extent. And I (foolishly) begged Livia not to tell him.

'I say, that's a bit thick,' blustered Nickie the first time he heard the title.

'It doesn't matter,' I said quietly. 'I'm little and I'm Jewish and proud of it – what else should she call me?'

'I don't know. Doesn't seem right to me. Still, as long as you're happy . . .'

'As long as David's happy,' I corrected. 'He cares for her so much.'

English newspapers were available a day late in the nearest town. We hadn't bothered with them until then. 'Who cares what's happening in dull, old England?' Livia would say. 'I don't need to know if some test Match has been rained off.' But Nickie couldn't survive without a daily diet of information, even if most of it was out of date before he got it. So he would drive into town every morning after breakfast to buy a newspaper and probably have a *marc* or two with the lads in the Café de Commerce. Most mornings, he bought *The Times*. One morning, his eye was caught by something different.

'Oh no, couldn't possibly,' I heard Nickie say as I wandered onto the terrace where a salad lunch was laid out. 'That wouldn't be right at all. Not fair.'

'I agree,' said Livia. 'Get rid of the thing.'

'Nonsense, we should show her,' Anne said firmly. 'It's for her own good. She ought to know.'

'Who ought to know what?' I asked, idly.

'Nothing. No one.' Nickie looked like a guilty schoolboy caught copying in an examination. He sat down quickly, but I could see the corner of a newspaper sticking out from beneath the seat cushion.

'Stand up, Nickie,' said his wife, briskly. She half-pushed him to his feet and pulled the newspaper out. 'I think you ought to see this, Judith. You ought to know.'

Clare's face looked back at me, terrible as an army with banners, gauntleted hand shading her brow, and I could see behind her the rows of menacing swastikas.

WHAT MISS NORTHAW WOULD LIKE TO SEE

screamed the headline in bold, black type.

WE Don't Agree With Her. Write to the Editor and Tell Us What You Think.

The Daily Mirror opens this page today to Miss Clare Northaw, Englishwoman and personal friend of Hitler. Would she get the same freedom for unpopular views in Germany? We say NO!

The rest of the page was devoted to an open letter signed by Clare.

> . . . those who believe that National Socialist Germany wishes to weaken England show a sad ignorance of Nazi ideology.
>
> And when discussing that ideology, one must remember that National Socialism is more to Germans than a political creed; it is a faith.

The print began to waver before my eyes.

> One of the foundations of Nazi ideology is the racial theory.
>
> Germans believe the Nordic race to be the greatest in the world, which indeed it is. They believe that the future of Europe stands or falls with the Nordic race. And they believe that enmity between the two great Nordic countries would mean its virtual suicide.
>
> Humanly speaking, friendship between England and Germany is the most natural thing in the world...

I folded the paper and gave it back to Nickie. The blood had drained away from my head, leaving it empty and light. I thought it might float away.

'Don't tell David,' I whispered. 'Please, don't tell David.'

'I'll burn the damn thing,' Nickie blustered. 'Why couldn't you just have kept quiet about it, Anne? Always meddle, meddle . . .'

'Then why did you buy it?' she retorted.

'I'm going to have a baby.'

Clare's voice cut through the gabble around the table, clear and incisive, a silver knife. No one could have thought they misheard her – no matter how much anyone may have wished to. A moth blundered around the candles. I heard a tiny fizzle as it hit the flame, beautiful and incandescent for a split second. Then it fell to the table, charred, in shreds.

'I'm going to have a beautiful baby,' she repeated and her face was so transfigured by joy, that I scarcely recognised the sullen Blackshirt I had first met.

'We heard you the first time,' Anne snapped. 'Is there some kind of tradition in this family for women to produce brats out of wedlock? First Olive – then you.'

'Isn't the pot calling the kettle just a teeny-weeny bit black, darling?' cooed Livia, sweetly. 'After all, you may have gone to your own marriage bed a virgin – did you really, I wonder? – but you popped out of it and into someone else's pretty damn quickly.'

'Steady on,' warned Nickie, placing his hand over his wife's clenched fist. 'I think that's rather uncalled for, Livia. I'll have to ask you to take it back, please.'

'To please you, Nickie, anything. But the truth always hurts. Congratulations, Judith. You seem to be the only woman at this table who's managed to get married without a shotgun and lived happily ever after – so far.'

'We were talking about my baby,' Clare broke in with a petulant glare at me.

'So we were, darling. Well, when's the happy day?' Livia asked, with a giggle. 'And how big a bouquet are you going to need to cover the bump?'

'We're not getting married.'

'Oh . . .'

Anne's tiny exclamation was the only reply. The rest of us were silent, still working out the correct response. I looked across at David. He'd gone quite white, haggard with shock. He was pleating and re-pleating his table napkin with urgent fingers, but his eyes never left Otto's face.

'Well, why should we?' Clare flung into the silence, defiantly. 'What is marriage anyway? Two healthy people have a duty to ensure that the purity of race is continued into the next generation. A few superstitious words spoken by an old man in a nightgown won't make our relationship any more holy. Ours is a union of free will, entered into freely.'

Everyone began talking at once, then – except David and Otto. We all had something to say – opinions to give, feelings to voice, with Nickie and Anne the loudest and most indignant.

'Nicely spoken, poppet,' said Livia with a little laugh. 'You've learned your lines nicely for Uncle Otto. Perhaps he'll give you a sweetie if you're a good girl . . . oh, grow up, Clare, do, for goodness sake. All that Nazi twaddle he's primed you with . . . I expect the real reason he won't marry you is that he's married already.'

'I am, actually,' said Otto, quietly, the first words he'd spoken, and we all stopped quarrelling to listen. 'But I consider it an honour that Clare has consented to bear my child and I will do my utmost to care for them both. As a mother, she will have a position of respect among the German people.'

He spoke seriously and firmly. His confidence was impressive and no one interrupted him. For the first time, I tried to see him as a man and not as a figurehead in uniform. But I couldn't do it. He carried the *Totenkopf* symbol with him wherever he went. Perhaps I was the only one who saw it. He bore it on his forehead like the mark of Cain. I couldn't separate the man from the death's head.

The extraordinary thing was that every one else seemed to trust him.

On the opposite side of the bed, the sheets were chilly. David had been out of bed some time. With sleep-blurred eyes, I looked towards the window, from where his shadow streamed back, wavering and pale. He didn't stir as I moved beside him and laid my cheek against his shoulder.

'You can't live her life for her,' I said softly.

'I wanted to kill him tonight,' he answered, in a toneless whisper, flat and controlled. 'I've never felt like that before. I've never believed in violence as an answer to anything, but I felt like pulling him to pieces. It's a shock.'

'I think he really will look after her. He cares for her, in his way. It's not our way, but none the worse for that.'

'But what will happen to her? And what will that child grow up to be? It'll be indoctrinated from birth, twisted and warped. They'll turn it into a monster, between them. I can't allow it to happen.'

'You don't have any option. Clare is an adult woman who's made a choice – just the same as you've made a choice. She's scandalised your family – but so have you. You're so like each other, but you're *not* the same person. Let her do what she has to.'

David turned and buried his face between my breasts. I could feel him shuddering and I put my arms around him, holding him close.

'I can't,' he whispered.

I stroked his hair, soothing, murmuring sweet, silly words, as a mother to a child who's wakened from a nightmare, but finds the bad dream still has a grip and won't let go.

Gradually he relaxed and his embrace altered subtly. We were a man and a woman again. His body was beautiful in the moonlight, each hollow and curve silver-edged, gleaming. His loving was warm and generous and piercingly sweet.

And when we were exhausted, we lay for a long time

together, kissing now and again in a sleepy, idle way, stroking each other with relaxed, undemanding fingers, until the moon disappeared. In the dark hour before the sun rises, I shivered.

David rose and, bending over, picked me up easily and carried me back to the bed. He knelt beside me and stroked the hair back from my forehead.

'Are you happy?' he asked.

'Mmm – very.'

'All the time?'

I laughed softly. 'Silly – who is? Most of the time.'

'I want you to be happy all the time,' he insisted.

'I am – nearly.'

'All the time . . .'

He wasn't joking. I thought he had been asking silly questions in the way lovers do, never expecting a serious answer. But now his fingers were hard on my shoulders. I couldn't see his face, but I could hear his urgent breathing.

'David . . .'

'What will make you happy, Judith? Tell me.'

There was only one answer and I didn't want to give it. It wouldn't be fair.

'Tell me,' he demanded.

'I want to find my family.'

I am a British citizen. My passport is blue, stiff, gold-embossed. This border guard with the swastika arm-band is to allow me to pass freely without let or hindrance, or he will have to answer to His Britannic Majesty's Secretary of State. He cannot shove me roughly into his guardroom, like that old man there. He cannot drag me off, never to be seen again. He must lift his red-and-white-striped pole and let me pass with my husband beneath the snapping blood-coloured banners. I am a married woman and a British citizen.

So I must stop cracking my knuckles and biting my nails. I must sit coolly and look as though I belong to the nation whose schoolrooms are still decorated by maps coloured with great red splotches. I may watch other, lesser mortals being interrogated as to their reasons for visiting the Reich. I might allow myself to look impatient – that would be in character – but I must definitely not look afraid. Whatever have I to be afraid of? I have a magic talisman and its power will protect me wherever I go.

If anything, the town looks more prosperous than when I left. There are signs of full employment. The river is thronged with barges waiting their turn to use the lock lift. The boatyards echo with the noise of riveting, clanging and hammering. Above the arcaded entrance to the Rathaus an eagle spreads proud wings. It grips in its talons a laurel wreath encircling a swastika. The prices displayed in the shops are very reasonable. But shutters cover the windows of the Sachs's shoe shop and, round the corner, the Frankl's newspaper shop is still open, but has a deserted look, as though whatever news they sell is long stale.

Women still gossip in the streets, baskets over their arms. I can hear snatches of their dialogue as I pass and the thick, country accents are as wholesome as bread and butter. They look well-off and comfortable. Then a long, black car glides down the street. The gossiping women drift away into shops, look into windows, shut their doors. I am alone in the street with the occupants of the black car. Two men look out of its windows. They scarcely see me, yet I feel as though I am standing naked under their gaze.

And here is our house, looking bright and well cared for. The window boxes brim with scarlet geraniums. They've just been watered. The ground is damp and

the air smells spicy. A few fallen petals lie spilled as
though the unseen waterer had cut a finger. There are
new net curtains in all the windows. A perambulator
stands at the door. I stoop to pick up the stuffed bear
that the baby has dropped. I peer into the pram and the
child, blond curls and chubby cheeks, holds out fat
hands for the bear.

There is a smell of cinnamon and apples. Mother is
baking, I think, there will be *strüdl* for tea when the
boys come home from school. Then the baby's mother,
a stranger, comes out of my house. She has a broad,
peasant face and wears a flowered pinafore. She says
guten Tag and looks at me incuriously.

'A lovely baby,' I say and watch the mother's face
blossom with pride. Then I walk on.

I'm perversely glad that someone is caring for our
house so well.

Frau Hummel opens her door to my knock and turns
so pale that I think she's going to faint.

'*Du lieber Gott,*' she gasps and slams the door.

David and I had booked into a small *Gasthaus* outside
the town where there was little chance of my being
recognised. I don't know what I hoped to achieve by
our visit. I knew already that my family had disappeared
and it was over-optimistic to imagine that anyone
would be prepared to tell me where and when. Frau
Hummel's reaction had made that perfectly clear.

I was an unwelcome ghost. People would be happier
not to see me. I reminded them of too much.

'I wanted to see . . . to know . . .' Even though we
were the only guests at breakfast, I felt the need to talk
to David very quietly. That morning, for the first time
for a year, I had found myself giving the *deutsche Blick*,
the German look, a furtive glance over each shoulder
before I spoke. How quickly I had adapted to the

old ways again. 'Someone must know, there must be a clue . . . Can we go back to the house again? Perhaps to Uncle Rudi's factory? Someone there might know.'

'We can,' agreed David, doubtfully. 'But unless someone is prepared to speak to you, I don't see what you can gain by just looking.' Seeing my expression, he went on, quickly. 'Whatever you like – we'll go to the factory, anywhere, but you must be prepared to be disappointed. Unless we attract attention to ourselves by asking questions and being a nuisance, we'll find out nothing.'

And I didn't want to attract attention to myself. I didn't have that much faith in my new, blue passport.

'Perhaps the best thing to do,' suggested David as we went out the front door into a drizzly, humid morning, 'is for me to go to the Rathaus by myself and ask a few straightforward questions.'

'What?' I squeaked in amazement. 'Are you mad?'

'Saner than you think. What good will it do skulking around, acting suspiciously? I'm a foreigner. I'm enquiring about some old family friends. I don't suspect anything underhand, therefore I don't act in an underhanded fashion. I go straight to the officials and ask. What's wrong with that?'

'Well, nothing . . .' I hesitated. 'If they've simply moved, then you'll get a straight answer and that will be that. But I know the way these people work. If . . . if anything else has happened, then they'll fob you off with polite answers and have you followed for the rest of your stay. At the moment, you haven't attracted any attention, but if you do, then every movement you make will be watched and analysed. You won't be able to draw breath without someone making a note of it.'

'Then what do we do?'

'I don't know yet. Coming here was the easy part.'

I was wrong. We had already attracted attention. We opened the door of the car David had rented. On the driver's seat was a folded piece of paper.

We got into the car and drove off before unfolding and reading it. There was one word scrawled in pencil on the paper: *Hermannsdenkmal.*

'What does that mean?' asked David.

'It's a monument. Look, on the hill, you can see it from here. It's a popular Sunday walk. There's a café and footpaths and so on.'

'Yes, but what does it mean?'

'I suppose we have to go there.'

'Do you think it's safe?'

'I don't know – but I'm going anyway.'

Since the message didn't give us a time or a date, we decided to go straightaway and see what came of it. The road followed the river a little way, then began to wind sharply up an escarpment shaded by beeches.

Seven-eighths of the way up the hill, we passed a woman pushing a bicycle.

'That's Frau Hummel,' I said, turning to stare backwards. David slowed the car, but the woman made a flicking gesture with her hand, urging us on.

On a Sunday, the area would have been thronged with enthusiastic hikers and the café full of people eating cream cakes, but on a drizzly Tuesday morning, there was no one in sight. Like a pair of bored tourists, David and I stood at the bottom of the monument, looking up at the massive, cross-gartered legs of the German hero, Hermann. Oddly foreshortened from this angle, he stood in his winged helmet with his sword arm raised.

'Good heavens,' murmured David. 'Why are all the heroes in this country so big?'

When we turned round, we saw Frau Hummel standing with her bicycle in the shelter of the trees.

Before I could frame a single question, she took both my hands in hers and kissed me. 'My dear, they are gone,' she said, gently.

'All?' I gasped.

She nodded.

'All? The boys too? But they were just children. What had they done?'

I was suffocating. There wasn't air fit to breathe in the whole of Germany.

'All,' she confirmed. 'When your aunt and uncle still lived, they told me that your parents had been sent to Oranienburg. Why I don't know – who knows these things – maybe they upset their landlord, maybe they got involved in politics, maybe someone was jealous or wanted your father's job or apartment, maybe they wouldn't pay their grocer black market prices, maybe they are in the wrong place at the wrong time, who knows? Such terrible things happen these days, you wouldn't believe. People are so spiteful. If they don't like the way you wear your hat, they denounce you. Your aunt cried on my shoulder and told me that your whole family had been picked up at five o'clock one morning and not even allowed to dress. She showed me a postcard from your father asking for strong boots and warm clothes. Such a parcel she sent, full of everything they asked for and more – tinned food, money. Then nothing.'

David stood with his head cocked to one side, straining to understand the flood of German in a dialect that almost defeated the rudiments I had taught him. Yet he could follow the drift, if not the details.

'But what can we do?' he demanded.

'Believe me – nothing. If they are dead, they are lucky. Then your uncle, God rest his soul, he never got over the way his Oskar died – terrible, terrible . . . He put his head in the gas oven one night. Your aunt found him in the morning, the kitchen full of gas and the house ready to blow up. I'm sorry, her heart was never strong . . .'

Frau Hummel was a tough old woman. Her tears were hard and hot. They trickled down the seams in her cheeks and into the corners of her mouth.

I walked silently away. I walked around the monument. My feet scuffed through drifts of crisp leaves that rippled, gold and brown, around the base of the steps.

All. All gone. The love and the warmth and the happiness. In fragments, in snatches, a ragbag of memories, their faces, their voices teased me: Mother lighting the *Shabbat* candles, their glow softening her pinched face, making her young again; Father standing on the teacher's podium, his saturnine face intent, reciting Milton in beautiful, accentless English; Aunt Lotte half-laughing, half-scandalised at one of Uncle Rudi's jokes, her ring-laden hand on her heart. 'Oh, that man will be the death of me . . .'

In the place in my heart where I had kept safe my love for them all, I felt a surge of hatred, deeper and blacker than I'd ever have believed possible. It darkened the sky. It blotted out the sun.

I didn't know words bad enough to curse and blast the men who had done this. My grief was wordless, timeless, centuries old.

When I came back, Frau Hummel was wheeling her cycle off. I fell into step beside her.

'I can't stay. Who knows . . . I haven't much time. Listen, there is a child I know of. A little boy – six years old. His father has disappeared and his mother is frantic to get the boy to safety. She will do anything – even give him away. Take him . . .'

She put one foot on the pedal and scooted off down the hill.

'We can't do that,' shouted David.

'Tomorrow,' she called back over her shoulder.

The border guard is taking so long with the car in front. What's he doing? Why's he taking so many notes? The shiny grey Mercedes with blue leather upholstery is driven by a man in a matching grey suit and blue shirt. His face and head match each other, too, shining pink and clean. The pretty blonde beside him, her hair wrapped in a blue silk scarf, is examining her red nails. They only want a drive in the Belgian countryside for an afternoon. Yes, they have money. No, they have no permit to take out such a large amount. So the border guard writes out a receipt for the man's wallet and solemnly hands him a small amount of *Taschengeld*, pocket money, a few coins only. They'll be lucky to have two cups of coffee on that amount, let alone hire a hotel room for an hour or two.

Such attention to detail. I'd persuaded David to go to a busy crossing instead of the quiet one he'd chosen because I thought the guards would be too occupied to pay anyone much attention. Yet they worry about the contents of the pockets of people who have every intention of returning to the country in an hour or so. How can we hope to take out a child with no travel documents, when even the lining of one's wallet is scrutinised? We must be mad.

My blouse has dark, damp patches under the arms. My top lip is sweating – I can feel the prickle, I long to scratch. I look across at David. His hands are relaxed on the steering wheel. His knuckles are not even white. The breeze is flicking through his hair. A smile, a very small smile, just curves his lips. How does he do it? He's actually enjoying himself.

Our turn. David rolls the car gently forward down the slope a yard or two, without bothering to put it into gear.

'Heil Hitler.'

'Heil Hitler,' we respond, obediently, and the words sear my lips.

The boy begins to grizzle. He throws down his red tin car and rubs his eyes. Oh, God. He's going to cry for his Mutti and Vati, he's going to talk in German. I twist round, kneeling in my seat, pick up the car and try to interest him in it.

'Look, Henry darling,' I say brightly in English, 'the bonnet opens. Look inside.'

By the time I turn round again, we're in Belgium.

We've done it! We've done it!

Just a nice young English couple with their little boy going home after their holiday. The guard had flicked through David's passport, but he didn't even bother with mine – hadn't I simply been described on entry as *Ehefrau*, David's wife, not an entity in my own right – let alone wonder about the child. We were so ordinary.

Never, never again.

David turned the car down the next narrow lane that led nowhere. When we were out of sight, he jerked to a halt and pulled me across to him. He had never been so forceful. His lips sealed around mine as though he were trying to steal the breath out of my body. His hands roved over me, trembling with the excitement that had passed and the reward to come. He lit a flicker in me that flared up as suddenly as a brush fire. I would have given myself to him gladly at that moment. He had a right to anything I could offer.

'David,' I managed to say, 'David – the child!'

With a little, embarassed laugh, David sat back and flicked back his hair.

'Gosh!' he said. 'I aged about fifty years back there!'

And little Henry, or Heinrich, went to live with a childless civil servant and his wife and was sent to Stoatley

Rough School, near Haslemere, run by the Quaker-organised German Emergency Committee – God bless them. Would he ever see his parents again? Would he remember them in ten years time – next year, even?

At least he didn't have to join the long lists of children offered, along with pianos, secondhand fur coats and pedigree puppies, in the small advertisement columns. The lists were getting longer, the pleas more frantic, with every month that passed.

Please, please help. Give my children a home. Two boys and a girl, clean, intelligent, hardworking.

Which family will take a boy, 15 years old, from a first-class orthodox Frankfurt family and give him a chance to continue his education? He has had to leave school and his father (a jeweller) is penniless.

And everywhere committees were trying to help, in their own ways, with their own special interests at heart, scarcely one liaising with another. The League of Nations special commissioner, James MacDonald, beavered away in isolation in Geneva. The *Reichsvertretung der Juden in Deutschland* did the same. The Jewish Refugees Committee, in return for a relaxed interpretation of entry regulations, promised the British government that no Jewish refugee would be a charge on public funds. The Central British Fund for German Jewry raised a quarter of a million in less than a year. The Chief Rabbi's Religious Emergency Council ran orthodox refugee homes, one for boys and one for girls. The little people, good people: Anna Essinger's school, Bunce Court, in Kent; Greta Burkill's house of safety in Cambridge, financed by Jesus College.

Why didn't they *talk* to one another? No concerted effort. No government-led assistance. Why didn't they *make* the governments listen? Only governments had the resources to cope with the undreamed of volume of human misery. Volunteers couldn't and couldn't be expected to cope. The Jewish Refugees Committee received up to a thousand calls a day. Only the Dutch showed some official humanity.

Of course, now we know that the English did come to their senses, when it was nearly too late. From 1938, ten thousand children were brought out of Germany and German occupied lands. Maybe two million remained and died. How many more could have been saved, if their rescue had begun sooner?

So many people helping. So many needing help. So few helped.

Send them to China. Send them to Northern Australia. Send them to Central America, to South West Africa . . . The bigger, the emptier, the less hospitable the land, the more Jews it was thought could be transported and dumped there. Had no one learned geography at school? Send them to Palestine. Ah, if only . . .

'We've done it once,' David said. 'We can do it again.'

'We'll never be so lucky again.'

'No,' he agreed. 'That was a stupid escapade. It could have ended in disaster. But with planning – who knows . . .'

David the dreamer was growing up into a practical man.

Without Chris's contacts and inside knowledge, we couldn't have started. First of all, we needed passports with the names of fictitious children written in. Two, at most, we decided. We just weren't old enough to have any more children, scarcely old enough for two.

'How precocious we must be,' laughed David, patting my tummy. 'Two's quite enough. You can have as many children as you like later on!'

The plan was that we would visit Germany quite openly, entering at one point without children and leaving at another with two children tagging along. We would be as natural as possible and make no attempt to hide our movements. We'd be the young married couple on holiday.

In addition, we'd probably need more than one passport each, as entry and exit stamps would otherwise mount up to a suspicious level. We didn't want someone asking why we went on holiday so often. Also we needed to allow for different possiblities: one boy, one girl; two girls; two boys; sometimes we might go by car, sometimes by train.

We sat up late in Chris's flat, talking through the snags. The air was stale with cigarette smoke and beer fumes. Chris had stretched out over the floor and had kicked off his shoes. His eyes were closed and I thought he'd fallen asleep.

'You're mad,' said Chris at last, without opening his eyes.

'Is it mad to want to *do* something?' David demanded. He was perched on the edge of his chair, alight with eagerness. His elbows rested on his knees, giving the impression of gawky limbs, all tangled together. 'What has all your banner waving and shouting actually *achieved*? Sometimes it feels as though everyone I know is protesting – but we're all running like mad and getting nowhere. Has daubing slogans on walls saved a single life? Has getting yourself arrested pulled a single person out of a concentration camp?'

'I suppose you put him up to this?' Chris queried, opening one eye and squinting lazily at me.

'No,' I answered quietly. 'David is not a boy any more, to be led here and there by other people's demands. This is his own idea. But whatever he does, I'll do too. I'd put a bomb under Hitler, if I thought I'd

408

get near enough. I'd burn down the Reichstag if someone hadn't already done it. I'd do *anything*. This is a
small thing – we'll be able to take so few – but I think
we'll succeed. If we don't, it won't be because we
haven't tried hard enough.'

'You're definitely mad. But the mad are under the
special protection of the gods, they say. Yes, I can get
the documents for you, but they'll be expensive. They'll
be genuine British passports, not fakes. My contact is
a professional. Can you pay?'

'We'll pay.'

And David, cap in hand, went back to his parents.
He asked the father whose money he had scorned since
he'd walked out of university for enough to buy a
house.

He didn't take me with him. I couldn't have faced his
father with a lie like that. The poor man was pleased to
help, pleased that his only son had grown out of his
socialist madness. Such deception. David spun a terrible
tale of a little Georgian terraced house for sale in Lime-
house for £150.

'It has a marvellous view of the river. Judith loves it.'

'You can do better than that,' his father had said. 'I
know just the place for you round the corner, not very
big, but room for a nursery and a couple of servants.
You'll be needing a nursery soon, I shouldn't wonder.
Or what about a cottage in the country? Let your
mother look out for something nice for you – she's got
a good eye.'

But David dug his heels in. To his credit, he had the
grace to blush when he showed me the generous cheque
his father had written, there and then, for far more than
he'd been asked for. Thank goodness his father didn't
have the energy to come and look at 'our' house.

Perhaps, after all, he didn't care.

'I don't like it,' I murmured. 'It seems so deceitful.'

'Chris would say that the end justifies the means.'

'I know. He would. Hitler says something like that, too, and Stalin, I shouldn't wonder. Does that make it better?'

'I'll give it back if you're unhappy, darling. But I really do think that this is too important to quibble over middle-class scruples.'

And I thought about that day beneath the grotesque grandeur of the Hermannsdenkmal when Frau Hummel had wept to tell me of my family's annihilation. The seed of hate had taken root in my heart then and I had watered it every day with my tears.

'We'll do whatever we have to,' I said.

'That should do it,' said Chris, pocketing the cheque. 'Don't worry. There'll be some change.'

The main drawback, as far as I could see, was that we could only take children whose families could afford to pay. With the new documents, Chris had handed back less change than we'd hoped for from David's father's cheque. There were tickets or fuel to buy for every journey and we just didn't have the money. I worried about only being able to offer freedom to those who could buy it. It felt like blood money. God knows, I'd have taken every child free, if I could, but the world doesn't work like that and a sweet smile doesn't buy very many ferry tickets.

Sometimes, a synagogue or church community would club together to ensure that a needy family, perhaps with a father in concentration camp or a sick mother, could get their children to safety. That made me feel better. I didn't want to sell liberty.

David and I had done a lot of thinking since our first crazy attempt. As well as credible documents, we needed to make sure that the children looked English. What English children wore leather coats or very short

410

shorts or caps of that particularly German cut, wide and flat across the top? So in our suitcases we always carried a schoolboy's cap, a blazer, a smocked dress, a cardigan (*only* the English could have invented the cardigan!), Start-rite shoes and long socks.

In addition, we had to persuade the children that, although they could talk when we were alone, they were on no account to open their mouths if a man in uniform was around. That wasn't difficult. These children had learned at an early age that uniforms meant trouble.

Karl and Ulli. Klara and Rosina. Recha and Johann. If I close my eyes, I can see their faces looking back at me, aged beyond their years, eyes that have seen too much, trusting so little in their distorted lives, but trusting us because their parents have told them to. In my dreams, they walk hand in hand in a crocodile behind me, clutching their little parcels, on their way to the good people who would take them in.

Jew and Christian. Catholic and Protestant. Pole, Russian or German. They were all children.

Only once were we forced to use a train. Never again!

David's car had broken down and we felt it would be dangerous to wait around, because we'd already made contact with the family of the children who were coming with us on this trip. So we decided that he'd stay to get the car repaired, while I went ahead by train with the children, as they were entered on my passport.

How can any mother be so desperate that she's prepared to hand her children over to strangers? How can any mother be so afraid that she'll take a journey half-way across the country, to where she's not known, to where there are no prying eyes to say, 'Who was the stranger I saw your children going off with, Frau X?', and then go home again without them?

The mother was a little woman who'd once been

plump and pampered. Some man had loved her, had worked hard to provide the fur coat, the smart frock that now hung loosely from her shoulders, the dainty shoes. Perhaps she knew where he was, but dared not say. Perhaps he'd not come home one night to the fine meal she'd cooked. Perhaps a registered package had been delivered. Had she opened it, full of curiosity, to find inside a swastika-stamped cigar box of ashes and fragments of charred bone?

She'd had a merry face once, young for her age, but beneath the sealskin hat that matched her coat, her cheeks had fallen in, emphasising too-bright eyes and a prominent nose. Her soft lips drooped, giving her the look of a once-loved doll abandoned in the attic.

'This is Rolf,' said his mother, gently pushing forward a slight, pale child with too-wise eyes. 'And this is Lisl. What do you say to the kind lady?'

Rolf clicked his little heels and bowed over my hand. '*Guten Tag, gnädige Frau.*'

Lisl just looked at me, silent and blank. Already she'd learned that strangers were dangerous.

'Look, Lisl,' I said. 'I've brought you some new clothes to wear, you and Rolf. Try them on and see what you look like.'

Her little arms and legs were rigid. We had to force them through armholes and into socks.

'She's a good girl,' her mother kept repeating. 'She won't be any trouble, I promise. Rolf will look after his sister, won't you, Rolf? You're such a big boy now. She's a good girl. She'll do anything you ask.'

With some children, I'd managed to make it a game. We'd had a laugh and a joke. But not with Lisl. She was like a little, baleful, old woman, glaring at me in helpless fury with eyes that said, 'If I were bigger, I'd bundle you downstairs, you and your pretty clothes.'

'I'm sorry,' the mother said, 'she didn't use to be like

412

this. Since her father was taken away . . . she saw, you know . . . she saw things a child shouldn't see.'

Eventually, we managed to turn the two children into reasonable imitations of English schoolchildren.

'We're all going for a walk,' I said, 'Mutti, too. We'll all go together. Do you like trains, Rolf? Would you like to go on a big one?'

She handed over her children to me without a tear, although I knew her heart was breaking. She kissed each one, but briskly, as though she was a family friend or an aunt. Her fingers lingered on Rolf's tie as as she straightened it and when she laid a hand on Lisl's hair, I saw that it trembled, but not once did she allow the children to see her grief.

'Think what fun you'll have,' she said brightly, 'a train and then a big ship, all the way to England. Lucky you. I've always wanted to go to England.'

'Then you come, too,' said Rolf. He didn't look such a big boy any more.

'I will, darling. I promise. I have to wait for Vati, then we'll both come for you.'

Across the heads of her children, her eyes spoke to me: 'Be good to my little ones,' those black eyes said. 'If I never see them again, I must know that they're safe and loved. Take care of them for me.'

'I promise,' I said out loud.

She kissed them both again, less briskly this time. Rolf was impatient to get on the train. It took us a while to climb up the high steps and to find our carriage, but when, eventually, we looked out, I saw her walking down the train, looking in at each window, half-running, half-holding back, scurrying down the platform with a little, frantic shuffle. We stuck our heads out, to let her know where we were, but the train gave a hiss and a lurch. The guard blew his whistle and waved his wand with the green disc on the end.

Lisl gave a squeal – thank God, without words. Her mother looked up and saw her children disappearing. She started to run, one hand held outstretched, but the train kept going. There were knots of people between her and us, waving or chatting or walking away. She pushed her way through them roughly. Running. Running. But the train wouldn't wait. Hazily, through a cloud of steam, I saw her reach the end of the platform. She was quite still, both hands clamped over her mouth.

'I promise,' I whispered again, although there was no-one to understand.

It was a nightmare of a journey, not that the children were naughty – far from it – they were unnaturally good. Having been warned of the dire consequences of speaking German in front of other people, they naturally attracted attention because they didn't speak at all.

'What good children,' remarked one woman, peering over to look suspiciously into their faces, '*Ich hoffe dass sie nicht krank sind* – I hope they're not ill.'

'I'm afraid I don't speak German,' I said, trying to capture the bright, confident tone of the Englishwoman abroad.

They wouldn't eat the sandwiches that their mother had made for them.

'They're so naughty,' I said in English to anyone who might be interested, knowing that no one understood me, but feeling that any mother might naturally make some sort of remark, 'they've just never taken to German food. Never mind, darlings, home soon and Nanny will make you cinnamon toast and hot milk.'

The children looked at me warily, as though I were some sort of performing animal that just might be dangerous. I tried to amuse them with a card game and the one English picture book I'd brought, but they couldn't rouse themselves to show any interest.

Oh God, I thought, what do I think I'm doing, taking

over Your role? Do I know better than You? Isn't it cruel to take these children away from the only parent they have left, more cruel than leaving them? Wouldn't they be better with their mother, after all, than being dragged off to live with strangers, however kind?

What shall I do? Shall I take them back? How shall I find their mother again?

The effort of trying to appear natural made my head ache. Someone had closed the windows and the compartment smelled of varnish and orange peel, of bodies in winter clothes and the throat-catching sting of smoke that seeped through everything.

Everyone had fallen asleep except me. Rolf's head was against my shoulder and Lisl had pillowed her head in his lap. Across the compartment, a soldier slept, his head lolling, his legs in hefty boots thrust out across the floor, taking up most of the room. An old man, who might as well have had 'Jew' written all over him, huddled in a corner, trying to look as inconspicuous as he possibly could, even in his sleep.

Is this the right way for people to live? I thought. Which is worse – to take children away from the only family they have left or to leave them here to become a new, despised generation of *Untermenschen*, of less than men?

I didn't seem to have an answer.

It was getting dark by the time we reached the last station in Germany. The compartment door slid open and a man in a green uniform looked in.

'*Guten Abend*,' he said. '*Passkontrolle.*'

Good evening, not Heil Hitler. It was good to hear – an omen.

The compartment was nearly empty by this time, just one middle-aged couple and ourselves.

'Good evening,' I said and handed over my passport. He flicked through it, noting the entry stamp and date.

415

Then he looked sharply at my two children, who bore not the slightest resemblance to me.

Lisl jumped up. With one hand she dragged at my sleeve. The other she clapped to her body. '*Ich muss Pipi machen*,' she informed us all in a hoarse, urgent whisper.

I couldn't think, couldn't move. That she should have kept silent for so long, then burst into German at the very moment freedom awaited them. Poor child. Poor children. I'd never asked, never given a thought to their physical needs all day . . . but now . . . I could have wept with anger and frustration.

Lisl started to cry and a steaming, yellow puddle spread out across the floor, soaking her socks and sandals.

The customs man laughed and handed me back my passport. '*Gute Fahrt*,' he wished us. 'Have a good trip.'

They say that every thief grows greedy after a while and when he grows greedy he becomes careless. And what were David and I but thieves? We stole children away, spiriting them off under the very noses of the law. Like Pied Pipers, we arrived in town and stole away with people's most precious possessions. Wherever we went, a line of children danced after us into the hollow hill, never to be seen again – at least, not by those who loved them.

This country is too stupid, we said, too avaricious, too blind. It doesn't deserve to be allowed to keep such treasures.

David felt the strain, I know. He scarcely ate enough to keep a child alive and he'd got terribly thin. Yet every time we drew up at a customs post with our dangerous contraband, he'd be as negligently relaxed, as good-mannered yet firm, as English gentlemen traditionally are.

His was the sort of courage that made him come back

416

again and again for punishment – the schoolboy who finally makes up his mind to defy the class bully. You may knock him down, but he'll stand up again – and again and again – and you know he'd rather die than give up. David may have been drawn as fine as a thread, but I knew he'd never snap.

And I – well, sometimes I'd look in the mirror and wonder how we ever thought that we were inconspicuous. We were too bright-eyed, too excitable. We laughed too much. In that country of tense, watchful people, we shone like stars.

It's a heady mixture – danger and success – and we were young enough not to notice that we were becoming drunk on it.

Christmas in Germany is like nowhere else and although my family had not celebrated the birth of Christ, I had always enjoyed the atmosphere – in a land where everyone loves to be *gemütlich* on every possible occasion, Christmas is the purest essence of *gemütlichkeit*.

The Nazis had done their best to replace every Christian festival with a pagan invention of their own: Corpus Christi was overshadowed by the Midsummer Solstice when wreaths in memory of Party martyrs were tossed into blazing bonfires and incendiary incantations, *Feuersprüche*, were intoned; *Alleheilige*, All Saints, was replaced by parades on 9th November, in solemn veneration of those who had fallen in the 1923 Putsch. But nothing could dislodge Christmas, with its combination of Christian and old Germanic traditions, from its place in German hearts.

Christmas Eve. David and I took the road south. This time we weren't working, but staying with people we'd met on our travels, Gerhardt and Christina Lüben, people we trusted.

The Christmas markets were still open, but their

stalls, though brightly lit, were nearly empty. People hurrying home had their arms full of parcels. The air had that heavy, still quality – dense enough to touch, cold enough to freeze your breath into crystals – that means snow isn't far away. In the centre of every village, no matter how small, the *Christbaum* stood, a star on its very tip.

Here a man pulled a handcart heaped with holly, scarlet and green. There a woman set a row of white candles in the window, ready to light as a guide to the travellers to Bethlehem. A girl with Gretchen plaits could scarcely get sideways through a gateway, hampered as she was with a basket of bright apples in one hand and a basket of hazel nuts in the other.

The road rose higher, through forests of pine so tall they shut out all but a glimpse of sky. The thin, resinous air was fragrant enough to clear every passage in one's head, better than any medicine. Here, snow had already fallen and the tyres made a squeaking sound on the tight-packed surface. In the beam of our lights, tracks of deer crossed and criss-crossed the road ahead.

> Bald ist Heilige Nacht,
> Chor der Engeln erwacht –,
> Hört nur, wie lieblich es schallt,
> Freue dich, Christkind kommt bald.

Yes, it was a Christian carol, but I'd heard my friends sing it, long, long ago, before the world went mad, and the tune was beautiful. At the sound of my voice, David reached over and lightly touched my hand.

At the entrance and exit of every village, and sometimes in front of individual houses, the signs made a mockery of the holy season.

★

418

JUDEN DÜRFEN HIER NICHT BLEIBEN.

JEWS MUST NOT STAY HERE

DEUTSCHLAND!
ERWACHE AUS DEINEM BÖSEN TRAUM,
GIB FREMDEM JUDEN IN DEINEM REICH
NICHT RAUM!

GERMANY!
AWAKE FROM THY EVIL DREAM,
GIVE THE STRANGER JEW IN THY KINGDOM
NO ROOM!

JUDA, ENTWEICHE AUS
UNSEREM DEUTSCHEN HAUS!

JUDAH, VANISH FROM
OUR GERMAN HOUSE!

I stopped singing and David grew silent as we drove on through the dusk.

The Christchild's mother would have found no place to bear her son in this land.

Our hosts, Gerhardt and Christina, were very generous and made us welcome, giving us a room with a huge bed under a thick, white feather quilt. The chimney of the blue-tiled stove below ran up the inner corner of the room and kept it comfortably warm. From the window we could see a garden covered with snow as snug as the feather bed.

We'd been told that supper would be early, to make time for carol singing, the compulsory listening to the government broadcast and for those who wished to go, Mass. We stood drinking white wine that tasted like luscious fruit syrup – *Eiswein*, made from the last grapes on the vine, touched by frost and highly prized. It went to my head immediately. I managed to forget the insulting banners we'd passed. I felt warm and cuddly.

419

David put his arm around me and I leaned my head against him. The early supper went further and further back.

Christina had pulled the bell by the fireplace two or three times, I'd noticed, but no one came. Finally, while still joining in our conversation, she stood and pulled the bell repeatedly until a maid appeared.

'Is there a problem in the kitchen?' she asked.

'The cooking is done,' answered the maid, 'but I cannot serve it. There is a Jewess amongst you.'

If she'd slapped my face, I couldn't have felt sicker. David's arm tightened around me, holding me back. Keep out of this, he was saying, keep calm, keep your dignity.

But the other guests weren't looking at me. They were looking at a tall, quiet woman standing near the window.

'Don't be cheeky,' snapped Christina. 'You have served Frau von Wehlau every Christmas for eleven years. She is a Catholic, her father and her grandfather were Catholics, not that it's any business of yours, Anna-Liese.'

'She is a Jewess. I do not serve her any longer. I am a good German – a *Kerndeutsche*.'

'This is disgraceful. You know very well that the lady is a good German and that her husband was as *Kerndeutsch* as anyone. He died for our country at Arras.'

'She is a Jewess.' The maid's voice was blank, toneless and very, very stubborn. 'I obey the Party. I do not serve food to a woman of Jewish blood ever again.'

'Very well,' our hostess answered. 'You may go. You may pack your bags and leave as soon as Christmas is over. I don't want to see you between now and then.'

'You can't dismiss me. I belong to the Party.' She brought out the word like a talisman against evil.

'That will do,' Gerhardt rapped. 'Go downstairs.'

420

'No, it will not do and you'd better not cross me.' I felt spite ooze out from the woman, like mud underfoot. The Party had taken her out of whatever poor peasant's cottage she had been born in and made her important. The Party had taken the place of the saints she used to venerate. What had the saints ever done for her? 'I know too much about you – you and your pacifist friends.'

'Get out! I am master here.'

She stepped forward, her rosy, homely face twisted with venom. 'I have a notebook with every telephone call you have made and every visitor you have received written down – with hour and date. You read *The Times* from England and you entertain important English people. You have a wireless set tuned to foreign stations. You visit the borderlands . . .'

'Get out!'

She went, but left her spirit with us.

'I'm so sorry,' said Gerhardt, 'it's Christmas Eve and we should be at peace with each other.'

'I had better go,' said Frau von Wehlau quietly. 'I'm so sorry. I should not have come.'

'No, no, Erika,' our hostess begged. 'You come every Christmas. Why should this year be different? Gerhardt, don't let her go . . .'

'Aunt Erika, Aunt Erika,' the children cried. 'You mustn't go.'

'She's not leaving, I promise. We are all Germans here – no more, no less. Come along, Erika – all of you. The children will serve supper.'

I don't know what we ate. None of us noticed, I think. The table was so beautiful, decorated with an evergreen garland and gilded pine cones, and we all sat round it, pretending to eat. The children served the soup, but with the next course, a man came upstairs. I knew who he was. He was the chauffeur who had carried our bags indoors.

'Let me do this,' he said. 'Cook and I both think that woman has gone mad.'

He served and got the little ones to take round the plates, trying to make them laugh by humming under his breath, '*O Tannenbaum, O Tannenbaum, wie treu sind deine Blätter* . . .' because after the meal would come the tree ceremony. But even the children scarcely smiled.

Towards the end of the meal, Gerhardt slipped away. The rest of us rose and went to stand in the hall outside the closed doors of the drawing room. The hall was almost dark – there was just a glow from behind other open doors – and cold enough to make our breath smoke in the fir-scented air. The children wriggled with excitement, nudging each other and whispering. Beyond the door, we could hear rustling and, once, a cough. Then from inside, Gerhardt called for one song after another. In voices thin and clear as icicles, the children sang the verses and we all joined in the chorus. Just when we were thinking that we didn't know another, single carol, the door opened . . .

And there was the tree, a mile high, soaring to the ceiling, green and sparkling in the darkened room with tiny, white candles. Beneath it was the *Krippe* – all the figures at the holy child's birth.

It was so strange to me, strange and alien, almost pagan. Yet I could see the beauty of the story. Was I really the same girl who'd thought that St Paul's Cathedral might fall on her head?

My eyes were stinging, but not with the sentimental, easy tears that Christmas so often brings. The fresh, fair faces of the children were beautiful, but they were not the faces I was looking for.

But I realised, too, that the bitterness that had been driving me ever since I'd learned of my family's fate had been misdirected. My father had fought for this country. He had thought it was worth spending four, terrible years in the trenches for Germany. He was both a German and a Jew. I had thought it wasn't possible to be both any longer, I thought I had to choose, I was being forced to choose, but perhaps I might be wrong. When I looked at the faces of the friends who surrounded me – good people, decent people – I forced myself to remember that beneath the filth still lay something worth salvaging. And I knew it was more important than ever that this should survive.

All the precious, secret, handmade presents were distributed to everyone in the house – parents, children, guests, cook, chauffeur, gardener and all their families. Only the quarrelsome maid was missing, but, like the uninvited fairy at Sleeping Beauty's christening, she made more impression in her absence.

In the middle of the gift-giving, Gerhardt switched on the wireless for the compulsory broadcast. Goebbels' voice filled the room. It rose up on the warm, scented air as high as the star on the top of the Christmas tree:

'The world knows today, and politicians of other nations have recognised, that thanks are due to the Führer alone that the peace of Europe was preserved during the past year . . .

'Germans abroad need no longer be ashamed of their Fatherland. They can be proud of it. No doubt many other nations prefer that other Germany which bowed to every foreign command, no matter how humiliating . . .'

Christmas was over - it had never really begun.

We were on our way to visit Clare. Mad, you might say. Perhaps. Probably. I didn't understand then, and still don't, the mystic relationship that binds twins. But I did know that David needed to see his sister again. He said that he wanted to satisfy himself that she was being properly treated by this man she was living with, but we both knew that this was only an excuse. The real reason was that he simply couldn't go on any longer without seeing her.

Besides, I'd managed to persuade myself that such a visit, to a woman who was involved with a high-ranking SS officer, could only make our position in Germany safer. Who'd dare question us afterwards? Had we not just come from spending a short holiday with SS-Untergruppenführer Otto von Darmheim? Would he not vouch for our probity? We'd be inviolable.

Yes, I'd do anything – truckle to the SS, *anything* – if by doing so I could snatch a few more children out of the pit.

Yet the thought of staying under that man's roof made me feel frightened enough to want to turn tail and run back to England. He got into my dreams. He stood, black and dangerous, between me and my husband. I'd wake, sweating and shivering at the same time, clutching at David, crying out his name. David would soothe me back to sleep, or thought that he did, but long after his breathing told me he was sleeping, I'd lie in his arms and wonder how long we might have together.

Clare had been installed in a house overlooking the Tegernsee, the most fashionable of the Munich lakes, favoured by quite a few of the Nazi higher ranks. Otto had rented a substantial farmer's house on the eastern shore and there his mistress lived alone, except for her dog.

Clare was waiting, with Corsair like an heraldic statue by her side, as our car drew up to the house. She looked as though she had been standing there for a long time.

'You're late,' she accused as we got out the car.

'Sorry,' said David, grimly. 'We were held up by a parade. I wonder what it was this time – were they celebrating the New Year, perhaps, or simply crucifying another Jew?'

'Oh David, please don't let's quarrel – not so soon.' Clare put her arms around her twin and kissed him. Although her lips only touched his cheek, it seemed to me that she didn't kiss him as a sister kisses a brother.

'All right.' David's rather fierce smile softened. 'I promise to wait until we're inside the house.'

Clare tucked her arm through David's and led him off towards the open door, leaving me standing in the snow with the suitcases at my feet. Well, what else did I expect – to be welcomed with open arms? But at the door, David turned and ran back to me, with such an expression of contrition on his face that I could only laugh and forgive him.

Two's company, three's a crowd. Four's a – what – a disaster? Clare monopolised David's attention throughout our stay. Yes, I'd expected that. I'm intelligent enough to be able to enjoy my own company for a few days. I was also secure enough to know that David's relationship with his sister posed no threat to our married life. The problem was Otto von Darmheim.

Can you imagine those evenings? David and Clare chatting away, enthusiastic as children, about past events and people they had known. Otto and I, equally excluded, polite as two bishops, exchanging very small talk about the scenery, the weather, conscious all the time of those subjects we *must* not mention.

Between us lay the pit, blacker and fouler than I could ever have believed a year before, and we tiptoed around its rim, wary as wrestlers, each daring the other to be the first to take a step over the brink.

Left to himself, I imagine that von Darmheim would have made very short work of me. He and his like walked over untold thousands of people like me and never even noticed that we were there. But I had David – and David had Clare. And whatever Clare wanted, Otto would give. A house in the country? A car? She could have them. A baby? Certainly. Protection for her beloved brother and his misalliance? No need to ask.

Thank God.

Four days. Five nights. The days I could stand. We'd go for long, hard walks over mountain tracks, up the Wallberg perhaps, or, more gently, along the Zeiselbachtal to the Aueralm, the pasture where cattle grazed all summer long and where there was always a glass of milk to be had, fresh from the morning's milking. The cattle were down in the villages now and the summer steadings deserted. David and I had the blue-and-silver landscape to ourselves.

Clare never came with us. Otto wouldn't allow it. Their baby wasn't due until May, but already he treated her like a Dresden shepherdess. More like a spider in a web she sat, waiting for evening and for one man or another, for David or Otto, to come back to her.

Those evenings.

The tiny windows were shuttered fast against the winter wind and the heat from the ceramic *Kachelofen*, that warmed the whole house, made my head muzzy and stupid. Clare might enveigle us all – even me – to play *Skat* and we'd slap down cards fast and furiously, but mostly she and David just talked – or she talked and David listened and watched. I'd catch him looking at me across the dark, low-ceilinged room. The shadows from the oil lamps patterned his face at strange angles. Sometimes I'd not be certain if I was really looking at my husband or at his other, female self.

And always in the background, never silent, there was the wireless. I'd go to bed with my head thumping to the rhythm of a military band or the heroic idiocies of Wagner. The speeches, the voices, would get into my sleep and posture there, mocking me and my tiny efforts. Do you think you can really get away with it, they'd say, do you think you can escape us? We are

426

Germany and Germany is us. There is nowhere to go that we cannot find you.

On the last evening, Otto suggested that we might all go into Bad Wiessee for dinner. Clare looked across at me dubiously.

'Do you really think . . . ?' She let the question trail away.

'You go,' David said quickly. 'You haven't been out for ages. Judith and I will be quite happy with a quiet evening here.'

'But it's your last evening,' Clare complained. 'I suppose she's quite presentable really – no one need know . . .'

I squeezed David's hand – hard – before he managed to blurt out the furious response that I felt surge up in him.

We went to the Hotel Hanslbauer and were shown to a table with such obsequiousness that I could feel my toes curling within my shoes in disgust. But an SS-Untergruppenführer would be treated thus anywhere in the country. To be fair, I don't think Otto liked it any more than I did. Having one's boots licked came with the rank, so to speak – a nuisance, but what can one do about it – along with a big, black car and a driver.

I looked nervously around. No notices here informing Jews that they were unwelcome. No need now. What Jew would dare walk in here? Wasn't it 1935? We'd been taught our place in the world by this time and it wasn't in an hotel patronised by highly-placed Nazis.

'Just think,' whispered Clare penetratingly, as we slid into our seats, 'it was in this very hotel that Röhm was arrested. The Führer really showed how unselfish he is, to give up his greatest friend for the greater good of Germany.'

'I don't remember you saying that at the time,' David remarked, acidly.

'Well, I know better now,' Clare snapped.

'It was necessary,' said Otto quietly and ended the conversation. 'Now, what will you have? I can thoroughly recommend the *Kalbsrahmbraten* with noodles – or perhaps you'd prefer something a little more cosmopolitan?'

It was dust and ashes in my mouth. Clare ate hugely and finished off with a mountainous ice-cream confection – with chocolate sauce, walnuts, almonds, pistachios and I don't know what else – called *Nussknacker*.

'I've got something very special to tell you,' she said, as she spooned out the last scraping of whipped cream from the goblet. 'Otto and I are getting married tomorrow.'

'But I thought . . .' David gave a little, embarrassed cough. 'I thought you . . .'

'My wife died two months ago – quite suddenly. She always had a weak heart.'

'I'm not sure whether I ought to offer you my condolences or congratulations,' David said. His face had become pinched all in a moment, his lips colourless.

Struck with a sudden horror, I looked again at David and saw my suspicion mirrored on his face. Surely, not even they . . . Oh no, oh surely, no . . .

'My Aunt Lotte had a weak heart,' I murmured. 'She couldn't withstand a shock.'

All at once, I wanted to weep. I wanted to mourn the people I had loved and all those I hadn't even met – the unknown, the unloved, the unmissed, the victims. I could feel my eyes filling with tears. Hurriedly, I looked down at the table. The cutlery blurred. Two small, damp spots spread across the tablelinen and joined up into a big one.

Not now. Not now.

'Well, really – this is supposed to be a celebration, you know,' Clare said fiercely. 'Won't either of you congratulate us?'

David's voice was so soft, I could scarcely hear him on the other side of the table. 'If it's what you really want, Clare – and you're quite certain – then I hope you'll be very happy.'

'You will come to our wedding, won't you – both of you? Stay just one more day.'

It was a nightmare.

Clare and Otto were married according to the neo-pagan rites of the Germanic tribes. The ceremony was conducted by Otto himself in the presence of his comrades.

In a panelled room decorated by runic carvings – mystical no doubt, but to me nonsensical – and hung around with fir branches and dried sunflower heads, the symbol of the wheel of the sun, Clare and Otto plighted their troth.

They faced a short column crowned by a basin in which a smoky flame of eternity flickered, casting long shadows that left the corners of the room dark enough to hide the ancient, evil presences that had gathered to watch. I could sense them there, licking their lips, waiting for Clare's soul to fall into their hands, and I sent up a silent, half-forgotten prayer to deliver her from their clutches.

Before the flame lay two rings, engraved with runes, and a wooden platter of bread and salt, emblems of the earth's fruitfulness and of its purity.

Clare had discarded her uniform (the skirt would no longer fasten around her bulk – thank goodness) and wore a long gown of soft, undyed wool, fine as lace, embroidered with green oak leaves and with a row of black swastikas around the hem. Her hair, loose and gleaming, was crowned by a woven wreath of wheat, acorns and fir cones. She was a Norse goddess come to life, bold as a warrior, fertile as the earth.

It was grotesque and yet, watching her fierce face softened by torchlight, I felt that I came closer to understanding her in that moment than I ever had. Her pagan soul had become misplaced. It had wandered the earth looking for a body and had found one in 20th century England, a thousand years out of its place and time.

Then Otto flung a handful of salt into the fire. It flared, blue and green, with a fizzle and an acrid smell, jolting me back into the present. This ceremony was no more than romanticised nonsense. It wasn't a real marriage. It was a travesty, alien to the laws of God and humanity. My skin crawled as I looked round the black uniforms and watching, empty faces.

' "Marriage I will call the will of two," ' Otto intoned solemnly, quoting Nietzsche, ' "to create one which is more than they who created it." '

He placed one of the rings on his new wife's finger. I watched him put it gently in place, then fold his hand around hers. I saw his hard, scarred face soften in a smile that was so much more than a displacement of the lips.

Dear God, I thought in amazement, he really does care for her.

Clare put a matching ring on her husband's finger and the thing was done. As a last gesture, Otto gave into her keeping his SS dagger, as a symbol of his wife's *Wehrhaftigkeit*, her capability of bearing arms.

Then all the waiting black figures came to life, clapping Otto on the back and kissing the bride. David hovered on the brink of the boisterous crowd, excluded. I could scarcely bear to look at him. It was as though a living part of him had been torn out by cruel claws.

Clare's face was hectically flushed. Her laugh was

high and wild. 'David? Where's David?' she cried, looking from one grinning face to the next. 'Oh David, come here, do. You must wish me joy – please.'

David folded both of her hands in his and raised them to his lips. Then he kissed her once on each cheek, very gently. His voice broke briefly, as he said, 'I wish you happiness, Clare, wherever we go and whatever we do. And I'll always love you, whatever happens.'

Two more children – two boys, cousins, solemn as owls under English school caps, wound round with striped scarves over gabardine mackintoshes – sit rigidly to attention in the back of the car as we hurtle along the winding road that leads along the north shore of the Bodensee. We should have picked the children up yesterday, not participated in that farcical Teutonic ceremony. We should have been passing this point last night.

On a clear day, we might be able to see the frosted peaks of the Swiss alps across the lake, tantalising as a mirage, a new Promised Land. Not now. The towns on the German shore announce themselves through the darkness as prickles of light that blaze and blur through a curtain of snow. The wipers are clogged with it. It lies packed in a band of ice at the base of the windscreen. The wheels spin as David slides into a bend. The tail of the car swings out, then back, and he's in control again.

'David – darling – you're going too fast.'

I lay a hand on his arm. Through the overcoat, through his tweed jacket, I can feel the tension in his muscles.

'I know,' he grunts.

'Is something wrong?'

'I don't know. Nothing, probably. We should have got out yesterday. I just feel . . . this time I don't want to be around any longer than we have to.'

Meersburg. Birnau. Überlingen. And surely, there, that larger group of lights – that must be Konstanz and the border. Not far now. We're running for it like rabbits to a hole.

The boys are still sitting to attention as we pull up at the customs barrier. They're transfixed by the lights and the uniforms and the swastika banners hanging limp and snow-burdened.

David rolls up to the barrier and winds down the window, turning on his innocent, English smile like a lamp.

'Heil Hitler.'

'Heil Hitler,' David and I chorus, like a comedy double act.

We hand over our passports and the guard looks at them and then at the two boys in the back.

'Your boys?'

'Yes,' David answers. 'Back to school next week, I'm afraid.'

'Fine boys.' He puts our passports in his pocket. 'I must inform you, Mr Northaw, that kidnapping is a very serious offence.'

Baron von Darmheim. SS–Untergruppenführer von Darmheim. His name is a talisman. I chant it through lips that are stiff and swollen, lips that will scarcely open far enough for the words to be audible. Though I can feel my teeth shifting in my jaw, I call on his name as a pilgrim calls on his namesaint.

'Baron von Darmheim is my brother-in-law. The Baroness is my husband's sister. My husband and I have done nothing . . .'

'Jew-bitch!'

This time they make me scream. My back is a staircase and they walk up and down it. My face is ground into the stone floor. I'm choking in my own blood.

432

The boots thud into my ribs. Something, somewhere, breaks. I feel it give. Oh God, oh God . . .

When next they haul me to my feet, I blubber a pathetic threat through the blood and snot, 'If the Baron finds out what you are doing . . .'

There are long gaps between the questioning and these are just as bad. No, that's a stupid thing to say. Nothing could be as bad. But the silence is so terrible.

David. David. Where are you?

And I feel him answer me. I feel his mind just touch mine, fleeting as a melting snowflake, before he's gone again.

David.

When I open my eyes, I can't see, but only because there is no light and no window. I drag myself to my feet, my arms flailing like a drunk. Here is a straw pallet, here a wall, another wall, a bucket that stinks already. Here is a patch of slime, of . . . 'the Lord is nigh unto all that call upon Him, to all that call upon Him in truth.'

I lie in the darkness and listen to my own breathing, as rasping as a nightjar. Fear sits in the dark corner, fear of pain, fear of death, and with every breath he creeps nearer.

My passport, my lovely, new, blue-and-gold passport was as much protection as a paper umbrella. Things are done in this country in black secrecy. Who knows where we are? Who will ever know until it's too late? They can't keep us, surely. They daren't keep us. We're British citizens. But ponderous diplomatic statements of displeasure won't bring us back to life.

Someone, somewhere is screaming – a thin, high, animal sound that has nothing to do with human vocal cords – the sound of a human being reduced to a quivering bundle of nerve endings.

'Deliver me from mine enemies, O my God: defend me from them that rise against me.

433

'Deliver me from the workers of iniquity and save me from bloody men.'

David, where are you?

And he reaches out and touches me, sure and strong, like a voice in the darkness.

After each question, between question and answer, they stamp on my hands.

'Who organises your smuggling ring?'

Stamp.

'What smuggling ring?'

'Who finds the children for you?'

Stamp.

'What children?'

'How many have you abducted?'

Stamp.

'I don't know what you mean . . .'

The trouble is, you see, David and I never worked out a covering story between us. We didn't have time. No, I mean we never made the time. We were so confident. Nothing could hurt us. And now, I don't know what he's saying. I don't know if anything I say might harm him . . . one little, wrong word is all it might take . . .

My hands are pulsing. With each strong beat of my heart, the blood is pumped through my body and into my hands. With every beat, the pain knifes through them, great bouts and gobbets of pain, gushing through my hands as my heart beats.

'SS-Untergruppenführer von Darmheim . . . get in touch with him . . . he'll vouch for us . . . his wife is my husband's sister . . . if he finds out what you've done . . .'

I lie in the dark and think of poor Oskar, so long dead. I think of him lying in the night, at the entrance to Judengasse, alone, while his life seeps away through his ruptured organs.

The shadows in the corner creep closer. One more step, and they'll have me.

'When the wicked spring as the grass and when all the workers of iniquity do flourish, it is they that shall be destroyed forever.'

David. David.

I listen for his answer and this time none comes.

David . . .

They bandaged my hands and strapped my ribs. They washed me and gave me a painkiller that dulled the stab of broken teeth and the pulsing of my hands. They ministered to a limp, compliant body. All my energy was spent on calling out to David. Into the silence I called his name.

But there was no reply.

He'd gone from me and I'd never noticed the moment when he slipped away. I should have been listening. I should have been with him. Maybe he had called out to me in his agony and I hadn't heard.

I'd failed him.

They bundled me into a big, black car and drove me away from that terrible place. I'd gladly have turned round and gone back in again, if that could have brought David back to me. Rather lying in the dark fighting off the demons of fear, listening to David's mind touch mine with his comfort, than this void.

Forever. Such a long time without him.

The light flashed back off the snow and hurt my eyes. The lids were so swollen they wouldn't open or close properly. I tried to shut my eyes against the glare, but it crept under my lids and shone on my brain like the light that had stood on my questioner's desk.

Forever.

They drove me back to the house by the Tegernsee that David and I had left – how long ago? – yesterday?

435

– a week? – a lifetime? When they helped me out of the car, I fainted.

The short January afternoon was nearly over when I woke. The room was almost dark, but the reflection of the snow made the low ceiling bright. The room was very warm – someone must have stoked the *Kachelofen* to the brim with logs. In the great feather bed, the starched white cover was lapped up to my chin. It still smelled of the lavender and southernwood sprigs that kept away the moths during its summer storage.

I felt heavy and drowsy and very, very comfortable.

Until I moved.

'Would you like something to drink?' Clare bobbed up from a chair on the other side of the bed. I hadn't seen her there. 'Some water? A cup of tea?'

I turned my head away. Go away. Don't make me wake up. I don't want to be awake. I don't want to be alive.

David? Are you there? Are you listening? Tell me you can hear me.

Nothing.

I looked back across the days we had shared and they were pitifully few. I looked down the long procession of days to come and there were so many, all empty.

Clare was crying, not ostentatiously, but I could hear the catches in her breath and the bubbling sniff when her nose became blocked. Painfully, I turned my head back to her.

She sat in a carved, peasant's chair too small for her, looking oddly diminished in a woollen smock. The golden goddess had shrunk. I shan't be afraid of her ever again, I thought. I shan't ever be afraid of anything.

My voice was a faint, dry rasp – an old woman's voice. 'Why're you crying?'

She looked at me with the sort of amazement that might have been comical at another time.

436

'Keep your tears for yourself – you need them,' I whispered. 'Or cry for the people you don't know, for the unnamed people who have yet to die. Don't cry for David. Nothing can hurt him any more.'

'Oh no – oh no, you're wrong. David's coming back.' She shook her head as though the truth of her denial depended on its force. 'Otto's gone to fetch him. He's going to bring David home. He got you out, didn't he? You're here. Why not David? Otto won't let anything happen to David.'

I couldn't look at her. I couldn't bear to see the flare of hope in her china-doll eyes. She was his twin. How could she not know what I knew? How could not feel his absence?

'Then why're you crying?'

'It wasn't supposed to be like this!' she wailed. 'It was supposed to be clean and pure. It was good. It was a holy fight. It wasn't supposed to be . . .'

I was tempted to fill in the gap . . . it wasn't supposed to be a disease, a filthy sore . . . it wasn't supposed to be knocks on the door at night while neighbours turned in their beds and thanked God the knock wasn't on their own door . . . it wasn't supposed to be shame that would never be wiped out . . .

Too many words. I didn't have the energy to speak them.

Poor Clare. Where were her banners and her bands? Poor Clare.

Someone was coming, someone wearing heavy boots. I cringed, trying to make myself small under the bedclothes, and my mouth was foul with the bile of fear. But the boots weren't clanging along stone corridors – not any longer. There were no bolts to shoot back. They weren't coming for me.

I listened. Someone was coming up the wooden staircase. Someone in boots, who moved very slowly.

437

Otto was too tall to stand upright in the doorway. He stood with his head bent, for what seemed like a very long time, and we couldn't see his face. Then he just shook his head.

Clare started screaming. The noise went on and on.

EPILOGUE

The letter lies open on my lap. The ink has blurred where my tears fell, drying into three crinkled spots, dark on pale blue, obliterating the words beneath, but I know them by heart.

Sometimes, one has to wait so long for prayers to be answered, that one forgets what the problem was in the first place. But I haven't. I never forgot and I never stopped praying. It took me a long, long time to catch God's ear, but He finally turned His face to me and listened.

Willi. Big, boisterous Willi, who wanted to be allowed to go on hikes and camping with the other boys, who never wanted to be a Jew, is an old man now. (How can that possibly be? He was just a boy. Yet when I look down at my own age-spotted hands, I know it must be true.)

But he is alive and in Israel. He has been looking for me for as many years as I have been looking for him.

He didn't survive Oranienburg. He never went there. During those early days in Berlin, he had become attracted to the Zionist movement and joined their youth group – the only alternative to the HitlerJugend open to him, I suspect, but thank God for it. They ran an official camp in the Harz Mountains, recognised by the Nazis, who granted visas to a few young people every month, to enable them to emigrate to Israel. It was called *Aliyah Bet* – secret immigration – and was a thorn in the side of the British in Palestine. In the meantime, they supported themselves by labouring on local farms. Willi's turn to leave had come, just in time, before that escape route was closed by the Final Solution.

Red Cross records had eventually left him in no doubt of our parents' fate and of Max's, but my name he could not trace. Since then, he had been looking for me. It's been a long search.

My heart is hammering so hard that I can hear it, a squeaky, inefficient sound. It's a long time since it had to work so hard. I lift the letter and hold it to my cheek. The last hands that touched it had been my brother's.

'*Oma* Judith, I've brought you some tea and I've put out a cup and plate for your friend, when she comes. Shall I put it here? Can you reach? I'll pour a cup for you, shall I?' Lisl's daughter puts the tray on a low table by my chair. She glances at the letter crumpled in my hand, at my face. 'Not bad news, I hope?'

'No, love. Good news – the best, the very best.'

I can see my visitor coming across the garden, now. I'd like to get up to meet her, but by the time I manage to extricate myself from this deck chair, she's arrived. She greets me with a kiss on each cheek. We're exactly the same age, but you'd never think it. She has worn better than I. We meet once a week, for tea, on Saturday – *Shabbat*.

She plumps down on a chair, heavily and clumsily. She sits like an elderly games mistress, feet and knees well planted apart, hands spread on thighs. So many Englishwomen sit like that, hearty, tweedy, with a firm handshake and a taste for large dogs.

But her face is curiously unlined, with a baby-soft complexion and plump, pouting lips. She looks at my letter with open curiosity. Her eyes are not faded, like those of most old people, but a vibrant blue, wise and

442

childlike at the same time, but beneath the surface, behind the first, bright impression, is a blank.

Seventy-eight years old. You wouldn't think it. She puts her complexion down to rosewater and Pond's cold cream. That – and no makeup. The Führer couldn't abide painted women.

'Hello, Clare,' I say. 'How are you?'

Just before it grew light, Clare had walked into the Tegernsee and when it became too deep to walk, she started to swim. When she thought she'd gone far enough, she stopped swimming. A long, long time afterwards, she told me it had been so easy. She'd floated on her back for a while, staring at the brightening sky, but she knew that soon, in the bitter, glacial water, she'd stop floating and just disappear. That's all she wanted – just to disappear.

But she didn't sink fast enough. The helmsman of the little steamer that dots around the lake from hamlet to hamlet spotted her, bobbing in her nightdress like a pink log, and, although she'd gone down before they reached her, she was hauled up and pumped back into life.

The baby was born that night. A boy, Otto told me – and I wondered at the tears that glittered on his scarred face – small enough to lie in the palm of his great hand, and dead.

But for Clare there was a kind of mercy in it. She had been under the icy water long enough for her brain to be deprived of oxygen for a critical length of time. Her parents, at last, too late, taking responsibility, had her brought back to England. Her memory of that time, although clear, seemed to have been wiped of pain. The facts she remembered. The emotions seemed to have gone.

No one cared to put that theory to the test, however.

No one told her of Otto's suicide. After the failure of the generals' plot in 1944, the 20th July plot that failed to kill Hitler, he blew his brains out. Better that than the piano wire and meat hook.

I don't think Clare has suffered. I don't think she has endured any strong emotion since the day she almost drowned. Mercy comes in many guises. But I don't really know.

Two childless old women. How strange. We have known each other long enough to be easy in each other's company. Clare holds out her cup for some more tea. While I pour – steadily, for my wrists are rather weak – she chooses the last tiny eclair, popping it into her mouth whole.

'Mmm, scrumptious.' She licks her fingers and looks at my letter again. She's bursting with curiosity. At last, she says, 'You've got a letter.'

'Yes,' I answer and pass it to her to read.

Next year in Jerusalem?
Perhaps.